W9-AQG-010

So This Is
Christmas

Also by Jenny Holiday

So This Is Christmas

a novel

JENNY HOLIDAY

AVON

An Imprint of HarperCollinsPublishers

SO THIS IS CHRISTMAS. Copyright © 2022 by Jenny Holiday. All rights reserved. Printed in the United States of America. No part of this book may be used or reproduced in any manner whatsoever without written permission except in the case of brief quotations embodied in critical articles and reviews. For information, address HarperCollins Publishers, 195 Broadway, New York, NY 10007.

HarperCollins books may be purchased for educational, business, or sales promotional use. For information, please email the Special Markets Department at SPsales@harpercollins.com.

FIRST EDITION

Designed by Diahann Sturge

Gift boxes with bows illustration © AnastasiaSonne / Shutterstock

Library of Congress Cataloging-in-Publication Data has been applied for.

ISBN 978-0-06-295212-7

22 23 24 25 26 LSC 10 9 8 7 6 5 4 3 2 1

For Elle, who imagined Mr. Benz, and believed in him, before I did.

So This Is Christmas

Chapter One

Thirty-one days until Christmas

*A*s usual, the last thing that went in the suitcase was the Post-it.

> *change is the essential process of all existence.—Mr. Spock*

Cara plucked it off the mirror in her bedroom and set it on top of her toiletry bag. She wasn't sure why she always just laid it on top of everything when the rest of her stuff was so meticulously packed, clothing and shoes and notebooks nestled together as snugly as a game of Tetris. She supposed it was because she liked opening her suitcase at the other end of her trip, in a hotel room in Milwaukee or Madrid or Miami, and having it be the first thing she saw. But one of these days, an overly aggressive TSA agent was going to select her for a random screening and the Post-it would get lost in the shuffle.

Which would be fine. It was just a thing. A visual representation of a sentiment that existed independently of its depiction. She could write those words on a new Post-it any time. It wasn't even sticky anymore—it had to be inserted into the mirror's frame to stay up—and the ink was faded. She'd thought, over the years, about going over it with a Sharpie, but she kind of liked the way the emerald ink she'd used as an eighteen-year-old had faded to a dental-office mint. It reminded her how far she had come. How much she *had* changed, and therefore by definition that she was still here, not only not dead but thriving. Getting closer and closer to her goals.

A glance at her phone informed her that her Uber was ten minutes away. Time to get the big goodbye over with. She checked her last-minute essentials list against the contents of her shoulder bag: passport, phone, computer, chargers, briefing binder, sudoku book. Steeling herself, she took a quick look at her reflection in the mirror that hung by her bedroom door. She couldn't look like she'd been crying. And she hadn't been, really. If a few tears had escaped while she was showering, it was because she was over-tired. A mechanical response to exhaustion.

"You've never had to travel over Thanksgiving," her mom said as Cara clattered down the rickety stairs from her attic bedroom to the kitchen. It was four in the morning, and Cara had half hoped her parents would not be up.

But of course they were. They always got up to see her off. Especially today, the day Cara left for a trip that would cause her to miss Thanksgiving. Cara traveled more days than not in any given year, but she always made sure she was home for Thanksgiving, the holiest of holidays in her family, which was funny because they were Catholic. Which meant there were many other, *literal* holy days—Christmas? Easter?—one would think would be a bigger deal.

One would be wrong.

For what we are about to receive may the Lord make us truly thankful. That was said every day in the Delaney household, and it was meant every day, but never more than on Thanksgiving.

Mom was wearing her sad face. Because her mother loved her, Cara reminded herself, and was disappointed that she'd be away for the holiday. Though maybe *disappointed* was too anemic a word, judging by the tears that had been shed when she announced two days ago that she'd have to be gone.

"The person who was supposed to go broke a hip," Cara said for the tenth time, willing her voice to remain even. Cara had a tendency to soak up her mother's emotions, just like the second-hand smoke she used to inhale back in her mom's smoking days.

"I know. I've been praying for him. I just don't understand why *you* have to be the one who takes his place. You've given so much to that company for so many years."

"And 'that company' has given so much to me." *To us.* She tried to say it without any censure in her tone, in a way that wouldn't offend her mother's robust sense of pride.

It didn't work. "I know. I know," her mom said quickly, turning away and aggressively stirring the pot of oats she cooked every morning. As usual, her mother could hear what Cara left unsaid: "that company" had put a stable roof over their heads and was the reason her dad was going to be able to retire next year.

She sighed. She was being prickly because being prickly was easier than being disappointed. She had a tendency to lash out when she was feeling vulnerable. She started over. "I have to go because this is a big, important project that we've already put four months of work into, and I'm the one who knows it best, after the guy with the broken hip." She was his boss, and that's what you did when you were the boss. At least that's what you did when you were a senior associate who was someone's boss. She reminded herself that she loved her job. She loved the travel that came with it, too. It gave her a feeling of freedom, of expansiveness, of amazement, honestly, that she had carved out such a life for herself. Or at least it used to.

She'd been on the road so much lately; she'd only gotten back yesterday from a two-week stint in San Diego. She was tired—like, in-her-bones tired. She just needed some sleep, and she'd be done with this weird maudlin mood. Honestly. She'd missed holidays before, if not Thanksgiving, and she could do it again. Her annual performance reviews always made mention of her reliability. She was a team player. A respected leader. Those adjectives accreted. She had worked hard for those adjectives. Someday, she would make partner because of those adjectives.

"I just . . ."

Argh! Cara wanted to scream at the way her mother trailed off performatively, her back still turned as she tended her oats. "You just what?" Which refrain was Mom going to pull out? *I just don't know how you'll ever have time to meet someone when you're working so hard. I just don't know how they can expect people to work that hard and also have families. I just, I just, I just . . .*

"Honestly, I'd never even heard of Eldovia before last week," her dad said good-naturedly, setting down his copy of the *Post*. As was his endearing way, he was oblivious to the undercurrents swirling around Cara and her mother—or maybe he chose to ignore them.

Either way, she was grateful for the reset. "I don't think a lot of people have." And that included the partners at CZT, aka "that company," before they'd been invited to bid on the job. Cara had heard of Eldovia, but only because she had memorized every country and its capital for the seventh-grade geography bee, back when she was in a particularly aggressive education-is-the-way-out-of-poverty phase. "It's tiny. It doesn't do much." Except make luxury watches, and her parents were not luxury watch–type people. The small Alpine nation didn't even make that many watches anymore. Hence the big, lucrative contract. And the Thanksgiving trip.

Cara's mom set a bowl of oatmeal in front of her dad, her eyes shiny. Damn it. Cara didn't want to miss Thanksgiving any more than her mother wanted her to. She didn't want to spend her flight cramming—though she knew this file, she hadn't been heavily involved in the day-to-day details of the project in the last couple weeks because Brad had been ramping up for the trip.

Cara told herself Thanksgiving was just a day. Like the Post-it was just a piece of paper. The sentiment attached to Thanksgiving wasn't unique to the fourth Thursday in November.

A tear escaped the corner of her mom's eye.

Fucking Brad. On her good days, Cara thought of Brad as a management challenge. He existed, she told herself, to remind her of her Mr. Spock maxim. *Change is the essential process of all existence.*

Cara had no role in hiring Brad, even though he reported to her. He'd been parachuted in to Cara's manufacturing operations team by one of the partners, who was friends with Brad's dad. Cara was forever having to adapt to Brad's low-key bullshittery. But that was okay, because that meant she was forever adapting. The summer intern complains about Brad aggressively complimenting her outfits all the time? Have a conversation with Brad about it and rewrite the team's sexual harassment policy. Brad breaks his goddamn hip at age twenty-eight because he drunkenly falls off a rooftop patio in the Hamptons? Cara's off to Eldovia for Thanksgiving.

"We'll FaceTime on Thursday," she told her parents. "We'll FaceTime constantly. And I'll be back for Christmas." Barely, but she would make it. She was scheduled to fly out of Eldovia the morning of Christmas Eve, and with the time change working in her favor, she'd be home in time to cook dinner.

"I'm gonna miss you, lassie," her dad said as he stood and wrapped her in his arms. She let him hold her for longer than she normally would have, thanking her lucky stars that Patrick Delaney had chosen to claim her as his own. When she broke the hug, she avoided eye contact with both parents. "When I make partner, I won't have to travel so much." Partnership. The brass ring. The dream she'd had since her first day of work at CZT as a twenty-year-old intern. Once that happened, she would stop having to do Thanksgiving duty when someone fell off a freaking roof. She could be more selective about which projects she got personally involved in, and choose where, when, and how much she traveled. You paid enough dues, you stopped having to prove yourself.

She assumed.

That was the plan anyway, and she'd come too far not to stick to the plan.

"And when do you think you're going to make partner?" her mom asked.

Cara huffed a short, frustrated sigh. They had talked about this many times, and the answer hadn't changed. "Hopefully by the time I'm forty." No one had ever made partner younger than that. Her mother knew that, which meant her question had been a loaded one, a windup to what she really wanted to say.

"Do you ever . . ."

There it was. A spark of annoyance ignited in Cara's chest. Which was fine, actually. It would make it easier to leave. "Do I ever what?" She steeled herself for a conversation about the condition of her uterus.

Do you ever think about freezing your eggs? Do you think you'd be open to adoption later, if it ends up being too late for you?

"Nothing, nothing," her mother said, coming over and wrapping Cara in a hug.

That was a twist. Usually, Mom would not have hesitated to finish her thought. Cara was careful not to squeeze as hard as she wanted to, for fear of aggravating any joints. Her mom's rheumatoid arthritis had been flaring up the last few days. She inhaled the familiar baby-powder scent that was her mother and felt it physically relax her. She associated that smell with being tucked into bed at night, which long ago had meant books and lullabies, and, as Cara had grown older, the sharing of confidences. Her mom didn't tuck her in anymore, but when Cara was home, they often had a cup of tea together in the evenings before Cara climbed the stairs to her bedroom.

"I'm sorry," her mom whispered in her ear. "I'm being terrible. I'm so proud of you. You travel safe, okay?"

Damn it. Now Cara was actually going to cry. "I love you, Mom," she croaked.

"I love you, too, my girl, my greatest thing," her mom said, her voice back to its usual lilting warmth as she pulled away. *My girl, my greatest thing.* Her mother had appended that refrain to every good night and goodbye that had passed between them for as long as Cara could remember, whether Cara was leaving for a day at school or for a month in the Eldovian Alps. "We'll light a candle for you on Thanksgiving."

As MUCH AS he didn't want to, Matteo decided at the last minute to go to the airport himself. He could have sent a car. There was no reason he personally had to make the trek to Zurich and hold up a sign that said "Ms. Cara Delaney" in order to welcome the woman who would be Eldovia's undoing. He did it anyway.

When the king charged you with making sure that the hotshot American management consultant was properly welcomed, you didn't send a staff member; you went to the airport yourself. Matteo would freely admit that he was the sort of person for whom duty mattered. No, that wasn't it. That made him sound like a protocol droid. It was more that *tradition* mattered. And since Americans were so woefully underprovisioned when it came to tradition, Ms. Delaney was going to be welcomed by a representative of the Eldovian Crown whether she cared or not. He cared, was the point.

He scanned the arrivals terminal, his gaze snagging on a child standing alone crying. He hurried over to the boy. "Is everything all right, my friend?"

"I'm lost!" the boy, who looked to be about five or six, wailed.

"Well, let's get you un-lost, shall we?" Matteo offered his hand, the boy took it, and together they made their way to an information desk.

Within minutes, the boy's parents, who had been paged, were descending on them. Matteo smiled at their thanks and nearly tripped over a suitcase. "I'm sorry!" a teenager girl exclaimed. "The zipper broke!"

He bent down to help her repack the bag, and it turned out the zipper wasn't broken, just malfunctioning because the bag had been overstuffed. What chaos there was at the airport today. Matteo helped the girl shuffle some items to a backpack.

He had only just sent her on her way when, speaking of the forces of chaos, a woman burst into his field of vision, suddenly there when she had not been before. She was wearing a black pantsuit and the highest heels he had ever seen on a woman in Eldovia in the winter, or perhaps ever. He saw her catch sight of his sign, and she headed toward him at an impressive speed, given those shoes, pulling a small rolling suitcase behind her. The staccato clacking of her heels joined the steady buzzing made by the bag's wheels to create an ominous, crescendoing symphony. Her dark, almost black, hair was pulled into a severe chignon, and along with the black suit, provided a stark contrast to her skin, which was nearly as pale as the snow falling outside and seemed almost aglow, like a pile of that snow had accumulated and was glinting under the moonlight. She looked like an angel.

He huffed a self-disgusted exhalation. Honestly. He needed to take the hyperbole down a notch or several. Cara Delaney was not bringing good tidings of great joy. If she was an angel, she wasn't a good one. He arranged his mouth into the shape of a smile but took care that his eyes did not convey any warmth. "Ms. Delaney?"

"Yes." She stuck out her hand in that aggressive way Americans had. Her nails were varnished in a red so dark it was almost black.

"I am Matteo Benz."

"A pleasure to meet you," she said in a tone that suggested there was in fact nothing whatsoever pleasurable about making his acquaintance as she attempted to break his fingers.

"Likewise," he murmured, squeezing her hand equally hard. It was ridiculous, these displays of dominance, when everyone, except perhaps American management consultants, knew that when it came to getting what you wanted, soft power was a great deal more effective than brute force. Bone-crushing handshakes and shoes that should be subject to EU weapons regulations were not only empty signifiers, they suggested an underlying lack of confidence that could be exploited.

He made a mental note.

"I know you'd been working closely with Bradley Wiener to prepare for his arrival," she said. "I hope getting me instead isn't too much of a disappointment."

He was supposed to rush to assure her that she could never be a disappointment. Instead, he kept his face expressionless. "I do hope Mr. Wiener's recovery is continuing apace?"

Ms. Delaney did not address Matteo's inquiry about her colleague's condition. "I can assure you that Brad has oriented me to the file."

The file. As if an entire nation, its well-being and prosperity, could be reduced to something so pedestrian as a *file.* But he needed to remember that in her mind, it could. It already had been.

"I didn't realize you would be meeting me," she said.

He did not know if she was remarking on the fact that he hadn't merely sent a driver—as he should have—or if she was complaining that the king himself was not on hand to roll out the red carpet. "The king regrets that he could not be on hand this evening to personally welcome you. He had some last-minute business to attend to in Riems, which you may or may not know is on the other side of the country. He is—"

"Yes. There's a secondary Morneau factory in Riems," she said, interrupting him.

Though why should he expect anything less from someone like her? He practiced his breathing. *In through the nose, out through the mouth.* Just once, though, so he didn't look a fool. It helped. He picked up where he'd left off, not acknowledging the substance of the interruption. "He is, however, looking forward to meeting you tomorrow. In the meantime, I am equerry to His Majesty. Are you familiar with the role?" He asked because many people weren't. Americans in particular often thought he was a butler. Not that there was anything wrong with being a butler. It was an honorable way to make a living performing an important service.

"Yes. I've seen *The Crown.*"

God preserve him. His impassive facade almost slipped. *In through the nose, out through the mouth.*

"As far as I can tell," she went on, "being an equerry is like being an executive assistant. Everyone thinks you're a secretary, but really, you make the entire ship go."

"The ship? I beg your pardon?"

"It's a Star Trek metaphor. The captain can talk a good talk, but the person who actually makes the ship go is the engineer. If the engineer can't make the ship go—or doesn't want to—it's not going, no matter what the captain says."

Hmm. What a curious, and unexpected, analogy.

"But choose your metaphor," she went on. "The wind beneath your boss's wings. The man behind the throne." She cracked a smile, which she held for a beat, clearly trying not to laugh. She lost the battle and let loose a high, musical, delighted laugh that seemed at odds with her crushing-handshake, rudely-interrupting, corporate-goth persona. "Which I guess is not a metaphor in this case, because you literally are that."

"Well, not literally."

"What?"

"I don't literally stand behind the throne." There wasn't even a literal throne, at least not in the way she imagined.

She rolled her eyes ever so slightly. He would have expected "Don't roll one's eyes at the client" to be a basic principle. "You may not be aware," she said, "that many English-language dictionaries have revised the definition of *literally* to include *in effect*, or *virtually*."

He tried not to bristle overtly. He spoke English as well as or better than your average educated American, thank you very much. "I am aware, but that doesn't mean I approve. A word cannot also mean the opposite of itself simply because enough people agree." Another fact of which he was aware: he shouldn't be speaking to her like this, not when the king had expressly asked him to see her comfortably settled.

She stared at him for a beat too long before saying, "I see how this is going to be."

"Do you?" He was still doing it. He couldn't seem to stop.

"I do." Her voice had taken on a tone—probably to match his—and her eyes, which were the deep, dark blue of a mountain lake, flashed.

All right. Enough. He had one task here, one simple task, and that was to welcome Ms. Delaney. He had other, more important work to do, so he was anxious to tick her off his list. "Shall we go collect your bags?"

She nodded at the small suitcase of doom she'd been pulling behind her. "This is it."

"That is all you have for such a long stay?"

"I travel a lot. I have packing down to a science."

She probably had everything reduced to "a science," including how she planned to strip Eldovia of its identity and traditions. She was likely a card-carrying member of some efficiency cult or other that had a lot of Greek letters in its name but really did nothing more than teach you how to write a to-do list and drill into you the discipline to carry it out. "Well then, shall we?"

"We shall."

In through the nose, out through the mouth.

"MAYBE WE CAN use this time to get started?" Cara asked once they were settled in the back seat of a black BMW and Mr. Benz—he kept calling her Ms. Delaney, so she was thinking of him as Mr. Benz—informed her that the trip from the airport to the palace would take almost two hours. "I thought we could go over a few things."

"I believe your contract commences tomorrow."

"Right. Regardless, I'm fine to start informally now. Can we get up to speed?"

"Get up to speed?" he echoed, a quizzical expression on his face. He nodded toward the driver, who was separated from them by a clear plastic partition. "I assure you that Mr. Walmsley is as expeditious a driver as you could hope for and, more critically for when we begin our ascent into the mountains, a careful one. He's former Eldovian army."

"That was an idiom. To get someone up to speed means to catch them up." Was that a bad way to explain it? Another metaphor that might not make sense to a non-native English speaker? "To 'orient them to the file,' you might say?"

"Yes, exactly. To teach them what they need to know as they start something."

"And here I thought you were already oriented to the file." He looked at her evenly. This Mr. Benz guy had a great poker face most of the time. Occasionally, though, he would do this thing where he flared his nostrils and pursed his lips—but only for a second, and then the poker face would be back.

It was a surprisingly handsome face, regardless of which mode it was in. He had gold-flecked green eyes, close-cropped dirty-blond hair, and stupidly full lips. His jaw looked like it had been chiseled out of granite—it looked like it could chisel *through* granite, actually, and also all kinds of bullshit. It was odd: if you really looked at Mr. Benz's face, he was probably in his thirties, but his general demeanor brought to mind someone older. It was partly his suit, which was clearly well-made but was a three-piece style—not something you saw much of these days. There was even a watch chain attached to one of the vest's buttons that disappeared into a small pocket. His formal way of speaking, which she suspected went beyond the fact that they had different native tongues, also contributed to his old-soul aura. He looked like a millennial dressed up as a boomer. A fancy boomer. With a great poker face.

A great poker face that occasionally slipped, and she knew what those slips signified. He was pissy about her being here. She hadn't expected that. To be fair, she hadn't expected anything. She knew this file—she had taken the lead on the pitch and had been checking in on it since CZT won the contract. But Brad, given his background as a mechanical engineer and his fluency in German, had been the project lead—and the point person for the Eldovians.

So Cara was going into this trip without a bead on any of the players, which was suboptimal but couldn't be helped.

But she knew clients. There were only so many types of clients. The source of Mr. Benz's ire was almost certainly one of two things. First, it could be plain-old sexism. He could be annoyed that he'd been working with Brad but now had to deal with a *girl*.

The second option was that it wasn't personal, that he was pissed *anyone* was here. This happened sometimes when CZT had been tasked with coming in and cleaning house. Cara was here to begin an overhaul of the operations of Morneau, a historic luxury watch company in the vein of Rolex but smaller and, depending on who among the old-money set you asked, more exclusive. The royal family owned two-fifths of the privately held company, and Morneau's history and that of the throne were intertwined, so she could appreciate that hers was a delicate task.

As she understood it, Mr. Benz *was* the man behind the throne, even if he didn't like to phrase it like that. She had seen the royal family's org chart. Mr. Benz was his own, high-level box on that chart, but a *whole lot* of people had dotted-line reporting relationships to him. He had his hand in every department from the kitchen to public relations. And perhaps more importantly, he had, according to Brad, the king's ear and his unwavering trust. Cara knew the king wanted her here. He, in his role as chair of Morneau's board, had personally been involved in the vetting of firms vying for the job. What she didn't know was if anyone else wanted her here. Just because a boss wanted something didn't mean the rest of the team did, even if—maybe especially if—that boss was a hereditary monarch.

Was she going to be facing a lot of resistance? Were people going to help her? Undercut her? These were the kind of behind-the-scenes questions she couldn't answer until she was on-site, and she'd been hoping Mr. Benz might have some insight on the politics of the situation. And whatever happened, when heads *did* have to roll, this guy's wasn't going to be on the chopping block.

"I am oriented to the file on paper," she said carefully, returning to Mr. Benz's remark. "But as I'm sure you can appreciate, that's quite different from having boots on the ground in a place."

"Boots on the ground," he echoed quizzically.

"Sorry, that's another idiom. It means—"

"It's a military metaphor."

"Yes. I was hoping you might be able to give me an insider's view of the company and the context in which I'll be operating."

"And in this metaphor, you are an invading army?" He looked off into space and smirked as if at something amusing only he could see.

"Not at all. I'm merely—"

"What does that make me?" he went on, ignoring her, still entertained by his private joke. "The poor, backward village you're here to pillage?"

"Of course not," she snapped before she could think better of it. Damn. She hated that he was getting to her. She extra-hated that thanks to that snippy tone she hadn't been able to rein in, he would *know* that he was getting to her.

He turned his head slowly, finally giving her his attention. She really did think his jaw could cut granite. Or, okay, maybe just a very soft shale. But still. There was challenge in his gaze. "What *does* it make me then?"

Oh, for god's sake, this man was a lot. "You should give yourself some credit. You don't really seem like the backward-village type to me. Maybe you're actually a guerrilla fighter. Or a spy." She was trying to lighten the mood.

It didn't work. "Ms. Delaney, I am not on the board of Morneau, and as such am not privy to any, as you say . . . insider information."

Jeez. He acted like she was talking about insider trading. But okay. Whichever was the explanation for his standoffishness, sexism or a more generalized animosity—and it could be both—it was unfortunate. But she was adept at rolling with the punches. Change is the essential process of all existence, right? Her job now was to make sure Mr. Benz remained a neutral party rather than a saboteur. To do that, she needed to disarm him, to stick with the military metaphor. To do *that*, she needed to figure out what exactly the stick up his butt was made of.

But not literally.

Ha. Too many metaphors.

"Is something amusing, Ms. Delaney?"

He wanted to start tomorrow—Monday. Maybe he was a work-to-rule type who had a more European sense of work-life balance. She was aware that those sorts of people, and cultures, existed. Once on a job in Spain, the entire company shut down for two hours over lunch—and they'd hired CZT to find inefficiencies in their processes.

To test her theory, she asked, "What is there to do in Witten on weekends? I was just laughing to myself because I understand that Eldovia is known for its skiing, but I'm not a skier." She was *most decidedly* not a skier. She pushed away those memories. She was not that girl anymore. "I'm actually extremely talented at finding myself in places where I'm not able to partake in a signature activity. I once spent a month in Barbados without knowing how to swim."

"If you're interested in learning to ski, I can arrange lessons for you. But there are numerous other distractions this time of year. There's a skating rink in the village." She made a face, and he said, "I gather from your expression that you don't skate, either."

"I never had a chance to learn." Which was true about skating, if not technically about skiing.

She should not have brought up skiing.

"Workaholic, as the Americans say?"

"Something like that."

"There's some architecture of note in the village, particularly St. Matthew's church."

"Oh! Is there a Catholic church in Witten?" That had come out a little too vehemently. She'd been thinking that maybe she'd try to find one on Thursday. It wasn't Thanksgiving here, of course,

but she could still go and light a candle, do a little dorky, transatlantic communing with her mom. "If you can't tell by my very
Irish name, I'm Catholic. But not really."

"Cara Delaney," he said slowly, letting the syllables stretch out.
It felt like his voice was caressing her name. Which was absurd.
"How does one manage to be Catholic but not really?"

"By having extremely Catholic parents you love. By finding the
traditions of the Catholic Church comforting, even if you don't
agree with all—or most—of their takes." By having had her elementary Catholic school tuition paid for via scholarships that,
unlike her high school scholarships, had enabled a good, solid
education without marking her as the poor kid.

"I see. I'm sorry to report, then, that St. Matthew's is Lutheran.
There is, however, a small Catholic congregation in Witten. I'll
get you details on location and service times, though it's a French-
speaking parish. Regardless, might I suggest that St. Matthew's
is worth a visit? It's a rare example of modern architecture in the
village, and it's really quite striking."

She continued to question him, not because she cared about
what there was to do on the weekends in Witten, but because it
felt as if he were starting to thaw a bit. She was starting to sense
a pride of place in him, a streak of nationalism. Getting Mr. Benz
talking might help her understand both him and the place that
would be her home for the next month.

"There are a few restaurants in the village," he said, after she'd
asked about local food, "the best being Imogen's, which serves
pub fare, but impeccably done. There is a more upscale restaurant, which is usually of interest to expense-account types. But
the food isn't any better than at Imogen's."

Expense-account types. That was rich coming from Mr. Pocket-Watch-Fancy-Pants. "Is Imogen the name of the proprietor or the pub?"

"Proprietor. The pub is called the Owl and Spruce. She's called Imogen O'Connor."

"Imogen O'Connor!" Cara exclaimed, and immediately regretted the girlish enthusiasm in her tone. She didn't do girlish enthusiasm on the job. Or in front of men. Or in front of men on the job. She tried again, more sedately. "That's a proper Irish name."

"Yes. Her father was Irish."

Somehow, though Mr. Benz answered all Cara's questions cordially enough, they didn't have the effect she'd been going for—getting him to relax. Maybe even start trusting her. Was a two-way conversation too much to ask for? Yes, apparently. Every time she asked a question, he answered, and they lapsed into silence until she asked the next one.

Fine. She gave up. For now. Silence was better than invading armies or whatever they'd been doing before.

But then, after a good ten minutes, he suddenly spoke. "Witten is in a valley, and the palace sits atop a hill next to the village proper. When we clear this peak"—he leaned over and pointed out the window on her side—"we'll make our way down the other side of the mountain on a series of switchbacks. That will be your best view of the palace." He retreated to his side, but his scent lingered. He smelled . . . minty? Well, minty but with a darker, deeper undertone she couldn't quite place. She wondered if his minty aroma was a seasonal thing. He seemed like the kind of guy who might have seasonally rotating cologne. Mint for Eldovian winter. What would summer be? Alpine wildflowers? Edelweiss, maybe! Ha!

"Should you care about such things," he added, looking at her quizzically.

Right. *Get it together, Delaney.* She *did* care about such things. She'd worked in a lot of places, mostly pedestrian but occasionally glamorous—the Barbados gig, for example, had been for a company that owned resorts. But an actual palace? That was new. Like a lot of people raised on modern, Disney-inflected culture, she'd undergone a serious princess phase as a girl, in parallel with her still-going-strong Star Trek phase. She still remembered the day her mom brought home a hand-me-down Belle costume from one of her housecleaning clients. It had been one of those cheap, packaged, polyester Halloween costumes, but it might as well have been a priceless, hand-beaded gown, as much as her seven-year-old self loved it.

But Mr. Benz did not need to know any of that. She twisted to look out the window. The castle was something to see. It was indeed perched on the top of what she supposed counted as a hill here—that's what Mr. Benz had called it—nestled as it was against the backdrop of much bigger snow-capped peaks. But it was orders of magnitude bigger than any hill she'd ever seen. The castle itself was cream-colored with a dark roof studded with circular turrets. It looked like someone had dropped a castle-shaped meringue on the tip of a miniature mountain.

"It is rather lovely, isn't it?" Mr. Benz said with the hint of a smile that actually seemed genuine.

She was pretty sure her latest theory was correct. Mr. Benz

was house proud—country proud. So she would keep hammering away on that front. "What a beautiful castle. How old is it?"

"It's not a castle; it's a palace."

Well, la-di-da. "And if I ask you what the difference is, will you think me a boorish American?"

"A castle is a defensive structure."

"Ah, meaning castles have moats and drawbridges and those little holes to shoot arrows through?"

"Those 'little holes' are called embrasures, but yes. A castle might be home to royalty, but it needn't be. Regardless, its original purpose would always have been fortification."

"So this joint isn't fortified."

"This . . . *joint* is not fortified." Mr. Benz's poker face was slipping in favor of that nostril-flaring thing again. It was like a sniff of disapproval that stopped short of being an actual sniff. It wasn't audible, and he didn't stick his nose in the air or anything, but somehow he was doing an internal sniff.

God help her, this man was a lot.

"The palace is newer than you might think," he added as he raised the poker-face drawbridge again. "It was built in 1867 by the king's great-grandfather. A palace, if you haven't gathered from context, is the home of royalty."

"I have gathered, thank you." She paused. Once again, that had come out too snippily. She tried again on the making-friendly-conversation front. "It looks like a more realistic version of Cinderella's palace at Disney World."

"Indeed. I spend more time than you might imagine denying requests from film crews."

"Why would you deny them?"

"Why *wouldn't* I?"

Because you need money. She didn't say it like that, and of course Mr. Benz personally did not need money—although his suit was a little old-fashioned in terms of its cut, at least to her American eyes, it clearly wasn't actually old. Dark blue and paired with a lavender raw-silk tie, it was elegant and fit him to a degree of perfection that could only be attained by a tailor. And she assumed that not only did the equerry gig pay well, it was the kind of job you got by being a fancy person to begin with. *Eldovia* needed money, though. That was the whole reason she was here, even if these posh Europeans would never put it so plainly. The luxury watch industry was in decline, and this was a one-industry country. Unemployment was up, and GDP was contracting. Mr. Benz didn't need money, but his country sure as hell did.

As they wound their way up the hill, the palace disappeared from sight due to the steepness of the incline and the forested landscape surrounding it. When they emerged onto a gravel-lined approach, it appeared again, monumental yet delicate. It was imposing but somehow, at the same time, welcoming. A castle of contradictions.

She smiled to herself as she issued a mental correction. A *palace* of contradictions, though that was not as pleasingly alliterative a phrase. A palace of paradox?

Mr. Benz said something to their driver in German before turning to her. "Is something amusing?"

That was the second time he'd asked her that. She needed to rein in the smiling along with the sniping. "I'm merely happy to have finished my journey. I don't think I've recovered from the jet lag from my last trip." On cue, she yawned.

"The best thing to do is to force yourself to stay up until a reasonable hour locally, as difficult as it may be, and retire for the evening at a normal time."

For some reason, an anti–jet lag lecture from this dude annoyed her. "I'm aware." She was back to being snippy, but she couldn't help it. "I travel a lot for work."

"Do you now."

She was noticing this tendency of his to say something that should be a question—*Do you now?*—but to make it a declarative statement, and one that conveyed subtle, snobbish disapproval. "After this trip, I'll have logged more than two hundred days on the road this year."

"Mm," he said as they came to a stop in front of the palace. He opened his door, and she did likewise. The driver was extracting her suitcase from the trunk. "Your bag will be delivered to your suite if that suits?" Mr. Benz asked, making an "after you" gesture in the direction of a stone staircase that led to an oversize wooden double door.

"Yes, thank you." She made her way up the stairs, and the door opened to reveal a man and a woman. The man wore a plain black suit and the woman a black dress. Servants. They were servants. They probably didn't call them that anymore, and hopefully they made a decent living and had dental benefits and all that, but they looked like they could have come from the set of *Downton Abbey*.

"Ms. Delaney, welcome," the man said. "I am Ernst, and this is Frau Lehman."

Cara had no idea how she was supposed to greet them, but she stuck out her hand. Maybe that wasn't done, but she came from humble origins herself and she always made a point to be nice to service staff. Hell, her mother had cleaned houses—normal houses—for a living until her rheumatoid arthritis got bad enough that she'd had to stop.

Each of them shook Cara's hand in turn, with no indication that to do so was unusual. "The princess and the king are so sorry they could not be here to greet you in person," Ernst said as they made their way into an enormous foyer with marble-tiled floors and gleaming wood-paneled walls. There was a fireplace at one end with a massive, elaborately carved mantel over which hung a portrait of a very pretty woman. "Though I'm sure Mr. Benz has welcomed you in their stead," said Ernst.

"Yes," she said, though she wasn't sure *welcome* was the word she would use.

"I trust you will see Ms. Delaney settled to her satisfaction and to the high standards for which we are known," Mr. Benz said to Frau Lehman.

Ernst answered, apparently speaking on behalf of Frau Lehman. "Yes, of course." Cara wondered if Ernst was his first name or last name. Did Eldovians do the British-style one-name butler thing? She had read up on royal protocol on the flight but hadn't learned anything about servants. Servants! It still boggled the mind.

"You've had a delivery, Mr. Benz," Frau Lehman said. "Several boxes. I had them sent to your office."

"Thank you, Frau Lehman," Mr. Benz said warmly, and with a curt nod in Cara's direction, he set off down a corridor.

What a curious man. On the surface of things, he had been the picture of decorum, but there had been a disconnect between the actions he performed and the emotions that seemed to lurk beneath them. And he definitely had a tone problem.

But to be fair, so did she, apparently. He brought it out in her.

Cara gave up her attempts to make sense of Mr. Benz when they reached her room. Rooms, plural. It wasn't unusual for a client to put up a consultant on-site when the project was in a remote locale, but as far as she knew, never in the history of CZT had anyone been accommodated in a palace. As Ernst showed her around, she reasoned that theoretically, the space wasn't that different from a hotel suite. There was a bedroom, a sitting room, and a bathroom—a glorious bathroom featuring a large, free-standing soaker tub. Cara loved nothing more than to luxuriate in a hotel bathtub at the end of a long day. Her house in New York had only a small shower stall, so she considered hotel bathtubs a major perk of all her work travel.

Outside, the sitting room was broken up into four zones—a sofa and chairs arranged around a fireplace, another seating area in a corner centered on a television, an office alcove with a desk and a charging station, and a nook housing a coffee machine, microwave, and minifridge.

But everything was so much *fancier* here than a hotel room would be. Not the princess-fancy of her girlhood imagination, or that she might have expected when she first got a load of the Sugar Plum Palace, but understatedly elegant. Instead of being painted or wallpapered, the walls were paneled in a dark wood. The gray marble floors were veined with a subtle pattern, and antique-looking lamps and chandeliers cast the space in a warm glow. The minifridge was full of drinks of all sorts including half bottles of champagne. And there was a display of chocolate truffles she'd been told were a local specialty.

If all that weren't enough, before he left, Ernst showed her a long tasseled cord hanging in a corner—like, literally the kind people pulled in movies set in ye olden days to summon servants—and told her to pull it if she wanted anything. He presented her with a menu and told her that the kitchen could produce anything on it at a moment's notice and that if she wanted anything *not* on it, she merely needed to inquire and they would do their best.

Clearly, Mr. Benz, in his sermon about what there was to do in Witten on the weekends, had forgotten to mention "take baths while gorging on royal room service."

Her phone dinged. It was an incoming FaceTime from her mom. "How was the trip?" her mom asked.

"Fine. Just getting settled in. Get a load of this place." Cara reversed the camera and conducted a quick tour of the suite. Her mom made cooing noises over everything and directed her to zoom in on the marble floors. "Those are gorgeous."

"Add it to the list." Cara and her mom kept a half-joking wish list of features their future duplex would have. After a lifetime of bouncing around apartments, Cara had saved enough to buy their current house three years ago. But it was merely a planned stop along the way. The end goal was a duplex. She'd live in one side and her parents the other. According to her calculations, with the equity in the current place plus projected raises at work, she'd have enough for a down payment in about four years.

"I bet those floors are cold on your feet, though."

Cara took her shoes and socks off to test the theory. "Yep, freezing. I wonder if there is such a thing as heated marble floors—add *that* to the list."

"I'm sorry I made things difficult for you this morning."

Cara took the phone into the bedroom and studied her mother.

Her brow was furrowed, but Cara was pretty sure it was from guilt, not arthritis pain. "Aww, Mom. It's okay. We were all bummed I had to make this trip."

"I just don't want you to kill yourself working because you feel like you need to take care of us. We're fine."

"I like working." And they *were* fine. Cara knew that. They had beaten back the specter of financial ruin, which had loomed on the not-so-distant horizon for most of her childhood. But they weren't done. *Cara* wasn't done. Not until she had the duplex and partnership at the firm.

"I know. You always were so diligent. But you should be having fun, too. You're young. You should be dating." Her mom held up a hand. "And before you get your feathers ruffled, I'm not talking about getting married and having babies, although I'm not going to lie, I wouldn't be mad at any of that. But when was the last time you went on a date?"

Cara didn't date. At least she didn't date in the way her mom meant, which was going to the movies and, Cara didn't even know . . . probably sharing a milkshake at the Crosstown Diner. In some ways, Mom was a mystery to Cara. She was super-Catholic and, frankly, came off as kind of naive. But she'd gotten pregnant with Cara as a twenty-year-old, when she still lived at home with her own super-Catholic parents—who had kicked her out. She'd been four months pregnant and living in a shelter when she met Cara's dad. So it wasn't like she didn't know how the world worked.

"I don't think people date the way you think of it anymore," she said, hoping that would be the end of it.

"How do they date?"

Nope. They weren't having this conversation.

Cara couldn't bring men home, since she lived with her parents—though she supposed that since she paid the mortgage, it was more accurate to say that her parents lived with her. Either way, she had roommates, roommates who took a particular interest in her comings and goings. Well, one of them did. Her dad could and did sleep through anything, but Mom had supersonic hearing and would be all over Cara if she sneaked in late at night. Not that it had to happen at night. Theoretically there was nothing stopping her from, say, taking a long "lunch." It was more that . . . her mom would *know*.

Which was, logically, absurd, because her mother was the one all over her to "meet someone." She just didn't want Cara to meet someone the way people actually did in the modern world. So it was only on Cara's trips that she could get a certain itch, an itch that healthy, single, thirty-five-year-old women had, scratched. It was an arrangement that suited her. She was happily married to her job right now, but the odd casual hookup on the road reminded her that she was alive.

But there would be no itch-scratching on this trip. It wasn't like she could bring a dude into the freaking royal palace of Eldovia for the purposes of hooking up. "Mom, I gotta go. I have to do some prep work for my meeting with the board tomorrow."

"Sleep tight, my girl, my greatest thing."

After Cara finished unpacking in her bedroom, she took her suitcase out into the living room, intending to unpack the rest into the office alcove, but the sofa looked so comfy. Deciding to allow herself a moment of respite, she flopped down on it and thought of Mr. Benz and his sniffing. Maybe it wasn't so much that he disapproved of her; maybe he had a secret cocaine problem. Or maybe—

No. *Why* was she thinking about Mr. Benz right now? She was supposed to be relaxing.

Though *he* certainly wouldn't approve of this. She might accidentally fall asleep and violate the Anti–Jet Lag Protocol.

Okay, enough. Mr. Benz did not deserve this much mental real estate. She would worry about him tomorrow. She unpacked her sudoku book. Time to turn her thoughts to an easier puzzle.

Chapter Two

Matteo had only just started climbing the stairs to his suite when Torkel Renner, the former head of palace security, called. "Good evening," Matteo said, unlocking his door and kicking off his shoes. "What did you find?"

"Not much. Thirty-five years old. Born in the Bronx, New York, to Saoirse Delaney-nee-McGrath. Adopted at birth by Patrick Delaney."

Hmm. That Ms. Delaney had been raised by a man who was not her biological father was not relevant for Matteo's present purposes, but it was an interesting fact. He filed it away.

"Both parents are Irish, obviously. Irish-Irish in the mother's case—she came over as a child. The father is third-generation. He's a longshoreman; there's no employment record for her."

Such a working-class background did not accord with his image of Ms. Delaney, with her designer suits, stilettos, and bruising handshakes. But Matteo of all people should know that appearances could be deceiving.

"They all live together in a house in the Woodlawn Heights section of the Bronx. It was purchased three years ago. The deed is in her name. Before that they moved a lot—seven times in the previous ten years. Always apartments, always in the same neighborhood."

Matteo had to weave around the boxes covering most of the open space in his apartment as he made his way to the kitchen. He would be glad when Christmas was over. "Anything else?"

"She graduated top of her class from Dutton, which is a prestigious private high school in Manhattan."

Matteo wondered how *that* had happened given her apparently modest background. But again, he had to check himself. People were always more complicated than their circumstances would suggest.

"She has a BA in economics from Hunter College, where she was part of the Army ROTC, and she did two years in the military after graduating."

"I beg your pardon?" Ms. Delaney was *military*? He thought back to that ridiculous little argument about nothing they'd had earlier, with all the military metaphors.

"Reserve Officers' Training Corps. It's a U.S. military program that pays for university in exchange for—"

"I know what it is. I'm just . . . surprised." Matteo cleared his throat. "Go on."

"After she was discharged, she returned to CZT, where she'd spent a year interning while still in school, and she's been there ever since. She did an executive MBA at Columbia part-time, finished two years ago."

Matteo put the phone on speaker and attempted to pour himself a scotch, but the bottle was nearly empty. He ended up with less than a teaspoonful. "Boyfriend? Or"—he shouldn't make assumptions—"girlfriend?" He assumed she wasn't married. He would have noticed if she'd been wearing a ring—her red-varnished nails had drawn his attention several times.

"Not that I can tell."

"So that's it?"

"I can dig a little deeper, but that was what I could find on a quick first pass. Honestly, I don't know what you were expecting. She's a management consultant, not a jewel thief with an Interpol red notice."

Matteo sighed. He hadn't been expecting anything, not really, and ultimately none of it mattered. It was just that he preferred knowing with whom he was dealing. And since Ms. Delaney had been dropped in at the last minute to substitute for her injured colleague, he hadn't done any homework on her. Hence the favor called in to Torkel, who had quit the palace last year to go to work for the House of Aquilla. Torkel's boyfriend, Sebastien von Hansburg, was the younger brother of the Duke of Aquilla. Princess Marie was always laughingly accusing Matteo of having underworld connections, and while he did have a number of people, some of them tending toward the unsavory, on whom he could call for all manner of things, the true source of most of his knowledge had been Torkel.

He missed Torkel, and not only because of the man's connections. He and Torkel had spent many a day working side by side, first in the army, and later to protect and advance the interests of the royal family. Like Matteo, Torkel understood that a life devoid of higher ideals was an empty exercise.

He shook himself out of these fruitless thoughts. "How is life in Riems? How is Mr. von Hansburg?"

"He's well." Matteo could hear the smile in Torkel's usually gruff tone. "I could use your help with something, actually."

"Of course."

"I want to, uh . . . propose."

Matteo held back a laugh. Torkel was normally so unflappable. Huge and stoic, he looked like Hollywood's stereotype of a bodyguard, right down to the severe black suits and mirrored aviator sunglasses he favored. "That's wonderful."

"Indeed, but I, uh . . . don't know how to do it."

"I believe the tradition is to procure a ring," Matteo teased.

"I know that," Torkel said with a snappishness that would be off-putting if Matteo didn't know him so well. "I even know what ring I want—what kind he would want. The ring is not the problem. I just . . ."

Matteo sobered. This was the first time Matteo had ever known Torkel to be uncertain. "You want it to be special."

"Yes, and you're good at this sort of thing."

He was. At handling everything and fading into the background. From ensuring the king's victories in parliament to giving Princess Marie the nudge she needed to marry Leo Ricci, the interloper who had been entirely unsuitable yet singularly capable of making her happy. And Matteo enjoyed his job. There was satisfaction in being able to take credit for things running smoothly in the lives of the royal family.

"I realize it's a bit out of your scope," Torkel said.

Matteo made a dismissive noise. "I interpret my scope broadly.

You know that." The way he thought of it was he had his official mission, and he had his extended mission.

"Indeed. How are the baskets coming this year?"

"Slowly." Matteo regretted the word as soon as it was out of his mouth. It would activate Torkel's guilt complex.

"I'm sorry I'm not there."

"It's not that. It's this tiresome American management consultant come to upend Morneau. I can tell that she's going to be very . . . time-consuming."

"Well, if you need any help, you need only call on me. I can come down for a few days and you can put me to work."

"But what excuse would you use?" Wait. "Have you told Mr. von Hansburg about the Christmas baskets?" Matteo understood that he couldn't very well ask Torkel to keep secrets from his partner, but the fewer people who knew about the baskets, the better. That number was currently three—possibly four—and he strongly preferred to keep it that way.

"I haven't. And I'd think of something."

"Well, we don't need you. We have it in hand. Now, back to your proposal."

"Right. I was thinking about how you were responsible for getting the princess and Leo together, and about how you helped Daniela and Max after the late duke died. I don't need that much help. I just need . . . an idea."

"Allow me to give the matter some thought."

"Thank you." Torkel paused. "How are you?"

Tired. He always was this time of year, but this was more than that. He felt existentially tired, though he wasn't sure why. Nothing about this year was different from any of the previous, except of course the presence of Ms. Cara Delaney. But being visited by a corporate-goth management consultant bent on dismantling Morneau, while annoying, was not a sufficient explanation for this degree of weariness.

"I'm fine," he said in answer to Torkel's question, and he even sounded reasonably convincing. "Life unfolds apace."

"As it always does with you at the helm."

"Mmm."

After they hung up, Matteo loosened his tie, took his scotch, such as it was, to the window, and tried to put his mind to Torkel's proposal, but thoughts of Ms. Delaney intruded. Matteo's apartment, at the top of the original stable, faced west, and the days were so short now that the sun was already starting to set even though it wasn't yet five o'clock. Sunset over the mountains was always spectacular, and he made a point to observe it as often as he could. He cued up a record and sank into the chair he kept angled next to the window for this very purpose. He should have told Ms. Delaney to look for the sunset out her windows. He had told Frau Lehman to put her in the green-wing guest room specifically because it faced west. Not alerting Ms. Delaney to the wonders that lay outside her window hadn't been very hospitable of him.

Neither had been taking his leave earlier without so much as a goodbye. Or the several occasions when he'd been snappish with her.

Rolling his neck, he made a conscious effort to relax his tight jaw and let the soothing sounds of Sarah Vaughan wash over him as he savored his thimbleful of scotch.

Scotch didn't taste very good with a side of guilt.

Inhospitality was not something to be proud of. Mother had drilled that into Matteo and his siblings. *Share what you have. Make people feel comfortable. Kindness costs nothing.*

But, he argued with himself, it wasn't his job, at this moment, to make Ms. Delaney feel comfortable. The king had asked him to welcome her, and he had done that. Going personally to the airport to collect her had already been above and beyond the call of duty. Ernst and Frau Lehman had assumed guardianship of her. They would make sure she knew how to order food or put out her clothes to be laundered.

But would they tell her—or show her—how to get down to the village? Would they offer her horseback riding or anything else to do? She *had* asked him what there was to do on the weekends.

He yawned. He was so *tired*.

Like she was.

Would she fall asleep in her room right away? Would she order anything to eat before she did? And if she didn't, would Frau Lehman send a footman to check on her?

He disliked thinking of her rattling around that huge, mostly empty palace by herself, even if he disliked *her*.

It was confusing.

She was confusing.

Damn it. He sighed, and, half against his will, stood and tightened his tie.

CARA HAD FINISHED all of two sudokus before her brain was back trying to figure out the mystery that was Mr. Benz. He didn't want her here, and she was leaning toward resistance to her mission rather than misogyny as the reason. Either way, he had clearly washed his hands of her until his boss, aka the king, was back on the scene, and he would probably be less than no help next week.

Which was fine. Even though she hadn't gotten any useful information out of him, knowing where she stood with him was its own kind of useful information.

But when she answered a knock on her door to find him standing there, she had to admit she'd been wrong. The man remained an enigma.

"Ms. Delaney, I was going to walk down the hill to the Owl and Spruce in the village, and I wondered if you'd care to join me."

Okay, well, here was her next chance to try to figure him out.

"That would be great." She scanned his body. He was wearing a heavy wool coat but appeared to still have his suit pants on, so she would take that as a cue to remain in her own suit. "Let me get my coat."

He looked at her feet, which . . . right. She hadn't changed out of her suit yet, but she had taken off her shoes to test the temperature of the floors when she'd been talking to her mom.

He kept looking, staring really. There was nothing remarkable about her feet. She kept herself in pedicures. She considered it part of her professional grooming budget, even though no one ever saw her toes at work. She could have sworn her feet got hot under his scrutiny, even though the marble beneath them was chilly.

"I'll, ah, put on some shoes, too," she said awkwardly, and that had the effect of dislodging his attention from her feet.

"You can't walk down the hill in those shoes."

He sounded pissy again, almost as if he were baiting her. Also, what did he mean by "those" shoes? Her shoes were nowhere in sight.

She went to her suitcase, which she had open on a chair in the living room because she'd never gotten around to unpacking the office stuff that she wanted to keep out here. She pulled out socks and a pair of boots. They were smooshy and packable and collapsed down to not much bigger than the size of their soles. She shook them out and put them on along with a pair of socks, uncomfortably aware of Mr. Benz's attention throughout the process.

They made their way through the palace's drafty, art-bedecked corridors without speaking. It was a long way out, and eventually the silence started to feel awkward. It was a relief to get outside into the crisp twilight. Exercise and fresh air were both welcome after the long flight, and they would help with the jet lag.

And was the air ever fresh. This place smelled like the real version of the pine tree air freshener people hung on their rearview mirrors. She thought back to Mr. Benz's minty cologne from the car. Maybe everything—and everyone—in Eldovia smelled like a variation on Christmas.

"Are you quite all right, Ms. Delaney?"

The question made her realize she'd been sniffing like a coke addict. "I bet the walk back up this hill is quite the workout," she said, changing the subject. At least they were speaking again.

"We can summon a car for the return trip if you like. And you know, you're free to call a car at any time should you care to venture out. I hope Frau Lehman explained that."

"Yes, thank you." Access to cars and drivers had been part of the "stay at the palace" offer.

The silence returned. Usually, Cara was good at filling lulls in conversation, or, alternatively, at being comfortable in them. She could do small talk; she could do companionable silence. Social skills played a big role in her line of work. But with this guy, things were awkward in a way she wasn't able to overcome. It was like he was infecting her somehow, like proximity to him was making her socially clumsy.

She tried to let the bracing air restore her and to enjoy the crunch of snow beneath her feet as he led her off the main road and onto a footpath that disappeared into the woods. This would be a great setup for a murder. Lure the unwelcome management consultant into the forest just as it was getting dark. "This could be the opening to a horror movie."

He had been walking a little ahead of her, and he turned, his brow wrinkled in confusion. "I beg your pardon?"

It took her a moment to register that he'd stopped moving. She tried to put on the brakes, but she bonked into him—the jet lag must be making her brain slow. His reflexes didn't seem to be in tip-top shape, either: he put his hands up as if to stop her, but they came up only as she was making contact with him. She got another whiff of that dark mint, and ugh, why did he smell so *good*? And what was that note underneath the mint? Cedar? Sandalwood? She had no idea what either of those things smelled like, but she imagined they would smell like this—kind of masculine and woodsy. Her nose was at about his neck level, and since she'd already crashed into him like a complete dolt, she allowed herself to list ever so slightly closer to him so she could take one more covert breath and allow the—

His hands landed on her upper arms. She tilted her head back. It was almost fully dark now, but his eyes seemed . . . intense somehow. Her heart started beating like maybe he *was* going to murder her. Either that, or—

He took a big step back.

Right. He'd been using his hands to physically put her at arm's length.

Probably because she was sniffing him.

"Sorry," she said breezily. "Lost my footing there. Anyway, I was just thinking that this would be a great setting for a horror movie. If you were only pretending to be a loyal employee of the Crown and . . ." *You wanted to murder me.* "Never mind." She tried to laugh it off, but it sounded like she was choking rather than laughing.

She had succeeded in making things even more awkward. They set off again, and the silence became positively oppressive. Soon enough—thank goodness—they were off the hill. The village looked like a movie set, as if Maria von Trapp might come twirling out of one of the quaint half-timbered buildings that lined the narrow main street singing about bluebirds and apple strudel. As they walked, Cara noted a few restaurants, an antiquarian bookstore, a candy shop, a store that seemed to sell nothing but pastry-making equipment, and another that sold only leather gloves. There were also "real" establishments: dry cleaners and butchers and a dental office. Eventually, the street widened into a square with a huge pine tree in the center. There was a small skating rink on one side with a dozen or so skaters zipping along. The whole square was lit with strings of lights.

She had to hold herself back from rolling her eyes, but she also couldn't help smiling. "Well, isn't this too much?"

"What do you mean?"

"Is that hot chocolate being served over there?" She pointed to an outdoor bar that was serving steaming mugs of something, and she knew Eldovia had a cocoa festival at Christmas. There were people sitting on stools at the wooden bar—which was a giant slab of wood with one of those live edges that people in New York would pay a pretty penny for—warming their hands against bright-red mugs. Everyone looked happy, like stock-photo people in a "winter fun" shot.

"It is hot chocolate," Mr. Benz said. "You can get it plain—milk chocolate or dark—or with various syrups or liqueurs mixed in. There's coffee, too. Cocoa and coffee mixed together is a popular libation in Eldovia."

"I assume that's a Christmas tree?" She nodded at the huge pine.

"Yes. It just arrived. It will be decorated over the coming week, and there's a lighting ceremony next weekend, should you care to take it in."

"Happy people skating and drinking cocoa. It's like a magical fairyland where everyone's always happy and it's perpetually Christmas."

Mr. Benz pondered the idyllic scene as if he were seeing it for the first time. "This is not necessarily representative."

"So people are allowed to be unhappy in Eldovia?" she asked, following him as he resumed walking.

She'd been kidding, or trying to, but he didn't react. Of course he didn't. She was the newly crowned queen of awkwardness here, and Mr. Benz did not have a sense of humor. What a pair they made.

But to her surprise, he did answer, a full minute later, as he was holding the heavy wooden door of the Owl and Spruce for her. "People are allowed to be unhappy in Eldovia." He opened his mouth as if he were going to say more, then shut it abruptly. They stared at each other for a beat before she broke with his gaze and hustled through the door.

She scanned the pub, which was crowded with what looked an awful lot like more unnaturally happy people. Even though the building itself, from the outside, looked like the rest of the village, with its half-timbered stucco architecture, inside was one hundred percent Irish pub. She could have been back in any number of bars in Woodlawn Heights. Except not, because this was much nicer than any of the places she and her dad occasionally hit for a drink on Saturday afternoons.

"I customarily sit at the bar." Mr. Benz nodded at a huge, gleaming wooden bar that was about half full. "But perhaps you'd rather procure a table?"

"No, the bar is great." It was her preference, too, whether she was with her dad or alone in a hotel bar. At a bar you could watch the happenings, listen in on conversations, feel like you were in the thick of things even if you were by yourself. Equally, bars were good places to meet people for the kind of "date" Cara's mom didn't understand. Not that Cara would be meeting anyone at *this* bar. She was, unfortunately, already here with someone. Just not that kind of someone.

Mr. Benz pulled out a stool for her and hovered, waiting until she was situated before taking his own seat. He was so weirdly chivalrous given the strained vibe between them. The woman behind the bar came over, and he performed introductions. "Imogen O'Connor, meet Ms. Cara Delaney."

Imogen flashed Cara a grin and set a coaster in front of her. "You're the New York hotshot."

"The New York part, yes. The hotshot part, not so much."

"Cara Delaney. That's a fine Irish name."

"Yes. I'm second-generation on one side."

"Me, too. My da was from Dublin," Imogen said with an exaggerated Irish lilt. It reminded Cara of her mom, whose own accent came out when she was sick or tired—which she increasingly was. "But I'm extremely Eldovian on the other." She was pouring a glass of scotch as she spoke, and she set it in front of Mr. Benz. He must be a regular. "What can I get you, Cara Delaney?"

"Imogen has a very fine scotch list," Mr. Benz said.

"I also have a handful of even finer Irish whiskeys," Imogen said with a wink.

Cara liked Imogen. She was friendly and warm, which she supposed were job requirements for a bartender, but those qualities in her seemed genuine. And honestly, it was a relief to have a third person present to break up the . . . whatever it was between her and Mr. Benz. Awkwardness, tension, thinly veiled animosity? All of the above? "While I'm sure your inventory of both scotch and whiskey are second-to-none, both categories are wasted on me." She usually had one of whatever her client was having before switching to water, but she hated the taste of hard liquor without a mixer. "I'm a bit of a lightweight—an embarrassment to my heritage, I'm afraid."

"If you've a sweet tooth, I can do homemade cocoa with a shot of Baileys or Frangelico or any other liqueur you like. Or if you're partial to beer, I have a pumpkin stout I brew on-site. Or I can get you the wine list."

"I'll try the stout, thanks." She pointed to a chalkboard that listed the day's specials. "And the lamb stew, please."

As Imogen pulled the pint, Cara started aggressively yawning. "Jet lag?" Imogen asked sympathetically.

Cara was about to agree when Mr. Benz said, "Ms. Delaney is tired from a year spent traveling the globe to save hapless, backward companies from themselves."

Cara blinked, taken aback. Mr. Benz blinked, too, as if he were surprised by his own outburst. So much for the almost imperceptible snubs. Shit was getting perceptible here.

For once, Cara wasn't racking her brain trying to think of something to say to Mr. Benz. She was going to let him stew in his own bitterness. She picked up her beer and took a sip. "Mm," she said to Imogen, who was also blinking. A round of blinking for everyone, courtesy of Mr. Benz! "This is really good. Like an alcoholic pumpkin spice latte."

"Ta. I'm rather proud of it, if I do say so." She glanced down the bar. "Move over to this empty stool." She was speaking to someone Cara couldn't see, someone at the bar but on the other side of a large column. She couldn't hear the person's response, either, but it must have been a refusal, because after Imogen pointed at the empty stool next to Cara and said, sternly, "Kai. Get your misanthropic butt over here. Meet our guest from New York."

"Oh, that's okay," Cara said. "There's no need to—" Whoa. Okay. *Hello.*

"Kai Keller, this is Cara Delaney from New York."

"Nice to meet you," Cara said. Kai was tall and dark and scruffy and *gorgeous.* He wore a blue-and-black plaid flannel shirt, jeans, and heavy work boots.

Maybe she *could* meet someone at this bar. What were the

chances a man this good-looking was single? She glanced at his hand. No ring.

"Kai is a carpenter," Imogen said. "He moonlights doing these." She gestured at the shelves behind her. They were lined with bottles except for one, which was filled with snow globes. Imogen pulled one down and set it in front of Cara. It was a tiny replica of the bar building set in a glass globe that rested on an elaborately carved wooden base varnished to gleaming. She picked it up and shook it, smiling as the snow swirled around the scene. "It's beautiful."

"Come on now," Kai said to Imogen. "I only make the bases." He turned to Cara. "A local artist makes the miniatures for me. The bases are easy."

Imogen snorted as if she disagreed with Kai's interpretation. She gestured at the collection. "All the notable buildings in town are represented." She pointed at one. "There's the palace."

"Do you have an Etsy shop or something?" Cara asked. "My mom would love these."

"A what shop?"

"He doesn't make them for money," Mr. Benz said from her other side. Cara had been so blinded by Kai's rugged Alpine masculine beauty, not to mention his carpentry skills, that she'd almost forgotten about Mr. Benz.

Well, that wasn't true. Mr. Benz was difficult to forget. There was something about his presence that . . . took up space. You knew he was there even if he was silent. Maybe that's what had been wrong with her on the walk down the mountain. She didn't know how to deal with the juxtaposition between Mr. Benz's literal silence and his attention-commanding demeanor.

"He *should* sell them," Imogen said. "I get people trying to buy them all the time." Kai merely grunted. "But no, he's too busy being a hermit." She turned to Cara. "Kai lives alone in the woods in the cutest log cabin you ever saw."

Kai rolled his eyes. Kai, she was sensing, was a man of few words, but if he *were* prone to using words, he would probably expend a few objecting to his home being called *cute*.

Hmm. An absurdly good-looking, talented-with-his-hands man of few words who lived alone.

Was it possible things were starting to look up?

She glanced at Mr. Benz, feeling the ever-present magnetism of his attention. He was already looking at her, his expression as impossible to read as ever. She needed to get rid of him. Not just now, as it related to Kai, but, elementally. It was starting to feel as though the success of her project here depended on it.

To Matteo's surprise, Ms. Delaney wanted to walk back up the hill. He'd been prepared to call for a car. He wouldn't have minded. Spending time with Ms. Delaney was oddly innervating, and he was tired.

"Why don't we have it out, then?" she said as soon as they cleared the crowded village square.

"I beg your pardon?"

She stopped walking and turned to him, her pale skin illuminated by one of the village's gas streetlights. "You clearly don't want me here, and that's fine. Message received. But is this the attitude I should expect from everyone else? From the king?"

Matteo had to admit she'd disarmed him with her forthrightness. He was accustomed to the subtle currents of palace politics, where achieving one's goals sometimes required a bit of strategy. Almost like playing a game of chess. He wasn't used to being called out so directly. But he supposed he also wasn't used to working with American management consultants.

"Come on," she said with an air of impatience. "I don't want to do this covert warfare bullshit. If there's going to be warfare, let's have it be overt. You don't like me. All right. I can live with that. I don't like you, either." She was waving a hand around in the air, and it was ungloved. It was too dim to see the red of her nail polish, but her fingertips read as "dark" against the relative paleness of her skin. It was difficult to look away from them. "I can't play your game if I don't know the rules," she said when he took too long to speak.

He took a step back. He scrambled to think what to say to regain the upper hand. It wasn't lost on him that she'd used the word *game*. He had just compared his usual methods for advancing his agenda to playing chess. Paradoxically, though, being seen through so completely made him want to *stop* playing.

All right, they would do things her way. For now. "I *don't* want you here. And . . ." Should he say the rest? Well, she'd started it. "I *don't* like you. It's nothing personal, mind you. I'm sure you're very good at your job." She stared at him, assessing. He could almost see her mind spinning up. She was a worthy adversary. In another circumstance, one with lower stakes, he would have enjoyed facing off with her. "Are you going to lay people off?"

"*I'm* not going to do anything other than the job I've been tasked with, which is to report to Morneau's board of directors on how Morneau can modernize and become more profitable."

"You know what I mean."

She continued to look at him evenly, her face betraying no emotion. He didn't like that. He was used to being able to read people more easily than this. "I think it's very likely that there will be layoffs, yes. Demand for Morneau's products—"

"Which are *watches*," he interrupted. That was the problem with people like her. Everything was interchangeable to them. Morneau could be making any kind of widget, and it would be all the same to her. He sniffed, feeling more like himself. It helped that she had redonned her gloves, so he didn't have to look at her fingernails.

"Demand for Morneau's watches," she said smoothly, unbothered by the correction, "has fallen by thirty-nine percent over the past decade. Do you know what's happened to the company's workforce over the same period?"

He did not, which was embarrassing. He knew the current size of the workforce, roughly speaking—he read the company's annual report every year—but he didn't have the figure from the previous year memorized, much less that from ten years ago.

He resolved to do better.

"Morneau's workforce is up two percent over the last ten years," she informed him coolly.

"Is it now?" He smirked. He couldn't help it. That two percent was probably down to him. Not that she needed to know that.

"How does that make sense when productivity is down?" she went on, not unkindly, he had to concede. Her voice had lost its earlier confrontational quality. She was speaking softly now, as if she knew she was breaking bad news.

He didn't like that she thought she knew him, that she thought he was the kind of person she needed to treat gently. He didn't like it *at all*. "Your organizing principle here is that productivity is the be-all, end-all of human civilization, correct?"

"Well, since it's my job to 'save hapless, backward companies from themselves,'"—she made quotation marks with her fingers, and damn it, he was back to thinking about her nails even though he couldn't see them—"I suppose I'm going to have to go with yes."

He winced. That remark at the bar had been too much. He had lashed out, his aim to belittle her, which wasn't something he was proud of. "I apologize for saying that. I made things personal when they weren't."

His apology seemed to crack her facade. She huffed a little sigh and looked into the distance. "I'm trying to answer your question honestly. I don't think there will be a way to avoid layoffs. If it's any consolation, I don't relish delivering that news. I never do."

She *was* being honest, he thought. He decided to respond in kind. "To answer *your* question honestly, no, I don't think you can expect the king to be as resistant as I am to your . . ." He cleared his throat. "Charms." She was still looking off into the distance, but she smiled at his euphemism, which was gratifying. He didn't often make attempts at humor, so he hadn't been sure it would be effective. "I interpret the mandate of my job broadly," he added, because admitting he disagreed with the king about something to the consultant who had been hired by said king was perhaps unwise.

She returned her attention to him. "What does that mean?"

"I'm equerry to the king, yes, but as you said yourself, I'm not a mere secretary. I'm not a lackey who carries out his every command literally and promptly."

"You're an advisor. A courtier. A man of influence."

"Yes."

"And you hate that you were charged with babysitting me today."

It was his turn to smile. He had to admit that her straightforwardness, though disarming, could be rather refreshing. "I do." He rushed to add, "But only because you and I have different ideas about the future of Morneau. Because we have different degrees of understanding about how changes to Morneau will affect the people of Eldovia."

"And because we don't like each other," she added, and he dipped his head. She'd said it, not him.

"Again, it's not personal."

"So you interpret your mission broadly. You never answered that. What does that mean?"

"Did you know that the royal family of Eldovia has a mission statement?"

"Yes. It's something about heritage and values."

"'To steward the heritage of Eldovia, to advance its values in the world, to lift up its people.' I interpret *my* mission as a bifurcated one. On the one hand, in a pragmatic sense, I am charged with advising the king, with seeing that his will is carried out. On the other, the royal mission is also *my* mission. I strive in all I do to lift up the people of Eldovia."

"What if your interpretation of 'lifting' differs from the king's? Does that ever happen?"

"I don't think it's so much that we disagree, but sometimes we have different ideas about how to arrive at the same outcome."

"The outcome being that the people of Eldovia are lifted up?"

"Indeed."

"Hmm."

They stared at each other for a long moment, and despite the cold air, he felt his face heat. He broke the stalemate by making a gesture to indicate that they should keep walking. He half expected her to resist just for the sake of it, but she fell into step beside him.

Perhaps there was something to her plain speaking, to her American-style airing of grievances. It felt rather refreshing to have spoken so freely. He reminded himself, though, that putting to voice their mutual dislike hadn't actually changed anything, practically speaking. Ms. Delaney was still here to bring bad tidings of great doom.

When they passed through the gatehouse at the bottom of the hill, they lost the illumination that had been provided by the streetlamps in the village. Ms. Delaney tilted her head back as they began their ascent. "You don't see stars like this in New York."

"No. I've noticed that." He looked up, too, and beheld the star-studded blanket of blackness. He didn't stop often enough to do this, to admire the Eldovian sky. Here, the slice of it they could see was bracketed by the tall pines that lined the road, silent, timeless sentries. He was so habitually focused on the preservation of the culture of Eldovia, on the well-being of its people, that he sometimes forgot to properly appreciate its natural beauty.

His mother used to talk about the accident of birth, and she was always quick to clarify that she didn't mean their family's noble bloodlines. Yet she also didn't mean, he'd come to learn, anything about how impoverished their once-great family had become. She merely meant that they had "food to eat, family to love, and beauty all around them." She always said it like that. They were lucky, was her point, despite the challenges they faced.

"Eldovia is home to several natural hot springs," he said, in an attempt to make conversation. It was an olive branch, of sorts, he supposed.

"Hot springs!" she exclaimed.

He had noticed she did that occasionally, dropped her usual smooth facade and burst out with an expression of surprise or delight. She'd done so when she first saw the palace earlier today. "Yes. They're on the other side of the mountain ridge, so they're not nearby, but you really haven't lived until you've seen the night sky while immersed in one of them—that's what made me think of them. A dip in an Eldovian hot spring is particularly satisfying in the winter, when you get the juxtaposition between the hot water and the cold air."

"It sounds divine."

It really did. He and his siblings and mother used to go quite a lot—there was a spa in the next village over, an hour's walk from their home. But now he took the waters only when accompanying members of the royal family and/or their guests. He never went by himself, just for the sake of it. Perhaps he would make some time to do so after all the work of Christmas was over.

"So you've been to New York?" she asked, huffing a little on the steep slope. "You must have if you've noticed how starless it is."

"Yes. The king and the princess travel to New York with some regularity, either on business for Morneau or for diplomatic reasons—the princess does quite a lot of work with the United Nations. I generally accompany them. So I've been many times, but in some ways I haven't truly experienced it, as I'm usually working steadily." He'd enjoyed the New York trips, though. The city had an energy, an ever-present thrum of activity that he found exciting. Which he realized might sound contradictory, as he loved Eldovia so thoroughly, and Eldovia, with its forests and mountains and Alpine lakes, was in many ways the opposite of New York. But both places were so vital, so very much themselves.

He had always idly thought he might take a leisure trip to New York sometime and actually play tourist. But of course he didn't really take holidays, both because he sent most of the money he could back home, but also because he wasn't a holidaying sort of person. If he couldn't even find half a day to visit a local hot spring, how likely was it that he was going to jet across the ocean for no reason other than his own amusement?

"I love New York," Ms. Delaney said, with a vehemence in her tone he hadn't heard before. He wasn't sure what to say in response. He wanted to ask her why, what specifically she liked about New York, but although the conversation was flowing more easily than it had on the way down the hill, he wasn't sure he wanted to get into a discussion of such a personal nature. He had meant it when he said his antipathy toward her wasn't personal. And as such, there was no need to *get* personal. Every flash of curiosity needn't be satisfied.

Though he did rather wonder about those boots of hers. Collapsible boots. Probably an American innovation, but, he had to admit, a clever one. And she'd had painted toenails. Unlike the deep, almost-black red of her fingernails, they'd been a dark silvery-gray. He'd never seen nail lacquer that color.

"What's the story with Kai?" she asked, startling him—but, he had to admit, startling him because he'd been lost in thoughts of her *toes*, for god's sake.

"The story with Kai? What do you mean?"

"He's very . . . quiet." She huffed a little breath that might or might not have been a chuckle, as if something were privately amusing.

"Yes, he doesn't talk much. It's rather refreshing."

"He certainly is . . . talented." It was too dark to see Ms. Delaney's face, but why did Matteo get the impression that every time she used an adjective to describe Kai, she was smiling? It was as if he could *hear* it. She was huffing more overtly from the steep incline now—it was a strenuous climb if one wasn't accustomed to it. "I still think he could make a fortune selling those snow globes," she panted.

He wondered if her skin was pink. The dark prevented him from knowing, but her skin was so naturally pale, it seemed likely that exertion would turn it pink. "He probably could. And you should see the gingerbread replica of the palace he makes a little closer to Christmas."

"So? What? He doesn't like money?"

"Not everything needs to be monetized." He paused. That had come out too sharply. It wasn't Ms. Delaney's fault she came from the land of the quick buck. He needed to do a better job separating his distaste for her mission from his conduct toward her personally. He tried again. "Kai makes a good living doing custom carpentry—bookshelves and the like—and he and Leo, the princess's husband, have a business making custom log cabins."

"Kai builds log cabins? Like, by hand?"

"Well, he and Leo do, yes."

She whistled.

Ah. He understood now what all these questions signified, what those smiles he'd heard in her voice were about. He felt simple for not seeing it sooner. Simple, but also annoyed. He was trying to give her the benefit of the doubt, trying to do a better job conversing with her, and she was pumping him for information to fan the flames of a crush? How gauche. *In through the nose, out through the mouth.*

Matteo had learned this breathing exercise years ago when all the business with his father had come to light and his mother had hauled him and his siblings to a counselor who had taught them some strategies to combat anger and anxiety. Ms. Delaney's presence was making him resort to the technique more than he had in years.

"Is Kai single?"

How to answer? *Whether* to answer—it really was none of her business. "Yes and no." There. He wasn't lying, but he wasn't encouraging.

"What does that mean?"

He might as well tell her the truth. It would temper her expectations. "He is, but he's in love with Imogen."

She laughed, though this time he hadn't been trying to be amusing. "Does Imogen know that?"

The real question was whether *Kai* knew it, but Matteo wasn't getting into it with an interloper.

Matteo liked to think of himself as the kind of person who meddled for good causes. He had described, earlier, what he thought of as his extended mission. By which he meant that he looked for opportunities to help people. Usually that meant economically—a job, a connection. And, of course, the Christmas baskets, which were the main expression of his extended mission. But occasionally he resorted to playing Cupid when presented with two people too idiotic and/or stubborn to get the job done on their own. Torkel had once accused him of being a closet romantic. It wasn't that so much as it was Matteo couldn't stand to see such blatant displays of stupidity endure when he had the power to do something about them.

He had wondered, in recent months, if he should turn his attention to Imogen and Kai. They were so obviously smitten. But so far he had held his tongue—and his bow and arrow. He wasn't precisely certain why. Perhaps because he sensed a deep well of . . . something in Kai. Pain of some sort, he thought? But he didn't *know*, and as such he didn't know if whatever it was would get in the way of Kai's actually being happy even if he got what—who—he wanted.

"I'll walk you to the door," he said to Ms. Delaney as the palace came into view, deliberately not answering her most recent question. If she wanted to fruitlessly pursue Kai while she was here, that was her business.

"You don't live in the palace?"

"No. I have an office in the palace, but I live in an apartment above the original stable building."

"Huh."

Huh. He despised that word. It was inelegant. Vague. "I beg your pardon?"

"I'm surprised you don't live in the palace."

Why? Because she knew so much about him, about his job, about Eldovia, about how the monarchy functioned here? "Historically, the position of equerry was related to overseeing the stable." He could hear the lecturing tone creeping into his voice, but he didn't care. "It was traditionally filled by an officer of the king's cavalry. The role has evolved over the years away from that into more of a . . ." How to explain?

"Ship's engineer?" she suggested with an irritating degree of cheeriness, though that metaphor she was now invoking for the second time wasn't bad.

"The royal family still keeps horses," he continued without acknowledging her interruption, "but they're in a more modern stable. And of course these days, they're for recreation and ceremonial events rather than for military campaigns. I personally have nothing to do with them. But there was an old apartment above what used to be the main stable."

"What is it now?"

"It isn't completely unrelated, I suppose. We house the main sleigh there."

"The main *sleigh*?"

"Yes." Was he not being clear?

"As in Santa's sleigh?"

"Of course not." Honestly. "It's not pulled by magical flying reindeer, but by horses—that's why I say the current use of the building isn't unrelated to its historical identity. In modern times, equerries to the Crown have lived in a suite in the palace. But in the nineteenth century, they lived in the apartment attached to the stable. I favored the idea of returning to tradition, of living where many of my predecessors had." He liked the privacy, too, especially at Christmastime. "So I undertook a bit of a renovation."

"You really are a sucker for tradition, aren't you?"

He didn't know what to say to that.

When they reached the foot of the staircase that led to the main entrance of the palace, Ms. Delaney said, "I'm fine from here, thank you." He was struck again by how little her face gave away what she was thinking or feeling—or plotting. She turned partway up the stairs, illuminated by the lights mounted around the palace's large entrance, which threw into relief the dark circles around her eyes. He feared he had a matching set. "Thank you for making me feel so welcome today."

Matteo didn't know if she was being earnest or facetious. He studied those dark circles, as they were the only hint on her face as to what was going on below the surface. It felt as if a lifetime had passed since he collected her at the airport. She probably felt the same. "I hope you sleep well." He meant it.

He watched her disappear into the palace and thought about how beastly he'd been to her today. *Overtly* beastly. So beastly that she'd called him out.

He resolved to do better.

Chapter Three

Thirty days until Christmas

*M*atteo thought *he* had a policy of arriving early for appointments, but the next morning when he arrived at the palace breakfast room a few minutes before Ms. Delaney was to meet the king, she was already there.

Matteo had had to scramble to get here when he'd learned that the king had unexpectedly summoned Ms. Delaney—he generally liked to be more than five minutes early. It irritated him when the king deviated from the agreed-upon schedule—His Majesty and Ms. Delaney had been scheduled to meet in the car on the way to their morning engagement at the Morneau production facility and to breakfast there—but Matteo supposed he should count himself lucky it didn't happen very often.

"Good morning," Ms. Delaney said as Matteo made his way to the coffee urn. Her tone was pleasant enough, but she was eyeing him warily.

He was considering how and whether to say anything about

yesterday—not apologize exactly, but perhaps acknowledge that he hadn't acted as well as he should have—when the king appeared in the doorway. Honestly. How was he supposed to get anything done if *everyone* insisted on arriving early?

"You must be Cara Delaney." The king swept into the room. He had a regal air about him that came naturally, from being born knowing one's destiny. Ms. Delaney was remarkably at ease, stepping forward and shaking the hand the king extended. Foreigners meeting the king often stumbled. A handshake was the correct form of greeting if one was not Eldovian and therefore not a royal subject, but foreign visitors, especially those from outside Europe, often did not know that. Their impressions of monarchies were formed primarily by television, or, god help him, those dreadful Hallmark movies. The result tended to be a great deal of awkward bowing and curtsying that was not only not needed, but was, frankly, embarrassing for all parties. Matteo, an admitted devotee of tradition, merely dipped his head in deference to the monarch, unless they were at a formal occasion where more ceremony was called for.

"It's lovely to meet you," Ms. Delaney said smoothly.

"You as well. I asked you to meet me here because I was hoping to speak to you privately about a sensitive matter before my daughter joins us for the trip to Morneau," the king said.

Matteo whipped his head up from his phone, where he'd been composing an email to a group of parliamentary aides he was hoping to get on his side for a project. He had no idea what the king could have to say privately to Ms. Delaney. He was not accustomed to having no idea about things to do with palace business.

"Of course," Ms. Delaney said, glancing at Matteo.

The king followed her gaze. Were they going to ask him to leave? He made to leave before he had to be asked. Less humiliating that way.

"No, stay, please, Mr. Benz. None of this will surprise you."

Thank goodness for small mercies.

The king served himself a cup of coffee and sat at the breakfast table, motioning for Matteo and Ms. Delaney to join him. "My wife Josepha died five years ago."

"Yes," Ms. Delaney murmured sympathetically.

"I loved her very much. It hit me hard."

"I'm so sorry."

"Thank you. The relevant point is that, to be frank, I neglected both Morneau and my royal duties for years."

Why was the king telling Ms. Delaney, a stranger, this? This had nothing to do with the business at hand. And honestly, he was overstating things. Matteo and Princess Marie had kept things going just fine while the king was grieving.

"My daughter had to step in." He looked over at Matteo. "And poor Mr. Benz's job was made very difficult, I fear."

"Not at all, Your Majesty," Matteo demurred. It wasn't empty talk. Although he wouldn't wish the grief of losing a beloved spouse on anyone, he'd enjoyed taking a more active role in affairs of state during that time. In some ways, he missed that, having a wider canvas, and scope, for his work. Being in the foreground instead of the background, though such a vainglorious sentiment, did not reflect well on him.

"I didn't want to put this in writing or say it over the phone," the king said, "but I harbor guilt that some of Morneau's problems are my own doing."

"Your Majesty," Matteo interjected, for he couldn't remain silent, "you are too hard on yourself."

The king waved away his protest. "My daughter and others tried for years to persuade me to consider, for example, producing a smart watch."

Matteo wrinkled his nose, and somehow Ms. Delaney knew—she glanced briefly at him before turning back to the king.

"I'm afraid my neglect has put the company, and by extension the country, in jeopardy. There's no undoing the past, but I wanted you to know. You're conducting interviews with Noar Graf and the other senior executives; it's bound to come up."

Matteo rolled his eyes, but only because no one was looking at him. He'd thought. But the gesture drew Ms. Delaney's attention again. Was she in possession of extra sensory abilities? But honestly, Noar Graf, Morneau's CEO, was such an idiot that anything he said in an interview with Ms. Delaney should be taken with a very large grain of salt.

The king followed Ms. Delaney's gaze this time. Matteo tried to belatedly school his face but must have failed. The king said, "My equerry is protective of me, Ms. Delaney."

"As he should be," she said with the same maddeningly impenetrable expression she'd deployed several times yesterday. He couldn't get a read on her the way he generally could others. It was as if she induced facial blindness in him.

"And perhaps a bit skeptical about the work we are poised to undertake," the king said.

"Mr. Benz and I spoke a bit yesterday about my mission to modernize Morneau," Ms. Delaney said mildly.

All right. He could hold his tongue no longer. After all, as he and Ms. Delaney had discussed, his role was not merely to be in compliant agreement at all times. "I simply do not understand why it's a foregone conclusion that Morneau must modernize. I fail to see why *modern* has come to be assigned such moral value."

"Mr. Benz values tradition a great deal," the king said. Matteo refrained from pointing out that the continued existence of the Eldovian monarchy was attributable to tradition. The monarch was no longer the governmental head of state. The king's role was symbolic, his leadership carrying moral rather than legal weight. Would he rather Eldovia go the way of the Americans, throwing off the mantle of consistency in favor of the new and novel no matter how untested, or even reckless, it might be? "I often think of Mr. Benz as my moral compass," the king added, and Matteo wasn't sure whether he should be gratified or insulted, whether he was being complimented or patronized.

"Tradition is important," Ms. Delaney said, "and it's good to have someone on hand to keep traditions alive. The task before us, though, is existential. There can be no tradition if we don't save Morneau."

"So what you are saying," said Matteo, trying to rein in his annoyance, "is that there can be no tradition without moderniza-tion. A bit like a word meaning the opposite of itself?"

"Yes," she said with more of that supremely irritating mildness. "Exactly like that."

She turned her attention back to the king, apparently having dismissed Matteo and his concerns. "I appreciate your forthright-ness more than you know, Your Majesty. One thing I will never do is lie to you, or sugarcoat things. So perhaps you will take some comfort from my initial reaction to your concerns, which is that given Morneau makes only one category of product, and considering the state of the worldwide market for that category, I sincerely doubt that any neglect on your part could have had as great an impact as you fear."

"Ms. Delaney, are you telling me I'm not as powerful as I think I am?"

Matteo watched, astonished, as Ms. Delaney smiled mischievously and said, "That is what I'm trying to tell you—only as it relates to this matter, of course—but I'm trying to do it without being disrespectful. Did it work?"

The king cracked a smile, and Matteo's jaw dropped. "I think we are going to get on rather well, Ms. Delaney."

Well. At least *someone* around here liked her.

AT MORNEAU'S FACTORY on the outskirts of Witten, Ms. Delaney continued her campaign of American-style dogged honesty. As per her instructions—"All hands on deck," as if this were a pirate ship—the entire Witten-based staff was in attendance. Everyone from the corporate office was present: human resources, sales representatives, the marketing staff. The factory workers were also on hand: the jewelers who worked on some of the higher-end, diamond-encrusted models; the assembly workers; those who worked in packing and shipping. Ms. Delaney had even asked them to round up as many of their external suppliers as were local and willing to come. They had a tanner who worked on the leather for some of the straps and a representative from an engineering firm to which they subcontracted some of their mechanism design. And of course the company's small board of directors representing the families that had owned Morneau for generations: King Emil and Princess Marie; Max von Hansburg, the Duke of Aquilla, whose family mining company supplied some of the trace metals used in Morneau's watches; Lucille Müller, a member of parliament whose family had a long history of political and philanthropic activity; and Daniel Hauser, who came from an old-money family that didn't really do anything except use their money to make more money.

So there they all were, standing on the production floor, which was the only space big enough to hold everyone. Ms. Delaney had suggested that the board members and senior leadership not stand apart from everyone else but rather mingle with the crowd. The result was the director of sales next to a mail clerk, the chief financial officer next to one of the cafeteria workers. It was particularly novel to see CEO Noar Graf standing among the workers. Matteo wouldn't pretend to know anything substantive about the watch industry, and Noar had been wooed from Blancpain, so Matteo would defer to the man on matters of business. But Matteo *thoroughly* disliked him. Noar would never be one of those American-style CEOs who worked in cubicles alongside his staff or invited them to one-on-one lunches, but even so, he struck Matteo as unjustifiably self-impressed. It was satisfying, somehow, to see him looking as uncomfortable as he probably felt as he was forced to mingle with the masses.

Matteo continued to survey the crowd. He would have thought he knew many of Morneau's employees. He had, after all, been responsible for getting quite a few of them their jobs. Matteo considered a word to the king about a family he knew needed some help part of his extended mission—which he still could not believe he'd told Ms. Delaney about. He caught the eye of one such woman he'd assisted in this manner, Florina Ulmer, who had fallen on hard times when her husband, who had been employed at the factory, died several years ago. Matteo had gotten her a job at Morneau as a payroll clerk. She smiled and waved, and Matteo nodded in return.

Seeing everyone amassed showed Matteo that he didn't know as much about Morneau's staffing as he'd thought. That, combined with Ms. Delaney's questioning revealing that he didn't know how much the company's workforce had grown, was unsettling. He liked to think he knew the ins and outs of the company, even though he had no direct hand in its doings. And he certainly knew the company's history, given that it was so intertwined with Eldovia's. He carried in his vest pocket his great-grandfather's Lange 8522, a simple but timeless white-gold pocket model from the late nineteenth century. His grandfather, who'd been given it by his own father, had given it to Matteo directly, and as such it had survived Matteo's father's indiscretions. Matteo had wondered if perhaps that was why his grandfather had skipped a generation with the heirloom. Perhaps Grandfather had known, somehow, what the future would bring.

But, he reminded himself, just because he didn't personally know everyone who worked at the company didn't mean he didn't care about them. He wished there were a way he could protect them from what was coming.

He glanced at Ms. Delaney. She was dressed in another suit, this one a mid-toned gray. She wore a black blouse underneath it, and the shoes of death from the airport. Her hair was up in the same style of chignon as yesterday. She was so dark and so . . . tightly coiled. She reminded him of a snake about to strike.

And yet her demeanor could be so easy and friendly. With people other than Matteo, anyway—witness breakfast with the king. The juxtaposition was disarming. Or would have been if Matteo had been the type of person prone to disarmament. He was not easily manipulated.

Princess Marie arrived at Matteo's side. "The translator we arranged has not arrived."

He pulled out his phone. "I can find someone else."

"I was hoping you might do it."

Oh, for god's sake. Translating for the angel of doom was not part of his vision for this meeting.

"I would do it myself," Marie went on, "but I fear a member of the board translating for the consultant the board itself hired won't look right. And you have such a high degree of fluency in English."

He sighed. The princess's conclusion was sound, and Matteo often functioned as unofficial translator when one was needed. "Very well." He made his way to Ms. Delaney's side. "Apparently your translator isn't here. I've been pressed into service."

She narrowed her eyes at him. "I need you to translate exactly what I say."

"Of course," he said, with a snappishness he hadn't intended but couldn't seem to control.

"I don't need you and your 'extended mission' getting creative with my words."

"Shh!" He glanced around. Thankfully, no one had heard her. *Why* had he told her about that? "Most people here have at least some degree of fluency in English, and several are entirely fluent, so even if I wanted to, as you say, 'get creative,' I would be caught out."

"Good. You'll just have to find some other way to sabotage me."

"I'm not sabotaging you. I merely want you to understand that Eldovia is—".

"I think we're all ready, don't you?" She smiled brightly as she interrupted him. Again. She waved at the king, who was a few feet away, signaling that she was ready for him to introduce her. After he'd done so, she began. "Thank you for coming." She smiled widely at the crowd, but as she turned to him expectantly, her eyes narrowed.

Matteo barely managed to refrain from growling as he translated. "*Vielen Dank, dass Sie gekommen sind!*"

"When I come in to do work on a company, I like to start by getting everyone together and addressing the elephant in the room: Are you going to get laid off? The answer is maybe."

A collective gasp arose from the English speakers in the room that Matteo, to his chagrin, joined in on. So much for not being easily manipulated. He translated, and there were more expressions of shock.

"I know that sounds dramatic." She went on to review the history of the project, and they slipped into a rhythm whereby she spoke a sentence or two, glanced at him, and he translated. Soon, he had internalized her speech patterns and was able to anticipate when she would break for the translation. They worked well together. It was too bad that everything coming out of her mouth made him bristle.

After she'd finished her review, she said, "My core operating principle on a project like this is that gossip is the enemy of an efficient, productive process, and without an efficient, productive process, we can't get an optimal outcome."

"What's an optimal outcome?" someone shouted, a man Matteo recognized as the union steward from Morneau's smaller plant in Riems. Ms. Delaney was scheduled to make a visit there late next week, but the man had muscled his way into this gathering.

Ms. Delaney did not seem to mind being interrupted—perhaps she was so prone to doing it herself, she could tolerate it from others. "Good question. This, in a nutshell, is where we stand now: the luxury watch industry is on the decline. Your company makes luxury watches. In English, there's a turn of phrase that goes: 'Change, or die.' It's a bit of a motto of mine, and it applies here, I'm afraid."

Oh, for god's sake. That was a bit melodramatic. But he dutifully translated. *"Eine Englische Redewendung, die ebenfalls ein bisschen mein Motto ist und hier leider zutrifft lautet 'Ändern oder Sterben.'"*

"And your company represents sixty-six percent of your country's GDP. In the plainest possible terms, I see my job as helping Morneau, and by extension Eldovia, change. So the best outcome is change."

Goodness. Melodramatic *and* oversimplified. Ms. Delaney really had an entire arsenal of nonsense at her fingertips, didn't she?

Thinking about her metaphorical fingertips made him think about her actual fingertips. They were as darkly red as ever. Matteo knew very little about nail lacquer, but he did recall his sister going through a phase of polishing her nails weekly and complaining about how easily her polish chipped. He wondered how Ms. Delaney preserved such an impeccable finish.

"Change," she went on, jolting him from his mental detour, "that is not necessarily as least disruptive as possible, because often disruption is exactly what a company needs, but change that is as *humane* as possible. I would say that's the best possible outcome. I think of my job as having three stages. The first, which is complete, was learning about you on paper."

How complete could that stage be if she only found out she was coming a week ago, Matteo wondered as he translated.

"The second is me learning about you *not* on paper, and learning about the context in which you do your work. That's where we are now, and this stage is scheduled to continue for the next month. And this is the part where I truly believe that transparency is essential. That's why I'm not going to stand up here and spout platitudes. I'm not going to promise your jobs are secure, because I *can't* promise that. We all know that if nothing changes, none of your jobs are secure, not in the long term. So my pledge today is that I'm not going to lie to you. I can also tell you that I haven't been hired to come in and close down this factory or the company generally. I have had jobs like that, but this is not one of them. The leadership of Morneau wants it to succeed. We are all on the same team here, which I realize sounds like one of those platitudes I just said I wasn't going to spout, but it's true. So my time here will be spent learning about you, getting to know you, poking around, perhaps testing a few ideas and systems."

"And what's the third stage?" shouted the steward from Riems, interrupting both Ms. Delaney and Matteo, who had really gotten a flow going. It irritated Matteo how the man was *yelling* at Ms. Delaney. He was sympathetic to his point of view, but there was no need to interrupt so vociferously. When a person giving a speech said she was going to discuss three stages, you could safely assume she was eventually going to get to all those stages.

Ms. Delaney was, as ever, unruffled by the disruption. "The third stage is a report. I will present it to the board, and I understand that they have committed to making it public."

And then what? She would swan off to New York, leaving them to clean up the mess she'd left in her wake—which really meant leaving Matteo to do it. People out of jobs, people who were too old or set in their ways to start over, the factory being retooled to churn out some sort of flash-in-the-pan "smart" watch, throwing away a tradition of workmanship that was literally—to use her word, and to use it *correctly*—centuries old.

"I know you probably have lots more questions. I'm here for them. I will be around in the coming days and weeks. I'll be having meetings with many of you, or with representatives of groups you're part of, but I want to invite any of you to talk to me at any time. I'm going to give you my phone number."

Well. He hadn't seen *that* coming. There was a murmuring through the crowd as she rattled off her number. He stumbled over his translation and had to ask her to repeat the number.

"Anyone can call or text at any time," she added. "I will ask, though, that you give me a week's head start. I can't tell you much now, so we'd only be wasting both of our time. And obviously, I'm not crazy. I don't *want* to be flooded with phone calls. I'd like you to believe me when I say I'm committed to transparency, so if you can trust the process, I would greatly appreciate it. But if you have something you feel is urgent, I respect that, and I'm here for it."

The crowd quieted after he'd finished translating that last bit. She'd surprised, and, he dared say, impressed them. Though for all he knew this was merely part of her show, and she had a separate phone for calls from the masses—and perhaps even a person back in New York to answer it.

He couldn't get away from her fast enough after she was done. The impromptu translation duties had thrown him off-kilter, and he needed to regain his command of the situation. The board was meeting with Ms. Delaney next, so he'd go see that all was in order in the conference room. He started through the crowd, nodding at and murmuring greetings to people he knew until he was halted by a hand on his arm. It was Mrs. Ulmer, the widow.

"Mr. Benz, we've had the most wonderful news."

"Have you?" He kept his eye on the king, who was on the move with Ms. Delaney.

"My Erika has been accepted to the University of Geneva. She's waiting to hear from several other schools, including some in the United States, but who wouldn't want her?"

"That's wonderful news." He wasn't surprised, though, except perhaps that enough time had passed for Mrs. Ulmer's daughter to be university-bound. When he'd met the Ulmers, Erika had struck Matteo as an exceptionally bright and inquisitive young teenager, but she'd fallen into a depression and her marks had suffered. He'd arranged for some short-term tutoring both to supplement her education and to give her something to focus on besides the tragedy of having lost her father. He was glad things had worked out so well for the family. "Congratulations."

"Oh, it's not my doing. She's worked so hard."

"Well, you are her mother, are you not? So it must be at least a little your doing."

She smiled again, this one a little teary, but he thought they were happy tears. "I suppose you're right, but you helped us when we were in a bad spot. Things could have gone very differently."

He smiled at Mrs. Ulmer, made his excuses, and made for the meeting room. He surveyed the space, checking that everything was in order. Each of the five spots at the board table was laid with a notebook and pen. A coffee and tea service and a breakfast buffet had been set up on a console at the far end of the room. Although he usually wouldn't concern himself with such details, he had personally made sure that the buffet would contain not only the usual breads, cheeses, fruit, and muesli, but things he'd thought a visiting American might like: bacon, egg wraps, and even disgusting little donuts coated with altogether too much icing sugar. He hadn't known, when he'd arranged for the food, that the king was going to summon Ms. Delaney to breakfast at the palace. She hadn't eaten earlier, though, so perhaps his work here had not been in vain. But it was not to be. When she and the king entered, they parted ways. She helped herself to a coffee but did not appear to be interested in any of his food.

The food. Not *his* food. It didn't belong to him, and it didn't matter to him at all whether she ate it.

Lucille Müller sat next to Ms. Delaney and started gushing about how she'd handled herself earlier. Matteo refrained from rolling his eyes but only just. They should let her deliver her blasted report before they started pronouncing her their savior.

"Mr. Benz."

It was Max von Hansburg, the Duke of Aquilla—and the brother of Torkel's boyfriend, Sebastien. "Your Grace." Matteo mentally switched gears for a moment. Perhaps he could glean something of use for Torkel's proposal.

"Any idea how long this meeting is going to last?"

"None whatsoever."

The duke huffed a resigned sigh. He was new to the board—because he was new to the dukedom. His father had died unexpectedly a year ago, thrusting Max into the title he had never wanted. Though Matteo had to admit he was doing a surprisingly fine job of it. Better than the late duke, though that wasn't saying much. "Will you and Ms. Martinez be attending the Cocoa Ball this year?" Matteo asked. He had seen a preliminary seating plan the other day, and he didn't remember seeing their names.

"No, we're spending the holidays in New York with her family."

"But your brother will attend, I trust?"

"Oh, actually, I wanted to talk to you about that. Yes, he'll be there. But have you invited Torkel?"

"I assume so. Certainly Mr. von Hansburg is welcome to bring a guest."

"Right, but here's the thing. Last year at the ball, Torkel was working as head of palace security. I might be mistaken, but I wonder if a dedicated invitation addressed to him would make him feel a bit less like the poor country cousin. He's very proud."

"Ah, yes. I understand." Matteo was sorry he hadn't thought of it himself. "Of course. I'll see to it personally when I get back today."

"Good man, Benz."

Matteo returned his attention to Ms. Delaney, almost against his will. It was as if his eyes, of their own volition, sought her out before his brain could make other arrangements for something else—anything else—to look at. This was an unfortunate tendency: looking at Ms. Delaney was rather . . . destabilizing.

The steward from Riems who had been badgering Ms. Delaney

earlier suddenly appeared at her side. He wasn't a board member, but he also wasn't the type to let that stop him. Matteo glanced around, wondering if he should eject the man. He moved nearer, close enough to eavesdrop.

"Ms. Delaney. Leon Bachmann from Riems." Leon Bachmann. Matteo made a mental note. "I asked you some questions out there." *Asked you some questions.* As if she wouldn't remember his heckling. "Might I have a quick word before your meeting starts?"

"Of course." She gestured to the empty spot next to her. For god's sake, did she have to be so accommodating? Perhaps she would like to fetch the man a cup of coffee, too.

"I'm sorry if I was a pain in there. I'm the union steward from the Riems plant, so it's my job to be a pain, you understand."

She smiled. "I do. And I don't mind people keeping me honest."

"I can tell. Which is why I'm going to do you a good turn."

Matteo didn't want to be seen listening in, so he pretended to be surveying the food. He adjusted the plate holding those odious little sugary donuts, as it was too close to the edge.

"The factory in Riems is smaller than this one," Mr. Bachmann said. "And of course we don't have the corporate office attached, which if you ask me is a blessing." Nobody *had* asked him, but of course that wasn't going to stop him. "But it also means we're out of range, so to speak. News takes a while to reach us. This has created a perception that we're an afterthought."

"Ah."

"I'm going to level with you. Folks there are quite concerned about their jobs. Some people are saying that since you're not coming to have an initial meeting with us until the end of next week, it means we're in trouble, that we're going to be the first to go." Ms. Delaney made an indistinct noise Matteo thought signaled objection, but Mr. Bachmann interrupted her, as was apparently his modus operandi.

Matteo *detested* Bachmann's persistent interrupting of Ms. Delaney. His hatred of it was so strong, he could feel his own rude interjection rising up through his body, from his diaphragm up his throat. Alarmingly, it was like a sentient being, this objection, a palpable *thing*—a thing he didn't have control over.

He grabbed a donut and stuffed it in his mouth to prevent himself from speaking.

Oh! This was not as bad as he would have thought. The sweetness of the sugar melted on his tongue and gave way to a fresh, soft pastry leavened with just the right amount of airiness.

"Even if that's not true," Mr. Bachmann said to Ms. Delaney, "even if you're not planning to close up the Riems shop, there's already an underlying perception, you understand?"

"I do. Well, I didn't, but I do now, thanks to you."

"I can't imagine why I'm helping you."

"Perhaps because you understand the task at hand."

"I don't want to see any layoffs or concessions. I'll fight them with everything in me."

"Of course. That is your job, after all. Still, thank you."

Matteo could not deny what Mr. Bachmann had said was true. Ms. Delaney's trip to Riems was scheduled for next week because she was also scheduled to take a meeting with Max von Hansburg—she was holding one-on-one meetings with all the board members over the coming week—and bundling that meeting and her visit to the Riems factory saved a trip over the mountains. But Matteo could see how a simple logistical decision would look like a slight from a certain point of view. Perhaps it even *was* a slight, albeit an unintended one. Perhaps they *didn't* pay enough mind to the Riems operation. He resolved to assimilate this information and consider it further later.

The king cleared his throat, and everyone stopped talking.

Matteo turned, intending to make his way over to the king, but of course his eyes found Ms. Delaney first. To his surprise, she was already looking at him. She made a quick, restrained gesture, pantomiming wiping her face, and to his utter horror, he realized she must be signaling that he had icing sugar on his. He whipped out his handkerchief, dragged it over his face, and, with his head held high—what else could one do when caught out enjoying tawdry American pastries?—said, "If everyone has everything they need, I shall excuse myself."

"Please stay, Mr. Benz," the king said. He looked around the table. "Unless anyone has any objections."

No one would. The king was here in his capacity as a member of the Morneau board, but he was still the king. And Matteo was widely viewed as the palace's chief executive. He waited the requisite few beats, though, pretending he was entertaining the notion that someone might suggest the meeting be closed-door.

The meeting did not begin as he would have predicted, mostly because Noar Graf started talking. "Ms. Delaney, might I ask what became of my suggestion that we postpone the CZT visit until Bradley Wiener is recovered?"

"I was happy to come. It looks as though Brad's recovery is going to be a long one. The break was complex and will require more surgery."

"Yes, but several of us worked closely with Mr. Wiener in past months. You'll forgive me for being blunt, but I have to question whether a colleague of his will have the same grasp of the situation."

Ms. Delaney blinked and waited a beat before saying, "I'm not Bradley Wiener's colleague; I'm his boss."

Noar sat up straighter in his chair, startled. Matteo tamped down a spike of irritation. Like Noar, Matteo didn't want Ms. Delaney here. But *unlike* Noar, Matteo had never implied that she wasn't qualified to do her job. This was why striving to be cordial and fair, even in the midst of one's distaste for a situation, was a good policy. Less chance of putting one's foot in one's mouth. Matteo might not be succeeding in that endeavor, but he *was* trying.

"I've been working on this file from day one," Ms. Delaney said, and there was that blasted word again. *File.* "I'm not fluent in German as Brad is, and for that I'm sorry, but otherwise, I can assure you that I'm up to speed."

Up to speed. He still hated that phrase. *In through the nose, out through the mouth.*

Ms. Delaney looked at him suddenly, before returning her attention to Noar. Did he still have sugar on his face? He performed a very undignified swipe of his face with the back of a hand.

"Yes." The king looked pointedly at Noar. "You will recall that Ms. Delaney was involved in the tendering process last year and led CZT's bid for this project."

He spoke in a manner that silenced Noar. The king had a way of making a statement that was, on the surface, a neutral statement of fact, but imbuing it with a kind of palpable, withering disdain. He hadn't pulled out that tone for a while, not since the princess's husband first came on the scene.

With Noar chastened, the meeting unfolded as expected, beginning with some preliminary business unrelated to Ms. Delaney—approving the minutes from the last meeting and reappointing the members of the health and safety committee. Ms. Delaney watched with great interest that must be affected. But then, perhaps it wasn't the content of the meeting that interested her. Perhaps she was attempting to get a handle on the players. That's what Matteo would be doing in her place. She did seem to be looking at Noar whenever the opportunity presented itself, and she would look at him for a beat longer than was called for. It caused Matteo to do the same. The man did not look happy.

"Is there anything we need to add to the agenda before we begin?" the king asked as they reached their main item of business— Ms. Delaney and her modernization mission.

"Yes," Ms. Delaney said. "I'm wondering if it would be possible to visit the Riems facility earlier than I'm scheduled for? I'd rather not have visits to the two factories scheduled so far apart. While I understand the logic of grouping trips to Riems, I'd like for everyone to hear an introduction from me more or less at the same time. I don't want the folks in Riems to feel that they're an afterthought. I'd be more than happy to make as many trips as it takes to make sure we get off to a good start."

"Yes, of course. It's a good idea. Mr. Benz can take you whenever you like." The king shot a questioning look at Matteo, who nodded. What else could he do? He had thought collecting Ms. Delaney at the airport and organizing today's meeting would be the end of his nannying duties, and taking Ms. Delaney to Riems was the absolute last thing he had the time or the desire to do right now. But he would manage it somehow. He always did.

"Perhaps we could go on Friday?" she asked, looking down at her phone. "I'd really like to get there this week."

"We do have the artisans breakfast Friday," Matteo reminded the king, who waved a hand dismissively and said, "We'll muddle through that without you."

The meeting commenced with the group going over last year's annual report and answering a steady stream of questions about it from Ms. Delaney. During a break, she stayed where she was, making herself available for informal chats with board members, who flocked to her like flies to honey. She never even got out of her seat.

She never ate any of his food.

Chapter Four

Matteo finished his workday, as he always did, by checking in with His Majesty. It wasn't a formal meeting—it never appeared on the king's schedule—but it had become a tradition, and for Matteo, a valuable opportunity to gauge the monarch's mood. Much of the intelligence that informed Matteo's work arose from these meetings.

When they were both in residence, their end-of-day check-in generally took place in the palace library, where the king tended to sit for a while before dinner, and indeed that was where Matteo found him. He dipped his head and lowered himself to the chair by the fire across from the king.

"How was the rest of the board meeting?" After the break in the meeting earlier today, Matteo had decided his time would be better spent working on his second, seasonal job—since his presence wasn't adding anything to the meeting, he might as well seize on the unexpected few hours of time to get some work done.

Instead of answering, the king said, "You never knew my mother."

"No. I never had the pleasure." Matteo was three decades the king's junior and had only been working for him for five years. But of course he knew of the queen mother, and his parents had always proudly displayed Christmas cards from her—and they had actually been from *her*, not merely generic cards from her office. Matteo's late grandmother and the king's late mother had been close friends at school and beyond. And Matteo's parents had always been invited to the palace's annual Cocoa Ball. Sometimes, when Matteo thought about all the hard times, he held on to the memories of watching his parents—before his father's troubles—dress for the ball. The family would have lunch together on Christmas Eve, then his aunt would come to stay, or, when they were a bit older, they'd be left in the charge of his older sister. His parents would make the long drive back home after the ball, to be home for Christmas morning, even though they were always welcome to stay at the palace. That was something he and his siblings had been proud of—their parents were invited to stay at the palace. But his mother had always drilled into them that they were not supposed to say as much to other people, because it was conceited. It made other people feel lesser. *Kindness costs nothing.* And in this case, she would add, *And sometimes the kindest thing to say is nothing.*

But sometimes, these days, Matteo marveled that he worked at the same palace he'd watched his parents set out for every Christmas Eve. He could have chosen to *live* in that palace, but he'd surprised himself by opting instead for his apartment over the stable. Or perhaps it wasn't a surprise. Perhaps he was his mother's son. He liked to think so. He liked to think he had internalized some of her guidance, not only about how to treat people but about how to be in the world. What to value and how to preserve things that matter in a world full of disposable, fleeting pleasures.

"My mother was a very straightforward woman." Matteo had to shake himself back into the present. "You could say a lot of things about her, and my late wife did"—the king smiled fondly—"but you always knew where you stood with my mother."

"That's admirable."

"You think so?"

"Well, I suppose the answer to that depends on where you stood with her."

The king laughed. "I'd like to invite Ms. Delaney to dine with us this evening." Matteo took a moment to make the jump to yet another seemingly random topic. "Will you join us?"

"Of course."

"Ms. Delaney reminds me of my mother."

Ah. Now Matteo understood. Well, he understood the invocation of the late queen mother. He *didn't* understand the comparison itself. The queen mother had been a lifelong Eldovian patriot. She'd been a patron of the arts and the founder of the now-famous and much beloved Witten Cocoa Fest.

Had the queen mother a motto, it would never have been *Change, or die.*

Cara checked in with Tonya when she got back to her room at the palace that afternoon. She'd promised the CZT partner a report at the end of day one.

Cara: Hi. First day wrapped. It went fine, I think. Definitely two or three tricky people

I have my eye on. But the king seems very
on board, which is the important part.

Her phone rang. Tonya had a tendency, when she wasn't immediately busy, to reply to a text with a call. It was probably the
generational difference between them, but Cara liked it. Even
though she'd risen steadily through the ranks at CZT over the
years, some part of her still felt like the college intern, starstruck
by the founding partner who had taken an interest in her. Back
then, Tonya had been the only female partner. It had been hugely
flattering to have such a mentor. It still was.

"Hi," Cara said.

"Hi, yourself. I'm eating lunch. Thought I'd call."

Cara could picture it, Tonya with her salad at her desk. Sometimes Tonya invited Cara to join her for lunch when both women
were in town at the same time. "How's Brad?" she asked, because
that was what decent people did—they asked after injured colleagues. Fucking Brad.

"He's having a second surgery next week, then he's supposed to
move to a rehab hospital. He's agitating to skip that step."

"Can he even walk?"

"He cannot. Not even with crutches. But he says he's young
and will bounce back. Anyway, tell me about these tricky people."

"Well, there's a union steward, but he's surprisingly okay. Or
at least, he's straightforward. He's kind of declared war on me,
but he's *declared* it, you know? He seems smart, like he gets the
big picture even if he's not happy about it. He actually gave me a
logistical tip that's really going to help."

"Respect organized labor."

Tonya always said that. One of the reasons they clicked professionally, Cara thought, was that they both came from union families. "And then, perhaps more surprisingly, I'm getting the sense that the CEO might be a problem."

"Noar Graf?"

"Yes."

"Hmm. He was noticeably quiet during the virtual meetings."

"Yes. Here, not so much. He wanted to wait for Brad, which is fine." She chuckled. "He reminded me a bit of Brad, actually." Brad was good at his job when he chose to be. He had some specialized skills, and he spoke a couple foreign languages, which was super handy in their field. But he was also one of those guys who'd never had to work for anything in his life, but acted like he was god's gift to the consulting world—and he bristled at having to work under Cara, even though she was older and more experienced. She never complained about him, though, to Tonya or anyone else. He was her cross to bear, and she strived to be as professional as possible at all times. "Noar's allowed to be upset that he got me instead, but—"

"He's *lucky* he got you instead."

Aww. There went Cara's inner teenager again, flushing at praise from her mentor. "Well, my point is, I can deal with that. And maybe that's all it is, but I'm getting a sense that there might be more there. It's hard to put a finger on."

"Trust your instincts, or at least don't ignore them."

"Hopefully I'm being paranoid, but I'll keep an eye on him." Having the CEO of the company working against her would be a giant pain in the ass. "We have a one-on-one the day after tomorrow. It was supposed to be today, but he canceled it." Which was also suspicious. One would think a meeting with the consultant tasked with ruling on his company's future would be a priority. In his shoes, she would want to get in early and help shape the narrative.

"And number three?"

"Number three?"

"You said there were two or three people who are potential roadblocks."

Right. "I guess I meant two." Which was a lie. For some reason she couldn't articulate, she didn't feel like getting into roadblock number three, which was, of course, Mr. Benz.

There was a rap on the door. "Hang on a sec. There's someone at my door." She heaved herself off the bed where she'd sprawled out, exhausted, after she got back to her room. "It's probably a footman. How wild is this: They have people here whose literal job title is *footman*. And there's a housekeeper who keeps sending these footmen to check on me. There's some serious fairy-tale-grade stuff going down here."

"Well. You know what I think of that."

It was funny, having grown from being Tonya's protégé into . . . well, not a peer exactly. But the gulf between them didn't seem as wide as it once had. Years ago, Tonya had given Cara all kinds of unsolicited advice. Unsolicited hadn't meant unwanted, though. Cara had appreciated the hell out of it. She was super close with her parents, but neither of them were going to be able to tell her where to buy business suits and how to make sure men didn't take credit for her ideas in meetings. But somehow, without Cara even noticing, that kind of stuff had faded out of her interactions with Tonya. Cara still felt like the mentee, but Tonya no longer treated her that way, even though she was still technically her boss. In fact, these days, *Tonya* asked for *Cara's* advice on projects and staffing. And these days, when Tonya would normally have opined on a topic, instead she merely said some variation on *You know what I think about that.*

And Cara did. "Well, first you probably think they should be called foot*people*, and I couldn't agree more, and then you'd say, 'Fairy-tale endings are for cartoon women.'" That had been one of Tonya's adages from the early days.

"Damn straight," Tonya said as Cara opened her door.

It was Mr. Benz, as if Cara had conjured him, as if thinking the words *roadblock number three* had summoned him from his apartment above the stable, which for all she knew was a Batmanesque lair full of high-tech gadgets he used to survey the kingdom.

"The king has asked that you join the family for dinner."

Ugh. She would much rather have ordered something from the menu, called her parents, and spent the rest of the evening working. It had been a long, public-facing day, and she was not in the mood to be "on," any longer. But of course one didn't decline an invitation to dine with one's client at the outset of a project.

She opened the door wider and motioned Mr. Benz inside and toward the sitting area. "If you'd just give me a moment." She held the phone back up to her ear. "Tonya? I've got to go."

"I heard. Dinner with the king! Good luck, and I'll speak to you again soon."

"So, dinner," Cara said to Mr. Benz, who, naturally, had not taken a seat as she'd indicated he should. "Give me a minute to change?"

"Of course."

She went to the bedroom, and as she reapplied her lipstick she considered what to wear. She was a superlight packer and generally brought a skeleton wardrobe of business clothes, a pair of pajamas, a pair of jeans, a pair of yoga pants, and a comfy old T-shirt. She was wearing the yoga-pants-and-T-shirt combo now, having thought she was off duty for the day. For this trip she'd also thrown in a dressy jumpsuit, reasoning that she might have to attend the odd event that would call for something a step above her work suits. Was the jumpsuit *too* dressy for dinner, though, she wondered as she stepped into it. Maybe the suit she'd been wearing earlier was better? She'd ask Mr. Benz to opine. Put his know-it-all tendencies to work for her.

"What should I be wearing to this dinner?" she asked, when she returned to the sitting room. "Is this okay?" He blinked, and his gaze slid down her body. The jumpsuit was a simple black, scoop-neck, crepe number, and she'd belted it with a dark green belt that was, for her, a rare pop of color.

Mr. Benz's eyes had gotten stuck at her feet. Did she have a run in her stockings? She rotated her ankles—the pants were fitted and came to just above her ankles—one at a time to check, which seemed to have the effect of sending his attention back upward.

He cleared his throat, and there was a pause before he said, "You look fine."

"Are you sure?" That pause had planted a seed of doubt.

"Yes," he said brusquely, but he kept eyeing her like something wasn't quite right.

"So . . ." He seemed a little stuck. If she hadn't met him earlier and been presented with ample evidence to the contrary, she might have thought him a bit slow. "Dinner?" she prompted when he still didn't say anything.

That seemed to dislodge him. "Yes. Right. I'm here to collect you for dinner, but I came a little early because I thought you might want to see the portrait gallery."

Cara was, in fact, indifferent to the portrait gallery, but the invitation didn't seem like something she should refuse, so she said, "Sure," and let him lead her up to the third floor and down several long, empty corridors until one of them widened into a doorless room that was indeed full of paintings of people.

"Oh, there's the king, right?" She pointed to an oil painting of what looked like a younger Emil.

"That's his father." Mr. Benz walked over to the painting and looked at a small gold plaque on it. "He would have been about twenty at the time of this painting. Right about the age at which he met Emil's mother, Celeste." He pointed to the next portrait, which was of a fair-haired, unsmiling woman. "She was French." He paused. "She was famously blunt. That's what everyone always said, anyway, but I think she was . . ."

"What?" she prompted when he trailed off, seemingly censoring himself. She had the sense that Mr. Benz knew things, and that the things he hesitated to say were probably the most useful things he knew.

"I was going to say she was misunderstood, but I never had the pleasure of meeting her. She was a friend of my grandmother's, though." He moved on to the next portrait. "Here she is with her children. *That's* Emil, and those are his two sisters. You can see that Celeste is wearing a Morneau in this painting. In fact, if you look around, you'll see a lot of watches in these paintings, going back generations." He crossed to the other side of the room. "This is Arthur, the king's great-great-great-grandfather. He's wearing an Abendlied."

"Morneau still makes that model," she said. "The Evening Song, I believe it translates to?"

He glanced at her, looking a little startled. He shouldn't be. She was the kind of person who did her homework. Homework was the path to success. She'd known that since she was a little girl. You win the geography bee, they give you a medal. You win the Rotary Club essay contest, they give you a scholarship. You do enough good work, they make you a partner. Eventually. Hopefully.

"Yes," Matteo said, "and that particular watch is still in the family. Emil wears it sometimes on ceremonial occasions."

"Here's Princess Marie, I think?" She pointed to what must be a wedding portrait. "And this must be Prince Leo?"

"Leo, yes, but not a prince. He refused the title when he married Marie."

"He's from New York, too," she said, to cover the fact that she'd gotten something wrong. She'd read up on the royal family but she hadn't realized that the husband of the princess wasn't a prince. This stop in the portrait gallery wasn't going to be a waste, after all. It was good to get the lay of the land. This was exactly the kind of information she'd been hoping Mr. Benz would share with her on the car ride from the airport.

"Yes. You'll meet him at dinner."

She did, and meeting Leo Ricci was like meeting an old friend. Not only was he from New York, he was from the Bronx.

"I was born and raised a few blocks off Arthur Avenue," he said. "I'm basically an Italian stereotype."

"And I'm basically an Irish one—from Woodlawn Heights."

"Nice. There's a great bar up there that I used to go to sometimes before my parents died. I had a hockey-league buddy who lived nearby, and I'd drive him home after practice and we'd have a beer. It was called Saint's. Do you know it?"

"Know it? I go there with my dad every Sunday I'm in town!"

"What a delightful coincidence!" Marie exclaimed.

Cara had been less than thrilled about being summoned to dinner, but she was tickled to discover common roots with Leo—he had insisted she call him Leo. Marie had also asked Cara to use her first name. So she was dining with Marie, Leo, Leo's thirteen-year-old sister Gabby, His Majesty, and Mr. Benz. What an odd collection of people and monikers, and what a far cry all this was from anything she'd ever imagined for herself when she was younger.

The dinner itself was formal, with fine china and crystal and servers bringing out plates, but for the most part, the atmosphere was not. Leo, Marie, and Gabby were dressed down, and they chattered and laughed like any other family. The king, who wore slacks and a sports coat, was a touch stiff, though Gabby was able to make him smile by imitating someone Cara gathered was a fictional character in a book both she and the king liked. If anything, Cara was overdressed, compared to everyone except Mr. Benz, who was wearing one of his fancy, old-timey suits. He looked good in it, she had to admit. Today's tie had a green-and-yellow floral pattern that almost seemed custom-designed to make his gold-flecked green eyes pop. It also seemed uncharacteristically whimsical.

As the dessert was being served, the king turned to Cara. "Today went well."

She switched on the work part of her brain—so far, the conversation had not touched on Morneau. "I'm glad you thought so. I never know, coming into a company, how open the culture will be to change."

"Mm. A year ago, I wouldn't have been."

"What changed, if you don't mind me asking?" She had an idea, given their chat at breakfast, but she always liked to hear from people in their own words.

He shot an affectionate look at Marie. "To put it frankly, my daughter made me see that ignoring an existential threat doesn't make it go away."

Mr. Benz cleared his throat, drawing everyone's attention. He looked annoyed.

"Everything all right, Mr. Benz?" the king asked.

"Yes, yes. I just was thinking Ms. Delaney should see Gimmelmatt at some point while she's here."

"That's a fine idea," the king said.

"Gimmelmatt is a UNESCO world heritage site," Marie explained. "It's the quintessential Eldovian village. Very picturesque."

"I thought Witten was awfully picturesque," Cara said, because she didn't have time to play tourist.

"Oh this is much more so," Mr. Benz said. "Older, too."

The king nodded decisively, as if some grand decision about her schedule had been made. "Gimmelmatt really is not to be missed. I'm sure you can find the time at some point over the next few weeks. Mr. Benz can take you."

"I'd be happy to." Mr. Benz's smile involved only his lips. His eyes were doing something else.

She knew what he was up to. Well, she knew he was up to

one of two things. He was either trying to fill her time with distractions, or he had some notion of showing her the "traditional" Eldovia. The latter would only serve to distract her, so either way, the end result was the same.

"There's some wonderful skiing that way, too," the king said.

Cara accidentally dropped her fork, and it clattered against her plate, drawing everyone's attention. Her heart kicked into overdrive. Ignoring it, she pasted on a smile, reminding herself that she was an adult. No one could make her do something she didn't want to do.

"Yes," she said carefully to the king, "I understand that you have some good skiing here. Unfortunately, I never learned."

"Mr. Benz is quite an accomplished skier." Of course he was. He probably golfed and played polo and did all the rich-people sports. "He can teach you."

"I'd be happy to," Mr. Benz said again.

She was about to demur, to put an end to any and all skiing plans, when the king added, "You can't work the entire time you're here." He looked at Mr. Benz.

"I completely agree," Mr. Benz said to the king before turning to her. "We probably have time for one or the other—skiing or Gimmelmatt—on the way back from Riems on Friday. And you'll be heading back over the mountains at least one more time, so we can tack the other on to that trip. Think about which you'd prefer for this week, and we can discuss details later."

No, they would discuss sooner, like as soon as she could get Mr. Benz alone. She needed to nip this in the bud.

"I'm not sure I can find my way back to my room," Cara said as they were saying their goodbyes. She aimed a smile at Mr. Benz that was probably as false-looking as his had been earlier. "Since we took a rather roundabout route to get here and all. Would you be so kind as to walk me back to my room, Mr. Benz?" He couldn't say no. Not in front of the king.

"Of course."

As soon as they'd rounded the first corner, she said, "I have no intention of going skiing." She paused to let that sink in—for herself as much as for him.

"Fine."

"Or of visiting quaint Alpine villages you think are going to open my eyes to the wonders of Eldovian culture and somehow influence my work."

He blinked, taking a moment to absorb her admittedly pissy declaration. "Fine."

It was her turn to blink—in surprise that he had agreed so easily.

"I shall take you directly to the Riems facility and directly back, and we shan't waste a moment talking about anything other than work, as god surely intended."

Argh! He was maddening. She wanted to grab that stupid green tie and . . .

What? What did she want?

She wanted to get control of herself. She stopped walking. It took him a moment to realize she had done so. When he stopped a few steps later, she could see him steeling his shoulders before he turned.

"Mr. Benz, forgive my bluntness, but why are you making this so difficult?"

"I am doing no such thing. In fact, I must ask *you* to forgive *me*. I thought you might like to see some of the sights we are known for here in our little country." His sarcasm made her roll her eyes, as did the performance of his signature sniff. "I can see now that I was mistaken."

She ignored what he said and addressed the real issue. "I'm not sure how many ways I can explain to you that if things don't change, your economy is going to decline even more than it already has. Surely you can understand that."

"What I can't understand is how this vague entity called 'the economy' can be more important than people," he shot back. "Specific people, I mean. People with children and bills. People who've worked hard all their lives."

"That's a little rich coming from you." She wondered if the idiom about being born with a silver spoon in one's mouth was familiar in Eldovia.

He raked the fingernails of one hand through his hair. Curious. She hadn't seen him do anything like that. It seemed a very casual gesture for such a buttoned-up man. His hair wasn't long enough to really get messed up, but ended up a little askew. It reminded her of the sofa at home. It was made of a sort of velour, and you could rub it the "wrong" way and it created a kind of visual disturbance.

"There's a lot you don't know about me," he said with a hint of peevishness.

"I know you don't get to be equerry to a king without being born into a fancy family. I know your grandmother and the king's mother were friends. That's not exactly man-of-the-people territory."

"Did you ever read *Pride and Prejudice*?"

"What?" That was quite the non sequitur. It also made her realize that she was still looking at his hair instead of him.

"It's a novel by Jane Austen," he added.

"I *know* that."

"Have you read it?"

"No." His nostrils fired up, and she added, just to annoy him, "I've seen the movie, though." He pressed his lips into a harsh line, and she took perverse delight in doubling down on being the annoying, crass American. "I also read an article once about how Jane Austen fans are basically like Trekkies who think they're fancy. What do they call them? Janeites or something?"

She did not succeed in bothering him. He merely blinked. Which was probably good. Look at her: *trying* to rile a client.

"If you've seen a cinematic adaptation of *Pride and Prejudice*," he said, "you may recall that the family is genteel but poor. The Bennet sisters must marry well."

"Yes, but—"

"You, who have never read Austen, are going to school me on her?" *He* rolled *his* eyes as he interrupted her, and even though she wasn't supposed to be doing battle with him, she took perverse satisfaction in having inspired an overt eye roll.

And, yep, she was going to school him. "One, they still had servants. They lived in a big, fancy house."

"Yes, but they were only in that house until Mr. Bennet died. It was entailed."

She had no idea what that meant, but whatever.

"Then," he went on, "it was going to be inherited by their lout of a cousin, and the sisters would be out on the street."

"I am fairly certain you are a boy. And doesn't Eldovia have absolute primogeniture? Or is that only for the royal family?"

"I'm not saying my situation is exactly the same as that of the Bennets, merely that it's possible for a family to be genteel but poor."

"Fine." What were they even fighting about? Rich poor people? Who cared? More importantly, why couldn't she seem to make herself take the high road here, as she *always* did with clients when things got sticky? Why was she letting this dude get to her? She took a fortifying breath. "The point is, I do not intend to go skiing, nor to visit a village other than Riems."

"And I already told you that was perfectly acceptable, so I'm not sure why you persist in picking fights with me."

"You know what? I know where I am now. Thank you for accompanying me this far. I can make it the rest of the way on my own."

"Fine."

"Fine."

"Good *night*, Ms. Delaney."

"Good *night*, Mr. Benz."

He turned, and she watched the back of his head get smaller as he retreated. She was seized with the strangest urge to run after him, but for the life of her, she couldn't figure out why.

Chapter Five

Twenty-seven days until Christmas

Cara pulled out a stool at the Owl and Spruce around seven
o'clock on Thanksgiving Day—not that anyone here knew it was
Thanksgiving—and ordered a giant dinner to go with her melancholy.

"Thanks," she said, putting her phone down when Imogen appeared with her food.

"Working through dinner?" Imogen nodded at the phone.

"No. I'm staring at it wishing it would ring."

"Ah." Imogen's eyes twinkled. "Waiting for a man to call, then?
Have you got a fella at home?"

"Waiting for my *mother* to call. How's that for pathetic?"

"You should eat while everything's hot," Imogen said, but instead of leaving Cara to her food, she propped her elbows on the
bar. "Missing your ma, are you?"

"It's Thanksgiving at home, and . . ." What? She was a thirty-
five-year-old woman who missed her mommy and daddy? Well,

yes. That was exactly it. She shrugged. "I'm an only child, and we're tight. My mom has an autoimmune disease that causes a lot of pain and she gets tired easily, and I know she's going to be overdoing it today. Normally she'd be doing the bossing around, and I'd be doing the shopping and cooking and all that. I tried to get them to let me have dinner catered, but it's like she's trying extra hard to make everything the same as it always is."

"Ah, but everything can't be the same as it always was. It never can."

"Yes. Exactly." *Change is the essential process of all existence.* Imogen got it.

"In my experience, trying to hold on to something is the surest way to make sure it slips away." She looked down the bar quickly but then back at Cara, who had to stop herself from looking over her shoulder to see what—or who—Imogen had been glancing at.

A woman Cara didn't know appeared at the bar a few stools down, and Imogen excused herself to go serve her, so Cara did the covert look down the bar she'd refrained from earlier. Kai. Which meant Mr. Benz had probably been right about Imogen and Kai.

Even though she'd only known Mr. Benz for five days, she hated it when he was right about something.

Cara picked up a fry—or a chip, as it was called on the Irish-inspired menu—and almost groaned as she bit through the crispy exterior into a soft, creamy interior. Imogen, she'd learned, was famous for these thick-cut chips. Apparently the secret was that they were double fried in garlic-infused oil. Cara had come down to the pub for dinner after work the last two days, and these potatoes had become a favorite.

"I notice you didn't answer my other question." Imogen was

back with a mischievous look in her eyes that Cara was beginning to recognize as her default expression.

"What question?"

"Have you a fellow at home?"

"Oh, no. *No.*" When Imogen raised her eyebrows—she was probably questioning the vehemence with which Cara had issued that *No*—Cara added, "I live with my parents."

"It would seem to me the solution to that is to select a man who *doesn't* live with *his* parents."

Cara chuckled. "Yeah, I know, but there's also the part where I don't have time for a boyfriend—or the desire for one. I'm married to my job. Happily married. But . . ." She looked around to make sure no one was listening, though she wasn't sure why. Imogen, sensing a secret about to be dispensed, leaned in. "I travel a lot for work, and I do look forward, on my trips, to occasionally . . ." She raised her eyebrows and waved a hand around.

Imogen cracked up but played dumb, pasting on a teasingly innocent expression. "To what?"

Cara ignored the question. "But not on this trip. I can't 'entertain' any visitors in the palace, if you know what I mean."

Imogen was back to laughing. "Yes, I see your dilemma."

"Also, I've noticed that there don't seem to be a lot of locals on the apps—I had a look out of curiosity. So if you know anyone here who, as you say, doesn't live with his parents . . ." Cara winked to show she was kidding. Which she was. Mostly. But, damn, she really had the itch this week. It had been a long time.

Imogen had glanced down the bar again, and Kai must have felt her attention. He looked right up at her. After a beat, he transferred his attention to Cara and gave a curt nod. She gave a little wave.

"Not him," Imogen said quickly.

Message received. Cara's itch scratching was meant to be low-conflict. She wasn't wading into these troubled waters.

"He's not worth the drama," Imogen added with a breeziness that struck Cara as put-on.

"Got it," Cara said, though Kai seemed about as low-drama as they came, considering that he basically never spoke.

"I know everyone in the village. I'll arrange something."

"You'll *arrange* something! What does that mean? I don't need you to set up a sexual assignation for me!"

"Not a sexual assignation. Just a regular assignation. What you do with it is up to you." With a wink, Imogen was off to serve another customer.

WHEN MATTEO ARRIVED at Imogen's, he spied Ms. Delaney sitting at the bar. Which was good. She was the reason he was here. They had matters to discuss. They hadn't spoken since dinner Monday night, but it was Thursday and they had to be at the factory in Riems tomorrow morning.

He eyed her. She was in her uniform: gray pantsuit with white blouse, hair in its ever-present chignon. He could see her dark-red nails from here, clutching a glass of water.

Even though he'd come here looking for her, he was unsure about how to approach. He felt sheepish about his behavior Monday, and sheepish was not a feeling with which he was familiar. It was not a feeling he enjoyed.

What had come over him, lecturing her about *Pride and Prejudice*? He had accused her of picking a fight with him, but the next morning he'd had to ask himself if the reverse wasn't true. Or at least if they weren't jointly guilty. He'd awakened Tuesday feeling almost as if he had a hangover. Not physically, but he'd had that morning-after sense of dread, of being unsure if he had comported himself honorably. Not that he had a great deal of experience with that feeling. He'd only been drunk enough to be hungover the next day a handful of times in his life.

When one's father gambles away one's entire life, one is very careful about potentially addictive behaviors.

He had come to the conclusion that even if they were jointly at fault, he needed to apologize to Ms. Delaney for the way he'd spoken. He just . . . hadn't had a chance to yet.

Well, no, that was a lie. He'd known her schedule this week, and he could have intercepted her at any time. At least, he'd known about her official meetings. He scanned the bar and was relieved to see Kai at one end of it, far from Ms. Delaney. Of course, he cared if she and Kai became entangled only to the extent that he preferred she not leave any more wreckage in her wake than necessary. Who was going to be on cleanup duty when it came to that wreckage?

"Ms. Delaney," he said as he came to a stop next to her. "I was beginning to wonder if you subsisted on air alone."

She turned to him with her fork paused halfway to her mouth. He'd startled her. He watched her register him, and her surprise was replaced by a flash of annoyance she quickly tamped down. "I'm sorry?"

"I never see you eat." Matteo regretted the observation the moment it was out. It sounded like he was watching her closely.

Which he was. But only because that was his job. He considered elaborating, but saying, "I watched you not eat two breakfasts the other morning" was not going to help matters.

"Oh, I eat." She nodded down at her plate, which contained whatever was today's savory pie and a generous portion of salad. She also had a side plate of chips. "I have a bad habit of getting distracted by work, not eating all day, and realizing in the evening that I'm ravenous."

He pulled out the stool next to her. "I thought we might discuss tomorrow's trip to Riems. It's a two-hour drive. Building in a bit of a cushion, I think we ought to leave around six o'clock if that suits?"

"That's fine. But I'm quite happy to go on my own. As you yourself have pointed out, Herr Walmsley is a more-than-competent driver. You don't need to make the trip with me."

"Oh, I'm quite happy to accompany you," he said, lying through his teeth.

"Well, I can't imagine that's true."

He winced, unsure both how to reply and how he'd gotten himself into this mess to begin with.

"I haven't seen you the last few days," she went on. "I thought maybe you were cooling it on the babysitting duty, but I guess you'll do as a chaperone for my road trip." For the life of him, he couldn't tell if she was being flippant.

"The king has asked me to accompany you."

"But no cute villages and no skiing," she said.

"Correct. No leisure activities whatsoever." Oddly, he couldn't tell if *he* was being flippant, either. Not knowing the intentions behind the words that came out of one's mouth was a most unsettling feeling.

Her phone, which she had resting on the bar, lit up, and she started. "Oh! I have to take this."

Imogen appeared. "Is it your mother, m'dear?" Ms. Delaney nodded, and Matteo wondered how Imogen was in a position to know that. "The last snug over there is empty if you'd like some privacy."

Ms. Delaney, in the process of picking up the call, waved her thanks and hopped off her stool.

Imogen set a glass of Matteo's preferred scotch down in front of him. "She's homesick. She misses her mum."

"She *does*?" He turned and caught sight of her disappearing into the snug. He was truly astonished. *Homesick* was not a word he ever would have thought of applying to Ms. Delaney.

"She and her mum have been playing what she called 'telephone tag' with each other all day."

"Hmm."

Imogen tapped the bar. "What are you plotting?"

"Nothing." He truly wasn't. He was taken aback. Clearly, he needed to do some mental rearranging of his image of Ms. Delaney. It was difficult to imagine such a corporate warrior missing her mother. It was difficult to imagine such a corporate warrior *having* a mother, frankly, but of course she'd mentioned her parents. Still, he rather imagined her having been spontaneously birthed from a copy of *The Seven Habits of Highly Effective People*.

She never came back. Every time he looked over his shoulder at the snug, there was no change. After nearly twenty minutes, Matteo said to Imogen, "Do you think perhaps I should check on her?" He eyed Ms. Delaney's plate. Her slice of pie had only a few bites out of it. He thought of her saying she was ravenous.

Homesick he couldn't do anything about, but ravenous was easily solvable. "Perhaps I should deliver her dinner?"

Imogen's eyes were twinkling a great deal, even for her, but he chose not to try to determine why. One woman behaving uncharacteristically at a time. "That's a fine idea."

The half-dozen snugs at Imogen's lined one side wall, a row of overlarge, elaborately carved floor-to-ceiling wooden booths that formed their own small rooms. Most were full of villagers chatting and dining, and their doors stood open. As Matteo approached the one on the far end, he could see that the door wasn't closed, as it had appeared from his vantage point at the bar, but was standing a few inches ajar. He lifted a hand to knock. His intention was to whisper a brief apology for interrupting Ms. Delaney's call, set down her food, and retreat, but he could see through the opening in the door that she *wasn't* on the phone. She was sitting there, staring into space. She looked positively forlorn.

This continued to be unexpected.

He almost left. Her melancholy was none of his business. But once again, the word *ravenous* surfaced in his mind. Better to be melancholy and satiated than melancholy and ravenous. So he pasted on a neutral expression, rapped, and briskly pushed open the door. "Ms. Delaney, apologies for the intrusion, but I thought you might want your dinner."

She blinked, seeming to take a moment to register what he'd said, who he was, even. He was supposed to be retreating, but she looked so befuddled, he entertained a momentary fear that something was truly wrong.

She shook her head as if to rouse herself, and her face rearranged itself into an expression he suspected was supposed to be pleasant, but he saw through it. "Thank you. That was kind of you. I shouldn't be taking up this large table by myself. I'll . . . go back to the bar."

That last sentence had come out sounding rather tentative—and puzzled, as if she were bewildered by her own hesitation, unfamiliar with a strange new emotion she couldn't quite name. He knew the feeling. "You needn't if you'd rather not. I'm certain Imogen would be quite happy to have you stay here if you're comfortable." He paused, wondering if he should say more. Offer to fetch her a box so she could take her food back to the palace? Call her a car?

"Would you like to join me for dinner, Mr. Benz?"

It was his turn to blink, startled. She smiled, and this one seemed real. "I promise, no talking about work. We don't have to talk at all, in fact. You can just sit there." She looked away quickly, then back at him. "It's Thanksgiving in the United States, and I'm finding myself missing my family."

He was astounded. He wasn't sure why. What she'd said was not unreasonable. He gathered that American Thanksgiving was a family-oriented holiday. He just never would have expected Ms. Delaney to be so forthcoming about a vulnerability.

She must have taken his shock for disinclination to accept her invitation, because she quickly said, "I'll go back to the bar."

"No, no. I'd be delighted to join you," and, strangely, it was the truth. "I'll go retrieve my beverage and be right back. May I bring you anything to drink?"

She looked down at her plate. "I was only drinking water, but I think a glass of red wine would be lovely with this pie. Maybe you can have Imogen recommend something?"

He nodded and was back in a few minutes, sliding into the booth across from her with her drink and a plate of chips for himself. Before they settled into the combativeness that seemed to be their default, he asked, "What do you generally do on Thanksgiving?"

"Nothing that out of the ordinary. My father and I usually go to mass with my mother—she can take any nonreligious holiday and make it into a religious one. Heck, she can take any random weekday and make it into an occasion to go to mass. I was just talking to my mother, who told me she lit a candle for me today at church, which was . . ." She paused to clear her throat. "Nice. So to answer your question, we usually go to church, then we watch some football and have the typical big dinner."

"Turkey, yes? Or is that just on television?"

"Definitely turkey. And mashed potatoes and stuffing and all that. Pumpkin pie."

"And are you joined by other family members?"

"No. It's just us. My father's parents are dead, and his only remaining sibling lives in Florida. My mother is . . . on her own."

It seemed like there was a story there, but he wasn't going to press. His aim was merely polite conversation.

"And what about you, Mr. Benz? Does Eldovia have any kind of harvest holiday?"

"No. I think that would merely get in the way of our collective obsession with Christmas."

She laughed, and he was pleased to have been the source of it. "I have to say, even in the few days I've been here, I've seen things ramping up. I thought that first day, with the tree and the hot chocolate in the village square, and the snow globes here at the bar, that you already had a lot of Christmas going on. But every day there seems to be more."

"Oh, you haven't seen anything yet." He waved dismissively. "In the coming weeks there will be hay rides, organized caroling, a live nativity, and an ice slide constructed in the village."

"And I understand there's a cocoa-themed ball on Christmas Eve?"

"Indeed. There's a cocoa festival during the day and a ball in the evening. In between, the royal family holds its annual Christmas levee. Are you familiar with the term?" Americans often weren't.

"I am. It's like office hours for the peasants, right?"

He could not help but laugh at that, which he hated doing. She *was* funny, though.

"I'm a bit sorry I'll be flying out the morning of the twenty-fourth," she said. "A person—or at least an American commoner—probably only gets one chance to attend a royal ball. I admit to being tempted when the king invited me to stay for it, but I'm already in enough trouble at home for having missed Thanksgiving."

"Ms. Delaney, I can assure you the king would welcome you back to the ball any year of your choosing." Indeed, the king seemed impressed with his hired gun. She'd apparently already uncovered a major inefficiency in Morneau's contracts for the boxes the watches came in.

They ate in uncharacteristically companionable silence for a few minutes until Ms. Delaney asked, "If Christmas is such big business, particularly at the palace, with Cocoa Fest and the ball, that must mean you don't get to spend Christmas with your family?"

"It does mean that, unfortunately. It's part of the job." Although that wasn't entirely fair. The king would not object to Matteo taking some time off at Christmas. He probably would not even object to him skipping the ball. It was more that Matteo's expanded mission required his presence over the holiday. "I've grown accustomed to it, though," he added, because Ms. Delaney was looking at him with sympathy. "I've developed my own traditions of sort."

"What are those?"

He almost didn't tell her. It sounded so silly.

"What?" she prompted in a good-natured yet persistent tone.

"Well, if you must know, after all the Christmas hullabaloo is done, I'm usually too wound up to sleep, so I tuck into my apartment and watch Star Wars movies as the sun comes up."

"You do not!"

"I do. I'm something of a fan."

"You *are*? How did *that* happen?"

He had well and truly shocked her, which made him smile. He thought about how to answer, about how to tell the truth without trotting out the specifics. "There was a time in my life when I was in need of some escapism. It was right around the time the new movies started, and let's just say that at that point, a galaxy far, far away seemed like somewhere I would like to be."

"*Really?*"

She was still shocked. He had said too much. "We all have our struggles," he said vaguely, hoping that would be the end of it.

"I guess. It's just that you don't seem like the struggling type."

"Mm." He wasn't sure how to explain without sparking another argument about *Pride and Prejudice*.

By the time they'd finished their meals, he realized they hadn't spoken about work at all—about Morneau or watches or their upcoming trip to Riems. Their discussion had been entirely personal—and entirely pleasant. How odd. He'd thought the other day that he wasn't the type of person who was easily disarmed, but it seemed Ms. Delaney had managed it yet again.

"This was wonderful," she said, and he initially thought she meant dining with him. But then she said, "Imogen's pies are becoming a habit, I'm afraid. And those potatoes." She shook her head as she grinned. "I'm not a cook, but I would kill for this recipe. She says it's a family secret."

Of course she had been talking about the food.

She yawned suddenly, and he could see her try to extinguish it, but it became one of those oversize ones that went on and on. "Excuse me," she said when she regained control. "I'm still not caught up on my sleep." She eyed him, and he had the sense that she was wondering if he was going to say something unkind.

He was not. "Ms. Delaney, I must apologize for the way I spoke to you Monday evening. It wasn't like me. I don't know what came over me."

"Well, if you're apologizing, I should, too. I wasn't exactly the poster girl for how to treat one's clients." She smirked, and it was, he thought, at least partially self-deprecating. Before he realized what was happening, she reached out and rested her hand atop his. He nearly jumped out of his seat, from surprise but also from the sensation of tiny electrical currents prickling his skin. Her nails were still that same dark red with undertones of black, their matte finish utterly flawless.

He told himself she was patting his hand sympathetically, as if she, too, understood what it was like to lose one's cool when one was normally firmly in possession of said cool.

That was all that hand pat meant. If he was feeling it as something . . . more intense, that was an error of interpretation on his part. He cleared his throat and slid his hand out from under hers. He didn't want to be rude, but he couldn't have her touching him any longer. To smooth over any potential awkwardness, he said, briskly, "I was thinking I'd call a car for the return trip. Would you care to join me?"

It became apparent to Cara, a few minutes after leaving the pub, that they were not going directly back to the palace. After conversing briefly with Mr. Benz in German, the driver pulled away and turned down a little cobblestoned street that took them off the village main street.

"Where are we going?"

By the time she'd finished her question, they were pulling up in front of a small church labeled Saint-Sulpice. "This is the church we spoke about. The building, and the congregation, are rather small, Catholicism not being the dominant faith here. But I thought perhaps you'd like to know this was here. If you'd care to go inside and light a candle, I'd be happy to wait for you."

"Oh!" Again with the exclaiming she kept finding herself doing in Mr. Benz's presence, but she found she didn't mind it so much in this context. "I would love that." She opened the car door. She studied his face for a moment. The warm illumination and shadows created by the overhead light made his jaw look extra sharp. "Thank you."

He smiled—for real—and said, "You are most welcome."

Inside, Cara spent more time pondering Mr. Benz than she did

God or Thanksgiving or her faraway parents. If she'd had to answer the question of what the stuffy equerry did over Christmas,
a Star Wars marathon would not have been on the list. It wouldn't
have been in the same room as the list—no, it wouldn't have been
in the same *star system* as the list. But seriously, Mr. Benz had
gone from being a thorn in her side to a puzzle, and unfortunately,
she was a sucker for a good puzzle.

When she emerged from the church, he was sitting in the back
seat of the car looking down at something she couldn't see—a
phone, probably. The overhead light was still on, and from this
angle, he looked almost angelic. She rolled her eyes at herself. Too
much church.

She opened the car and was hit with a wave of . . . jazz music?

"Oh, Ms. Delaney. You made quick work of that." He said something to the driver in German, and both the music and the light
cut out. They didn't talk as the car made the short climb up the
hill, but as with the lulls in conversation at dinner, it was a companionable sort of silence.

They pulled up in front of the palace, and although Mr. Benz
got out when she did, he kept the car door open. Her gaze was
drawn to his hand, which was resting on the handle. She had
noticed earlier, in the snug, that he had surprisingly good-looking
hands. If you looked just at his hands, which were large and veiny
in a way that was inexplicably attractive, you might think *he* was
the one that built log cabins for a living.

"If there's nothing else I can do for you, I'll be on my way."

Right. *Stop ogling the equerry's hands.*

"I have something I need to see to this evening, otherwise, I'd see you inside," he added. You could say a lot about Mr. Benz, but you could never say he didn't work hard. She respected that.

Also, he was polite. When he wasn't snipping at her.

What he wasn't saying, since he *was* being polite right now, was that she was holding him up, standing there like an idiot staring at his hands. She dragged her gaze up to his face. It was harder than it should have been. "Thank you for everything this evening."

He nodded curtly but not unkindly. "I'll see you tomorrow morning." She started up the steps but paused and turned when she heard him call, "Ms. Delaney."

"Yes?"

"Happy Thanksgiving."

She smiled. "Thank you." She wasn't sure how he had done it, but Mr. Benz had made what had started out as a bummer of an evening into an almost enjoyable one.

When she entered the palace, it was to a completely transformed foyer. It was as if someone had, at some point today, hit the on button for Christmas décor. Beribboned garlands hung everywhere, and at the back, where the space opened up under a giant, vaulted ceiling, stood an enormous Christmas tree decorated in red bows, crystal ornaments, delicate silver bells, and tiny white lights. It was gorgeous, but absurdly, it made her miss the shrimpy artificial tree her parents would be putting up at home next week, with its mismatched lights and its plethora of not-thematically-consistent ornaments, many of which she had made as a kid.

Still, the perfect palace tree was buoying. Seeing such an over-the-top sign of Christmas meant her Thanksgiving melancholy could come to an end. Though if she was being honest in assign-

ing credit for the dissipation of her Thanksgiving blues, it probably had to go to Mr. Benz.

KAI RESPONDED TO Matteo's unannounced late-night visit by silently letting him in and going directly to the little bar cart he kept
in a corner of his cabin and cracking two bottles of beer. Matteo
heaved a sigh as he raised his bottle in thanks and drank deeply of
Imogen's amber ale. "You have no idea how long this day has been."

"You have the list?" Kai asked, getting right to business, as was
his way. "Shall we go to the workshop?"

"I don't have the list finalized yet."

Kai furrowed his brow. "Shouldn't it be made and in the process of being checked twice at this point?"

There was a beat before Matteo chuckled. Kai, normally so
taciturn, occasionally let slide a wry remark like that, but it always
took Matteo by surprise. "Soon. I promise. The visiting American
has taken up more of my time than I'd like. But yes, let's go to
the workshop and take an inventory—see where our holes are. I
came to tell you that I've been pulled away on some palace business tomorrow, so I won't be able to help you sort the food delivery." Kai's brow furrow deepened. It was interesting how no one
knew that underneath his gruff, seemingly unflappable exterior,
Kai was actually quite a worrywart. "Don't worry. Every year we
think we're not going to make it, but it always gets done. It's only
nonperishables arriving tomorrow, so take delivery and I'll come
Saturday morning and we'll deal with it all."

"It's going to be a lot of work this year without Torkel."

"We'll manage."

Kai grunted and grabbed his coat. Matteo was still wearing his—Kai wasn't the kind of person who took guests' coats. They tromped across the crunchy snow to Kai's workshop, which, like his house, was a log cabin. Unlike his house, which was cozy and well-appointed on the inside, the workshop was a mess. To Matteo's eyes, anyway, but it always seemed to be a kind of organized chaos Kai effortlessly navigated, so Matteo never remarked on it. As he'd said, the job always got done.

Kai led him to a table stacked high with books. "I picked these up in Zurich last week. They didn't have your whole order in, so I'll have to go back next week."

"I'll do it. I have to be there anyway on the twenty-second to pick up the Christmas cakes—I assume that won't be too late for the rest of the books. Books are easy to slide into baskets last-minute. And I'll take these with me tonight." Matteo generally kept books and some of the other small items at his apartment in the run-up to Christmas, in an attempt to clear actual workspace in Kai's cabin.

Kai grunted again, which Matteo took to signal agreement. "What else?" he asked.

"Toys." The next table contained a mixture of store-bought toys—games and dolls and science kits—and Kai's handmade creations. Kai was known for his handcrafted wooden marble runs and train sets. "Everything is under control here, assuming your final numbers aren't a lot higher than last year's."

"I really will have the list done, and broken down by family and category of need, by the middle of next week," Matteo vowed, to himself as much as to Kai. They moved on to a table piled high with clothing. "I've a major donation from Helly Hansen—fifty children's coats. May I have them sent here?"

"Yes."

"Thank you." He tried to infuse his thanks with the urgency he felt. Over the years, his Christmas project had expanded beyond his ability to contain it within the walls of his apartment. He wasn't sure what he would do without Kai. His workshop was large, and it was remote, both of which were key to the success—and secrecy—of their mission.

"You look tired," Kai said, startling Matteo. "Is it the American?"

"She's been here less than a week, so I don't think I can blame her. Alas." He was trying to be glib, but he was now worried that his existential exhaustion was outwardly visible.

"I have some unfortunate news," Kai said, startling Matteo.

"All right," Matteo said, bracing himself.

"I think it's possible that Imogen is onto us," Kai said.

Matteo relaxed. "I'm fairly certain she is."

"She is?" Matteo had to chuckle at Kai's shocked expression.

"She's made a few remarks that suggest she knows it's us. Is it really that surprising? Imogen's a smart woman."

"Mm." Matteo could see Kai adjusting to this new information. "She is that."

"In fact, I've often thought about coming clean and enlisting her help," Matteo went on. "She's very well-connected. Perhaps too well-connected, which is why I hesitate. If this endeavor gets any bigger, we won't be able to pull it off in one night." Though as soon as the observation was out, he wondered if perhaps it *was* worth thinking about bringing in someone else. Matteo had been trying to reassure Kai, but they were already feeling Torkel's absence.

Perhaps they needed a management consultant. He barked a laugh and immediately clamped a hand over his mouth. Kai hadn't noticed, though. He was staring into space, probably thinking about Imogen. Matteo cleared his throat. "Well then, if everything is in order here, I'll be going."

Kai grunted and waved his hand, dismissing Matteo. Time to go home and get as much done as possible before he blew an entire day tomorrow wrangling Ms. Delaney.

Chapter Six

Twenty-six days until Christmas

The next morning, Cara met Mr. Benz at the appointed time in front of the palace and was surprised to find him behind the wheel of a car.

"No driver?" she asked when he got out and held the passenger-side door for her as if he *were* a professional chauffeur.

"It seems rather wasteful to commandeer a driver when we'll be gone the entire day and I'm perfectly capable of driving."

"Is this your car?" It was a silver Audi, rather than the ubiquitous black BMW she'd ridden in before.

"It is. You're more than welcome to sit in the back if you'd like to spread out and do some work."

"I'd like to sit in the front if that's all right. We're going over the mountains, yes?" He nodded. "I do have work to do, but I think I'd better not pass up the opportunity to take in these views."

"You won't be disappointed." He flashed her a great, wide smile, as if he were personally responsible for the views she would soon be admiring. He had always been fine-looking, if a bit starchy, but with the skin around his eyes crinkling as he smiled, he was positively handsome. She had assumed that whatever warmth had been between them last night would be gone today, that he'd merely been nice to her because she was being a sucky baby with her pathetic "It's Thanksgiving and I miss my mom" story.

When Cara got back to her rooms at the palace last night, embarrassment had set in. She had exposed so much of herself. Not so much in what she'd told Mr. Benz. Though she generally didn't talk about her family on the job, she hadn't told him anything terribly personal about her parents. But somehow, having him waiting for her outside that church while she lit a candle inside it had felt strangely, intensely intimate. Which made no sense: there had been a solid, stone wall between them. Perhaps it was more that she'd shown a kind of vulnerability, both by admitting she missed her family, and by allowing Mr. Benz to intuit that she was the kind of person who could be comforted by the lighting of a candle in a church. She hated showing weakness to clients. But her mom's false cheer—speaking of false smiles—on their call last night had gotten to her. Cara could see how a day spent standing in the kitchen had aggravated her arthritis, exhausting her and making her face go so drawn that after a few minutes on the call, she couldn't even fake it anymore.

This morning, Cara felt sheepish, but as they wound down the hill and exited through the gatehouse at the bottom, Mr. Benz gave no sign that his impression of her had changed. Or, more accurately, he gave no sign that his impression of her had changed for the worse—the bar was probably pretty low to begin with.

Suddenly, she wanted more than anything to keep yesterday's

version of Mr. Benz for the day, rather than the argumentative version who so clearly resented her.

"Mr. Benz, may I propose something?"

"You may propose anything you like."

"I sense a *but*. I may propose anything I like, but you'll cheerfully disregard me?"

One corner of his mouth turned up. He schooled his face so quickly, though, she wondered if she'd imagined it.

"I'm giving you too much credit, aren't I?" she asked, extinguishing her own nascent smile. "There probably won't be cheerfulness involved. You'll cheer*lessly* disregard me."

"Try me, Ms. Delaney, and I shall attempt to infuse my disregard with good cheer."

"I propose a truce." He raised his eyebrows but gave no other reaction. "I know you don't approve of me, or of my work here. But what if we . . . put that on hold?"

"You are suggesting we enjoy the drive across the mountains and refrain from talking about watches and gross domestic product?"

"And from talking about *Pride and Prejudice* and the scourge of modernity. What do you say?"

"Gimmelmatt is so lovely this time of year," he said mildly.

"Are you *bribing* me?"

"Of course not," he said censoriously—but his eyes were twinkling. "Whatever gave you that idea?"

"Did you or did you not just strongly imply that you'll be nice to me if I go see your cute village?"

"You're the one who keeps calling it 'cute.' *I* would never use such a word." The smile she'd seen a shadow of before was threatening anew to escape.

She was having the same problem. She turned to look out the window. "I don't know what part of this isn't a bribe, but all right. Be nice to me today, and I'll go to your cute village."

"Today," he said.

"I'm not sure we have time for it today?" She had added a full day's worth of meetings to her schedule for Riems today.

"We don't. I meant I'll be nice to you today. No guarantees beyond that."

She snorted. "Fine."

He lost the battle and let loose an audible chuckle. "We'll do Gimmelmatt another day."

"But no skiing."

That had come out too intensely. He turned, his eyes briefly searching her face before returning to the road. "No skiing," he echoed, and not unkindly.

After that, conversation flowed as easily between them as it had last night at dinner.

It started, oddly, with him taking an interest in her work. "Can you overhaul any sort of company or operation?"

"I like to think I could, if they were willing."

"Do you apply your methods to your own life?"

"Not really. You might be surprised to learn that I'm a bit of a procrastinator in my personal life. I've tried to apply GTD at home, but I guess it's a case of the shoemaker's children going shoeless."

"GTD?"

"It stands for Getting Things Done. It's a productivity management system."

"A productivity management system called . . . Getting Things Done?"

She did hear how that sounded, and she waited for him to mock her, but he just smirked. She changed the subject. "Where did you grow up?"

"Not far from Riems, in fact."

"Do you have a big family?"

"I'm the second of four siblings. I've one older sister who's a teacher, and a younger brother and sister—twins—who still live at home."

"And your parents?"

"Are not together," he said quickly, a hint of his old brittleness returning. "My father is not around. It's just my mother and siblings and me."

She could respect the desire to shut down this line of conversation. If not for her dad, Cara would herself have had a very different life. And besides, they were making nice. No need for either of them to trot out family baggage. So she made an observation about the view, which, as they ascended into the mountains, was as spectacular as she'd imagined. The narrow road hugged blue-gray rock ridges and was lined with deep-green coniferous trees.

"You should see the approach to Gimmelmatt," Mr. Benz said, back to trying to tamp down a smile. "It's just like this, but at the bottom, in a valley, you have the world's *cutest* village."

THE FACTORY VISIT went well. Cara was good at this part, having developed a song-and-dance routine that disarmed people. Though she shouldn't call it a song-and-dance routine. It was genuine. She believed all the stuff she said about transparency. It wasn't that she was going to tell everyone everything at every step along the way, but being secretive didn't serve anyone. That had been another Tonya adage, and later, when Cara started heading up projects on her own, she learned it the hard way—she'd been on more than one project where the client's obsession with secrecy or spin-doctoring ended up sabotaging the whole thing. But happily, neither Morneau nor the Eldovian royal family had an overzealous communications department that needed to be managed. As she'd told Tonya on day one, her barriers here were going to be individuals. Leon Bachmann, for sure. He'd been quite snippy with her today, though she could appreciate that he was doing his job—and probably doing it more vehemently because he was in front of his hometown crowd. More worrisome was the CEO, Noar Graf, who for reasons she hadn't yet uncovered, was hostile. She'd had her rescheduled one-on-one with him, and he'd been either unwilling or unable to answer most of her questions. It was possible he was incompetent. That happened sometimes. People failed upward until they were left in charge of people or operations they weren't equipped to manage.

She glanced at her watch. Five minutes before four, which was her final meeting of the day. She'd been meeting with reps from different employee groups all day, and her last was some folks from the shipping department.

She sighed and rolled her shoulders. It had been a long day. Final push, though.

"Ms. Delaney, I thought you might be hungry."

Mr. Benz appeared at her side just as she was about to head back into the break room where her meetings were taking place. As he set a packet of almonds in her palm, his hand paused. She noticed again how weirdly attractive his hands were. He had prominent veins and long fingers. As they were making the transfer, one of those fingers sort of . . . caressed her thumbnail. She would have said it was an accident, but it was an oddly specific gesture. The pad of his index finger found her thumbnail and circled it, twice. Each time he made contact with the flesh of her cuticle, she shivered.

She forced words out. "Thank you."

He quickly retracted his hand. She thought he'd been about to say something when Leon, who was sitting in on all the meetings with unionized employees, appeared. Mr. Benz retreated, and Leon laid his index finger across his lips and leaned toward the door and beckoned her to do the same. It took her a moment to readjust to work—or to espionage, which it seemed they were doing. There were agitated voices coming from inside the break room. Leon frowned as he listened.

She didn't actually expect him to tell her what they were saying, but he surprised her by doing exactly that. "They are talking about how you're not to be trusted. Well, one of them says she liked what you said earlier, but another counters that you're staying in the palace and therefore not a neutral party."

She'd never thought of it that way. Perhaps she should have. But she hadn't known there was going to be this regional inferiority complex, whereby the Riems crowd felt like second-class citizens. "Where I'm staying has no bearing on my work, or its outcome," she whispered.

"They already think you're here to close the Riems plant—they think it's a foregone conclusion. Their observations about your lodging may merely be, what do you say in English? Confirmation bias? But . . ."

But perceptions mattered.

The interesting thing was that the meeting was extremely productive. One of the senior mail clerks pointed out that instead of shipping finished watches from Riems direct to their retail destinations, they sent them first to Witten, and all the outbound shipping happened from there. "What kind of sense does that make? We make all the Abendlieds here, so in cases where that's all we're shipping, we're wasting time and postage," he said, and Cara had to agree. There probably weren't enough savings to be had there to make much of a difference, but this was part of what these meetings were designed to uncover—aspects of the company's processes and culture that were so ingrained they weren't questioned.

Mr. Benz was waiting for her outside the meeting room when they were done. She wondered if their truce would hold. She wondered why her cuticle was tingling at his reappearance.

Her cuticle. Was tingling. She ordered herself to get a grip.

"If you're amenable," he said as they pulled out of the parking lot, "I have an idea for dinner on the way back."

"I'm amenable. And hungry. You probably noticed I didn't eat anything at lunch." The idea that Mr. Benz had been watching her closely enough to notice what she did or didn't eat should have been disconcerting, but from him it just seemed thorough. He was the sort of man who noticed things. It was probably a big part of why he was good at his job. "That's probably why you brought me . . ." She dug around in her purse and produced the bag of almonds. "This."

"Which you did not eat, apparently."

"I got waylaid."

"You did have a rather hectic day."

Hmm. Sympathy from Mr. Benz? Apparently their truce *was* going to hold.

They started ascending the mountain and hadn't gotten far before he pulled off into a small clearing that seemed to be carved out of the mountain itself. It was on the outskirts of a hamlet she'd noticed on the way over—not more than a half dozen buildings clinging to the side of the mountain. "This is an exceedingly informal place," he said as they pulled up to what amounted to a shack. "There is an item on the menu here I thought you might like. But perhaps you'd prefer something more conventional. There's a good restaurant in the next village."

"This looks great," she said, and it did. The restaurant was a lean-to made of roughly hewn wood. It was like the Alpine version of a taco stand, or one of those old-school ice-cream places where you walked up to a window to order. There were two bonfires burning in the clearing, each flanked by picnic tables and wooden benches and chairs.

They joined the small line at the counter. "You order your food here," Mr. Benz said. "It's mostly sausages, but there are some cold meat options. Everything comes with potatoes and various pickles. Then there's raclette service over by the fires."

She followed his gaze, and sure enough, a man was walking around with a comically large wheel of cheese and scraping gooey blobs of it onto people's plates.

"Is he heating that cheese over the fire?"

"He is."

Wow. What was next? Yodeling? Nuns exhorting them to climb every mountain?

They were almost at the front of the line, and Mr. Benz nodded at a handwritten chalkboard menu. "I thought of this place because they have a wild turkey sausage on the menu. The owner's son hunts them himself. It's not quite American-style turkey dinner, and of course, it's a day late, but . . ."

Oh my god, he had taken her out for turkey dinner, or as close as he could manage. Tears were there, suddenly, but she choked them back and ordered, with him translating the menu for her, a turkey-apple-sage sausage and a hot elderberry-ginger tea.

When their food arrived, Mr. Benz led them to a high-backed bench. The snow had begun to fall again, and it made her think of Kai's snow globes. It almost felt like they were inside one of them.

"I hope you won't be too cold?" Mr. Benz asked as he sat next to her so they were both facing the fire. He grabbed a heavy wool blanket that had been draped over the back of the bench and arranged it over their laps. Cozied up with Mr. Benz: what a strange turn the day had taken. Though where else was he supposed to sit? The next nearest chair was probably four feet away, which would have made conversation difficult. It was all very proper.

It just . . . didn't feel that proper.

But that was her problem. He remained unperturbed as he said, "We Eldovians are known for embracing outdoor activities year-round. There's a kind of collective belief that spending a good deal of time outdoors in all seasons improves one's mood in the short term and one's character in the long term. The Danes would probably have a word for it."

"I'm sure it does improve both those things. It's delightful out here, and a little cold reminds you that you're alive."

"Spoken like a true Eldovian."

The cheese dude arrived and said something in German. "He's asking if you would like cheese on everything?" Mr. Benz translated.

"*Ja, bitte*," she said to the man, who used a knife to glop a truly enormous volume of molten cheese on top of her potato and sausage. Her stomach rumbled.

"What would you do before Thanksgiving dinner at home?" Mr. Benz asked once they'd both been raclette-ed. "Say a prayer? Please don't let me stop you."

She smiled. The idea of saying grace over cheese-drenched turkey sausages in front of a bonfire with the equerry to the throne of Eldovia was too absurd. "That's all right. I'm not personally religious."

"So you said." His brow furrowed, as if he was trying to square her claims to secularity with the fact of her lighting a candle in church last night.

"I was upset last night because I missed my parents, of course, but also because my mother has an autoimmune disease that causes her a great deal of pain at times. She pushed herself too hard making Thanksgiving dinner. I would have done all the shopping and cooking, had I been home. I was feeling . . ."

"Guilty?" he suggested gently.

"Not so much that. I support my parents financially, so they understand I need to work. Just sad, I guess." Though that word didn't seem adequate. "A bunch of things mixed up, actually." And, *wow*, she needed to stop talking. Hadn't she been thinking this morning that she hated showing weakness to clients? Especially enigmatic clients she couldn't get a read on. Clients who resented her yet were kind and did thoughtful things like bring her snacks. And made her cuticles tingle.

"I know this mixture of feelings. My older sister has multiple sclerosis, and I also . . ."

She didn't push him to finish that sentence. "Then you know."

"I also . . . miss my family." He had finished his aborted thought, after all, and she sensed that he wasn't the kind of person who usually said things like that, much less to complete strangers. Well, good. They were even. Perhaps they could chalk up this interlude of disarming intimacy to the cozy setting. The gently falling snow, the fire, the outdoor meal—all these things conspired to make it feel as though reality was on pause.

"You don't see your family often?" she asked, wanting to keep the conversation going, wanting, strangely, to hear more real things about his life.

"My job keeps me rather busy, especially this time of year."

She understood. This was the part of the conversation where most people would spout some platitude about the importance of family. But she wasn't that kind of person, and she somehow knew Mr. Benz wasn't, either. She turned her attention to her food, slicing off a bit of sausage. As she lifted her first forkful, it steamed in the cold air. Her mouth literally watered as she took her first bite. "This is *so* good. I think the cold makes the food taste better. Is that possible?"

He smiled. "I think it is."

When they were done eating, Mr. Benz took their dishes back to the counter. Cara didn't want to leave. Somehow, the alfresco winter dining had unwound her. She felt as relaxed as she could remember being in a long time, like something that was usually taking up all the space in her chest—was it worry? She wasn't sure—had dissipated. She was pretty sure it would be back, though, whatever it was, when real life resumed. Reluctantly, she retied her scarf, which she'd loosened as the fire had heated them up, preparing for the trek back to the car. But when Mr. Benz came back, he said, "Shall we sit a few moments longer?"

"I was hoping you'd say that."

The smile he flashed her almost seemed fond. This time, when he sat, he left very little space between them. They didn't speak as they stared at the fire. The dancing flames were mesmerizing. She sighed, letting the smoky, piney air permeate her lungs. Though maybe that pine was him. He was awfully close. She yawned. Her eyelids were so heavy. If only there were a way to have a wee nap.

Well, damn: she had a wee nap. She assumed. Because the next thing she knew, she was snorting herself awake only to realize that she was cuddled up to Mr. Benz.

Dear god. She started to sit up, to issue apologies. He shushed her, placing his finger against her lips. It was cold, and her lips were warm.

"Truce," he whispered. And then he kissed her.

And then he kissed her.

Sort of.

Well, he did. His lips touched hers.

But only for a second, and only with the lightest of touches. It was as if they were connected by breath more than by flesh. It wasn't a sexy kiss. Per se.

Or it wasn't *meant* to be a sexy kiss, she didn't think. It did, however, wake her the hell up. Every cell in her body started buzzing, with alarm or delight, she couldn't tell which—maybe both. But the shape of the kiss, its design, wasn't sexy. It was probably some chaste Eldovian tradition that the Danes would have a word for. Kissing your comrade after a day spent outside. Hail fellow, well met: that sort of thing.

She had no idea what to say, so she experimented with not saying anything. She turned back to the fire and tried to feel if the lump in her chest was still gone. It was.

Eventually, he said, "We should go back."

"To Witten, you mean?" She wasn't sure why she was asking. Of course that was what he meant.

He looked at her quizzically. "Yes. Unless you have anywhere else you need to be?"

The lump returned. She didn't want to go back to the way they'd been before, to the antagonism and sniping. "No," she said quietly. "Let's go back."

AT THE CAR, Matteo popped the trunk to extract a blanket for Ms. Delaney, who he reasoned must be cold. The fire had staved off the worst of it, but they'd been outside for nearly two hours, and even he was starting to feel it. He paused, though, hidden by the raised trunk, and asked himself what in god's name he was doing.

He had *kissed* Ms. Delaney.

He had no way to explain it, except that he had felt, for a moment there, like he was out of time. Not out of time in the sense of being up against a timer, but outside the normal time-space continuum. Far from the palace, far from his Santa duties. The whole evening—the truce, the snow, the fires, the companionship—had felt like being inside one of Kai's snow globes. The world had shrunk to a cozily manageable size.

When she fell asleep and listed toward him, ending up snuggled against his side, he'd let it be, reasoning that she was asleep and would never know. And it felt good, to prop someone up, to stand guard while they rested. He had seen a different side of Ms. Delaney, when she'd told him more about her life, her parents. He saw the person inside the corporate goth, and that person was tired. He thought perhaps he could tell that in a like-recognizing-like sort of way. And if she was able to set her burdens down, even for a moment, he was all for it.

And then she'd awakened, and he'd been treated to a slideshow of facial expressions. The first had been, he dared say, contentment. She'd looked at him like it was normal to wake up from sleeping against his shoulder, like she was *happy* to be doing so. Astonishing. Next up had been befuddlement. Reality setting in. He knew the feeling. He could tell when she had collected enough information to be horrified, and that she was ramping up to apologize. The idea that she would apologize for falling asleep, for letting her guard down, felt so *wrong*.

He'd wanted to stay in the snow globe.

So he'd kissed her?

It made no sense.

He was trying to think how to handle things, whether to say anything, when she appeared by his side, probably wondering what was taking him so long. He handed her the blanket. "You can use this in the car until it warms up."

"You keep blankets in your car?" She peered into the trunk. "Is that an axe?"

"Yes." He pointed to the closed box that contained the rest of his kit. "And flares, sand, first aid supplies, and so on. Standard survival kit for traveling in the mountains in the winter." He reached for a brush to clean off the car and shooed her inside it to wait. They should not have lingered after dinner.

Once he was situated behind the wheel, he started the car, aimed the heat vents at her, and said, "Ms. Delaney, I must apol—"

She held up a hand. "No need. I'm the one who fell asleep on you."

"Yes, but—"

"Let's chalk it up to too much truce-ing and forget it."

Could it be that easy? "An overcorrection, if you will."

"Exactly. And now we'll go back to disliking each other." Her eyes twinkled under the dim lights illuminating the parking areas.

He feared his eyes were doing the same. "Very good, Ms. Delaney."

She fell asleep again a few minutes into their ride, which allowed Matteo to glance at her from time to time, to study her without her knowing. As she'd slept earlier, he'd been next to her, so he hadn't had a prospect of her face. The evening had done a number on her chignon. Some of her hair had escaped its bindings. Her head had lolled to one side, which had the effect of exposing one small, perfectly shaped earlobe studded with a small pearl. The cold had pinked her cheeks, and her lips were an even deeper pink. Her upper lip had a deep V in it, like an upside-down heart, almost, that he hadn't noticed before. He had never seen her without her signature lipstick, but he supposed the combination of the snow and the raclette had washed away her war paint.

He hadn't seen her naked lips before now, but he had felt them. Tasted them momentarily. They'd been—

No. He needed to do what she'd said and forget about that kiss.

He returned his attention to the road and, because she was asleep, did a few full sets of his breathing exercise. The car smelled faintly of smoke—they'd spent enough time by the fires that the scent had permeated their clothing.

Matteo's father used to smoke a pipe, and his car had always carried the scent. Mother never let him smoke in the house. She hated the smell, but Matteo used to like it. There was something comforting about that peaty smell. As an adult, he could see that it was probably just an association. When Father smoked, he was happy. And silent. It was the easiest time to be around him, and even though it embarrassed him now, as a child, Matteo had wanted nothing more than his father's attention and approval.

Matteo made a note to tell Frau Lehman to have Ms. Delaney's suit cleaned. She seemed to be rotating between a gray one and a black one, changing them up with different blouses and accessories. If she only had two, which seemed likely given the remarkably small size of her suitcase, she couldn't afford to have one out of commission for more than a day. He glanced at her again. She was—

Her phone rang, startling them both. He looked away quickly.

"I don't recognize the number, which means it's probably someone from the Riems factory."

"Has it been your real number you've been giving out?" It boggled the mind.

"It has been." Her brow wrinkled as she punched at the screen.

"And do people actually call it?"

"A few have." She answered the call. "Hello, Cara Delaney here." Her face changed from guarded to delighted. "Hi!" There was a long pause. "Are you *kidding* me?" Another pause. "I didn't think

you were serious! I'm on my way back from Riems. I don't know;
hang on." She lowered the phone and whispered to Matteo, "How
long have I been asleep? How long until we're back to Witten?"

"An hour or so until we're back."

"We're still an hour away. Tell him I'm sorry—" She huffed a
disbelieving chuckle as she listened to whatever the other person
was saying. "Okay, okay, I can't pass that up. Do I have time to
go change, though? We were out in the snow, and I'm sure I look
like a drowned rat." She pulled down the sun visor, slid open the
little mirror there, and winced. "Confirmed. I'm definitely giving
off waterlogged rodent vibes." She listened for a while, and the
chuckling of before became outright laughter. "Yeah, point taken.
Okay, then I'll be there in about an hour."

"Everything all right?" he asked when she disconnected her call.

"Yes. That was Imogen."

"Imogen?" He could not hide his surprise.

"Yes, she, ah . . . has something to show me at the bar. Do you
think you could drop me there before you head up the hill?" She
started rummaging in her bag.

"Certainly." He very much wanted to ask her what Imogen
could possibly have to show her that was so urgent, but his desire
not to be the kind of person who cared what Ms. Delaney did in
her free time was stronger. After a few seconds of silence, though,
he couldn't stand it anymore. But he limited himself to an observation that obscured the real question. "I didn't realize you and
Imogen had become so friendly."

"Mm," she said noncommittally as she adjusted the angle of
the visor to better study her reflection. Her "mm" morphed into
another vague syllable, but one that definitely signaled distress.

She started pulling pins from her hair. When it was all down it was so much longer than Matteo had imagined. It came almost to her elbows. She started raking her fingers through it, all the while curling her lip at her reflection.

"*Scheisse!*"

"What?" she said urgently. "What's wrong?"

What was wrong was that he'd nearly run them off the road watching her try to untangle her hair. What the hell was the matter with him? These were dangerous roads at the best of times, and it was dark and still snowing. "Can you please close that mirror? The light is distracting me."

He felt her attention for a long moment, as if she were trying to decide if he was telling the truth or was just out to sabotage her beautification efforts. She slid the mirror closed, flipped the visor up, and they spent the rest of the journey in silence. He felt miles away from the easy intimacy they'd shared this evening, and he didn't only mean that kiss. Dear god, he had told her about his sister. And last night, too, when he'd been prattling on about Star Wars and the solace it had brought him when he'd been younger. He'd allowed her to know that he'd been the kind of person who *needed* solace.

Ms. Delaney never put her hair back up. When he pulled up in front of the Owl and Spruce, it was still tumbling down her back. When she opened the car door, she triggered the overhead light. They stared at each other for several seconds.

She was right about the kiss. They needed to bury it. So instead of apologizing again, which had been his impulse, he said, "Are you going to lay people off?" He might as well ask. The question had been tormenting him, and now that she'd had her Riems meetings and had completed her first week of work, she probably had a preliminary sense of the scope of her planned destruction.

She looked startled, but only for a moment. "Undoubtedly."

He was surprised that she'd answered so easily. They continued to stare at each other. It was almost as if he could feel whatever goodwill remained from their truce disappearing, like the heat from the car dissipating into the cold night. It was more dismaying than it should have been.

He thought back suddenly to her confusion, back at the fire, when he'd said they should "go back." He'd meant to the castle, but had she been talking about this? This thing they did when they weren't in a truce?

"If you're on a sinking ship and you don't have enough lifeboats for everyone, do you say, 'Well, sorry, if we can't all go, we're all going to drown together'?" she asked, breaking with his gaze. Well, there it was. They were back to "normal." At least he had won the staring contest.

"I didn't say anything." He should be enjoying that she was having a one-sided argument here, imagining him saying things to which she was responding. It should be giving him a satisfying sense of superiority, knowing he was getting to her.

Somehow, it was not.

"Is a long, slow death preferable?" she asked, no longer even trying to keep the annoyance out of her tone.

"A long, slow death would give people time to adjust," he parried. "It would allow people to steer their children into different career paths, while *they* still have jobs."

They resumed staring at each other until she finally said, "Thank you for your company today," in a way that made him wonder if she had enjoyed his company at any point over the course of the evening or if she was just being polite. "And for dinner."

"You are most welcome," he said tersely. He *had* enjoyed their dinner, so he meant it. And yet, he could hear with his own ears how it sounded like he didn't.

Chapter Seven

*C*ara had had sex with a lot of different kinds of men. Doctors and lawyers. A plumber, a carpenter, a librarian. She wasn't picky, was the point, at least not about occupation. That kind of stuff only mattered if you were in the prospect for something long-term. She'd even hooked up with a professional archer once, when she was on a job in the same city as the Olympic trials for archery.

But goat herder was a new one for her.

Yes, Imogen had set her up with a dude named Johannes who was a goat shepherd. Wait. Did shepherds only do sheep? Maybe *goatherd*, like in that song from *The Sound of Music*, was the correct term.

According to Imogen, Johannes rarely came into the pub on account of how much time he spent with his goats. He was, no joke, a lonely goatherd. Funny that a couple hours ago, Cara had been by a fire with Mr. Benz, taking in a scene so stereotypically Alpine it had brought to mind *The Sound of Music*. Now here she was, preparing to meet her very own goatherd.

She paused before pushing open the door, trying to shake off the uncomfortable vestiges of the staring contest she'd had with Mr. Benz. She was a little alarmed at how she'd answered his question about layoffs. She shouldn't have answered it at all, let alone so easily. Maybe that kiss had actually been a spell. Maybe his plan all along had been to put the whammy on her in order to ferret out information. She didn't relish layoffs. She never did. But in that moment, she'd felt defensive, so she'd acted like layoffs were a foregone conclusion, one that didn't bother her. She'd felt the need to keep the upper hand, though she wasn't sure why. Well, probably because he'd been dropping her off at the pub so she could bang a goat herder named Johannes whom Imogen had set her up with. It all sounded so tawdry when put that way. And even though Mr. Benz was apparently a poor rich person, she knew in her bones that he didn't do tawdry.

No, he just did sweet, gentle fireside kisses.

Enough. She wasn't going to let Mr. Benz slut-shame her. Though to be fair, he had done no such thing. Okay, she wasn't going to let her interpretation of what Mr. Benz would think allow her to slut-shame herself. Resolved, she took a deep breath and pushed open the door.

She scanned the pub with a frisson of nerves. Imogen waved her over to the bar. "Hello, hello! He's having a round of darts while he waits for you. I'll take you over."

"Hang on a sec. Let me catch my breath." And by "catch her breath" she meant execute a super suave arm stretch–yawn thing to try to get a look at the lonely goatherd without him seeing her.

Wow. He looked exactly the way an Eldovian goat herder named Johannes should. He had long, slightly messy blond hair, and he was wearing a blue wool sweater with a red-and-white pattern knit into it. His back was to her as he threw darts, so she couldn't see his face, but this boded well. She took a fortifying breath as she turned back to Imogen, who winked and set a shot in front of her. "In need of a little liquid courage?"

She was so not this kind of drinker, but, hey, when in Eldovia . . .

When in Eldovia and about to bang a goatherd . . .

She threw back the shot and immediately started coughing. In her very limited experience with shots at home, they were always sickly sweet. This one was aggressively herbal, almost medicinal. She waved her hand in front of her face as she got control of herself. If any vestiges of sleepiness had been clinging to her from the drive home, she was now fully awake.

"Ready?" Imogen asked.

"I have one thing to ask you first. I need to find somewhere else to stay for the rest of my time here. Do you have any rooms? I'm here through the twenty-fourth."

"Ah, trouble in paradise?" Imogen pulled out a big, old-school calendar book from behind the bar.

"No trouble. I realized that the optics of me staying at the palace aren't great. I need to come off as more of a neutral party."

"The only room I have left is a small one without a private bathroom. It's clean and comfortable, though."

"I'll take it from tomorrow night."

Imogen waggled her eyebrows. "Are you sure you don't want to take it from tonight?"

"I thought you said he met the doesn't-live-with-his-parents criteria!" Meaning the goatherd had somewhere they could retreat to.

"He does, he does. I'm merely teasing you. He has a room in a boarding house in town. I'm told it's very small and cozy." More eyebrow waggling ensued.

"You're told or you know?" Cara could dish it out, too. She did her own eyebrow dance.

"I'm told," Imogen said firmly, and she didn't glance down the bar, but Cara wondered if that was only because Kai wasn't here this evening. Imogen came around the bar. "Shall we?"

"Why do I suddenly feel like you're my pimp?" Had she thought this through sufficiently? With an app, you messaged a bit, got a sense of the other person, and his expectations. "What exactly did you tell this guy?"

"I told him Eldovia was hosting a very pretty American woman who was desperate to have sex."

Cara gasped.

"Relax. I asked him if he was interested in a blind date with a visiting American. All you have to do is have a drink with him, play some darts. He's not expecting anything beyond a little company."

"Okay, okay." Cara dug around in her bag. "Let me fix my makeup first." Which she hadn't been able to do in the car since Mr. Benz had made her turn off the light. He was so—

No. No thinking about Mr. Benz. She pulled out her lipstick. She needed her armor.

MATTEO DROVE UP the hill. And then he drove back down.

It had only been three hours since dinner, but he found himself hungry. A plate of Imogen's chips would be just the thing right now.

Ms. Delaney was nowhere in sight when he entered the pub.

Not that he was looking for her. Just that he knew she was supposedly here, so it was notable when she turned out not to be. He took his usual seat at the bar, and soon Imogen was setting a glass of his preferred scotch in front of him.

He ordered his chips and considered moving to a table. Sometimes, a change of scenery was nice. Imogen reappeared as he was looking over his shoulder trying to decide if he should move.

"Looking for your Ms. Delaney?"

"No. I didn't even know she was here." And she wasn't *his* Ms. Delaney, but he feared saying that would sound like protesting too much.

"I thought you dropped her off."

"I did. But I was under the impression that you had something to show her, and since you're here and she's not, I'm assuming that has already happened."

"She's over there playing darts with Johannes Miller."

He twisted the other way in his seat, his gaze following Imogen's gesture to a little alcove that contained dartboards. Sure enough, there was Ms. Delaney with an enormous blond man. "I don't think I know him."

"He doesn't come in much. His family has a goat farm over near Feldkirch, and when he's working, he prefers camping on the mountain. But he keeps a room in the village in the winter. Pops in here from time to time."

Johannes Miller and Ms. Delaney were laughing, and he had his arms wrapped around her as he helped her aim a dart. For god's sake, it looked like a clichéd commercial for . . . he didn't even know. Chewing gum. Mass-produced American coffee. Something wholesome. They let loose a dart together, and when it hit the center of the target, they high-fived. Ms. Delaney's hair was still down. It was long and bouncy, and with it all in one mass like this, he could see that it wasn't a solid color as he'd always thought, but rather black streaked through with a dark mahogany.

He sniffed and turned back to Imogen, who said, "What?"

"Excuse me?"

"What was that sniff? Did I detect a note of misogyny in that sniff?"

"I *beg* your pardon?"

"I notice that when a woman goes in search of a casual sexual encounter, it often gives men a lot of feelings."

All he could do was blink. "When a woman goes in search of a *what*?"

"A casual sexual encounter," Imogen said matter-of-factly. "I think the Americans call it a 'hookup.'"

So if Ms. Delaney and Mr. Miller were in a commercial, it *wasn't* a wholesome one.

Something was happening to Matteo's blood. It was getting colder, and it rather felt as if it were slowing down. Turning to sludge. A delayed reaction to all the outdoor time earlier, perhaps. His mind flipped through a series of things to say to Imogen, who was standing in front of him with her elbows on the bar looking pleased with herself. *Ms. Delaney doesn't know this man. I don't know this man. She's here to work.* But of course, verbalizing any of these sentiments would only prove Imogen's point, and the degree to which that was unflattering was greater than Matteo's desire to speak. He didn't think of himself as someone who had different standards for women than for men. No, that was Noar, and his stubborn resistance to Ms. Delaney because she wasn't her male colleague. But what could his knee-jerk opinions about Ms. Delaney's use of her free time mean if not that?

He resolved to do better.

JOHANNES WAS PERFECT. His English wasn't that good, but that didn't matter. He was friendly and flirty and ridiculously hunky. It started out well. They played darts, and Cara would have said he did that stupid thing men do when they show you how to do something sporty by wrapping their body around yours to put you into the proper stance, but in this case, she really did need the help. Her first try had sent her dart bouncing off the wall several inches off the actual dartboard.

And more to the point, they both knew why they were here, and it wasn't to play darts. So his wrapping his body around hers could be seen as an efficient step on a path that ended with them wrapping their bodies around each other in a different way.

So what was the matter with her? Why wasn't she feeling it?

She told herself she was rusty. She just needed to smile and laugh and touch his arm and do all that stuff a person does in these situations. Fake it till you make it.

Hopefully she wouldn't have to fake it later.

"Should we evacuate?" Johannes asked.

She should be finding his tendency to use not quite the right word endearing. He had a certain earnestness that reminded her of Mr. Benz. Although Mr. Benz had a sense of humor beneath his starchiness. She thought back to his crack about cute villages on the way down the mountain. Johannes, who was still looking at her expectantly, seemed not to have a sense of humor at all.

Which, again, she reminded herself was fine. She didn't need him to tell her jokes. After tonight, she would never see him again.

"Or perhaps you would favorite another drink?" Johannes asked when she didn't answer his question about evacuation.

"Yes. I would favorite another drink," she said, even though it was a bad idea. When she joined Johannes, he had been working on a bottle of wine. She'd accepted a glass, then another. And she'd already had that shot.

He smiled his agreement and was off to the bar before she could tell him that on second thought, she'd have a Diet Coke. Well, hell, it was Friday night. She didn't have to see any kings or surly union stewards tomorrow. Or any maddening equerries. She'd probably see a lot less of Mr. Benz once she moved out of the palace. Which would, of course, be a huge relief.

She used Johannes's absence to ask herself a question, namely, what was her problem? She couldn't still be jet lagged. It had been a long day, yes, but normally she could and would rally in these types of situations. Plus, she'd had *two* catnaps this evening. And Johannes was *so* good-looking. If Mattel made a Goatherd Ken doll, it would look like Johannes. She turned toward the bar to remind herself of this fact.

And made eye contact with Mr. Benz.

He wasn't sitting at his usual place at the bar, but at a small table in the middle of the room, and he was facing her. Had he been watching all this time?

Was *that* why she couldn't get into the mood? Because her minder had been spying on her? Yes, the truce was over, but the idea that he was so quickly and easily back to his old ways, that he could go from kissing her to sitting there *judging* her, made her blood boil. How *dare* he?

She marched over there and slammed her glass on his table, but she forgot it was empty—and also perhaps that this wasn't appropriate behavior—so she miscalibrated. She bonked it too hard, and the stem broke clean off the bowl of the glass. Still, she'd come this far. So she might as well say what she'd come here to say, which was: "Why are you spying on me?"

He looked up at her—he hadn't stood at her approach, which was out of character for the scrupulously chivalrous Mr. Benz—and blinked. As if he was confused. The gall.

Eventually he spoke, but not until they'd stared at each other for a long moment. "I assure you I am not spying on you, Ms. Delaney. Lord knows, I haven't the time for that. I found myself rather peckish, so I came in for a bite." He gestured toward the table. She dropped her eyes long enough to take in the half-finished plate of chips. When she met his eyes again, he was still gazing at her evenly, supremely unbothered.

"Oh, come on. You're here to bust up my date."

"Are you on a date? And here I thought you were playing darts."

More of that blasted blinking, like he was a supremely patient adult and she a child making outlandish claims. "Yes. I am on a date. And you are ruining it." She needed to shut up. Even though what she was saying was true, the vehemence with which she was saying it, and with which she was throwing around glassware, was unseemly.

"*I* am ruining it? How is that possible? I'm merely sitting here eating my food, minding my business."

"Why aren't you sitting at the bar like you usually do? Why are you sitting *here*?"

"Well, if you must know, when I arrived, the only open seat at the bar would have put me next to someone I don't particularly care for."

She looked at the bar, wondering who that someone was.

"The bar was much more crowded when I arrived," he added with a touch of petulance in his tone.

It was currently about half-full and home to several swathes of open stools where a solo diner could sit and have a buffer on each side. But whatever. Why was she so pressed about this?

She glanced over her shoulder. There was Johannes, smiling and waving—and holding up another bottle of wine, god help her. Johannes was the reason she was here, so why was she wasting all this energy on Mr. Benz? She took a deep breath, hoping to settle both her ire and her nerves. "Good night, Mr. Benz."

There was a beat before he replied, "Good night, Ms. Delaney. Enjoy your . . . darts."

She intended to. She spun on her heel and made her way back to Johannes. She couldn't help marveling at how, a handful of hours ago, she and Mr. Benz had been sharing a meal and talking earnestly about their families. What had happened to that Mr. Benz? Or forget that, even—a handful of hours ago, she and Mr. Benz had *kissed*.

"Ah, hallo!" Johannes hoisted the new bottle of wine. "May I be pouring you another glass?

When she didn't say anything, Johannes set the bottle on the table. "Or perhaps the time has come that you would favorite to be seeing my room?" He smiled with such goofy happiness that he looked like a puppy.

What a nice man he was. What a *gorgeous* man he was. But somehow, despite everything lining up on paper, the time had not come that she would favorite to be seeing his room. So she pulled out that most horribly transparent of excuses and hoped it translated. "I'm actually getting really tired." It wasn't working. He was still looking at her with the puppy-dog face. "Thank you for a lovely evening, but I'm going to say good night."

He got it then, and she was flattered by the disappointment that flashed across his face before he replaced it with a smile. The goatherd would have to remain lonely.

As would she.

And despite his protestations to the contrary, and despite the fact that she couldn't really articulate why, it was all Mr. Benz's fault.

BY THE TIME Matteo dragged himself back to his apartment, he was exhausted. And embarrassed. While he had admitted to nothing, Ms. Delaney had been correct. He had been spying on her. And so overtly, too. He had innumerable people he could call on if he needed intelligence, and even in situations where he wanted to handle something himself, he was usually a great deal more subtle than he'd been tonight.

He resolved to do better.

He didn't turn on any lights as he shed his clothing on his way to bed. Lord, he was tired. But also jumpy. Before, he'd felt his blood thicken and grow sluggish. Now, he had hot soup zinging through him, and he feared that despite his exhaustion, sleep would not come.

When even a Nina Simone record failed to settle him, he sighed and got up to pace in the dark. He very much did not want to think about his own life, so why not turn his attention to someone else's? He picked up his phone and glanced at the time. Nearly midnight. But Torkel was a night owl.

"Hello?" Torkel answered.

"I think you should do it at the Cocoa Ball."

"You do? Hmm."

Matteo sat down, enjoying the way Torkel knew exactly what he was talking about, the way the two of them dispensed with formalities. It caused a kind of calmness to settle over his scattered self. He continued to miss Torkel.

"The ball two years ago was where Princess Marie and Leo got together," Torkel continued.

"Yes," Matteo agreed. They both knew that had been Matteo's doing.

"And to hear Sebastien tell it, the ball last year was a rather significant . . . episode in the romance between the duke and Daniela." He paused. "The word 'episode' is a euphemism here."

Matteo held up a hand even though Torkel was not there to see it. "Say no more. I can imagine." That had not been his doing, but he *had* helped arrange things later so those two fools didn't let each other slip away out of sheer pride and stubbornness.

"My point is," Torkel said, "there seems to be a bit of a tradition of romantic entanglements advancing themselves at the ball. I like that."

Matteo liked that he liked that. He liked when other people noticed and valued tradition.

The image of a dart-playing angel of destruction popped into his head. She was probably following her evening activities by working on her layoff list.

Unless she was sleeping over with the goatherd. Cuddled up with—

Enough. He forced himself back to the task at hand. "There are two general approaches. One is you do something big and attention-grabbing. With an audience. That's the Hollywood version—and I don't mean that in a derogatory way. Beyond the thrill of the spectacle, I imagine there might be a certain poetic justice in a public proposal. Give the naysayers a bitter pill to swallow."

"Well, the primary naysayer is dead."

"Indeed." Torkel was referring to Sebastien's father, the late duke, who had been nothing short of a beast.

"Then there's his mother, but she's been largely defanged. And bless Seb, he still holds out hope for some kind of reconciliation."

"Indeed," Matteo said again. He didn't know Sebastien von Hansburg well, but he seemed to have resisted the world's corrupting ways. He tried to see the good in people, perhaps even when there wasn't any there.

Matteo was happy for Torkel. He was so happy, for a moment, that his chest seized. What must it be like to have found a person you not only loved, but *liked* enough to want to spend the rest of your life with? Someone you trusted enough to give your entire self over to?

Matteo hadn't had a girlfriend since he was in the military. Anna had been a true companion, and he'd loved her. But he had known, all along, that they weren't destined for marriage. They'd been likeminded souls in a sometimes stressful setting, and being together had been a balm. But when he'd gotten tapped for the

equerry job, neither of them had harbored any delusions that they
would stay together.

And though he missed Anna as a person, he didn't miss dating.
His job was all-consuming. It required him to give over all his attention, all his care, to Eldovia. He was fine with that.

Wasn't he?

"And the other?" Torkel said.

"Pardon?"

"You said there were two general approaches."

Matteo ordered himself to shake off whatever this odd storm
of intensity in his chest was. "Yes. The other isn't showy. Perhaps
a few words whispered in an ear while dancing. I could arrange a
favorite song to be played. The point is merely a heartfelt declaration against the backdrop of the ball. A private moment in a swirl
of dancers, the calm eye of the storm. The—"

He was getting carried away. Imagining details that weren't his
concern. It just . . . sounded nice. To be allied with someone in a
crowd. To whisper words of love and belonging, and to hear them
returned.

Goodness. He needed to take a holiday after Christmas. A
proper one. Perhaps he'd finally visit New York as a tourist.

"That sounds perfect," Torkel said. "Sebastien is shy. He won't
want attention. He'll like it better if it's private."

"You do know that there will be a certain amount of attention
paid to the both of you, though. You've never attended the ball as
a guest."

And lord knew, it was going to be difficult to get Torkel to *be-
have* as a guest. The man had protection in his bones. Matteo
made a note to get the evening's security plans and pass them on to

Torkel ahead of time. Hopefully that would preempt any fretting he would otherwise be doing upon arrival.

"Right," Torkel said, and there was an uncharacteristic note of uncertainty, of unease, in his voice. "And will that be because we're both men, or because he's the brother of a duke and I'm military special ops turned thug-for-hire?"

Matteo didn't see any need to mince words. "A bit of both, I'd imagine. Mind you, no one is going to give you any trouble." No one would dare say a word against the mountain of a man that was Torkel, at least not within earshot. "It's handy sometimes, being a professional thug, don't you find?"

When Torkel didn't chuckle, when he didn't say anything at all, Matteo realized his apprehension was genuine. He switched into business mode. "Don't worry. As to the logistics of the proposal, we'll do it toward the end of the evening. Make sure you dance together a few times before the actual proposal. Let people get their gawking out of the way. And beyond that, just remember that it's worth it."

It was, yes? At least it was for normal people, people whose jobs didn't require the sublimation of their person lives?

"And I'm not just talking about the proposal," Matteo continued. "I'm talking about muddling through whatever rubbish you need to in order to take your place as the husband of the brother of a duke."

"Well, I don't think of it like that. I don't care about the title."

"Of course you don't." That was what made Torkel such a good man. "My point is, are you going to let a little discomfort keep you from the life you want with Sebastien?"

"No. You're right. Of course it's worth it. *He's* worth it."

Ah, there went the odd chest pressure again. "I'm sure he is, but you are, too, don't forget." Normally, Matteo would never say anything so sentimental, but it seemed to need saying.

There was a long pause, and Matteo worried that he'd overstepped, but Torkel cleared his throat and asked, "How'd you get so smart?"

Matteo ignored the question. Torkel still sounded a bit shaky, so Matteo said, "If you have a particular song you'd like played, or you want any other arrangements made, let me know. Beyond that, you concentrate on what you're going to say, and don't worry about a thing. Anyone who so much as raises an eyebrow in your direction will have me to deal with."

For some reason that, which he hadn't meant to be amusing, drew a chuckle from Torkel. "Everyone always said I was so intimidating, but the person to truly fear, either at the palace or on a military deployment, was you."

Matteo knew Torkel was in jest, but he also knew there was a kernel of truth in what he'd said—and he didn't know how he felt about that. On the one hand, he wanted to be respected, to have influence, and power. But not through fear. And he wasn't interested in power for its own sake. He'd seen enough of that among a certain type of soldier during his stint in the military.

But he was overthinking this. Torkel had been teasing. And Matteo had been silent too long. The humor had dissipated.

"Matteo," Torkel said with an odd sort of urgency.

"Yes?"

"Thank you."

He'd infused that *thank you* with enough heartfelt vehemence to make warmth blossom in Matteo's chest. "You're quite welcome. I can't wait to celebrate with you both."

Moving day dawned cold and bright, and Cara greeted it with a minor hangover and a major case of regret. She wasn't sure what had come over her last night, accusing Mr. Benz of spying on her. She heaved herself out of bed to start packing. When she was done, she figured she ought to inform the palace that she was decamping. Not quite able to make herself pull the tasseled cord in the corner of her room to summon a servant, she set out for the breakfast room. Frau Lehman had told her, when she first arrived, that there was a buffet set up for the family each morning, and that Cara was welcome to join. She hadn't yet, on account of the fact that she rarely ate in the mornings, but she headed there now—imagine having an entire room devoted to just one of the day's meals—hoping she might find the king.

She found, instead, his daughter.

"Oh, Cara! Good morning! Won't you join me?"

She helped herself to some coffee and grabbed a croissant. "I'm glad to find you here. I'm going to be moving to a room at the Owl and Spruce, and I wanted to explain why."

She explained her reasoning, and Marie said, "This seems like a smart move. I hadn't thought about the optics. But I guess that's why we have you."

"You'll explain to your father? I don't want to cause any offense."

"Of course, and don't worry, you won't. My father is quite keen for this project to be successful, and—"

Mr. Benz came sweeping into the room. "Your Royal Highness,

if I might trouble you for a moment . . . ." He trailed off when he registered Cara's presence, and his eyes flicked down to her plate. He quickly regrouped. "My apologies, I'm interrupting."

"Not at all, Mr. Benz," Marie said. "Join us."

He pulled out a chair. "It's about Torkel."

"Oh, how is Torkel? I do hope everything is all right?"

"Yes, everything's fine. He and Sebastien are planning to attend the Cocoa Ball. I need to speak with you regarding some of the details."

"Good. Max was making noises about being in New York for the holidays, but I selfishly want him to come here, so if his brother is coming, it will be another arrow in my quiver." She turned to Cara. "I'm sorry. You have no idea who any of these people are. Except Max—Max von Hansburg from the Morneau Board. He's also my best friend. His brother is Sebastien, and Sebastien's boyfriend is Torkel. You'll meet them at the ball."

"I would love to attend the ball," Cara said, "but I'm planning to go home to my family for Christmas. I'm flying out very early on the twenty-fourth, so I'm afraid I'll miss it."

The princess made a good-naturedly exasperated noise. "Everyone with their families!"

"We can't all marry orphans," Mr. Benz said fondly. Cara had noted that Mr. Benz showed flashes of affection for all the members of the royal family, including the American interlopers, Leo and Gabby. It was odd to see that side of him.

As Cara pushed back her chair, Marie said, "Don't leave on our account, Cara!"

"Yes, don't let me chase you away," Mr. Benz said, but all that warmth Cara had just noted had drained from his voice.

"I need to be going anyway. You'll . . ." She glanced at Mr. Benz. "Pass my message on to your father with my regards?"

"I will indeed."

She could feel Mr. Benz's disapproving stare on her as she left. And, oddly, she could feel it all the way back to her room.

Chapter Eight

Thirteen days until Christmas

*N*early two weeks later, at the end of a very long day juggling both his jobs, Matteo ventured to the Owl and Spruce. He had been staying away from the pub that was now home to Ms. Delaney. He saw her often enough in the course of the average day, as she poked around, asked for information, and generally made a nuisance of herself. More than once, his own meetings with various people had been canceled to free them up to speak with her. It was vexing. As was the fact that she was always writing things down in an ominous fashion. She was like an evil Santa, keeping a layoff list instead of a naughty list.

The truce was definitely over. It seemed like it had happened in another lifetime, in a dream.

But as time passed, he started to grow annoyed at himself for letting her disrupt his routine. He often went to the Owl and Spruce for a drink in the evening. But now he couldn't do that because it would look like he was spying on her? This was his pub.

He had every right to be here, and if the side effect of that was witnessing Ms. Delaney leading up to a "casual sexual encounter," to use Imogen's alarming term for it, it couldn't be helped.

Anyway, Ms. Delaney had a meeting at seven o'clock tomorrow morning, and it was going on ten p.m., so surely she would be upstairs in bed. He knew about her meeting because the palace scheduler who had been seconded to help Ms. Delaney with administrative work had emailed Matteo Ms. Delaney's schedule that first week and had simply kept doing it without being asked— probably because she, like everyone, knew that Matteo was, to use Ms. Delaney's metaphor, the ship's engineer. He made things go.

So it was with resolve that he marched into the Owl and Spruce that evening and pulled out a stool at the bar.

That resolve faded as he caught sight of something in his peripheral vision. It was Ms. Delaney. She was not alone.

"Is that Bashir Hussein?" he asked Imogen, who had appeared in front of him.

She rested her elbows on the bar. "It is."

"What is he doing with Ms. Delaney?" Ms. Delaney who should be in bed by now, on account of her early-morning meeting tomorrow.

"Can't say as I know," Imogen said in a tone that suggested the exact opposite.

Bashir Hussein was the principal of the elementary school in the village, and he was the best sort of person. He did a lot of community work. In fact, he was usually the first person Matteo turned to when he was trying to help a family with school-age children.

The blood-going-cold sensation started up again.

Damn it.

Still. He wasn't about to embarrass himself as he had last time. He sat at the bar and did not turn around. Not even once.

"Would you help me with something?" Imogen asked, setting a scotch in front of him a while later.

"Of course."

"The ice machine in the back is jammed. I was hoping you might take a look at it."

What an odd request. Matteo was skilled in many areas, but ice-machine repair was not one of them. Still, people were used to the idea of him as a problem solver. "I'd be happy to have a look."

Imogen asked one of her regulars to watch the bar, and he followed her to the kitchen. They had to pass Ms. Delaney's table. He made sure to walk at a reasonable pace. Not too slow, because he wasn't at all concerned with what Ms. Delaney was doing in her free time. Not too fast, either, because neither was he avoiding her. He slowed ever so slightly as he approached their table and murmured, "Good evening, Mr. Hussein. Ms. Delaney." He looked at each of them as he spoke, and though he intended to keep moving, his gaze snagged on Ms. Delaney's when her sapphire eyes flew open in surprise.

He didn't let himself stay snagged for long, though. He kept walking. He left her to her surprise.

WAS MR. BENZ back to spying on her?

No. Cara had to be reasonable. Yes, he was in the pub on a night Imogen had set her up with a man, but that had to be an unlucky coincidence. She hadn't seen him here for weeks. And he had merely walked by her table, and he'd barely acknowledged her as he did. He'd seemed brusquely intent on whatever his destination was. Perhaps the restrooms at the back of the bar. She smiled. The thought of Mr. Benz having normal, bodily functions was kind of amusing. She'd never seen him in anything but one of his signature three-piece suits, and part of her felt like he had been born in a tiny version of the same.

She wondered what he wore for pajamas.

She wondered *if* he wore pajamas.

Mr. Benz might be the kind of person who slept in the nude. She could imagine him having a Nordic-style, practical belief that things needed airing out. He might just have two modes: three-piece suit and naked. He was—

". . . or perhaps not."

Oh no. She had mentally followed Mr. Benz out of the room when she was meant to be paying attention to Bashir. "I'm so sorry. I zoned out for a moment there. Please forgive me. You were saying?"

"I was saying that it seems as though you've met Matteo Benz."

Good lord. She couldn't escape Mr. Benz in reality, in her mind, *or* in conversation with other people.

"I have. He's been . . . helpful." Which was true. Sort of. He had been helpful when he wasn't too busy being unhelpful. He had been selectively helpful.

Bashir's face lit up. "Then you know what a wonderful, warm man he is."

"I . . . do?" If she was making a list of Mr. Benz's qualities, *wonderful* and *warm* would not be on it. Although he had been thoughtful to take her to church. And out for turkey sausages.

There had also been the kiss. That had definitely been . . . warm.

But then all that warmth had evaporated, and she hadn't laid eyes on him except in passing for what felt like ages.

Ugh. Why was he such a mystery?

"Yes," Bashir said. "One of the things I try to do in my role as a school principal is look after the overall well-being of my students and their families. Learning doesn't happen in a vacuum, so if there are problems at home—food insecurity, family instability, for example—I try to do what I can to help. Matteo has been a tremendous ally in those efforts."

"Really?" That didn't sound like her Mr. Benz.

Well, not *her* Mr. Benz. She issued a mental correction: that didn't sound like the Mr. Benz she knew.

"He's so well-connected, and he knows so many people. I can't tell you the number of families of mine he's quietly helped, either himself or by connecting them with resources."

"What kind of resources?"

"All kinds. Tutors, jobs for the adults in the household. Donations of sports equipment so the children won't be excluded."

Well. That one hit home, didn't it?

"Once," Bashir went on, "he even gave over his own apartment to a woman and a child fleeing an abusive situation for a night before I could make more permanent arrangements."

She thought back suddenly to her first night in town, to when she and Mr. Benz had walked down the hill. They'd stopped to watch the cocoa drinkers and skaters on the village square, and she'd posed an offhand, joking question, asking if people were allowed to be unhappy in Eldovia. He hadn't answered it until later, when he suddenly had. *People are allowed to be unhappy in Eldovia*, he'd said while he held the door to the pub open for her.

". . . though perhaps another time would be better."

Gah. She was being terrible. "Bashir. I'm sorry. My fractured attention this evening is absolutely not about the quality of the company. I'm more tired than I realized."

He smiled. He was such a nice man. "I was suggesting you might like to take a walk, but perhaps it's time to call it a night."

He was giving her an out, and she was going to take it. "I think so. Thank you for the company. I enjoyed chatting with you." *Until I got distracted thinking about Mr. Benz being a secret do-gooder. And about Mr. Benz naked.*

He really was everywhere, Mr. Benz, even when he wasn't.

Once again, she forced her attention back to the very nice man in front of her. Imogen had introduced him but had warned Cara that he wasn't going to be like Johannes. "He'll want to get to know you. You'll probably have to go out with him a few times before . . ." She'd winked.

Cara couldn't tell if Imogen was merely, from her vantage point behind the bar, an accomplished student of human psychology, or if she was on her way to becoming a professional matchmaker.

Either way, Imogen had been correct about Bashir, who, unlike Johannes, had not given off *We're gonna hook up tonight* vibes. He had been smart and attentive, and, having moved to Eldovia as an adult, he'd made some interesting observations about its culture, some of which were going to prove useful for Cara in her work.

"Perhaps we can do this again," Bashir suggested as they pushed back their chairs.

"Yes, anytime. I'm staying upstairs, so I'll be here." Though she found that, as with Johannes, she was strangely not in the mood. For hooking up, or for a chaste date of the sort her mother would approve of. For any of it.

She trudged up the stairs to her room. All she wanted to do was take a hot shower and crash. Well, what she *really* wanted was to take a hot bath and crash, but the shared bathrooms upstairs had only shower stalls. There would be no baths for Cara until she was on her next work trip. She changed into the shorts and camisole she slept in for the trek down the hall. She was more than happy to be at the Owl and Spruce given that it corrected an optics problem, but it *was* a bit of a comedown.

She grabbed her toiletries bag and randomly thought of Mr. Benz saying you hadn't lived until you'd seen the night sky while immersed in one of Eldovia's famous hot springs. Like being a secret fairy godfather to children and families in need, lounging aimlessly in a hot spring was not something she would have imagined Mr. Benz doing.

And now she was back to picturing Mr. Benz naked.

It wasn't as hard to do as the last time she'd tried to. Or tried not to. Whatever. Anyway, surely the kind of hot springs he'd been talking about—the public kind—required bathing suits? Because—"Ahhh!"

Yet again tonight, her thoughts of Mr. Benz were distracting her from her surroundings. She'd been locking her room for her trip to the shower, and she'd turned without checking that the coast was clear and bumped into someone carrying a very large box.

She apologized in the German she'd been learning, and again in English. "I'm terribly sorry, sir." Or maybe it was a ma'am. The box obscured the person's head and torso. She let her gaze slide down the person's legs. Horror dawned. She knew those pinstriped legs.

"Ms. Delaney?" He lowered the box.

Mr. Benz seemed surprised to see her here, which was fair enough. The feeling was mutual. They both said, "What are you doing here?" in unison.

Before she could answer, his brow furrowed. He glanced at her closed door, then back to her. His gaze traveled down to her feet and back up, and she felt her skin begin to buzz. There was nothing indecent about her pajamas, but they were very . . . small. And this was Mr. Benz who was, as ever, dressed to the nines in one of his suits.

But whatever. She was taking a shower in the bathroom in the inn she was staying at. As she had every right to. She straightened her spine. "I moved into a room here."

"Yes. Right." He cleared his throat. "How is Mr. Hussein?"

Huh? "I don't know. I assume he's fine? At least he was a bit ago when I said goodbye to him downstairs." When Mr. Benz didn't say anything, she said, in an attempt to extricate herself from this awkward encounter, "Well, I'm off to shower and then to sleep."

"You are?" His expression was lightening in real time. After a beat, he looked positively delighted by her planned ablutions. He was such an enigma.

But equally puzzling was why she cared. Let the man be a mystery. It didn't matter to her. Or it shouldn't. The more immediate question was what *he* was doing up here. "Are you spying on me again?" she asked.

"No!" he said, visibly bristling. "I'm moving some boxes for Imogen." His expression transformed from piqued to puzzled.

"Part of your extended mission?" she asked. "Lifting up the people of Eldovia, or just lifting their stuff?"

"That, Ms. Delaney, is a very good question."

Cara had always thought of herself as a puzzle person. She did the crossword when she was home, and she never traveled without her sudoku book. But Mr. Benz was beyond her. He was the Saturday *New York Times* crossword, a puzzle so challenging she knew enough—or should know enough—to not even try.

"Well," she said with false cheer, "good night." She continued down the hallway, aware that her thin jersey-knit shorts were riding up her butt but not wanting him to see her digging them out. Assuming he was looking. Which he almost certainly wasn't. But she couldn't look over her shoulder to check. In case he was.

Which he *wasn't*. Right?

And that was a good thing. *Right?*

It was official: Noar Graf was a problem. Two minutes into Cara's latest meeting with him, it was clear that he was actively obstructing her work. What she didn't know was why.

She interrupted him as he was saying a lot of words that didn't mean anything, though she did appreciate that to do so in one's second language was a skill. "So what you're saying is that you're not willing to provide any of the data we spoke about last time." The data the company had used for its most recent valuation exercise. The data she'd needed two weeks ago. The data he had agreed he would bring to this meeting.

He blinked. "I wouldn't say unwilling," he said with a hint of affront in his tone. "As I was just explaining, the data you seek are not readily available in the format you desire."

"Right." She pushed back her chair, startling him. He expected her to agree with him, or even to argue, but not to simply leave.

"Where are you going?"

"I don't see any need to prolong this meeting if the information that was meant to be the point of it isn't here, so I'm going to hunt it down myself." She kept her tone neutral, bordering on pleasant, to contrast with her words. She had learned that the truth coming from a woman with some power could feel to a man like an attack.

She left him blinking and made for the Owl and Spruce. She now had an hourlong hole in her schedule, and one upside of staying at the pub was that it was within walking distance of the Morneau corporate offices, which were on the edge of the village. She'd gotten into the habit of taking a coffee break at the pub when she had a long enough gap in the day.

"Hello, hello." Imogen, having learned Cara's ways, started pulling an espresso when Cara arrived at the bar. She added hot water to it and set it in front of Cara. "Americano for the Americano." Seamlessly, she pivoted and continued a conversation she'd been having with a young woman Cara didn't recognize.

Cara sipped her coffee and stared at the display behind the bar, which in addition to the snow globes now included the gingerbread houses Mr. Benz had told her Kai made every year. There was one of the palace, one of the Lutheran church that was famous for its modern architecture, and one of the pub building itself. Having spent more time around Kai—Cara couldn't say she'd gotten to know him, as he seemed like a serious lone wolf—she understood that he was never going to monetize his creations. But both the houses and the globes were really something.

"Actually, my friend here might know." Imogen switched into

English. "Erika Ulmer, this is Cara Delaney. She's here from New York on business." Cara and Erika shook hands. "Erika is waiting to hear if she's been accepted to some American universities, and she's wondering if they will be open next week."

Erika flashed Cara a self-deprecating smile. "I'm anxiously awaiting acceptance emails. Or rejection emails—I've already gotten one of those. I'm trying to tell myself that at this point, I won't hear anything until the new year, but Imogen said she thinks that unlike here, most of them will be open over the holidays."

"I don't know, to be honest," Cara said. "I think most of them probably will have staff working except for the actual holiday days. But that's a guess."

"I'm just being impatient," Erika said.

"It's nerve-racking," Cara said. "All that uncertainty, especially if you're thinking of moving continents."

"I'll probably end up attending the University of Geneva. I've already been accepted there."

"Well, however it turns out, congratulations. Acceptance at a place like that is an accomplishment."

"It really is, in my family," Erika said.

"I was the first person in my family to graduate from high school, much less attend college, so I get it."

"See?" Erika turned to Imogen. "This is what I like about Americans. They're so much more upwardly mobile than we are."

"I hate to burst your bubble, but I don't know if that's actually true," Cara said. "That's the perception, for sure, but I think the fact is wealth begets wealth." What followed was an interesting discussion on class, social mobility, and national differences. It sounded like Cara and Erika had a lot in common.

"But sometimes, you have to find reasons to hope," Erika said.

"Oh, for sure," Cara said. "I don't mean to sound like a doom-sayer here. I'm not talking about you, anyway, just this idea that anyone can make it in America if they work hard enough. You can always find individual cases where that's true—I'm one of them—but I don't think that's the same thing as upward mobility being baked into the system."

"A few years ago, we started getting one of those Santa baskets at our house." Erika looked at Imogen. "Does she know what those are?"

Imogen responded by looking at Cara with her eyebrows raised.

"Nope," Cara said.

"Well, there's this . . . Santa thing here. I realize that sounds ridiculous."

If she was saying that the Christmas mania in Eldovia extended to adults believing in Santa Claus, then yes, that did sound ridiculous.

"Four Christmases ago, my father was very ill," Erika said. "He had been diagnosed with an aggressive cancer, and he was declining quickly. After he died, my mother got a job in the mail room at Morneau, but for a year there, when he was so sick and my mother was taking care of him, we had no income other than what my sister and I could bring in babysitting and dog-walking. Things were very bad. That first Christmas morning after he fell ill, we found outside our front door the most enormous basket—two of them, actually. One contained the fixings for a Christmas feast, which wasn't something we'd been able to splurge on. The other contained presents for all of us. Mine was a voucher for the cinema. It wasn't much, but it *meant* so much. I still remember going to that film. It was only a silly romantic comedy, but I hadn't done something purely fun like that for so long that tears came to my eyes as the opening credits began. Those baskets came every year until we got back on our feet."

"How curious," Cara said.

"Yes, and it always seems like the people who need them, get them. Everyone always says that the baskets appear for people who need a little Christmas magic."

"Who sends them?" Cara asked.

Erika shrugged. "Nobody knows."

"Santa sends them," Imogen said, her firm tone at odds with the twinkle in her eye.

"But it's not really Santa," Cara said. *Come on.* "Is it you?"

"It is not me." Imogen held up a hand like she was swearing an oath.

"What is Santa, really?" Erika said. "That's what I wrote my university entrance essays about. I come from the land of Christmas, and Santa comes to my house." She grinned at Cara. "I know it sounds like one of your Hallmark movies—"

"They're not *my* Hallmark movies." Cara hated to interrupt, but she wasn't letting anyone assign her ownership of those drecky, borderline-unhinged movies.

"But what I said was that Santa for the modern world needs a new metaphor. He—or she, or they—can be a radical. Bringing not magic but actual, material help where it's needed. A selective Santa who doesn't distinguish between naughty and nice but between wealth and poverty. A redistributive Santa."

"Santa as Robin Hood," Cara said. It was a cool idea.

"Exactly," Erika said.

"But who's behind it? Don't you want to know?"

"No," Imogen said staunchly. "I do not. Sometimes looking at a thing too closely can ruin it."

Chapter Nine

Eight days until Christmas

*J*ust over a week until Christmas, which meant it was crunch time for Matteo and Kai. Unfortunately for Matteo, he was no-where near the workshop that was currently standing in for the North Pole. He was, in fact, sitting in his car in Riems, outside the home of Leana Hauser, a retired Morneau board member, waiting for Ms. Delaney, who was inside. As he was working on tracking down a shipment of panettone that had gone missing, a text arrived.

Imogen: Kai's at the bar, and he asked me to text you to ask you where you are.

Matteo: I had to drive Ms. Delaney to Riems. I told him that.

Imogen: He says, "When did you tell me this?"

> **Matteo:** I emailed you. Him.

> **Imogen:** You emailed him! LOL!

That *LOL* had no doubt been intended as Imogen's commentary on the matter, as Kai did not speak in internet slang. Matteo did realize that emailing Kai, who checked his messages every once in a while on an ancient desktop that took ten minutes to wheeze to life and connected to the internet via dial-up, probably hadn't been sufficient. But Kai hadn't answered his phone, and the last-minute nature of this trip hadn't left Matteo with any other options.

> **Matteo:** Ms. Delaney was called away on an urgent matter at the last minute.

An urgent matter she would not speak about, which annoyed him. He realized that he wasn't on Morneau's board, that much of his knowledge about the company was the result of the board trusting him—by not ejecting him from closed-door meetings, for example. Seeing him, as the king did, as an extension of the palace. As an asset.

It irritated him that Ms. Delaney did not also see him this way.

> **Imogen:** He says: "And you had to be the one to drive her?"

Yes. Well, no. But yes. He huffed a sigh. Ms. Delaney had said a version of the same thing, had in fact already made arrangements through the palace for a car when he caught wind of her plans. *I didn't want to pull you from your work at the last minute,* she'd said. He wondered if what she actually meant was *I didn't want you driving me.*

He had insisted. He wasn't even sure why, except that he felt he should be the one to do it. Not least because it was snowing something fierce. The drive back was going to be difficult.

> **Imogen:** Kai says to tell you it's eight days until Christmas.

> **Matteo:** I am aware.

He was also aware that by telling Imogen to convey all these impatient messages, Kai was very likely tipping his hand about the Christmas baskets. Matteo assumed Imogen already knew—Imogen knew about everything that happened in the village. Still, there was no need to call unnecessary attention to themselves.

> **Matteo:** Tell Kai I'll call him when I get home this afternoon. And tell him to answer his phone for once.

He eyed the door Ms. Delaney had gone through more than an hour ago. What could she want with Mrs. Hauser? The Hausers were an old Eldovian family and were friendly with the royals. They'd had someone on the Morneau board for generations, but their current representative was not Mrs. Hauser but her great-nephew, Daniel. Ms. Delaney had, of course, met with Daniel, as she had all board members, but going so far out of her way to interview long-retired members, especially this late in her visit, seemed to him to be taking her consulting mandate to unnecessary extremes.

He started thinking about that layoff list. Would she tell him who was on it? If so, perhaps he could begin making plans ahead of time. If—

She appeared suddenly outside the house, just as a great gust of wind did. She struggled to make her way down the drive, and Matteo got out of the car to help her. The wind blew off her hat before he made it to her side, and he went after it. They both struggled toward the car, almost comically.

"Whew!" she exclaimed when they'd both managed to make it back to the car and closed the doors against the elements. Ms. Delaney's cheeks were pink, and her hair was covered with snow from the minute she'd spent outside hatless. She must have found the struggle amusing, too, because she was laughing. "This is some country you have here!"

It was strange to see levity on her face. Relations between them had not improved since their encounter upstairs at the Owl and Spruce. Matteo had avoided returning to the pub since then—he was busy with the baskets anyway—and the ride over the mountains today had been mostly silent. Unlike their last trip to Riems, Ms. Delaney hadn't seemed interested in the view. She'd spent so much of her time absorbed in her phone that he'd been forced to conclude she was studiously ignoring him.

Now, though, he could feel his mouth mirroring hers, making him smile against his will. "Yes, you can get these sorts of sudden storms in the mountains."

"Would this be a bad time to ask you if we can make one more stop before we head back?"

"Where would this stop be?" She handed him a piece of paper with an address written on it. "That's not far from here, and it's on the way home. I don't see a problem with a brief stop, as long as the weather doesn't get any worse."

The weather got worse.

"This isn't looking good, is it?" she said a few minutes later.

"Can your errand wait? I will gladly take you back another day." Because he had so many of those to spare before Christmas. But Christmas wasn't going to happen if he flipped the car.

"Yes, of course. I don't want to do anything rash. It's just that I was hoping the element of surprise would work in my favor."

"If you don't mind my asking, who were you planning to see? To surprise?"

She waited a beat before saying, "Daniel Hauser. At his house."

"Well, he'll be in Witten next week, won't he?" There was a board meeting scheduled early next week, before everyone scattered for the holidays.

"That's the thing . . ."

He glanced at her to find her looking at him intently. "What's the thing?"

"Mr. Benz, even though we don't like each other, I feel as though I can trust you."

"I wouldn't say that we don't like each other."

"We have both said exactly that on more than one occasion."

"Yes, but we didn't mean it. Or we came around to not meaning it." He paused. "Or at least I did." When she didn't respond, he said, "Remember the truce we called last time we were in Riems? Let's do that again." He needed to know what was happening with Morneau here.

"Another truce," she echoed, as if she were turning the matter over in her mind.

"Yes."

"Except maybe without the kissing this time?"

He was startled. He'd thought they had silently agreed never to speak of that incident. But also amused, because it was clear from her grin that she was teasing him. This boded well for getting her to open up to him about what she was doing visiting two generations of Hausers. "Without the kissing," he agreed. "I shall endeavor to restrain myself this time," he added, deadpan.

"As will I. All right. Daniel Hauser is selling his shares in Morneau to Noar Graf."

"*What?*" The Morneau board was small, and, he would have said, stable. Two of its five members were the king and the princess, the princess having inherited her mother's shares. The other three seats had been in the dukedom of Aquilla, the Müller family, and the Hauser family for generations. The Hausers had helped shape Morneau for nearly as long as the company had been in existence.

Matteo was so shocked, he turned on his blinker and pulled into the parking lot of a cheese factory on the outskirts of Riems. Once safely parked, he turned to Ms. Delaney. "Can he do that?"

"Apparently he can. Most private companies have shotgun clauses in their board contracts, but not Morneau."

"Shotgun clause? I don't know what that is."

"It's a clause that specifies if a board member wants to step down or sell out, they must first offer their shares to the other members of the board. It's meant to keep the interests in a private company close. If you could just sell your shares to anyone . . ."

"Chaos would break loose."

"Potentially."

"I suppose we don't have these types of clauses because we traditionally haven't needed them."

He waited for her to say something snarky about an overreliance on tradition, but she merely said, "Yes."

"The CEO has always been an advisory member of the board, but not a voting one. And not vested," he said, his brain grasping to try to make sense of why Noar would be trying to buy in.

"That's right."

"Doesn't it seem suspicious that if Noar is looking to acquire shares, or if Daniel is looking to sell shares, neither has thought to mention it, given that there is a companywide overhaul underway?"

"It does."

The way she was responding calmly and briefly to his thinking-out-loud statements made him think she had a theory about what was happening. She had just opened up to him. He decided to give her more reason to do so. "I don't usually publicly criticize people."

"You leave that for behind closed doors."

He wasn't sure if that was a question, and if it was a statement it wasn't a flattering one. "I don't usually publicly criticize people, but Noar Graf is a raging egomaniac, and I detest him."

She burst out laughing.

"What, pray tell, is so amusing?" Once again, the way her face lit up made his start to echo hers. It was supremely annoying.

"You! You're so buttoned-up, usually. It's strange to see you so freely expressing emotion. It reminds me of the time Data—Forget it."

"Data from Star Trek? Were you about to compare me to an android?" He didn't know whether to laugh or to be offended.

"No!" She was trying and failing not to laugh as she turned her face away to look out her window. "I would never do that."

He waited a beat and asked, "What do you think is happening with the shares?"

His uncharacteristic display of emotion, be it human or android, must have worked. "I don't know yet, but . . ." She turned and looked into his eyes, searched them, as if trying to decide whether she could trust him.

"Do you remember an episode of *The Next Generation* in which Data befriends Tasha Yar's sister, only to find she was set on betraying them all?" he asked.

Her brow wrinkled. "I thought you were Team Star Wars."

"I am. But I'm well-read. Well-viewed. When it comes to science fiction, anyway. At the end of that episode, Data is talking to Riker. He's confused. He doesn't understand these human concepts of friendship and trust. Riker tells him that without risk, there can be no friendship."

The sense that she was trying to see into his soul deepened. He waited. Allowed her to look—allowed himself to be seen. It was difficult.

Finally, she said, "Are you calling *me* an android now?"

He chuckled. "No. I'm just saying that although we've had our differences, you can trust me in this matter. If one of the board members is doing something underhanded, that's bad news any way you look at it."

It felt like a triumph when she started talking. "Noar strikes me as unusually obstructionist, not just as it relates to my project here, but in terms of handing over *any* information about Morneau. I've spent weeks trying to extract data from him to no avail, then I stumbled on him having a one-on-one meeting with Daniel Hauser. It made me suspicious in a way I couldn't put my finger on. I did some digging and found that Daniel's shares came from his aunt, and that his aunt was a close friend of the late queen."

"All true." Matteo could have told her that and saved her the digging, but fine.

"So I asked Mrs. Hauser if I could pay her a visit. I said I wanted to talk to previous board members as part of my work. I didn't even have to ask about Daniel. She came right out with it, told me the moment we sat down that he was in the process of selling his shares to Noar. They had clashed over it, and she was upset. She hadn't known if she should go to the king, or to the rest of the board."

"What does all this mean?"

"I don't know yet."

"All right. I do not, as previously established, hold Noar in high regard, but let's think this through. So he has the Hauser shares, or soon will. It's not as if they're even close to being a controlling share."

"Right. You're right." She nodded—a little too vehemently.

"But?" he prompted.

"You're going to think I'm paranoid." She was back to staring out her window. He could practically see the wheels turning in her mind.

"I'm not going to think that. Your first hunch proved correct, did it not?" He wanted to see what she was seeing.

"What if Noar has been running the company down so it's worth less?" she asked. "And now that he has shares, he'll stop being useless, and run up the company's value?"

"But it's a private company. It doesn't trade on an exchange. Shares are worth what we say they are." He thought, anyway. But he wasn't an expert.

"Yes and no. Even if a company isn't privately traded, it still has value that can be assessed in more or less objective terms. There are accepted inputs, formulas we can use. We know that in Morneau's case, its value has gone down. When we look at five years ago versus two years ago, for example, it's decreased by fourteen percent. And even if that figure isn't perfect, we're looking at the same things at the two points in time, using the same inputs to arrive at our starting and ending numbers—it's an apples-to-apples comparison. So we can say with confidence that Morneau's value has gone down. We've been attributing that to the decline in demand and/or increasing inefficiencies of process. I'm here to sort that out, and to address those factors to the extent that I can. And I have no doubt those factors have contributed."

"But perhaps Noar has also contributed?" And if so, how much? And more importantly, how would his meddling—or lack of it—affect the looming layoffs?

She shrugged. "I can't seem to get anyone to give me last year's valuation. Or the raw numbers so I can do it myself."

Why was the idea of Ms. Delaney doing a bunch of math in order to single-handedly calculate the value of Morneau so . . . stirring? He could picture her holed up in her room at the Owl and Spruce, wearing those ridiculous pajamas that were nowhere near warm enough for an Eldovian winter, surrounded by spreadsheets. Or perhaps not spreadsheets. Perhaps she used some kind of specialist accounting software that made her computer screen look like it belonged on the bridge of a starship. Perhaps—

But that was not the point here. "This is an interesting theory. Might it also explain why Noar was being so beastly about your being here? Because he didn't want your work to turn things around too soon? Before he had the shares in hand?"

"You thought he was being beastly?" She seemed oddly cheered by the prospect.

"Of course he was. He was being inordinately rude."

"Hmm." She smiled. She certainly was doing a great deal of that today. "Maybe you *do* like me a little, after all."

He could feel his face heat. His fluency in English was very high, but it took him a moment to compute that she was teasing him. Honestly, the way Americans mixed business and pleasure was very confusing. "Whether I like you or not is an entirely different matter from your competency. I needn't like you to see that you're more than capable of carrying out your mission here."

"Well, thank you. I think."

"So your plan was to visit Daniel Hauser unannounced?"

"Yes. Not that I really expect him to tell me anything—and maybe there isn't anything to tell. Maybe what he's claiming—that he plans to retire early and spend more time in the Riviera—is true. But if there *is* anything more there, I thought an ambush was likely to be more effective than a scheduled meeting."

Matteo wrinkled his nose as he echoed Mr. Hauser's plans. "Retire to the Riviera."

"You make it sound like he's signing up for exile to Siberia."

"What is he? All of forty?"

"Thirty-nine."

"How old are you?" He probably shouldn't have asked. For some reason, Americans were more worked up about aging than Europeans.

She answered, though: "Thirty-five. Why? And how old are *you*?"

"Thirty. Would you retire in four years if you could?"

"No. I might not do everything exactly the same as I am now, but no, I would not."

That accorded with his image of her, and he agreed wholeheartedly. "Neither would I."

"All right, but your point is?"

"Oh, I don't know. Perhaps that my regard for Daniel Hauser isn't a great deal higher than for Noar Graf." He started the car. "So let's pay the former a visit."

"You don't think we should go directly back to Witten on account of the snow?"

"It's on the way, and really, how long does an ambush take?"

TWENTY MINUTES LATER, they pulled up at the Hauser mansion. "With any luck," Matteo said, "the snow will have muffled our arrival."

"Well, it's not as if we're going to sneak in James Bond–style."

Right. He restarted the car. "I think I'll keep the engine on while you're inside so the car doesn't get too cold. That way we'll be able to make a fast getaway, James Bond–style, if we need to."

She did not react, and he was more disappointed than he should be. It seemed unfair that American management consultants were allowed to make jokes in the line of duty but their clients weren't.

Oh, no, she was merely having a delayed reaction. Surprise flickered across her face, and it was replaced by delight. Laughter. It was very gratifying. Perhaps Matteo's regular demeanor *was* a little too android-like.

She sobered as she leaned over and took in the house. "Actually, would you come in with me?"

He was startled. And flattered. "Of course."

"Do you think whoever opens the door will speak English?" she asked as they trudged up the snowy steps to the front door.

"Most likely."

A woman Matteo didn't know answered their knock, opening the door just enough to see out. Cara said—in German, which Matteo had noticed she was increasingly showing mastery of— "Good afternoon. My name is Cara Delaney." She switched to English. "I'm so sorry to descend upon you unannounced, but I need to see Mr. Hauser. It's about some urgent Morneau business."

Matteo didn't know this woman, but she seemed to know them—or to know Ms. Delaney, anyway. Matteo had seen recognition flicker across her features when Ms. Delaney said her name.

"I'm terribly sorry," the woman said in English, "but it's not a good time. Perhaps you have a business card? I'd be happy to pass it along to my husband and ask him to call you."

Matteo fired up his mental rolodex. "Mrs. Hauser—Hauser nee Weiss, is that right? I believe I went to school with your cousin, Benjamin."

She thawed infinitesimally. "You know Bennie?"

"I do indeed. We played polo together. Bennie was a legend

on the field." He switched to German and lowered his voice conspiratorially. "I will admit to having been *wildly* jealous back in the day. I so *desperately* wanted to play number one, but he was too talented. I was always stuck with the feed." She smiled, softening a little more, leaning forward. He almost had her. He switched back to English so Ms. Delaney wouldn't get lost. "Oh! I'm just remembering: one of Bennie's cousins represented Eldovia in the last Olympics—as a skier, I believe. That wasn't *you*, by any chance, was it?"

The over-the-top, performatively awestruck question he already knew the answer to yielded a genuine smile. "It was."

"Well, athletic talent must run in the family. I'm *honored* to meet you."

"And you are?"

"Oh, I *beg* your pardon, I *completely* forgot my manners." That was a lie. Matteo never forgot his manners. He had been known to "forget" them, though, when to do so served his purposes. He straightened to his full height. "I am Matteo Benz, equerry to His Majesty King Emil. Delighted to meet you."

Mrs. Hauser's eyebrows flew up, and she stepped back and opened the door fully. "Let me see if I can interrupt my husband. Please come in."

She turned, and Matteo dropped his facade for a moment, making eye contact with Ms. Delaney and sending her a little eye roll. She sent back a furtive thumbs-up gesture.

He'd attempted to set a falsely conspiratorial tone with Mrs. Hauser, but with Ms. Delaney, it was real.

It was rather pleasant to be in league with someone. He wasn't sure when he had last been. Well, no, that wasn't true. He was in league with Kai every December. But this felt different. As he watched Ms. Delaney hand her coat over to a housekeeper, he was forced to conclude that it was rather nice to be in league with Ms. Delaney specifically.

Oh, dear.

THEY'D KEPT THEIR visit quick, but a dismaying amount of snow had accumulated while they'd been inside Daniel Hauser's house. After cleaning off the car, Matteo pulled out his phone to do a weather check, noting that this was the second time he'd lost track of worsening, potentially dangerous weather because he'd gotten carried away with Ms. Delaney. Last time it had been sharing confidences by the fire. This time, it had been talking their way into Daniel Hauser's house and confronting the man himself. He had done the former, and Ms. Delaney had done the latter, the two of them working together seamlessly. He'd felt almost as if they were Jedi working to defeat a common enemy.

But he had to remind himself that they were engaging in a strategic alliance. She wasn't his ally, not in the context of the wider war.

"How do you decide if it's safe to drive?" Ms. Delaney asked as he tapped through his weather app. "How much snow is too much snow?"

"It's partly accumulation, partly wind, partly visibility. It's a judgment call. But sometimes—" Oh, no.

"Sometimes what?"

He tapped on an alert that popped up. "Sometimes the choice is made for you because there's an avalanche in your way."

"What? What does that mean?"

He turned the phone to her. She couldn't read the German headline, but she could see the picture, and her eyes widened. "It means we cannot get back to Witten tonight."

He expected her to get upset, but she surprised him by saying, calmly, "All right. So what do we do?"

The snow was still falling, so much so that the car was re-coated in a layer of it even though he'd cleaned it off a mere minute ago. "We go to my mother's."

There was a pause, and she burst out laughing. "I'm sorry," she said. "I'm not laughing at you. I just didn't expect you to say that."

He smiled. "I told you before that I grew up near Riems?" She nodded. "It's about a ten-minute drive to the village I'm from, though in this weather it will take longer. There's an inn there."

"We're ten minutes away from your family? Why didn't you say anything?"

"It wasn't relevant."

"But you told me last time we were here that you missed your family. We could have stopped. Well, I guess we are now, but we could have regardless!"

"Yes, but we're working. A detour to visit my family was not on your agenda. Or mine." He thought back to his earlier text exchange with Imogen. Now he was going to be leaving Kai hanging even longer. He was going to have to start pulling all-nighters to get the baskets ready.

"Yes, but we're so close! You can't use work as an excuse not to see your family when you're passing right by!"

He smirked. "Is it ironic that the self-proclaimed workaholic is taking issue with my, what did you call it, work-life balance?"

She rolled her eyes good-naturedly. "That was your word, not mine."

"I beg your pardon?"

"You used the word *workaholic* in that conversation, and I didn't correct you." She huffed a little laugh. It sounded delightful and girlish and utterly out of character. "I might go so far as to say it takes one to know one."

"But—"

She turned to look out the window. "I don't want to tell you what to do, but what happened to the getaway car? Are we going to talk about going to your mother's while we get buried in front of Daniel Hauser's mansion, or are we going to your mother's?"

He tried to tamp down a smile but was not successful. "We're going to my mother's."

If Cara had room in her life for relationships, which she didn't, she would want to be with someone who was a good driver.

Mr. Benz was a good driver. As he navigated carefully but confidently along the twisty mountain road, she found herself relieved to be in his capable hands.

But also sort of . . . warm inside?

Competence was, in general, a turn-on. But so was, in a more specific sense, competence behind the wheel. Mr. Benz's eyes bounced from the road in front of him to the rearview mirror to the side mirror, and occasionally, like once in every half-dozen circuits, to her. She wasn't sure why. Because he didn't trust her? Because he was worried he was going to kill her by driving off the road? Both? Who knew? Regardless, to watch him, you would have no idea he was navigating a mountain road in the middle of a storm. He was attentive, yes—his hands were at ten and two on the steering wheel, and he wasn't attempting any conversation—but he didn't seem stressed. The knuckles on those hands were not white.

He really did have such inexplicably attractive hands.

Probably some of her admiration had to do with the fact that she lived in New York. She didn't know anyone who drove to work, except some of the partners at CZT. But Cara didn't even have a driver's license. To be so casual handling such a machine, and in such circumstances . . . But in some ways, this was not a surprise. Her brief tenure in Eldovia had shown her that Mr. Benz, as much of a thorn in her side as he could be, was the kind of person who got things done. Look at how he'd flattered his way into Daniel Hauser's house. He'd cracked Mrs. Hauser like an egg.

She shook herself and turned her attention to the snow, which was falling increasingly heavily. Even though she was in good hands—literally—she was starting to feel a niggle of worry. She was relieved when they exited the main road for a smaller one with a sign that read, "To Anderlaken." They got stuck on the way into the village. The road into town sloped upward, and the car, which had been struggling to make it up the incline, wheezed. Mr. Benz navigated them out of a few tricky spots, but eventually, they hit a patch that defeated them, and the wheels spun in place no matter what he did. The only sign that Mr. Benz was distressed was a tightening of his jaw. "I'll return momentarily." He went to the trunk, reappeared with a shovel, and began making a circle of the car, looking at each tire.

No way was she going to sit in here warm and dry while he dug them out. She got out, and before he opened his mouth to issue the protest she knew was coming, she held up her hands and said, "I'm helping. No arguing. Tell me what to do."

He stared at her for a beat before handing her a shovel. "Dig out around this tire." She got to work, and he went back to the trunk and reappeared a moment later with a long piece of what looked like grooved rubber.

"What is that?"

"I'm not sure what you would call it in English, but it provides traction for the tires." He placed it under the tire she'd been working on. "I think this should do it, but I have more in my arsenal if this isn't the main, or only, culprit." He straightened and eyed her. "Can you drive?"

"Nope. I know how to push, though." Their neighbors at home had a junker that was always dying, and she'd been enlisted more than once to help push it to the end of the block, where, handily, there was a mechanic.

Again, Mr. Benz looked as if he was going to object. Again, she held up a hand. This time, that was enough, and he went around and got back into the driver's seat. He rolled down the window. "All right. On the count of three."

He counted, and she pushed with all her might. The car inched forward, and the tire got enough traction from that cool mat thing that it started moving. A spike of triumph had her pumping her fist in victory. "Go!" she shouted. "Keep going, and I'll catch up!"

He did, and she did—eventually. He only went a little ways up the road, but the wind and snow were such that she struggled to make her way there. He was waiting for her outside the car when she finally made it, holding the passenger-side door and looking troubled.

"I'm going to get your car all wet," she said in dismay as he took the traction mat from her and hustled her in. She was wearing her boots, but because they were made of squishy fabric, they had been drenched by the deep snow.

"It's not the car I'm worried about." He turned up the heat and aimed the vents at her. After a few minutes, they were making their way along a charming village main street dotted with shops and cafés, all of them iced with dollops of snow, like someone had dropped a scoop of whipped cream on every gable. They turned into a drive next to a large building directly on the main street. It was of the same half-timbered style as many of the buildings in Witten, but it was much bigger—three stories. With the snow coming down all around, it looked like it belonged inside one of Kai's snow globes. Given what Cara knew about Mr. Benz—the fact that the king had called him an accomplished skier, the air of old money he had about him—she had imagined him growing up on a vast country estate where he rode horses and frolicked in nature.

But she could also picture him here, in this adorable-but-enormous house in the middle of a vibrant village. The building had a name carved into the decorative stone above the front entrance, though it was snowing too hard to make it out, and it wasn't in English anyway. Perhaps if there had been a divorce—she assumed that's what his curt assertion that his father was "not around" had meant—this property had gone to his mother, and his no-good father was left to gad about in the countryside.

He drove around back. There were a lot of cars parked there—

his family must be quite wealthy and/or be automobile aficiona-
dos. Perhaps that's where his driving skills came from.

This did make her wonder what he had been on about with all
that *Pride and Prejudice* talk. He had piqued her curiosity enough
that she'd bought an e-book of it and had read it on her phone.
Though she saw his point about the Bennet sisters needing to
marry well, she also thought *her* point stood. The Bennets were not
poor by any stretch of the imagination. And clearly neither was he.

"I probably should have texted them," he said as he cut the engine and leaned across her to look out her window. As on the ride
from the airport, he was sufficiently in her space that she caught
a whiff of that minty smell of his, though it was diminished compared to that first time—probably due to all the outside time. With
the mint less in evidence, she could smell . . . him. He smelled like
salt. In a good way—like the sea.

All right. She needed to get a grip. So Mr. Benz smelled like
salt-rimmed mojitos. So what? And more to the point, salty mojitos *should* be disgusting. "Should you call them now?" she asked,
eyeing the building he was still looking at. Lots of the windows
had lights on.

"No. We'll surprise them." A smile blossomed on his face, and
it occurred to her that there were two kinds of families, those
that would be happy to have you show up on their doorstep unannounced and those you really needed to call first. She had the
former. He appeared to as well.

He led them to a rear door, examining his key ring in the dim
light cast from a sconce mounted above it. The door, up close,
was more beat-up than she would have expected. It was made of
wood, like the one at the palace, but it was crisscrossed with deep

scars, and it had clearly been revarnished several times. Perhaps it was the servants' entrance. Ha. Mr. *Pride and Prejudice* had a servants' entrance. So much for the—

Holy shit.

She could barely contain her shock as her eyes adjusted to a dimly lit hallway. It was lined with numbered doors. This wasn't his mother's divorce-settlement village house; it was an *apartment* building.

Her entire mental picture of Mr. Benz began to rearrange itself, pixels falling out of place and reassembling into a different image.

She followed him silently up two flights of stairs, to a door adorned with the number 305 and a Christmas wreath. He rapped on the door, through which music was clearly audible.

Was that . . . *Britney Spears*?

It was. Someone inside Mr. Benz's family's apartment was listening to "Oops! . . . I Did It Again."

What was *happening*?

He tried the door again, knocking louder this time—pounding, really.

A clomping heralded someone's approach. The door was thrown open by a scowling boy who looked so much like Mr. Benz it was startling. It took a few seconds for recognition to dawn, but when it did, the boy's features rearranged themselves into a grin as he threw himself into Mr. Benz's arms. He hadn't fully pulled away when he shouted back into the apartment, "Mutti! Martina!" followed by something that she was pretty sure was a variation on "Mr. Benz is here!" except surely his family didn't call him Mr. Benz. Though who knew? He was so . . . Mr. Benzy.

No one responded, and the boy stepped back to let them in.

"My mother and sister are wearing headphones," he said, looking at Cara and switching to English, "so they do not hear me calling." She wondered how he could tell she didn't speak German just by looking at her.

"Armend, this is Ms. Delaney."

"Cara," she corrected. She and Mr. Benz had fallen into the formality of last names, but it seemed weird to have his younger brother call her that. She was off duty here.

"You are the lady from America!" Armend exclaimed.

The lady from America. It sounded like Mr. Benz's family already knew about her?

That was almost as startling as the fact that they lived in an apartment.

"At least take her coat before you ambush her," Mr. Benz said to his brother in a tone that suggested he was trying to convey annoyance. The affection in his voice was palpable, though.

An older woman appeared in the hallway wearing a quizzical expression and, as Armend had predicted, headphones—big, over-the-ear ones.

When she registered Mr. Benz's presence, she shrieked and immediately clasped her hand over her mouth as if trying not to cry.

Suddenly Cara was fighting tears, too. The reaction reminded her so much of her own mom, who acted like she'd won the lottery every time Cara walked in the door from a trip.

Cara was starting to be able to piece together simple phrases in German, but the rapid-fire speech of the woman, as she threw herself into Mr. Benz's arms, was beyond her. Mr. Benz answered his mother smilingly as they hugged, and Cara heard her name mentioned.

When they separated, his mother pressed her palms to her cheeks as if she were gathering herself, smiled warmly at Cara, and said, "Ms. Delaney, welcome to our home. We're so glad you're here. I am Matteo's mother, Inge."

"Please call me Cara." When Inge stepped back and gestured for Cara to come deeper into the apartment, Cara said, "Oh, but I'm headed to the inn. I gather there's one in the village?"

"No!" Inge protested as if the very idea pained her. "You must stay with us!"

"I can't intrude on you so unexpectedly."

"At least come in and let us lend you some dry clothes and give you a cup of tea to warm you up."

A pair of dry socks *did* sound like heaven right now.

And she was desperately curious, suddenly, about these people, and this place, that had given rise to Mr. Benz. So she allowed herself to be herded inside, examined, and proclaimed the same size as Mr. Benz's sister Martina, whom Inge called for.

A girl appeared with the same big headphones her mother had been wearing, and once again, Cara was witness to an over-the-top hug complete with shrieking. Cara sneaked a glance at Inge. The matriarch's eyes were bright with unshed tears as she watched her daughter and Mr. Benz embrace.

More introductions were performed, and Martina took Cara into her room and found her socks and a pair of . . . well, Cara wasn't really sure what they were. They were sweatpants, she supposed, but they were fancy sweatpants, made of sweater material, the kind of thing a Frenchwoman would throw on and be effortlessly chic in.

Back in the living room, Mr. Benz had changed, too. He was

also wearing sweatpants, and Mr. Benz was *so* not a sweatpants kind of person. Even better, on top he was wearing a Taylor Swift 1989 World Tour sweatshirt.

She failed to contain a snicker as she sat on one end of the sofa.

"My brother is an aficionado of popular music," he said with a touch of indignance.

"Not just an aficionado, a scholar," Armend said, with the same tone of affront. The two brothers were near-clones, differentiable only by age. Armend transferred his attention from Mr. Benz, whom he'd been glaring at, to Cara. "I am studying music engineering, and I want to be a music producer, so I immerse myself in pop music. Where are you from in the United States?"

"New York."

He seemed pleased by that answer. "Have you ever been to Los Angeles?"

"I have. In fact, I've spent several weeks at a time there, a few times over."

That pleased him even more, and he proceeded to interrogate her about the merits of New York versus Los Angeles, stopping only when his sister interjected with "Guess what? I'm pregnant!"

Mr. Benz paled. Instantly. All the color evaporated from his face.

"Just kidding!" Martina trilled. She turned to Mr. Benz. "I have this new method for getting Armend to stop talking. I say something really dramatic, and the conversation grinds to a halt."

Everyone laughed, including Mr. Benz, but he added, "While your strategy may be effective in the short-term, you should consider the longer-term potential for harm, namely, giving your other brother a stroke."

"Oh, you love babies." Martina waved dismissively and turned to Cara. "You should see him with our older sister's children. He turns into that emoji with the hearts for eyes."

"Martina," Mr. Benz scolded, but there wasn't much fire in it.

It was hard to imagine Mr. Benz getting gooey over a baby, but then, an hour ago, she would have said it was hard to imagine Mr. Benz growing up in an apartment with a Britney Spears–playing brother and a practical-joking sister.

"How are you finding Eldovia, Cara?" Inge asked when she returned from the kitchen with a tray containing a teapot, cups and saucers, and a plate of cookies with perfect little dots of red jam in the middle of them. "I understand you're here to drag Morneau into the twenty-first century?"

"Eldovia is lovely." It was. The people were warm—Imogen, for example, was becoming a real friend, and was someone Cara would miss when she went home. "And so . . . Christmasy."

"Yes. It can seem a bit much, but I try to remember the meaning behind Christmas—a time to be with family, treat oneself a bit, count one's blessings."

She sounded like Cara's mom. "That's a good way of thinking of it." She accepted a cup of tea, but Mr. Benz waved away the one his mother offered to him and got up and went to the window.

"How is it out there?" Cara asked.

"It's still coming down in earnest. I'll call the inn. No point in setting out in this unless they have a room."

"Are you sure you wouldn't rather stay here, Cara?" Inge asked. "You'd be most welcome."

"Oh, no, I couldn't."

"It's no trouble," Martina said. "I'll bunk in with my mother, and you can have my room. And then Armend can interrogate you about Los Angeles. Really, you'll be doing him a favor."

"But where will you sleep?" she asked Mr. Benz.

"My old room—Armend and I used to share a room." He shot an affectionately exasperated look at his brother. "Assuming my bed can be excavated from beneath your recording equipment."

It didn't take much to convince Cara. It was so warm and cozy here, which was only partly to do with the apartment. Mr. Benz's family was so welcoming, and so clearly fond of one another. Being with them reminded Cara of being at home.

After more lively conversation and a light dinner, Inge declared it bedtime, and Cara followed the family down the hall. Martina's room was across from Armend's. Cara hovered awkwardly in the hallway between them, her offers to help Martina strip and remake the bed rebuffed. Armend was moving stuff around inside his room and came out to set some speakers in the hallway.

"You know, Armend," she said, deciding to start earning her keep, "early in my career, I worked on a project at EMI in Los Angeles."

His head jerked up like a dog's upon hearing a silent whistle. "You *did*?"

"Yes, it wasn't as exciting as it sounds. It was related to how their A&R people kept track of contacts with artists they were scouting."

"That seems a far cry from watch manufacturing," said Mr. Benz, who had joined them in the hall.

"It was my first year working full-time for the company, and I was able to bounce around a bit, assist on projects in different groups. I eventually found my stride in manufacturing operations."

"Hmm. A passion for manufacturing operations."

"How and why people make things is actually pretty fascinating."

He looked at her quizzically for a long moment. "I suppose it is."

Martina emerged from her room. "All done."

Cara thanked Martina for surrendering her room and said good night. "We can speak about Mr. Hauser tomorrow?" she asked Mr. Benz. They hadn't learned a great deal from their visit. Daniel had been a bit defensive, but had confirmed that he was planning to sell his shares to Noar. He said he wanted to retire early, and that he hadn't thought it worth informing the rest of the board until the transaction was nearing completion. To Cara's mind, it all seemed suspicious, even if there was nothing illegal going on. But she wanted to discuss it with Mr. Benz, see if his impression matched hers. But there was nothing to do about it tonight.

"Yes, we'll chat about Mr. Hauser tomorrow," Mr. Benz said. "Sweet dreams, Ms. Delaney," he added, his voice low and almost . . . caressing?

Jeez. She was hearing things that weren't there. Time for sleep.

The walls were thin, and she could hear Martina go into Armend's room with her brothers. She let the sound of the three siblings talking and laughing lull her to sleep.

Chapter Ten

Seven days until Christmas

Ms. Delaney slept in the next morning, which was just as well because one look out the window confirmed Matteo's fears that they were not going anywhere for a while. A great deal of snow had accumulated, and the main street wasn't even passable yet, forget the parking lot out back.

He was not pleased.

"Cara seems nice," his mother said as he rejoined her and his siblings at the table where she was serving his favorite rösti that she always made when he came home.

"She's pretty, too," Martina said in a singsong voice.

Oh for god's sake. "She's here to do a job. I was escorting her to a meeting in Riems. And I wouldn't exactly call her nice." He shot Martina a quelling look, which she held for a long moment, her eyebrows raised. "What?" he asked, annoyed at her—and himself for falling so easily back into the bickering-sibling role.

"I notice you didn't refute the 'pretty' part."

To his complete and utter mortification, he felt his face heating. "I didn't—"

"Good morning! I'm sorry I slept so late." The sudden appearance of a sleep-mussed Ms. Delaney did not help matters. That her hair was no longer in her signature severe updo was a shock to the system, even though he had seen it that way once before. It was wavy and slightly messy, as if—

She produced an elastic seemingly from thin air and put said hair up in a haphazard ponytail, interrupting his fixation. Which was fine. There was no call to be fixated on anything about Ms. Delaney, least of all her hair. The image of her undertaking a valuation exercise with specialized accounting software was one thing, but her hair? No. He needed to get ahold of himself.

She made eye contact with him, and he prayed his face was no longer red. "I had a peek out the bedroom window, and I assume we're not going to make it back to Witten this morning?"

"Probably not until this evening at the earliest. It will take a while for the roads here to be cleared, and even longer for the mountain to become passable. I'm sorry." He truly was. Losing an entire day's worth of work was not what either of them needed right now.

"I have a wonderful idea," his mother said. "Why don't you two snowshoe over to Biel and take the waters? It's a beautiful day for it."

"Biel is the neighboring village, and it's home to a spa centered around some hot springs," Matteo explained to Ms. Delaney before turning to his mother. "I'm sure Ms. Delaney would prefer to spend the day working." He returned his attention to her. "We can set you up at the dining room table."

"Hmm," she said with a twinkle in her eye, "a day spent working or a day at a spa? Tough call."

"You would prefer the spa?" He thought that's what she meant, but he was surprised.

"I would prefer the spa," she said decisively. "I wouldn't want to risk becoming a *workaholic*, after all."

He felt his eyebrows shoot up. He needed to rein them in. "You would prefer the spa even if you have to snowshoe to get there?"

"I would prefer the spa even if I have to snowshoe to get there." When he didn't answer right away—he was still surprised—she said, "There's only a shower at Imogen's, and I'm quite the fan of a hot bath. I've never been in a natural hot spring, but it sounds like a bath on steroids. I'm all in."

He didn't know whether the "on steroids" qualifier was a good thing, but it must be, given her palpable excitement. "All right, then." He looked around the table. "Someone will have to stay back." He explained to Ms. Delaney, "We only have four pairs of snowshoes."

"Oh, I'm not going," his mother said. "I have a shift at the library."

"Me neither," said Armend, who, as that rare type of human who didn't particularly like immersing himself in hot water, usually had to be dragged along on the family's excursions to the baths.

As he turned his attention to his sister, he saw a look pass between her and their mother. "I can't go, either," she said cheerily. He waited to see what excuse she would come up with, but she smiled at him without producing one.

He knew what they were doing. They were completely misunderstanding the situation. But there was no way to tell them as much without making things extremely awkward. So . . . "Ms. Delaney, it appears it will just be the two of us."

"Why do you call her Ms. Delaney?" Martina asked. "You're so weird, Matteo."

"Oh, I call him Mr. Benz, so it's not just him," Ms. Delaney said quickly.

While Matteo appreciated that Ms. Delaney was defending him, she didn't need to entangle herself in whatever matchmaking mischief was afoot here. He frowned at Martina and switched to German to say, "It's called manners, Martina. You should try it sometime."

"I'M GOING TO assume that if you've never been skiing or skating, you've also never been snowshoeing?" Mr. Benz asked as he rummaged through a storage locker in the basement of the building. He extracted two pairs of snowshoes that looked very high-tech and not at all like Cara's image of snowshoes. She'd thought they would be made of wood and have a crisscrossed base. But then, her image of snowshoes was straight out of a picture book her mother used to read her about a family of bears who accidentally awakened from their hibernation and decided to try out winter activities.

"I have not. I get bad marks across the board when it comes to winter sports." She paused, thinking of the nonswimming trip to Barbados. "And summer sports."

Chuckling, he led them outside and pointed to a bench that, because it was under the building's awning, was free of snow.

"What are these made of?" she asked as she sat. "Fiberglass?"

"Aluminum, I believe."

"But coated with something. Powdered plastic, probably."

"I'm not sure."

"Where do they make them?" She wondered if they were mass-produced in the usual places, or made in a snowy place.

"You really do have a passion for manufacturing, don't you? I don't know where these were made."

She chuckled. "I just never thought of snowshoes as being mass-produced, which is, of course, stupid. I had this image of them made out of wood, and I don't know, rawhide or something?"

"Collectors prize those kinds of traditional snowshoes, but for actually getting around, I think newfangled is better."

"Excuse me. Do I hear you saying that the modern version is better than the traditional one?"

He smirked. "There are exceptions to every rule."

Mr. Benz helped her into her shoes, gave her a quick orientation, and they were off. Tromping down the deserted main street of the village was fun. The shops were closed, and the world was silent, blanketed with snow. They passed a few other snowshoers and cross-country skiers with whom they exchanged brief words of greeting. But other than that, it felt like they were alone in a world blanketed by snow.

At the end of the main street was a park, and he led them through it. "There's a walking path that connects to Biel. It's a straight shot from here, but there are some hills along the way, one in particular that's rather strenuous. The plus side is that since Biel is higher in elevation, the trip home is downhill."

She could do with a little exercise. She'd been working overtime to try to get to the bottom of this Noar Graf business even as she kept doing her actual job. "Lead the way."

He did, showing her at the first hill how to keep her weight at the front of her foot as they ascended and how to kick her foot when she landed to create a place to step. She got the hang of it, but it was hard work.

"You're a quick learner," Mr. Benz observed after they'd made it up the first hill.

"I've never been an athlete, but one thing I can do is walk. When I'm in New York, I walk fifteen blocks from a subway stop to my office."

"I hope you . . ." Mr. Benz trailed off and cleared his throat before starting again. "Wear sensible shoes."

He was so weird sometimes. "Do you play any sports?" He didn't seem to be finding their trek strenuous, whereas she had worked up quite the sweat under her winter coat.

"I did when I was young. Polo and football—or what you would call soccer. I also competed in dressage."

"Dressage. That's fancy people doing horses, right?" He barked a laugh, startling her. She was stupidly pleased to have drawn such an explosive laugh from such a serious person. It was as if he couldn't control his reaction, and she had the sense that there wasn't much in Mr. Benz's life that he couldn't control. "And polo. That's horses, too, right?" It was hard to square that with the notion that he'd grown up sharing a room with his brother in an apartment. It was a nice apartment—much larger than any of the ones she'd grown up in—but still.

"You are wondering about the discrepancy between what you saw of my family and the idea of us owning horses," he said, reading her mind. "My family used to be 'fancier,' to use your term, when I was younger."

"What happened?"

"Let's just say there was a fall from grace."

The *Pride and Prejudice* stuff was starting to make sense. She desperately wanted to know more, but she left it at that.

The conversation turned to Noar. Mr. Benz filled her in on what he knew about the man, which wasn't much beyond what Cara herself had already known or had turned up in her recent investigations. Morneau had hired a headhunting firm who'd presented him as a candidate—he'd been a senior executive at Blancpain in Switzerland before moving to Eldovia to take the top job at Morneau.

"I can find out more, though," Mr. Benz said.

"You can? Do you moonlight as a private investigator?"

"I have a great many connections."

She'd just bet he did.

They moved on to Daniel Hauser. It sounded like he was your classic rich kid who treated his inherited wealth as an entitlement. His tenure on the Morneau board had been uneventful.

"The way you talked us into his house was amazing," Cara said.

"False flattery works almost every time," he said dismissively. "I did go to school with his wife's cousin for a year but played it up to sound like more than it was."

"Well, thank you," she said, and she meant it. "We wouldn't have gotten in there otherwise."

"Yes, but we didn't find out anything we didn't already know."

"True, but at least he knows we know. Though to be honest, I'm now questioning whether that's a good thing. If there is something shady going on, we may have succeeded only in giving him incentive to hurry it up and/or drive it further into the shadows."

"Not to worry," Mr. Benz said with that same low, sure voice he'd used to wish her good night last night, the voice that sort of felt like he was touching her, which she realized made no sense. "I will get to the bottom of it."

The main street of Biel was more crowded than Anderlaken's had been. There was a lineup to get into the spa, and lots of people seemed to have come on snowshoes and skis. There was a festive air to the proceedings as they waited. A spa attendant came out and took orders for hot drinks.

"Oh my god, this is good," Cara said, taking a sip of her drink. She'd taken Mr. Benz's recommendation and ordered a local specialty that was half coffee, half hot chocolate. It was like a mocha, but not the sickly sweet Starbucks kind. It was piping hot and bittersweet, and she wasn't sure she'd ever tasted anything better, especially after their long tromp through the snow.

Listen to her. She sounded like she had drunk the Eldovian Kool-Aid. Well, the Eldovian hot chocolate.

"High-quality ingredients," Mr. Benz said. "A proper half-and-half—that's the literal translation; as far as I know there isn't an English word for this drink—is made with freshly pulled espresso with a little hot water—so, what you would call an Americano. But then in a separate pot, cream is mixed with melted dark chocolate. The two are then combined. It's a . . . very old recipe.

"You were going to say 'traditional,' weren't you?"

His lips quirked. They came to the front of the line and paid their entry fees. Cara had been assured she could buy a bathing suit in the gift shop, and sure enough, there was a small selection of sensible one-pieces.

She changed in the locker room, and on the other side a be-robed Mr. Benz was waiting for her.

"Oh, this is lovely!" The grounds were dotted with a series of steaming pools. She wasn't sure what she'd expected. Not mud pits full of water, but perhaps something more naturalistic. "I didn't expect them to look like . . . regular hot tubs." She stumbled in finishing her sentence because she was belatedly realizing that most people here were naked.

She tried to be cool. She tried not to stare at the parade of naked bodies of all sizes and shapes and ages. But damn.

"There are some hot springs in the countryside that are little more than holes in the ground, but here they've built infrastructure around the naturally occurring springs."

Mr. Benz was lecturing her about hot springs. She forced herself to tune in.

"The pools are fed from the earth, but they're treated with salt for hygienic purposes—and there's some meddling with temperatures. Most of the pools are just the temperature they are, but at the front here you'll find some that are artificially cooled so they're suitable for children or pregnant women or anyone who can't tolerate heat." He led her past a large, crowded pool immediately in front of them. "And in the summer, they have a few cold plunge pools. That's not possible in the winter, of course, since they would freeze. Most Eldovians prefer to roll around in the snow, anyway." His lip quirk was back. "It's the traditional way."

"Don't they get . . . cold?" She was still looking around. She couldn't help it, but she was trying to be subtle about it.

Apparently her ogling had not been subtle enough. Mr. Benz's lip quirk had become quirkier. "Perhaps I should have warned you that Eldovia tends toward the German practice of nudity at spas. We're not as dogmatic about it, but for the most part, the feeling is that bathing attire in a place such as this is not called for."

"Mmm." She nodded.

"Nudity is not considered sexual by default the way it is in America."

"Oh, totally." She laughed as if to communicate how silly those prudish Americans were. But then something terrible occurred to her: *Was Mr. Benz naked under his robe?*

"Shall we? Do you have a preference as to temperature?"

"As hot as possible." Perhaps that way she could attribute her flaming cheeks to the heat.

He led her to a small pool at the back of the property that was labeled with a sign that read "40 degrees." She did some quick math in her head to convert to Fahrenheit. Wow, they didn't mess around here.

She eyed Mr. Benz. They were about to get naked and/or half naked in front of each other.

In a totally nonsexual way. Because Americans were the only ones whose immature minds would go there.

"I'll hang up our towels and robes if you'll give me yours," he said, making her realize that she'd been standing there like a slack-jawed idiot.

"Thanks." She tried to be unobtrusive about watching him as he hung her robe at a row of pegs built into a charmingly rustic wooden lean-to and began shrugging out of his.

Her cheeks were *on fire*. Dear god. Was she going to see *Mr. Benz's butt?*

He dropped the robe and . . .

Nope.

She heaved a shaky exhale. He wasn't even wearing a tiny Speedo, as most of the not-naked men here were. Mr. Benz was wearing trunks.

Which was good!

They were on the shorter end of what would be considered normal in the United States, though, and they were actually pretty tight across his—Stop it. What was she *doing*? She needed to get a freaking grip. Without waiting for Mr. Benz to make his way back over, she turned, slipped out of her spa-issued rubber sandals, and stepped into the water.

"Oh my god," she moaned. The heat was nothing short of glorious.

"It is rather wonderful, isn't it?" Mr. Benz reappeared at the edge of the pool wearing those little trunks—except this time she had a frontal view—and Cara's head nearly exploded.

She thought back to their unplanned meeting in the hallway at the Owl and Spruce. Her mind had jumped to wondering what he slept in and then on to wondering what he looked like naked.

Well, now she knew. Kind of. Mr. Benz wasn't a bodybuilder or anything, but all those horsey sports must have done their work on him. He was lean and had a gently sculpted torso and arm muscles and sturdy, muscular legs.

She was discombobulated. It was the "What's wrong with this picture?" feeling of being face-to-face with Mr. Benz in his skivvies. He had seemed to her like the kind of man who was born in a three-piece suit. It was taking her a moment to adjust to the fact that Mr. Benz was hot.

Mr. Benz was hot.

Wow.

But okay. The world was full of hot people. She needed to accept the fact that Mr. Benz was one of them and move on.

Mr. Benz heaved a huge sigh of his own as he stepped into the pool, and the skin on his chest pebbled as he sank into the water. When he was all the way in, he tilted his head back so it was resting on the edge of the pool and closed his eyes.

So she let herself keep looking.

They didn't speak for a while. Cara reflected on how many different kinds of silences she had shared with her Eldovian tour guide. There had been awkward ones when neither seemed to know what to say, fraught ones when one or both had said too much, companionable ones when no one felt the need to speak. This was one of the companionable ones.

He righted his head and caught her looking at him. "There was a fall from grace because my father was, unbeknownst to us, a gambling addict who managed to gamble away our house, my parents' savings, a good chunk of *his* parents' savings, and every asset we had—every car, every horse, every piece of jewelry. He even lost a first edition collection of Rilke's poems that had been given to me by someone I greatly admired."

He was answering her question from before, the "What happened?" he had previously brushed off, returning to it unbidden, as if the glorious heat of the water was loosening his tongue as well as his muscles. She wasn't sure how to respond. She wanted to acknowledge that he'd told her something real, that her assumptions about him had been incorrect.

She also wanted to know who had given him the Rilke poems, but that was not the point.

"I grew up poor," she said. "My father was a longshoreman, and he worked a lot, so we weren't out on the streets, but things were always tight."

"That's why you got along so well with Leon Bachmann."

"Maybe. I know you think of me as the Big Bad Wolf, but I have a lot of respect for unions."

"Is that why you listened to him about hastening your first trip to Riems, and about moving out of the palace?"

"Mostly that was a question of understanding that he was right." She hesitated, wondering if she should say the rest. Well, hell. "That's what I meant in the car on the way from the airport, about getting the lay of the land. There are often—usually—forces at work that I can't know about until I arrive. What Leon said about the mood at the Riems plant made sense. I just didn't know about it."

"I didn't know about it, either," he said, and she was pretty sure what he was trying to say was that he hadn't been holding back that information.

They lapsed back into silence. It was still companionable. Eventually, he said, "I'm not ashamed of my family's modest circumstances."

"Of course not. Why should you be?"

"Well, it was quite the scandal. My mother lost a lot of friends. Many people couldn't get over the fact that we had to move to an apartment."

"Apartment living is normal in New York. I've lived in a bunch of apartments. We moved a lot, either because my parents thought they had a lead on a slightly less dumpy place, or because the rent would go up too much. It was only three years ago that we bought a house." He nodded as if he appreciated what she'd said, so she kept going. "My mom was pregnant with me when she met my dad—he adopted me—and she'd been living in a shelter because her parents kicked her out of the house. So she never took for granted having a reliable roof over her head, and she taught me not to, either."

"Yes," he said quietly. She waited for more, but there wasn't any. She started to think about Mr. Benz's family. Like hers, they might not be rich when it came to material things, but as cliché as it sounded, they were clearly rich in other ways. The affection and goodwill between them had been palpable. "Why do your mother and sister wear headphones when your brother is playing his music? Why doesn't he wear the headphones?"

Mr. Benz smiled. "Something about sound quality, needing to really hear the sound in its purest state."

"Your mother and sister are good sports. At least Armend has good taste. Who doesn't like Britney Spears?" She was partly baiting him, but she smiled thinking back to her own boy-band phase.

He rolled his eyes. "Aren't you too old for Britney Spears?"

"Is anyone ever too old for Britney Spears?"

"I . . . don't know." She lifted her head. His brow was deeply furrowed. He looked utterly bewildered. "Ms. Delaney, you are something of a mystery."

She didn't tell him that she'd been thinking of him the same way—as a puzzle she couldn't crack. "Do you think maybe your sister was right and you should start calling me Cara?"

"Do *you* think so?"

She shrugged. "At least while we're truce-ing." She looked around. "Which I assume we are. I don't think we would be sitting here chatting in a hot spring otherwise."

"Very well, then, Cara. And you must call me Matteo."

"Matteo," she echoed, and it felt strange in her mouth.

They smiled at each other sort of goofily for a moment before Mr. Benz—*Matteo*—went back to talking about his brother. "Armend is very talented musically. The twins were only six when we moved to the apartment, but in those days he had access to the best music teachers, and he was something of a prodigy. I always thought he would become a musician. I never thought about the production end of things, but it seems a good fit. In addition to having musical talent, he's always liked to build things."

"It's honestly probably less of a gamble than wanting to be a pop star."

"Yes. I just need to . . ." He frowned. "Get him set up. He wants to move to LA, but I'm trying to talk him into Stockholm. I understand it's somewhat of a hub for popular music production, and it's more . . . realistic than America."

It seemed likely that Mr. Benz, like her, was supporting his family. No, that *Matteo* was supporting his family. Her brain was having trouble making the switch to first names. "Your younger siblings are quite a bit younger, yes?" The way he interacted with them had been half brotherly, half paternal.

"Yes. My older sister is three years older than I. The twins are ten years younger. I think my mother thought another baby might mend things between her and my father. This was before she knew what was actually happening. She didn't understand that she couldn't fix his problems, that his long absences weren't about their marriage, but about his gambling. But of course a baby never solves marital problems anyway. And she got two for her troubles. Though I sound as if I'm saying they weren't wanted, which isn't the case at all. The twins are the light of her life. Of mine, too."

In some ways, it was a bit odd to think of the buttoned-up Matteo using "light of my life" in reference to other people. But in others, it was beginning to seem less odd. She really had misjudged him initially.

"We lost things when life changed," he said thoughtfully, "but they were just that—things. Experiences, too, I suppose. Travel and fine dining and such. But life was so much easier with my father gone. I think we would all agree that it was a more-than-fair trade-off. My mother is happy. She has a job she finds meaning in, as do I. My older sister is happily married with two children. The twins aren't at Oxford or Cambridge, but they're being educated."

He sounded a tad defensive, and she imagined that in his circles, he encountered his fair share of snobs who viewed his family's changed circumstances as a tragedy.

"Actually, it's a better life than we had before, though no one ever seems to believe that," he added, ratifying her interpretation.

"I do. I believe that."

He seemed startled, even though she'd spoken quietly. "Yes, I suppose you do, don't you?"

MATTEO WOULD HAVE been appalled by how much he had shared with Cara, except he was too relaxed to be appalled. He was the proverbial lobster in the pot, getting cozier and cozier until it was too late. He would have made a terrible prisoner. Apparently all you had to do to get him to talk was provide a hot bath and a sympathetic ear.

"What's funny?"

He hadn't realized he was smiling—chuckling, even. "I was thinking about how even though I've had training in anti-interrogation techniques, I would make a terrible prisoner of war. I just told you my entire sordid life story."

He waited for her to make a crack about how she wasn't his enemy, but instead she asked, "How have you had training in anti-interrogation techniques?"

"I had a brief military career before this job."

"You *did*?"

"It's an honorable calling." He shifted in place, cozy and warm giving way to cozier and warmer. "I retired as a captain."

"First Lieutenant Cara Delaney reporting for duty."

"Indeed." The sun was shining down, and as she mock saluted him, he saw a flash of what looked like a mole near her armpit, which was interesting because she had no traces of any other marks on her skin—no freckles, no age spots, nothing.

"What do you mean 'indeed'? Why are you not surprised? Most people are. Wait. Did you have me investigated?"

He smirked. "It's possible I had you investigated."

"I should be outraged."

"But you're not?"

"Well, you're nothing if not thorough."

"What did you do in the army?" he asked. Torkel hadn't given him any details, and he was extremely curious about young Cara Delaney.

"Logistics. Supply chains."

"Of course."

"Why do you say that?"

"You seem very inspired by the quest for efficiency."

She chuckled. "I found military logistics dull, to be honest. I had a standing job offer with CZT, where I'd interned during college, and I was counting the days until I was discharged."

"And you've been at CZT ever since? You must enjoy it."

"I . . . do."

Hmm. He had never imagined Cara as anything other than completely dedicated to her work. "You sound less than certain."

"I love the work. There has been outstanding mentorship and support from the get-go. No one in my family has ever gone to college, so I was in uncharted waters. One of the founding partners took me under her wing. I'm just tired. I'm gunning for partnership, which is still a ways off, so I've had my nose to the grindstone for a long time." She sighed. He wasn't sure if it was a wistful sigh related to her career or a satisfied sigh related to the hot spring. "It's okay, though. I'm in the paying-my-dues phase of my career. What about you? What did you do in school? And did you go directly to the military afterward?"

"I studied history."

"I am shocked."

He smiled. He sure had been doing a lot of that. Yesterday, too. There was something about getting away from the grind of daily life. There was also something about allowing yourself to be teased. Normally, he reserved that for family. "To answer your other question, I did go directly to the military after I finished university."

"What attracted you to that career path? I would have thought you'd be more of an academic type."

"Partly the same thing as you—money. Namely, I didn't have enough of it. But also . . ." He was going to sound ridiculous.

"What?" she prompted, and seemed genuinely curious.

"I'm a patriot," he said. "I believe in the notion of service to one's country. My grandfather had a long military career. I'd been considering it since before our family's changed circumstances."

He expected her to tease him about tradition or something similar, but she merely nodded as if what he'd said made sense. "And you went from there to your equerry gig?"

"Yes. I'd assumed I'd do a longer stint in the military, but when the king asked me to come work for him, of course I said yes."

"I suppose you don't say no to something like that."

"You don't," he confirmed, willing to say more because she hadn't seemed phased by his earnest expression of patriotism. "But it was more than that. Serving Eldovia seemed like a calling. How often do civilian jobs like mine come along? Jobs where such service is a central tenet? The equerry position seemed unique in that regard."

"That makes sense. Why does everyone call you Mr. Benz, though? Why not Captain Benz?"

"I was only early in my fourth year of service when the king came calling. I was never deployed anywhere. I suppose I'm entitled to the rank, but it felt disingenuous. And you?"

"Similar reasons. I was never going to be a careerist. And anyway, in my line of work, the rank doesn't do me any favors. People too often think of me as the invading enemy to begin with."

This was normally the part where *he* would have made a crack, but he found he didn't want to. He was too relaxed, or too . . . something.

They sat in silence for a minute before she surprised him with another question. "Favorite Star Wars movie?"

She certainly was in an interrogative mood. He was in a forthcoming mood, though, so it worked out. "Of all of them?"

"Yes."

"*A New Hope.*"

"Favorite of the prequels?"

"I don't acknowledge the prequels."

She nodded and emitted a sort of hum-grunt hybrid as if she approved of that answer. "Favorite of the new ones?"

"*The Rise of Skywalker.*"

"Argh." She let her head fall back as she made a dramatic choking sound. His approval streak was over.

"In fact," he said, deciding to double down, to needle her, because he was feeling mischievous, "it rivals *A New Hope* in my mind."

"What? Why would you *say* that?"

"Well, to begin with, the shock of Rey being Palpatine's granddaughter—the delicious shock."

"You would say that."

"I beg your pardon?"

"Star Wars is all about hierarchy and bloodlines. It might as well be a monarchy."

"I suppose there is the emperor."

"Sure, but there's also the Skywalkers." She snorted derisively. "The almighty Skywalkers. And just when they had a chance, with the setup from *The Last Jedi*, to blow the lid off the whole bullshit Skywalker blueblood thing, to have the next generation be a meritocracy, they have to stick in this last-minute 'Guess what? Rey is secretly Emperor Palpatine's granddaughter! Gotcha!' She can't just be a nobody from Jakku who has the Force. God forbid she's *actually* an unloved kid who was abandoned by her parents."

Matteo blinked. This was all a bit surprising. Yet he had to admit that her position was internally consistent. He didn't agree with her—he didn't think—but he couldn't say her argument wasn't logical. He decided to take another tack. "But if anyone can have the Force, it isn't special."

"But anyone *doesn't* have the Force. It's rare. It's still special. It just doesn't have to run in families or be the exclusive property of rich, privileged people."

"Hmm," he said, to cover the fact that she was blowing his mind. "Those children on Canto Bight in *The Last Jedi*. They were slaves, effectively. Nobodies, as you say. Yet there was a hint that they had the Force."

"Yes. Exactly. Give the Force to the people."

On the one hand, this was an odd sentiment coming from this elite management consultant. He knew what Morneau was paying her firm. But now that he knew her better, perhaps it wasn't so odd. "Regardless of one's opinion on the last film, there was certainly a storytelling error when you consider the arc of episodes seven through nine." He was sidestepping the actual topic, but honestly, he needed some time to process her argument. Not to mention the fact that he was sitting in a hot spring analyzing Star Wars with Cara Delaney, whom he had thought of, not so long ago, as the angel of doom.

"There sure as hell was."

"It was as if no one bothered to plan the whole thing from the get-go." That *had* bothered him, even if it hadn't detracted from his enjoyment of any individual film.

"Exactly."

"Cara, is this the first time we've enthusiastically agreed on something?"

She grinned and moved herself up to a higher spot to sit, putting her torso out of the water. "I think it is."

He watched the steam rise off her skin and thought back to her lack of surprise when he professed his affection for episode nine. "For the record, it wasn't Rey's bloodlines, as you called them, that made me like *The Rise of Skywalker*. It was the plot twist. I didn't see it coming." He paused, wondering if he should vocalize the rest. He cared what she thought of him, but he wasn't sure he wanted her to *know* that he cared what she thought of him. Well, hell. "I don't want you to think I'm a mindless monarchist."

"How can you not be a monarchist, given your job?"

"I *am* a monarchist. But it's not because I think the royal family is somehow better than everyone else. I don't believe in divine kings."

"See, that's what I always wonder. It's hard to imagine any modern person believing that. But you kind of have to, don't you? If you don't believe in the divine right of kings, what's so special about the king? What gives him moral—or actual—authority?"

"It actually isn't about the king, Emil specifically or kings in general—or queens. I know that sounds strange, but bear with me. It's not that Emil is rich or blue-blooded; it's that he happens to be in line. It isn't about him, it's about the consistency and value of the tradition." He eyed her, waiting for her to object.

Instead, she asked a good question. "What if everyone in Eldovia put their names in a hat, and you pulled one out every twenty years, and there you go, there's your next monarch."

He considered it. One thing he'd learned about Cara was that she often had interesting new ways of looking at things—witness the Rey discussion earlier. "I think I'd be fine with that. It sounds like the Dalai Lama, in fact."

"But isn't there some kind of divine thing going on there, too? The old divine dude is reincarnated in the baby divine dude? And it *is* always a dude. I'm not knocking it, but it's not exactly a shining example of populist power sharing."

"You're right. My larger point is that I'm fine with your hypothetical scenario, as long as the randomly selected monarch upholds the nation's traditions. It's the traditions I care about—the nation—not the person. The person is a symbol."

"Hmm." She nodded as if she didn't think his position ridiculous, and she was staring off into space as she did so. Perhaps *she* needed time to process *his* insights. Eventually, she returned her attention to him. "Well, anyway, Star Trek is the vastly superior space franchise."

"Because it's the anti-monarchist space show?" He smiled.

She did, too. "Maybe. It's also interesting from a management-consulting point of view."

He shot her a skeptical look.

"Seriously!" she protested. "So many different leadership styles!"

"Yes, I suppose. Don't they say Kirk was the heart and Spock was the brain or something along those lines?"

"Yes, yes, but beyond the archetypal characters of the original series, there are so many interesting questions about how to work together, when to question authority, all that stuff."

"Allow me to turn your previous question back to you: Which is your favorite incarnation of Star Trek?"

"*Voyager*," she said vehemently. "Which is funny, because Spock is my all-time favorite character. How often is a character created that is so entirely different from anything we've seen before, yet also so entirely himself? But favorite show? *Voyager*, even though I'm aware that objectively speaking, it isn't the best of them."

"Why is it your favorite even if it's not the best and it doesn't have Spock?"

"Because of Captain Janeway. It was the first show with a woman captain. It's kind of embarrassing, but my kid self found her completely inspiring."

"I don't think there's any call to be embarrassed. That sounds rather logical to me."

"Spoken like a true Spock."

He chuckled. "I do often get called ruthless. Unfeeling."

"I do, too."

"I'm sure some of it, in your case, is because you're a successful, powerful woman. I'm sure Janeway got called all those things, too."

She looked at him quizzically. "When I first got here and was trying to figure out what you had against me, I wondered if you were sexist."

He made an involuntary, vague noise of dismay. He could not let that stand. "That's—"

"That wasn't it. I know that. I figured that out pretty quickly when you defended me against Noar at that first meeting. Not that I needed defending, but I appreciated it."

"I told you ages ago that it wasn't personal. It was the idea of you. You could have been anyone, and I would have felt the same."

"Kind of like the king could be anyone?" she asked pointedly.

Another interesting, unsettling point. One he would think about, but not while she was staring at him. Not while he was sitting a few feet away from her in a swimsuit. "Ms. Delaney—*Cara*—I've grown overheated. Would you care to join me in a cool off?"

"Are you asking me if I want to go roll around in the snow with you?"

"I suppose I am."

She grinned. "When in Eldovia . . ." She started to lift herself out of the water, but he held up a hand to stop her.

"If I may make a suggestion, it's better to have a plan in place before you go."

"A plan beyond 'Find snow, roll in snow'?"

"Yes. Namely, what are you going to do after the snow? Right back in the water? Or into a sauna? There are also several heated buildings where you can relax at room temperature."

"I am in your hands, Matteo."

He liked the way his name sounded in her mouth. "All right. Snow over there." He pointed to a relatively untrammeled patch nearby. "Then to that building." He pointed again. "I also recommend that once you commit to this course of action, you truly commit."

"It's almost like you don't know me at all."

She was joking, but it made him think. They'd met less than a month ago. Yet in that time, they had almost come to blows several times, shared very personal things about their pasts, and faced Daniel Hauser as allies. She'd met his family, and now they were sitting half-naked in a pool.

An unsettling truth arose: if he knew her, she knew him.

He cleared his throat. "All right. On the count of three, we get out, we run, we roll, we go inside. Fast, decisive, committed. It's too terrible otherwise."

"Understood."

"One, two, three."

She lifted herself from the pool, and steam rose from her skin. She was wearing a modest bathing suit, but still, there was something about all that skin. Something about Cara Delaney, corporate warrior, drenched and trembling that . . . got to him. He wished he could get a look at that mole again, but it only showed when she stretched her arms up, and she was doing the opposite, hugging herself against the cold.

"What happened to fast, decisive, and committed?" she asked.

What had happened indeed? Embarrassed, and hoping he hadn't been ogling too overtly, he heaved himself up, and they ran.

She started shrieking the moment her feet hit the snow. "Oh, oh, oh!"

Matteo was glad it was so cold. He lay down on his stomach, just in case.

She flopped down next to him and flapped her arms in the same manner he was. It was as if they were swimming side by side. Except she was breathing heavily and occasionally omitting an "Oh!"

Matteo had given his life over, these last five years, to service of king and country, and he had done so gladly. That had meant giving up a lot of things. Vacations. Christmas at home with his family.

Relationships. He hadn't had one of those since he and Anna had parted ways. He hadn't had sex since then, either.

He hadn't minded.

He'd thought.

"I guess we should do our backs, now, right?" She rolled over, her arm hitting his in the process, and even though he was freezing, it felt rather as if she were electrocuting him.

AFTER ROLLING AROUND in the snow, Cara, breathing hard and feeling like she'd run a marathon, followed Matteo to a small building. It was full of lounge chairs, and she collapsed gratefully on one next to him, her entire body tingling.

She felt fantastic. Spent and satiated and . . . actually, she felt like she'd just had sex. She looked over at him to find him watching her. "What?"

"Nothing." He looked away rapidly.

"What's happening in my brain right now?" she asked. "That hot-cold cycling releases some kind of happy chemical, doesn't it?"

"I imagine it does." He smiled up at the wooden ceiling. "It really is a kind of relaxation that comes from this and . . ." She watched him swallow, his Adam's apple moving up and down. "Few other things."

Oh god, was he thinking about sex, too?

And *who* had given him those Rilke poems his father gambled away?

"I notice that your toenails are painted a different color than your fingernails."

It took her a moment to adjust to the new topic. "Uh, yes."

"Would it be more customary for them to match?"

She cast her mind back to her nail place at home. "I don't think necessarily." She extended both her arms and legs to examine her own mani-pedi. She had her usual dark-red on the fingers and a gunmetal gray on the toes. "What would be customary in my line of work is to have plain nails, or to paint them something boring and neutral." She shook her head. "Blech."

"So your nails are your little rebellion?"

"I suppose they are. Which is funny because I've worked hard to be taken as seriously as my male colleagues. You'd think I'd want to blend in."

"I wouldn't think that."

She rolled over to face him. "You wouldn't?"

He rolled over, too. Lying on their sides staring at each other, with the tingly sensations still very much present in her body, reinforced the whole post-coital vibe. "I would not."

"I do blend in in other ways. We have to wear dark suits. Plain heels for women. Mine are too high, but no one says anything."

"Is there actually a dress code?"

"Not a written one, but you learn pretty quickly. I was lucky to have one of the partners take an interest in me when I came on board as an intern—that was the mentorship I mentioned. When she hired me for real, after I got out of the army, she took me out to lunch and told me what to buy for a starter wardrobe."

"You went from army uniforms to corporate ones."

"I don't mind it. On the one hand, yes, we look like corporate clone troopers. On the other, it can be nice to have a uniform of sorts. It takes away one big avenue of stress. You don't have to worry about not fitting in—at least not based on what you're wearing."

"Do you worry about fitting in?" he asked quizzically.

Damn it. She had said too much. "Doesn't everyone, to some extent?" Though probably not him. Say what you wanted about Matteo, he didn't seem like the kind of person who cared what other people thought of him. Maybe that was the born-rich part. Maybe that kind of confidence never went away.

"I find it curious that you say your nails don't fit in, given the dress code you've described. They're almost black. It sounds as though your company culture favors black."

"If nails are painted, they're supposed to be ballerina pink, some kind of beigey neutral, or done in a French manicure."

"Hmm." To her complete and utter shock, he said, "I like your nails. They suit you." He smiled a slow, lazy smile that reignited the tingling inside her, except this time she couldn't attribute it to the snow.

Well, if it was going to keep feeling like they'd just had sex—without the benefit of actually having had sex—she was going to ask him something a little bold.

Not that she wanted to have sex with him.

Did she?

Oh, crap.

"What are you going to do about Noar and Daniel?" Matteo asked, jolting her back to reality.

She sighed. "Honestly, I don't know. I suppose I need to go to the king."

"If I may make a suggestion?"

"By all means."

"Goodness, the truce seems to really have taken this time." He winked. Matteo Benz *winked* at her. "Give me a little time to poke around before you say anything to His Majesty?"

"That makes sense. This all may be nothing. Noar may be arrogant and incompetent but not criminally so."

Matteo snorted in a way that suggested he was Team Criminal. "It's more that I don't want the king to act rashly. Depending on what we find, it might be a delicate situation, and the king can be . . . well, rash."

"You don't worry about keeping him in the dark?"

"It's not keeping him in the dark. It's waiting until we have as much information as we can gather. Sometimes loyalty to the Crown requires strategy. An eye to the long-term good."

"Is this that extended mission you spoke about?"

"Mmm," he agreed vaguely. "And I assume you will want to know what's been going on with the company's valuation before you submit your report."

"Yes, and that, in turn, might change my recommendations." Something happened to his face then, but she couldn't quite figure out what. "So the next step is you poke around. Will you tell me what you learn?"

"I will."

"Because we're allies now, allies who are on a first-name basis?" Allies in bathing suits.

"Yes. The truce endures." A slow smile blossomed. He really was so handsome when he de-starched himself. He extended a hand. He no doubt meant that they should shake on it, that he was agreeing, but he'd extended his top hand, which was his left—he was lying on his right arm. She sent her top hand out to meet his. They didn't shake, though; they just sort of held hands and stared at each other. "To the enduring truce," he said, his voice doing that weird caressing thing.

She had to swallow to get *her* voice to work. "To the enduring truce."

Chapter Eleven

Six days until Christmas

The next day, back in Witten, it really did feel like they were allies. Matteo texted to update her throughout the day as he poked around, trying to find out more about Noar. Maybe she shouldn't have been so surprised. She'd come to realize that there were two versions of Matteo. There was the formal, bordering-on-uptight equerry, and there was the man. For a while, she'd seen only glimpses of the man beneath the surface. Then, on their two trips to Riems, larger and larger doses of him.

Now, as if he had turned himself inside out, she saw more of Matteo the man than Mr. Benz the equerry.

"Good evening. May I join you?"

She was sitting at the bar finishing a late dinner when he appeared at her elbow. "Please do. I'd welcome the company."

She'd welcome his company specifically.

"I have some news from an associate regarding Noar," he whispered. "Something I didn't want to put in writing."

She had to shake off the sting of disappointment that he wasn't here because he wanted to hang out with her, but because he wanted to talk business.

And then she had to remind herself that business was the whole reason she was in Eldovia.

And also to stop thinking about him in his little swim trunks.

"Perhaps we can go to your room when you're done eating?" He was looking around at the crowded bar.

"Sure." She followed his gaze with her own, trying to see if anyone was close enough to overhear them. "I feel like a spy."

"One thing I've learned in my line of work is that walls have ears. It doesn't matter if they're palace walls or pub walls."

She settled the bill with Imogen, who handed over Cara's gray suit wrapped in plastic. "Grabbed it for you when I went to pick up my own things at the cleaners."

"Oh, thank you." To Matteo, she said, "Ready?" He nodded and headed for the back door.

"Where are you two going?" Imogen raised her brows after the departing Matteo in an exaggerated fashion.

"Oh come on," Cara said. "We just need to have a private chat."

"Oh, is that what they're calling it these days?"

"That is *not* what they're calling it these days," Cara said emphatically, but her face flamed. She wasn't even sure why. This certainly was not "it."

It had been so very long since she'd had "it." That must be her problem. Maybe it was time to recall the lonely goatherd.

She followed Matteo up the stairs and tried not to look at his butt.

He took the suit from her while she unlocked the door, and the inadvertent brush of their hands that resulted made her suck in a breath. She was becoming problematically obsessed with this dude's hands. She ordered herself to get a grip and unlocked the door. Inside the room, she pointed to the armoire. "Do you mind hanging that?"

"You really do pack light, don't you?"

"Pardon?"

Matteo was contemplating the interior of the armoire, and yes, it was nearly empty.

"I have it down to a science." She'd been an involuntary minimalist as a kid, but as an adult, she embraced an unencumbered approach. Even though she could buy pretty much whatever she wanted these days, she was careful not to accumulate too much stuff. Stuff tied you down. Stuff was for later. "What do you need, really need, that can't fit into a suitcase?"

"I don't know, a place to live?" He was smiling as he spoke, teasing her.

"Well, I have a place to live."

"Is it one of those absurdly tiny homes one sees on American television? Is it a house you can tow around? Then perhaps it does qualify as packable."

"No, it's a house in New York, and believe it or not, it's too small. As soon as I can afford it—and I'm aggressively saving toward it—I'm buying a duplex. I'll put my parents in one side and I'll take the other."

"That sounds lovely."

"I don't know many people who would say that living with your parents sounds lovely." But he would. He did. She loved that about him. Well, no, she *appreciated* that about him.

"Well, you're not going to be living with them; isn't that the point? You'll be very near, but not actually with them. Sounds ideal." He shrugged. "But I think perhaps I like my family—my father excepted—more than most people do."

"I think I do, too. It's funny. I've watched colleagues buy their dream homes. They're generally either Manhattan apartments or houses in the Hudson Valley. But not me! I'm looking for a duplex in the Bronx." She realized that the only place to sit was the bed. At least housekeeping had been in, so it was made. She kicked off her shoes and settled herself on one side, leaning back against the headboard and extending her legs. "I'm sorry I can't offer you a proper seat. This is quite no-frills compared to the palace."

"Yet you had no qualms about making the switch."

"Don't get me wrong, given a choice, I'd rather be at the palace, but the project comes first. I do miss that bathtub, though. I'm a sucker for a hot bath at the end of the day, and my house in New York only has a shower stall. I think that's why I enjoyed the spa in Biel so much." She was babbling. To her great horror, she was pretty sure it was because she was nervous. She patted the bed next to her. He hesitated. Was he nervous, too? No, he was probably worried about propriety or decorum or something. But there was literally nowhere else to sit.

He surprised her by kicking off his shoes, as she had, mimicking her position on the other side of the bed, and saying, "So your real estate ambitions are a duplex with a suitable bathtub."

"Yes. Or a bathroom I can rip out and rebuild centered on the tub of my dreams."

He looked at her.

She looked at him.

Something between them shifted—suddenly, with a lurch. The

air had grown heavy, like after a storm. She was extra aware of her own body in space, of where it stopped and the charged air began.

He leaned a little closer.

Oh my *god*, was he going to kiss her again? Her entire body started tingling. She wished she hadn't had that coffee downstairs. Her breath was going to be—

"Noar has approached Lucille Müller about selling her shares to him, too."

"Whoa!" He'd wanted to tell her a secret, not *kiss* her. God. She was an *idiot*.

"Whoa indeed," Matteo said mildly.

He was going to assume her shock was the result of his news, not their imaginary almost kiss, and she was going to let him. "How'd you find this out?"

"I, ah, accessed his calendar remotely."

"You *hacked* him?"

"I wouldn't say that, exactly." He smirked. "I called on some connections for information."

"Is that what we're calling it?"

"Noar had a meeting with Lucille, and I spoke to her executive assistant afterward."

"Her executive assistant in the *government*?" In addition to being a member of parliament, Lucille Müller was the leader of the official opposition party. She was a big deal.

"Yes, and that's how I found out they talked about the shares. Lucille apparently turned Noar down when he asked if she would sell to him."

Wow. Matteo had done this all in a day. It was remarkable.

"Lucille does seem very committed to Morneau. And very morally upstanding."

"Yes, I believe Noar was, as you might say in America, barking up the wrong tree. The larger question is what does it mean that he was seeking to buy shares from more than one shareholder? If we take Daniel Hauser at his word, if the sale truly was a matter of him wanting to retire, that's one thing. But doesn't it seem rather odd that Noar would then seek out further shares?"

"I wouldn't say odd so much as I would say alarming."

"Is this hostile takeover territory?"

"A hostile takeover of a private company isn't really possible—well, there are some arcane, long-game strategies involving setting up a bunch of shell companies who each buy in, seemingly independently, but that seems a stretch in this case. I think it's more likely that Noar is simply trying to amass a bigger stake. The question is, why? And why so secretly?"

It was strange, and oddly intimate, to be conversing with Matteo while they were both lying in bed. She was still sort of tingly from the kiss that wasn't.

"I'm starting to fear you might have been right, that it's possible the company isn't doing well *because* of him," he said. "Are you still operating with that theory?"

"Well, I haven't discarded it. If he can convince others that the company is on a downward spiral and to sell him their shares at a low price, then when things 'turn around,' the value of his shares increases."

Matteo tilted his head and emitted a skeptical sounding "Hmm."

"You think I'm being paranoid."

"No. I just wouldn't have thought Noar Graf smart enough, or cunning enough, to conjure and execute such a scheme. Or capable enough to suddenly start doing a good job to such an extent that it changes the trajectory of the company."

"Maybe it's not that, or not only that. Maybe he believes that the recommendations my firm makes will in fact turn things around."

"But how can he know that, when he doesn't know what recommendations you're going to make? Not to mention the fact that he doesn't seem eager to cooperate with you."

"I don't know." What a tangled web. "I'm just thinking out loud here, but what if Noar is a proxy for someone else? Is he married?"

"No."

"What about family? People he's been working closely with who are perhaps less than trustworthy? People who . . ."

Oh my god. Brad. Fucking Brad. Was this why Noar had been so hostile when Cara appeared at Morneau in Brad's place? Was this why Brad had made a point of conducting all his meetings with Noar in German? Had it in fact not been to show off but to add a layer of obfuscation?

No. Now she was one hundred percent being paranoid.

Right?

But then why was she getting that sinking feeling in her stomach? In matters of business that involved reading people, her instincts were usually right. That they hadn't been with Matteo was what made him such an enigma. She fumbled for her phone. "I need to make a call. It's rather urgent."

"All right." He started to get off the bed, but she gestured for him to stay.

"Cara?"

"Oh! Tonya, hi!"

"What's wrong?" Cara had told Tonya about the shares Noar was buying from Daniel Hauser, and that she and Matteo were doing some digging before telling the king about the transaction.

"Nothing, nothing. I just didn't expect you to answer." She'd been mentally rehearsing the voice mail she was planning to leave.

"You usually text before you call, so I figured it was important."

"How's Brad?"

There was a beat before Tonya answered what no doubt seemed to her a random question. "Improving. He's agitating to come relieve you, if you can believe it. We've told him he's being ridiculous. He's still in the rehab hospital. But what's wrong? You're not calling about Brad."

"I *am* calling about Brad, actually." Matteo's eyebrows flew up, and she watched him put it together.

"How so?"

She blew out a breath. She had to tread carefully here. "I know Brad and I have had our . . . issues."

"Yes," Tonya said mildly.

Cara would lay money on the fact that Tonya disliked Brad, too, but she had never said a negative word about him, even behind closed doors. Tonya never gossiped. "I don't know how to say this, but I have a hunch about something, and I'd like to ask you to look into a few things. I don't want you to think this is personal, though."

"Your hunches are usually correct. Consider your suspicions about the obstructionists. You were right about the CEO, weren't you?"

"Yes."

"And that equerry guy?"

"No," she said swiftly, darting her eyes to Matteo. She felt oddly
guilty. "He turned out to be . . ." Shit. He was going to know she
was talking about him. Well, hell. They were in this together now.
"The equerry turned out to be an unexpected ally." The smile
that earned her made any remaining discomfort evaporate. "He's
just discovered that Noar Graf is trying to buy *another* member's
shares."

"*Really.*"

"Yes, and we have the sense Noar isn't the type to be making
this move on his own."

"'We' being you and the equerry?"

"Yes."

"And you think Brad is involved?"

"I don't know. As I said, it's only a hunch. But Noar seemed dis-
proportionately upset that I was here instead of Brad. And Brad's
been having months of meetings—in German—with Noar one-
on-one. And . . ."

"And Brad is a sneaky little shit who would sell out his own
mother if it served his purposes." Wow. So much for Tonya's cool
professionalism. Tonya must have taken her silence for the shock
it was. "I think you and I have reached the point where we can
level with each other, yes?"

"Yes?" Cara said weakly.

"I know who Brad is. I see him. He's Roger's hire, so I can't get
rid of him without cause. And honestly, I don't *want* to get rid of
him without cause. Life is full of dickbags, and a person has to
learn to coexist with them."

Life is full of *dickbags*? This was *Tonya* talking?

"But there are dickbags, and then there are criminals." Tonya snorted. "I guess I should say *alleged* criminals. What do you need from me?"

"I don't know, exactly. I think we—Matteo Benz and I—need to go to the king with what we know about Noar and the shares. It's too big a deal to keep to ourselves any longer, even if I wish we had more information." She raised her eyes questioningly at Matteo as she spoke.

Matteo nodded as Tonya said, "I agree."

"I don't want you to do anything unethical, but I was hoping that since Brad was still out of the office, you might be able to poke around a bit. See if you can find anything about his relationship with Noar."

"Brad's computers, devices, and the content of his emails are the property of CZT, so I don't see any ethical hurdle here."

"It might all be nothing."

"And that's fine. But it might not be nothing. We owe it to our clients, and frankly to ourselves, to find out."

"But even if he is into something shady, he might not have left a trail. He might be using his own devices."

"He might. But remember, being a dickbag tends to be inversely associated with intelligence."

Cara burst out laughing. "I'm sorry. I'm not laughing at you. I'm just not used to hearing you talk like this."

"I guess I'm feeling rather informal today. Let me do some digging. I'll call you."

Cara hung up and turned her head to find Matteo looking intently at her. "Everything all right?"

She opened her mouth to reassure him that everything was fine, but the air shifted again. Suddenly, sitting a foot away from

Matteo in bed, everything was very much not fine. It was not fine that his stupid hands were so hot, or that he had made her feel comfortable enough to tell him *so much* about her life. It was not fine that he was turning out to be so smart and so cunning and so capable of using his wile for good.

She was in trouble. There was no denying what was going on here. It made no sense, but there was no denying it: she wanted Matteo.

She'd had Johannes the lonely goatherd and Bashir the handsome principal in her grasp, but she hadn't been able to get it up—metaphorically—for them because she wanted *Mr. Benz*.

She wanted him to kiss her. She wanted him to do more than kiss her. That's why she was fixating on his hands. And his butt.

Dear lord.

Well. You can't always get what you want. She'd learned that thoroughly and at a young age. So with great effort, she rolled away from him.

Which caused him to roll away, too, and get off the bed.

Which caused things to start feeling awkward.

No. They weren't backsliding to awkward.

She froze in place half on, half off the bed as a rogue thought arose: Was it possible all that awkwardness between them in the early going had actually been attraction?

"Is everything all right?"

"Sorry, I was taken aback by something my boss said that was a bit out of character, but it wasn't about Brad, or Morneau, or any of this. She is going to do some digging into Brad."

He opened his mouth like he was going to say something, then shut it. He wandered over to the small bureau at the foot of the bed and picked up her Post-it. "'Change is the essential process of all existence,'" he read aloud. "From Mr. Spock. You really are a Star Trek fan."

"I really am."

"What does it mean?"

She wasn't sure what exactly he was asking. His command of English was as good as hers, so surely he understood what he'd read. "Exactly what it sounds like. To survive in this world, you have to be adaptable. You have to keep moving."

He looked up, and their gazes met in the mirror. "But doesn't that grow tiresome, moving all the time?"

"Not really. Not when the alternative is stagnation. I like to be on to the next thing."

"But what happens to the first thing?"

"What do you mean?"

"If you're on to the next thing, what happens to the thing you left behind?" He turned, and even though he'd been looking at her in the mirror, his direct, unmediated attention felt more intense. She had no idea how to answer him, but she didn't have to. He changed the subject. "I suspect Lucille will be in touch with the king regarding Noar's offer, and it's probably better if he hears from you on the topic first. Would you like me to arrange a time for you to speak with him tomorrow?"

"I would appreciate that, but I would also appreciate if you'd join me." She paused, wondering if she should say more. "I feel like we're in this together now, don't you? And honestly, I could use the reinforcement."

He smiled at her in a way that seemed almost . . . fond? "I would be glad to accompany you."

After he left, she stared at the ceiling for a while thinking about how inconvenient it was that she wanted to jump his bones.

AFTER LEAVING CARA, Matteo headed downstairs and into one of the pub's single-occupancy restrooms. He locked the door behind him and stared at his reflection in the mirror. He wasn't sure what he was looking for. Perhaps signs of insanity? His face was a bit flushed, but other than that he looked the same as he always did.

Inside him, though, was a riotous commotion. And he knew why.

He had been trying to tell himself that his inexplicably good mood of late was because there was hope on the Morneau front. If Noar had been sabotaging Morneau, perhaps there wouldn't have to be any layoffs, at least not in the short term. At the very least, they would have to untangle Noar's impact on Morneau's fortunes and Cara would have to restart the whole modernization exercise.

Which was an enormous relief.

Still.

That wasn't the cause of the riotous commotion. He leaned closer and studied his reflection. He looked . . . *happy*.

He sighed. He couldn't deny it anymore, even though it didn't make any sense. He could understand being attracted to Cara when they were in their swimsuits. There was a certain logic there. After all, he was only human, as much as some people sometimes seemed to believe otherwise.

But when they were fully clothed? She was wearing one of her warrior suits today, and though it flattered her, it wasn't exactly the stuff of fantasies.

He wouldn't have thought, anyway.

Perhaps it had been the context—the bed. What had *possessed* him to lie down on it next to her?

He shook his head. It didn't matter what the source of this inconvenient attraction was; what mattered was whether he was going to do anything about it.

Normally, the answer would be a decisive *no*. There were so many reasons why not. She was here to work. He didn't have the time. It would complicate matters enormously.

And on the *yes* side of the ledger? Only his own inexplicable, maddening want—and a gut sense that he wasn't alone in feeling this way.

Whatever had possessed him to kick off his shoes and lie on her bed had also possessed her. She'd been talking about her real estate ambitions, and suddenly there had been something there between them. It had felt as if a weather system had blown in and settled over them like a storm over a mountain valley. He had almost kissed her again, for god's sake.

And the rub was that he was fairly certain that if he had, she would have kissed him back.

And if she had, would that have been the worst thing? Oddly, the stakes didn't seem that high. She wasn't here that much longer. Before he knew it, she would be "on to the next thing." Was he crazy to think that a brief affair with Cara the handful of days she had left in Eldovia might be just the thing?

Well, yes, he was.

But was he going to suggest exactly that anyway?

Unclear.

Well, he wasn't going to solve anything now. Kai was waiting for him at the cabin. He splashed cold water on his face. When he passed by the bar on his way out, Imogen was alone at it, a rare occurrence.

He paused. Perhaps that was providential.

It couldn't hurt to ask. He wasn't committing himself to any course of action by doing so.

"I need some advice," he said, keeping his voice low as he pulled out a stool.

"*You* need advice from *me*." She laughed. "The chief courtier needs the bartender to tell him what to do?"

"Yes. Keep your voice down."

"All right." She moved to stand directly across from his stool and raised her eyebrows.

"How does one . . ."

"Yes?" she prompted.

"How does one initiate a casual sexual encounter?"

"Are you *kidding* me?"

"I am not. I figure you—"

"Are you calling my morals into question?" she exclaimed.

"No!" Oh, wait, she was teasing him, as evidenced by the twinkle in her eye. He hadn't been referring to her personal life, though a woman as gregarious and pretty as she was certainly must have her share of offers. "I merely meant that as a bartender, you must see . . ." He waved his hand around. "Casual encounters." He kept waving. "Or the, ah . . ." More waving. "Lead-up to them."

"That's certainly true. May I ask with whom you would like to have this casual encounter?"

"You may not."

"Well, may I ask if you have a specific person in mind, or if any-one will do? Because if you're not picky, an app is the way to go."

"Oh, no, no apps. I do have a particular person in mind."

"You don't say." She smirked.

"Are you going to help me, or are you going to mock me?"

She sobered. "I'm going to help you. What seems to be the trouble? Are you—Wait." She lowered her voice. "Are you a virgin?"

"*No.*" Good lord. "Not that it's any of your business."

"Well, you *are* asking me for sex advice."

"I'm not asking you for sex advice! I'm asking you for . . . logistical advice." He did realize how ridiculous that sounded. All right. There was no reason not to level with her. "It's been a while. And in the past, I always limited my, uh, activities to within the context of relationships. So this manner of approach is new to me."

"All right. I understand." She had dropped her teasing manner, which he appreciated. "Do you have a reasonable sense that this person might be open to the kind of arrangement you're suggesting?"

He considered the question. He thought of staring at Cara in her bed as something shifted between them. "A reasonable sense? Yes. Am I certain? No."

"Well, I'm going to go out on a limb here and suggest you just . . . ask the person in question."

"Just ask," he echoed.

"Yes. You do this thing where you open your mouth and you form your lips into words."

"Is being that direct advisable?"

"Look, what I hear you saying is that you're not looking for romance, for anything long-term. So why not just ask? I mean, don't be gross about it. Take no for an answer."

"Well, of course." He was a little piqued that she wouldn't know that went without saying. "But you think simply asking is better than . . . making a move?"

"Do you have any moves?"

"Now you're insulting me." He smiled to show that he wasn't truly taking offense and considered her advice. *Just ask.*

Hmm.

LATE THAT NIGHT, Cara was tucked into bed with a book that she was having trouble concentrating on—what a day it had been!—when her phone pinged with an incoming text.

> **Matteo:** The king has made time in his schedule tomorrow to see us at 4 p.m. if that suits. I notice that he has a late dinner booked with Lucille Müller, so this is good timing.

> **Cara:** Sounds great. Well, not great, but you know what I mean. Thank you for arranging this.

> **Matteo:** I was also wondering if you would

Hmm. That was weird. Matteo always texted in full sentences, using proper punctuation.

> **Cara:** If I would what?

> **Matteo:** My apologies. I hit send there too soon.

The bubbles that indicated he was typing appeared, and they kept bubbling. Sure enough, when the next text arrived, it was long. And back to being very Mr. Benzy with an immaculately composed and punctuated paragraph.

> **Matteo:** I was wondering if you would care to join me for dinner after our meeting. I admit I'm a little unsettled by the prospect of what we have to tell the king, and I was thinking about how my customary way of relaxing after a particularly stressful day is dinner in front of Star Wars. Perhaps you'd care to join for such at my apartment? I'll even let you choose the episode.

Cara could think of nothing she'd like to do more tomorrow night than to debrief the day and watch Star Wars with Matteo in his apartment, and not just because she wanted to jump his bones. Which she still did. Unfortunately.

> **Cara:** I would love to join you, thanks. But I think we should watch Trek instead of Wars.

> **Matteo:** All right.

> **Cara:** All right?! I was kidding! I didn't expect you to capitulate so easily.

> **Matteo:** Well, if we watch Trek instead of Wars, then I don't have to listen to you

> monologuing about bloodlines and the divine
> right of kings. That doesn't actually sound
> very relaxing, now that I think about it.

And then he sent a winky face emoji.

Wait. Was she sure that it actually was Matteo on the other end of this conversation? Had he been bitten by a particularly accommodating zombie with a sense of humor?

Either way, she was irrationally excited to watch TV tomorrow with the equerry to the throne of Eldovia.

Chapter Twelve

Five days until Christmas

*M*atteo worried about the emoji all evening and into the next day. He worried about it so much that during a break in sorting and wrapping at Kai's workshop, he called Martina. Given the amount of time she spent on her phone, she should be able to advise.

"Talk to me about emojis."

"Huh?"

"I need a crash course on emojis. When should you use them? On their own or in concert with written text? To accentuate written text or to soften it?"

"What are you talking about? Just use an emoji if you want to use an emoji."

"The problem is, I already did. Now I'm concerned that it wasn't appropriate."

"Did you send the peach? Or the eggplant?"

"Why would I do that?"

She laughed. "Oh Matteo, you're adorable. Okay, tell me what you sent."

"I sent a text that I meant sarcastically. I immediately worried that perhaps it wouldn't be taken as such, so I followed it up with the emoji of the little face winking. My intent was to convey the fact that the previous text had been meant in jest."

"Sometimes sarcasm doesn't always come across the way you intend in print, so an emoji can help with that. So it sounds like you handled it perfectly, at least for an old person. A-plus, brother."

"But then she never replied. So I'm concerned that the spirit of my message wasn't conveyed."

"She?"

That was an oversight. He should have left it vague. "The recipient of my message was a woman, yes."

"Are you texting emojis to Cara?" Martina practically shrieked.

"No," he said immediately. Even he could hear what a terrible liar he was.

"Matteo." Her voice had softened. "I wouldn't worry about it. One of the other norms of texting is that you don't necessarily have to close out a conversation, especially if you've already communicated whatever it was you needed to communicate."

"I did that. We made arrangements for . . . a meeting."

"Great. So don't worry about it. You're fine. You can go on your date with Cara without any worries—on the emoji front anyway."

"It's not a date!"

Except it was, wasn't it? Or at least he wanted it to be.

"Yeah, okay, Matteo, I gotta go. Enjoy your *meeting*."

He hung up feeling marginally cheered about the emoji situation and headed back into the workshop.

"I have to go at two, I'm afraid," he said to Kai. He had brought most of the things he'd been storing in his apartment over here, and they were mostly done wrapping and packing the nonperishable items into baskets, but he still had piles of books as well as some small items like candles in his living room that needed to be hidden away so Cara didn't see them.

"Do you ever think you're getting too busy to keep doing this?" Kai asked.

He did. He thought that all the time. "I can't abandon the project. Too many people count on these baskets." He paused. "I'm sorry so much has fallen to you this year."

Kai shrugged. "I don't mind. I'm just wondering again whether we might need another body next year."

Matteo's first thought was that Kai was right. But then, next year, Cara wouldn't be here doing . . . Well, he'd been going to complete that thought with his usual reflexive idea that she was here to destroy Morneau and/or Eldovia. He was no longer sure that was what she was doing—or had ever intended to do.

Regardless, things would be significantly less busy next year, when Cara was not here. When she was on to the next thing.

That would be good.

Right?

CARA DIDN'T GENERALLY get nervous in the line of duty. No matter how harrowing a job became, she was usually able to separate herself from it emotionally, which in turn meant that the stakes never felt high enough to freak her out.

But she had never had to tell a literal king that the CEO of his family's company might be fleecing him.

She would be a lot less on edge, ironically, if she had hard evidence that Noar was fleecing him. She hadn't heard back from Tonya yet, so all she had now was the attempted purchase of shares from board members and a hunch that there was more behind it.

When she rounded the corner in the palace that would take her to the king's library, she found Matteo. He was standing beneath a giant wreath—the palace had even more Christmas décor on display than when she had last been here.

She wondered if they did mistletoe in Eldovia. But then she wondered why she was wondering. It wasn't as if she was going to be doing any under-the-mistletoe kissing while she was here.

"Hi." The greeting came out a little breathless.

"Are you nervous?"

"Kind of," she said, answering Matteo at the same time that she looked into his warm green eyes.

Damn. It was possible that some of this breathlessness was because of the whole *Matteo is suddenly a hottie, and I haven't had sex in months* thing.

It had also not escaped her how easily she had admitted to nerves. She rarely felt nervous, but if and when she did, she *never* admitted it.

He nodded but said only, "Ready?" as he raised his hand to knock on the door. She appreciated that he didn't spout platitudes or try to offer false comfort.

"Ah, Ms. Delaney." The king rose from where he'd been sitting in an armchair by the fire and gestured for her to take a seat on the sofa opposite.

She did, and Matteo sat next to her—very next to her. His leg was about an inch from hers, and she swore she could feel the heat of him through his pants and hers.

"I'm told you have something pressing to tell me?"

Well, here they went. "I'm just going to come out and say it." She paused, and Matteo cleared his throat, drawing her attention. "Do you want to tell him?"

"No, no," Matteo said quickly. "Go ahead. I am in complete agreement that the best way is to just come out with it."

"Will *someone* tell me what in the hell is going on?" the king, clearly irritated, demanded.

She steeled herself. "Noar Graf is in the process of buying Daniel Hauser's Morneau shares, and he tried to buy Lucille Müller's. I'm concerned about what that might mean, both in general and as it relates to Morneau's recent performance, which is what I have been taking as the baseline for my work."

There, it was out.

The king's eyes widened, and he said something in German Cara was pretty sure was not a nice word.

"Indeed," Matteo said.

Cara told the king what they had learned and how they'd learned it, and shared her theory about what might be going on. The king grew increasingly angry, but mostly at himself. "This is another thing I should have seen, another thing I let slide while I was buried in my grief. How could I not have known this was all happening under my nose?"

"Your Majesty," Cara said, "if I may, we don't yet know what is happening. The only verifiable facts we have at the moment are about the shares."

"But you suspect there's more going on, given the possibilities you raised."

She glanced at Matteo, who gave her a minuscule nod. "I do. But once again, I feel dutybound to say that I'm going on a hunch here."

The king stared at the ceiling.

"Your Majesty," said Matteo, "may I gently suggest that you not assign yourself sole responsibility for whatever is occurring?"

"I appreciate that, Benz, but I'm the king. And the chair of the board. What do they say in America?" He turned to Cara. "The buck stops with me?"

"They do say that, and it *can* stop with you. We will get to the bottom of this, and I know you'll take the right course of action." They talked it through, and decided that the king, the princess, and the Duke of Aquilla, who between the three of them made up a majority of the Morneau board and were the ones Noar had *not* approached, would see what they could reconstruct about Noar's hiring and his tenure at the company.

Cara explained that her colleagues in New York were also working on some information. She stopped short of telling him Tonya was spying on Brad. Fucking Brad. Even though she loathed him, she wasn't going to tarnish his name until she had reason to.

The king nodded, seemingly calmed by having talked it all through. "Whatever else happens, I believe it is time to rethink Morneau's board size and structure."

"Yes," she agreed, "and the wording of contracts as it relates to selling shares or to the passing of board seats upon death or retirement."

"But the larger issue," said the king, beginning to pace, and she could see him thinking through things as he walked and spoke, "is that, as you say, this means your company's assessment may be based on incorrect information."

"It might be."

"You might have to start over entirely."

"I doubt it." She tried to keep her tone calm. She didn't think now was the time to tell him that she'd spent all day looking at the draft of the report she'd written, and that even if Noar had been sabotaging Morneau, the company was still in trouble. "But I will be able to absorb any changes that need absorbing and deliver you my report as promised."

"Ms. Delaney is good at handling change," Matteo said. "She's very . . . nimble."

The king shot a bewildered look at Matteo, who seemed rather cheery, given the tenor of their conversation.

"Your Majesty," Cara said, "I think it's important that we not jump ahead. It's Friday. Let's take the weekend to see how things play out. You speak to the princess and the duke and Frau Müller. I'll touch base with my people. Then let's regroup on Monday, shall we? Nothing existential is going to happen between now and Monday."

"Yes, yes. You're right, of course." He walked over to a small bar cart in the corner. "I think it's time for a drink."

Cara sighed internally. She didn't want to have a drink. Well, she didn't want to have a drink here, with the king. She wouldn't mind having a drink with Matteo, in his apartment. Her curiosity about what kind of space Matteo would call home had been building all day. And she could practically see the opening credits of *Into Darkness*.

Matteo stood and murmured his goodbyes to the king, who waved absently from where he was pouring something from a crystal decanter. Cara laughed to herself. Here she was assuming the king was inviting them to stay for a drink when really he was dismissing them.

They were free!

They didn't speak until they emerged from the palace. She could sort of see now why Matteo had chosen to live in one of the outbuildings. Working for the king was intense.

"How do you think that went?" she asked as their feet crunched on the snow. "I thought he would have a more extreme reaction."

"He's still processing. That bewildered face he made initially was his processing face." He slowed his pace and turned to her. "You're still up for dinner and Star Trek?"

She'd been thinking of little else all day. But she managed a casual, "Oh, yeah, sure." She followed him across the grounds and toward the building he'd pointed out before. "Is there really a sleigh in here?"

"There really is." He led her to a row of windows. Following his lead, she peered in, and sure enough there was an enormous red sleigh in there.

"The ones in the village are newer. This is an antique. It was built for the king's mother when she was a girl. We can take it out tomorrow if you like." He paused. "Since we seem to have ended up with the weekend off."

"Oh, I—" She wanted to do that. She'd been about to reflexively decline, but she *really* wanted to do that.

"If in fact you meant it about there being nothing to do regarding Noar and Morneau this weekend," he said in a rush. "Probably you did not. Probably you're very busy regardless."

"No, I did mean it." It was her turn to pause. "And I would love a sleigh ride." There were the sleighs in the village he'd referenced, but suddenly she wanted Matteo specifically to take her. Would he be as good at driving sleighs as he was at driving cars? Would his hands on the reins be as stupidly attractive as his hands on a steering wheel? She feared they would.

"It's a date," he said.

It's a date. He probably didn't mean that the way her American ears heard it. She followed him around the back of the building and up a set of exterior stairs that led to a heavy wooden door with a small, tasteful brass nameplate that said *M Benz.*

"Here we are."

He gestured her in ahead of him, and she let loose an involuntary "Ooh." He lived in a loft. It was huge, and the walls were exposed brick, except for a few sections that had been drywalled and were covered with art. And not fussy old-fashioned art like you'd think the tradition-obsessed equerry would favor. No oil paintings of old-fashioned people, like he'd shown her in the portrait gallery so long ago. These were interesting modern pieces— some paintings, some photographs.

On one end of the large space was a small, open kitchen with a floating breakfast bar. On the other was a sleeping area with a bed tucked into an alcove. It was immaculately made with the same sort of plain-but-posh linens she'd encountered in the palace, and its frame was made of dark, elaborately carved wood.

"Come in, sit," he said, making her realize that while he had taken off his boots and hung his coat, she'd been standing in the entryway gaping at his apartment.

"This place is *amazing*," she said by way of explanation. "I can't stop looking at it."

"Thank you. I'm fond of it." He led her to the sitting area, which floated in the middle of the space and was demarcated by an enormous area rug and flanked on one side by a brick chimney that rose through the center of the loft. There was another huge piece of art hanging on the chimney, an abstract geometrical thing that was, perhaps counterintuitively, set in an ornate gold frame. That frame wouldn't have been out of place in the palace portrait gallery, but the painting was stark and modern. The juxtaposition was so cool.

Oh, no, wait. It was a TV disguised as art! He had picked up a remote and aimed it at the painting, which was replaced with a smart TV menu. "Wow," she said, which made her feel like an unsophisticated country mouse, but she couldn't help it. In fact, she said it again. "Wow."

"I am not a fan of the TV-as-altar look," Matteo said with a smile. "Can I get you something to drink?"

"Yes, please."

He handed her the remote. "Pick what you like." From the kitchen, he called, "I have some of Imogen's pumpkin stout. Or wine? I have scotch, too, but I don't believe that's your thing."

"A glass of wine would be great, thanks."

He came back with two glasses of wine, handed her one, and lifted his. "To hard things done."

"Well said. And to not having to do any more of them for a couple days."

They clinked. "What will you do with your free weekend?"

"I don't know. Honestly, it's a bit of a weird feeling. Even at home, I'm usually working on the weekends, and when I'm not, I'm tied up with my parents. Maybe I'll do some of the Eldovia Christmas stuff." Everywhere you turned, there was décor or music or food that reminded you of Christmas, and it was ramping up daily. But the holiday frenzy had been, for her, akin to a soundtrack playing in the background. She sat for a moment with the notion of spending the next two days Christmas-ing and found that she liked the idea. "Can we really go on a sleigh ride tomorrow?"

"We can indeed. The sleigh is used by the palace during Cocoa Fest, but we can take it out any time before then. Perhaps a late morning sleigh ride and picnic lunch tomorrow?"

"I would love that."

"Is something wrong?"

"No. Why do you ask?"

"Your face does not match your words." He set his wine on the coffee table, and to her complete astonishment, reached out and touched her forehead. "You say 'I would love that,' but your skin wrinkles here in such a way that suggests the opposite."

She hadn't noticed she'd been furrowing her brow, but it tracked. Some part of her was no doubt shocked by the words coming out of her mouth. She was not the kind of person who enthusiastically agreed to a freaking *sleigh ride*. But here she was, jonesing for those jingle bells.

Also, she was being electrocuted by Matteo's fingers, which were now *rubbing her forehead*. Was it possible he was actually a superhero? Uptight royal dude by day, harnesser of electricity by night? Maybe the Star Wars thing was a decoy and he was really the Clark Kent–esque alter ego of some kind of lightning-harnessing superhero? Wait. Was he actually Thor?

He kept rubbing, and he added a little smile. Shit. She had to get this back on track. "I was thinking about something else while I was answering you."

I was thinking about how distressing it is that you make me want to go on a sleigh ride . . . and possibly also make out with you while on that sleigh ride?

Matteo accepted the deflection. He leaned back against the sofa and sighed.

"Tired?" she asked.

He turned his head toward her without moving his body. "I'm always tired this time of year. It's more that . . ." He shook his head as if he didn't want to finish the thought.

"What?" she prodded.

"I don't know," he said, getting up and walking toward the kitchen. "I find myself almost existentially tired this year. I'm not tired in the sense that sleep will cure it. I'm *tired*."

She twisted to face him. "Burnout."

"Perhaps."

"Can equerries quit their jobs? You're not committed for life or anything, are you?"

He started pulling things out of a slim refrigerator hidden inside a cabinet. "I can resign anytime I want, of course. But the appointment is in many ways more than a mere job. It's a giving over of one's life, in a way. It's not unlike the military, in that sense."

"You know that song 'Wind Beneath My Wings'?"

"I do not."

"It's from a movie called *Beaches* that's about a famous singer and her nonfamous best friend who does everything for her and then dies tragically. The famous friend sings this song to the nonfamous friend about how she's the wind beneath her wings, about how everything she's achieved has been because of her support."

"Well, that's a nice sentiment."

"No, it's a bullshit sentiment. Why should the one friend efface herself fully in service of the other?"

"That's a very American way of looking at it."

She realized that he wasn't coming back to sit because he was working on their dinner, so she got up and walked toward the kitchen. "Can I help?"

He gestured to one of the stools at the bar that separated the kitchen from the rest of the apartment. "You can keep me company. I hope you don't mind a simple dinner. I've pre-poached some trout and was planning to serve it over a salad with some good local bread."

"That sounds wonderful." She seated herself on one of the stools. Another wonderful thing? Having someone cook for you. When she was home, she cooked for her parents. And when she wasn't, she ate in restaurants, but to have someone cook for you in their home, to direct you to sit down and *not* help, to want you to just sit there and *talk* to them . . . well, it felt suddenly as luxurious as the hot springs in Biel had. "What do you mean that my way of looking at that song is American?"

He paused in whisking the salad dressing he'd been making. "Well, it's a point of view that starts with the presumption that glory is the goal. That strikes me as rather American. You ask why the one friend should efface herself, but what if, for her, what you're calling effacement *isn't* actually?"

"What is it?"

He opened a cupboard and pulled out a large wooden salad bowl. "Service. And not in a subservient way. To have a cause, a deeply felt cause, and to serve that cause, can be a noble thing."

"Even when the cause is your narcissistic best friend?"

"We can't know what's in people's hearts that is driving their outward choices."

"That is . . ."

He glanced up from where he'd begun dressing the salad and raised his eyebrows.

"An interesting point," she finished. He really was a student of humanity.

He chuckled and smiled.

"Still, if Bette Midler was my friend, I'd murder her."

"I'm not sure murder is advised as a friendship-maintenance strategy." He paused in the middle of laying a place setting in front of her.

"What?"

"All this talk of friendship has me wondering: Are *we* friends?"

"Well, we only just got over being low-key at war with each other, so . . ." She made a face to show she was kidding.

"Right." He grinned. "Although it's possible we might have segued into being friends and we just haven't realized it."

She couldn't tell if he was teasing or in earnest. Either way, his theory wasn't crazy. "I think you might be right. But I'm going home soon, so it's kind of a moot point."

"Do you think we'll keep in touch?"

"Do you want to?" He wasn't even sitting that close to her, but she could feel the heat his body was throwing off.

"Do *you* want to?" he asked.

She shrugged, suddenly shy. She did want to. She wanted to text him when something funny happened at work, or something frustrating, or when "Wind Beneath My Wings" came on the radio.

"I would very much like to visit New York someday as a tourist, to be there and be the master of my own schedule," he said when she didn't answer the question.

The image of Matteo the man, rather than Mr. Benz the equerry, in New York was oddly appealing. "There's a lot you can do in New York that's off the usual touristy beaten path. I could show you some stuff."

He picked up his fork. "It's a date."

Another date. But not really.

"This is delicious," she said after her first bite. The fish was tender and flavorful, and the simple salad beneath it was dressed with a bright-tasting citrus vinaigrette.

They chatted easily as they ate. It all felt very natural. So apparently they were friends.

She got off her stool when they were done and picked up her plate. "Let me help you clean up."

"No, no, there's nothing to do. I'll return a few things to the refrigerator. You go sit. Turn on the TV and find what you want to watch. *Voyager* is on Netflix." He gestured at her empty wineglass. "Can I get you a refill?"

"Thanks, no, I'm perfectly full."

As she headed to the living area, she reflected on how the evening continued to feel very cozy and indulgent. Being hustled off to a big fluffy sofa so someone else could clean up, getting ready to watch a favorite TV show. There was a shelf in the living area that contained an old-school record player and a great many records. She leaned down to look at them. "I can see that you're not a Bette Midler fan—or a Britney Spears fan."

"But I am fond of American music."

"Jazz, it looks like." That was what he'd been listening to in the car while he waited for her in the church on Thanksgiving.

"Yes."

She wanted to ask him how that had happened, how an upper-crust European boy fallen on hard times who had grown up to be equerry to a king had become a jazz aficionado, but her phone rang. She glanced down. Tonya. "Oh, shoot. This is my boss. I have to take it."

"I can step out if you'd like privacy."

"No need." She picked up. "Hi."

"You were right about Brad."

She sat down with a thud. "Wow."

"We found months' worth of emails between him and Noar Graf. They started out coming from his CZT account, and they were above board. They became increasingly personal in nature, though, as they discovered interests in common. Then they stopped entirely, so we figured he had switched to a personal account except for emails that other people needed to be copied on. We were going to hire a forensic IT specialist, but then Dave"—that was the firm's IT guy—"figured out that Brad had his personal Gmail on his office computer, and it was set to stay signed in."

Fucking Brad. "What an idiot."

"Indeed. Although to be fair, he wasn't expecting to fall off that roof and not be back in the office for weeks. But it's all there in black-and-white. Honestly, I'm a little disappointed at how easy it was." She snorted. "Like, at least let me feel like a spy for a day?"

"Have you confronted Brad yet?" Matteo appeared at Cara's side with his eyebrows raised. She moved over to make room for him next to her on the sofa.

"No," Tonya said. "We're convening an external legal team tomorrow. We have more than enough to fire him, it's just a question of how far into criminal territory his actions go. It seems as though his plan—"

"I'm sorry to interrupt, but do you mind if I put you on speaker? I'm with Matteo Benz, the king's equerry, at the moment, and he might as well hear it directly from you."

"You trust him?"

"I do."

"All right."

Cara switched to speaker, performed introductions, and Tonya filled them in on what they'd learned from the emails. The plan had been for Noar to amass as many shares as he could. He would own them, but he and Brad were going fifty-fifty on their gains going forward. It didn't particularly seem like Noar was doing anything to drive down value, merely that they were counting on CZT's work to make the company more profitable. They'd even gone a ways toward pre-deciding what Brad's recommendations were going to be.

"Honestly, having read through these emails," Tonya said, "I'm not sure Noar Graf was smart enough to purposefully drive down the value of the company."

"I'd thought the same," Matteo said. "If he was dragging the company down, he was probably doing it without even trying."

The three of them shared a resigned laugh. "So you're firing Brad," Cara said, letting it really sink in.

"Unless you'd like to do it. You are his direct boss. We can probably work out a Zoom firing."

"No, no, go right ahead with my compliments."

"You spoke to the king today, yes?"

"Yes, but only about Noar, not about Brad."

"We'll need to take responsibility for our part in this—responsibility for Brad, basically. I think it's important that he hear from a partner."

"Of course. You want to fly in? We can set up a meeting." She looked at Matteo. "Right?"

"Of course," he said hurriedly. "I can arrange a meeting whenever you like."

"I don't think you need me to fly in," Tonya said.

"Okay," Cara said. "We'll set up a Zoom link."

"Actually, Cara, can you take me off speaker?"

"Sure." She made an apologetic face at Matteo as she did so.

"I was going to wait until you were back to tell you this—I was going to take you out to dinner and make a big fuss—but we were planning to offer you partnership in the new year."

Cara gasped, and tears appeared instantaneously in her eyes. She felt like someone had punched her. "What? What are you saying?"

She had alarmed Matteo. Fair enough. She had alarmed *herself*. Matteo moved closer and laid his hand on her forearm. She started to wave him off, to assure him that all was well, but actually, that hand on her forearm was helping. Its warmth and weight were anchoring her, tethering her to reality when she felt like she was about to float away.

Reality where she needed to say something in response to the bomb Tonya had dropped. All she could manage was a weak "But . . . I thought that was quite a ways off."

"You've been our top performer for years. Beyond that, you have all the qualities we look for: loyalty, judgment, leadership skills. And look what you uncovered!" Cara was trying to talk but making only vague squeaks, and Tonya laughed. "We can talk about it when you're back in town. I only raise it because it's relevant to the immediate circumstances. You can patch me into the meeting if you want, or you can handle it as you see fit."

"Was this why you were using the word *dickbag* the other day?"

"What?" Tonya sounded confused.

"You used the word *dickbag* several times. It seemed so . . . not like you."

She cracked up. "Right. Yeah, we're peers now. You'll be vesting into the company. We can talk about dickbags all we like."

"Does this mean I can travel less?"

"If you want to."

"I . . ." She *thought* she wanted to. That's what she'd always told everyone. That's what she'd told *herself*. After she made partner, she'd stop traveling so much, and she would do all the things. Buy the house. Have time for relationships.

Be still.

Aww, shit. Having the brass ring right there, so much sooner than she'd planned, was throwing her for a major loop.

"We can talk through details when you're back," Tonya was saying, and Cara worried that her internal freak-out was going to cause her to miss something important. She could freak out later.

"Right," she said. "Right."

"We've got meetings with lawyers all weekend, and they'll advise on if and how we're going to involve law enforcement. If you think you can hold off on updating the king, you might want to wait until I have more info for you."

"Okay." She was still squeaky. Her heart was hammering like she was climbing the hill to the palace at top speed. She cleared her throat. "Yes. Thank you so much, Tonya. I'm a bit overwhelmed with this news, but I'm thrilled."

"Is everything all right?" Matteo asked when she hung up, concern etched across his features.

She looked at his hand. It was still on her arm. He looked at his hand, too. He didn't move it.

"I've made partner." She could still hardly believe it.

His face lit up. "That's wonderful!"

And then, to her surprise, he hugged her.

Oh, shit. The tears that had been threatening were starting. She felt suddenly like a teenager again, reaching toward whatever was the next big thing: an A on a test, a summer job, a scholarship. Striving. Always striving. Always moving.

Now she could stop. She had what she'd always wanted. She'd thought she still had a good chunk of ladder to climb, but it turned out that she was already at the top rung.

Which made her cry?

No. She could not cry here, now, in front of Matteo. She needed to do something else, something that would forestall the crying.

"Congratulations," Matteo murmured, his mouth in her hair near her ear, and he was doing the low-voice thing again.

Yes. Here it was. The thing that was the opposite of crying.

She kissed him.

Chapter Thirteen

*C*ara Delaney was kissing him.

Cara Delaney was kissing him.

Matteo had never felt anything better. He was finally tasting her, after that maddeningly featherlight kiss by the fire, and she tasted *so* good. When she opened her mouth a little, he did, too, groaning when their tongues touched. The wet silk of her mouth was hot, and he let himself sink into it, surrendering as if to a hot spring. He felt that kiss *everywhere.* Perhaps he wasn't going to have to take the direct approach advised by Imogen after all. Although then he started to fret that Cara wasn't in her right mind.

With a great deal of effort, he pulled away. He was nothing if not accustomed to self-denial. "You don't know what you're doing."

Confusion washed over her face. "I only had one glass of wine. I'm not drunk."

"You might be drunk on good news."

He expected her to roll her eyes, but she laughed. Loudly. It echoed through the silent space, a long, delighted laugh that made his insides feel wobbly. He watched her with a sense of awe.

She was so uninhibited with her laughter. It made him wonder what she looked like when she came. "I *might* be drunk on good news," she finally said, "but I'm fairly certain that good news has no bearing on consent."

So she wanted to do this? There was only one way to find out. Really, Imogen had been right. Directness was best. He cleared his throat and tried to infuse his bearing with the seriousness called for by the situation. "Cara. I feel that you and I have come to a certain understanding. We've been calling it a truce, but I feel that it's evolved into quite a strong, and productive, alliance."

"Okay . . ." Her brow furrowed.

"Would you agree that our alliance has been characterized by a refreshing ability to speak openly with each other?"

She smirked. "Well, you *did* tell me you didn't like me on day one."

He chuckled. "Exactly. Which is why I feel comfortable asking you the question I'm about to ask."

"Okay . . ."

"Would you be interested in a casual sexual encounter?" He thought that direct question would have cleared things up, but when she didn't say anything, just blinked and looked as bewildered as ever, he added, by way of clarification, "With me."

She leaned closer, putting her face right near his, and one corner of her mouth quirked upward. "I'm pretty sure we were just *having* a casual sexual encounter before you started talking about it."

"Oh, yes. I see what you mean." His face heated. And then, heaven help him, she climbed on his lap, and *everything* heated. "Do I take this as a yes?"

"You take this as a yes." She undid the bottom button of his shirt, and he thought he might die.

"You don't think it's an ill-advised idea?" he rasped. "You don't think it will . . . complicate things?"

She paused in her unbuttoning. "Well, this is wildly unprofessional."

Oh. He hadn't been talking about that. He'd meant "it might complicate things" in the sense that one or both of them might develop feelings. But clearly she wasn't worried about that, so he resolved not to be, either.

"Sleeping with the client is generally frowned upon," she said even as she resumed her unbuttoning.

"I'm not the client," he said.

"That is a very good point." She pushed her blouse off her arms. She was wearing a black lace bra, heaven help him.

"I thought so. Morneau is the client. Or, I suppose, technically, it's the board of directors."

She reached around and unclasped the bra and let it slide off her shoulders, too. He entertained a momentary pang of regret that he hadn't gotten to look his fill at her wearing it, but he revised that thought immediately when presented with small, creamy, pink-tipped breasts. "Matteo, may I ask a favor of you?"

"Anything," he said, though one part of his mind was aware that promising things in the heat of the moment to a woman as smart as Cara Delaney was not a wise move.

"Shut up."

That he could do. He clamped his mouth shut and let her straddle him. She'd been sitting on his lap before, but she slid down and nestled herself right against him. He was already hard, a fact she seemed delighted by as she buried her face in the crook of his neck and ground against him.

He'd assumed they were going to kiss some more, but she seemed to be breathing against his neck. He hadn't known such a thing could be so . . . enjoyable. He slid his hands up her bare back as he let his lips brush her shoulder.

"You smell good," she said, speaking against his neck, and he felt as absurdly proud as if she'd complimented him on an actual skill. "I don't want to stop smelling you."

"Then by all means, carry on."

She started working on his tie, and though he'd always been quite comfortable in his clothing, he suddenly felt like he was suffocating. He batted her hands away—she was struggling to loosen his double four-in-hand knot—and made quick work of the tie while she held her hands up as if he were threatening her. *Him* threatening *her*. It was absurd.

"What's so funny?" she asked.

"Everything. This. You. Us."

She scowled. "Funny like 'Ha-ha' or funny like 'I never would have predicted it'?"

"The latter. Funny like 'Dear god, this is going to be amazing.'"

That charmed her, though he'd been in earnest. Finishing with his buttons, he shuffled around until he could get his shirt off his arms.

She poked him in the chest. "You are surprisingly fit."

"I move a lot of boxes." Especially this year, with Torkel gone.

"You move a lot of boxes?"

He had said too much. Happily, there was a way to deflect from that fact. He put his hands on her cheeks and pulled her head down and kissed her again. Kissed her senseless. Kissed *himself* senseless. So much so that when she started to pull away, he held on and grunted like a caveman. How appalling. The noise snapped him back to his senses, and he let go. He was relieved to discover that she had initiated the break so she could take her pants off. And she was hitching her head at his like she wanted him to do the same, and to be quick about it.

He did, and he was.

When she was back on his lap—she was on his lap!—he felt as though he should warn her. "I have to tell you that it has, ah, been a while for me."

"For me, too."

"*Really?*" All right, that had come out sounding entirely too delighted. But he couldn't help it. He had seen her upstairs—alone—after her dinner with Bashir Hussein, but he had no idea what had happened with Johannes Miller after the darts game.

"You're wondering about Johannes Miller," she said, reading his mind.

He dipped his head. "Not that it's any of my business."

"Not that it's any of your business," she echoed tartly. "But he was . . . Well, he was not the smartest goat in the herd. We said good night shortly after you saw us." She made a self-deprecating face. "So it's been a while."

"Still, I'm almost certain my version of 'a while' is longer than yours."

"What are we talking about here?"

"Five years."

"Wow." She wasn't saying that in a mocking way, more as though she was impressed.

"Yes, I've been . . ." She let her hand drift down his chest, and he emitted a strangling noise. "Busy with work. Which I . . ." The hand was drifting lower, and he thought he might die. Might actually go into cardiac arrest right here with Cara on his lap. Well, there were worse ways to go. "Which I mention only to warn you that, to my great embarrassment, things might move rather . . . rapidly if you—"

He'd been trying to say that he didn't want her to touch him yet. He wanted to pay her some attention first, but she interrupted him. Her hand had made its way down to his penis, and she took him in hand. "If I do this?"

"Cara," he warned, and oh god, his penis had a mind of its own.

"Or maybe this?" She squeezed experimentally.

He'd thought himself fully hard, maximally erect, but she managed to coax him to heretofore unheard of degrees of arousal.

"Or how about this?" She kept up the pressure, but pumped her hand, and he groaned. The sight alone, of her red-lacquered fingers moving up and down, was nearly enough to do him in.

"Matteo," she whispered, leaning forward so her breasts grazed his chest, even as her hand kept working. "I like this idea of you surrendering your famous control."

He was trying not to. He was trying *so very hard*.

"Of you going from zero to sixty so fast you don't even know what hit you." She let loose a noise that was half evil cackle, half delighted laugh.

Hold on, he urged himself.

"Don't worry about it," she soothed, dropping an absurdly tender kiss on his temple. "I'll get mine later. You just let go."

So he did, throwing his head back and shouting as he came in her hands like a school boy, but dear god, as his body heaved and shuddered, it felt like . . . relief. Like stepping into a hot pool in the cold winter air. Like that, but more.

When he opened his eyes, he half expected her to be gone. For this to have been a fever dream. But there she was, smirking at him as if she had defeated him, and he supposed in a way, she had.

But that wouldn't stand. She would, as she'd said, get hers. He was going to see to it immediately.

He shuffled her off him and guided her to lie back on the sofa. She started talking, and he didn't want that now, so he covered her mouth with his, even as he let his hand drift down her body.

He found her wet and, he thought, ready. So without wasting any time, he stopped kissing her—that kiss had achieved its aim in getting her to be quiet—and moved down and replaced his hand with his mouth.

"Oh my god!" she gasped in what sounded like a mixture of shock and pleasure. He would allow that kind of talking.

He threw one of her legs over his shoulder and started licking her, stopping just long enough to murmur, against her throbbing flesh, "I would like you to let go, too, Cara."

To his great satisfaction, she did. She shouted, and her flesh started fluttering beneath his lips. He'd been content— delighted—to settle in for a while, and he hoped he would get such an opportunity later, but for now, he lifted his head, shot her a smirk, and said, "Well then."

AFTERWARD, HE SAT up, pulled Cara's legs into his lap, and started running the fingers of his other hand up and down one of her calves.

She wanted him to stop.

Well, she didn't. The featherlight touch was doing something to her as her breath returned to normal. It was creating a slow pooling of warmth inside her. It reminded her of the feeling she'd gotten after coming off the snow at the spa. She was suffused with relaxation and goodwill. Though to be fair, that was probably from the orgasm.

And holy hell, had that been an orgasm. She tried to tell herself that it had been so intense because it had been a while for her. Not Matteo's five years, but at least that many months. But she was pretty sure the quality of that orgasm had been about the person delivering it.

With his mouth.

Which was another reason she shouldn't be worked up about his stroking her leg now. This was nothing.

And yet . . .

Beyond the physical sensations his touch was stirring up, it was also . . . tender. She didn't do tender. She couldn't lie here and let someone touch her like that with affection and gentleness when there was no *point* to it. And he wasn't giving her a massage or doing anything else productive with that hand. There was no *objective* here.

So, as good as it felt, she pretended she needed to stretch, extended her arms above her head, and righted herself so she was sitting next to him. The yawn that followed was real.

He stared at her and, after a moment, extended his arm and resumed stroking her, this time on her upper arm. It seemed almost mindless, like he wasn't aware of it.

Maybe he wasn't. Maybe all she'd been reading into it—tenderness and all that crap—wasn't really there.

"Can you . . . not do that?" She nodded at his hand, which he immediately retracted.

"My apologies," he said quickly, and something in his face shuttered.

"No problem," she said, pierced with a sudden, sharp guilt that she'd insulted him, or rejected him, or . . . something. "I'm just ticklish," she added, acutely aware that lying to spare a man's feelings was not something she had ever done before.

"Should we . . . discuss this?" he asked, scooching a little farther away from her and grabbing his shirt—it seemed he had truly gotten the message, and she continued to feel an odd sort of regret, even though that was exactly what she'd wanted.

"You mean like, what the hell this is, and is it going to happen again?" She was about to go in search of her own shirt, but he tossed her a quilt he had folded over the back of the sofa, and she wrapped it around herself instead.

"Yes. Both those things."

He seemed to be waiting for her to weigh in. "Well, on the last question, I hope it is going to happen again."

If his face had shuttered before, now it looked like someone had let a little light in. "You do?"

"I do, but only if we can answer the first satisfactorily."

"What this is . . ." He trailed off. "What is this?"

"You tell me."

"Well, I suppose it's a time-limited affair. How would you characterize it?"

"I was going to say a hookup, but your way sounds posher." She put on an exaggerated fancy accent. "A time-limited affair." She reverted to her normal voice. "Whatever we're calling it, I'm in, as long as it doesn't upend things."

"Well, you're headed back home in a matter of days."

"Professionally. I meant it can't upend things professionally."

"Right. Of course. That goes without saying. We simply need to cordon off our activities from the business of Morneau."

He made it sound so easy. Which it was. All right. What next? Should they shake on it? Last time they shook hands had been in the spa, and that had been very . . . unsettling.

"We also need condoms," he said, his eyes twinkling for a moment before his expression turned serious. "Assuming you would like to do things that require condoms."

"I would like to do things that require condoms," she said, so quickly it made them both laugh.

"It's a date."

It actually was this time. Sort of.

"This will sound like a non sequitur, but you haven't seen the bathroom yet. I have quite a nice bathtub, if I do say so myself. Would you care to avail yourself of it before you leave?"

Before she left.

So that meant he expected her to leave.

Which was fine.

It was good! It was tangible evidence that they were on the same page about the nature of the time-limited affair.

She just might have thought, given that it was late, and that they had sleigh-riding plans tomorrow morning, he would suggest she stay over. She was perfectly capable of doing that and not having it mean anything. But his way was better. Cleaner. "I would love to avail myself of your bathtub before I go, thank you."

He pointed at a pair of sliding, barn-style doors on one end of the loftlike space. "It's the left door. There are towels in the cabinet under the sink, and in the shower you'll find some body wash that may work as bubble bath if that's of interest."

Okay, then. His meaning couldn't be any clearer. Time to get out of the dude's bed. Sofa. She hadn't been in the bed yet. She eyed it. It looked really comfy.

"Would you like me to bring you a cup of tea once you get settled? Or perhaps another glass of wine? I'll drop it off and go, and leave you to enjoy your bath."

Man, this guy was too much. But she was going to enjoy it while she had it. "A cup of tea would be wonderful, thank you."

His phone rang. "I'm sorry, I have to take this. I'll be in with your tea in a bit." He got up and left through the front door. She heard him say, "What happened to the geese?" as he shut it behind him, and she smiled. The life of an equerry.

She heaved herself up and headed for the bathroom. Except she slid open the wrong door. It was a storage closet. Oddly, it was full of books and candles. The books were all in French or German, but she could tell there were a variety of types here—novels and picture books and cookbooks.

She picked up the nearest candle. She couldn't read what was written on it, but she gave it a sniff. Cranberry. The next one was cinnamon.

Oh my god! Was Matteo the mysterious Eldovian Santa?

No. She disregarded the idea as soon as it came up. While helping people anonymously was exactly in his nature, there was no way he had time. And anyway, he spent Christmas Eve at the ball.

She thought back to Bashir, the school principal, saying that Matteo had been such a help with many of his students. The books were probably related to that. The candles, though . . . Well, who knew? Maybe he gave them to visiting dignitaries—a token from the land of Christmas. She headed for the tub. His bathroom was plain but fancy, if that was a thing. The floor and walls were white marble, but with subtle gray veining. The tub was porcelain, a freestanding soaker with a sloped back. A vanity ran the length of one wall and was made of smooth dark wood. She opened one of the cabinets in search of a towel and found instead his stash of man products. Her attention was drawn to a small bottle that read *"Menthe Fraîche."* Ah, that had to be the source of his minty smell. She picked it up and spritzed a little on her wrist. Yep. That was him. She took another whiff. It smelled less complex, though, straight from the bottle. She sniffed again, but then she worried that he would arrive with her tea to find her trying on his cologne, or worse, *smelling* like his cologne. So she started the bath, and as it began filling, stuck her wrist under the hot water and scrubbed.

She needn't have worried. The gel she grabbed from his shower stall was also minty—a kind of warm, gingery mint, and he'd given her the go-ahead to use it. It did work as bubble bath, and the result, as she sank gratefully into the hot water, was divine.

She was almost asleep when he knocked. "May I come in with your tea?"

"Yes, thank you!" she called, grateful that the surface of the water was covered with bubbles. She wasn't sure why she was sud-denly shy. He'd seen it all just a while ago. Like, extremely up close.

He came in, set the tea on the vanity, and produced a tray from another cupboard. It was one of those ones meant to lay over a bathtub, and she couldn't help but emit an appreciative "Ahh," when he laid it in front of her. "Thank you."

"You're quite welcome." He paused, and his eyes snagged on her chest. Her hand instinctively went to the spot she knew he was looking at, on the side curve of her left breast, almost in her armpit. As if, after all these years, she could protect it.

"You have a tattoo. I noticed it while you were disrobing."

He probably didn't approve. "Yes. It's in a spot where it's almost always covered by my clothing."

"I admit I was surprised by it. At first I thought it was a mole."

"I don't seem the tattoo type?"

"No, you do. I'm surprised by that particular design. I would have thought you'd have . . ." He looked at the ceiling as if trying to conjure an image.

"Flowers? Butterflies?" She tried not to make her scoffing too overt.

"No. This, perhaps." He raised his hand in the Vulcan "live long and prosper" salute, and she laughed. "Or perhaps that Starfleet insignia they have on their uniforms?" he suggested, smiling along with her. "It's almost the right spot for that."

What possessed her to tell him the truth, she would never know. She'd never told *anyone* the truth. All she could think was that he was making to leave the room, and she wanted him to stay. She wanted to keep talking—to him. "When I was seventeen I was . . ." It was hard to say, to put the correct words to it. As she trailed off, he turned, shot her a questioning gaze. "Well, I was attacked, I suppose, by a boy I had a crush on." His eyebrows shot up, and something happened to his face. She waited for him to object, to exclaim, to do or say something to interrupt her narrative, but he did not. He leaned back against the vanity as if settling in for a while. He was going to stay. She was relieved. "There was a scuffle. I was trying to get him off me, and he scratched me here." She gestured to the small image. The Star Trek insignia would actually have been a great idea. "There was a scar. Not a deep one, and it probably would have faded eventually, but I couldn't stand looking at it, so I had this tattooed over it."

"A shoe."

She smiled. "Yes. I was wearing a very high heel at the time, and I took it off and stabbed him with it."

A bark of triumphant-sounding laughter escaped Matteo, but he quickly sobered and returned his attention to her. His commitment to letting her tell her story on her own terms was refreshing. But there wasn't that much more to tell. "It disarmed him enough that I could get away. And I lost my shoe! It was just a cheap shoe from Famous Footwear, but money was so tight in our house, and I had splurged on it for a dance we were attending. So, I don't know, I decided to memorialize it. The shoe that saved me."

He surprised her by coming back over, sinking to the floor, and resting his arms on the edge of the tub so they were face to face. "It sounds more like you saved you."

That was such a generous thing to say, and absurdly, it made her throat tighten with unshed tears.

"I find myself at a loss for words," he said. "I am sorry that happened to you."

"I'm not. I mean, I am. But I got away before he could hurt me." Matteo winced. It was the truth, though. "I look back on it now as a formative incident. It made me who I am. I'm always prepared now."

"You do seem fond of extremely high heels." He smiled to show he was teasing. "Still, I'm very sorry."

"It's not that uncommon a story, I'm sure," she said, suddenly wanting to deflect his earnest concern. "Lots of girls find themselves in these kinds of situations."

"Which must also mean lots of boys find themselves in these kinds of situations."

"Right, but it isn't formative for them. For them, it's just entitlement. Taking what's theirs."

"Whereas for you, what? It made you harder?"

"I was born hard." She'd meant it as a joke—even though it was true—but he didn't laugh, or even smile, this time. "It's more that it made me smart. I didn't experience it as a terrible trauma. It gave me a burst of self-confidence, a sense that I could do anything. It taught me that I can rely on myself. I'm not going to say that I'm glad it happened . . . but it did give me something valuable."

He still didn't smile, or speak—or anything. She had said too much. She'd told him this weird, personal story that didn't fit in with what they were doing here. This was a fling, and here she was trotting out her teenage sob story. Time to change the subject. "Well," she said with artificial cheer, "we should talk about when we're going to tell the king about Brad. CZT is meeting with lawyers this weekend, and they may end up calling the cops. Can we wait until after that, do you think, or should we talk to him tomorrow?"

"Why don't I make arrangements for us to speak to him first thing Monday morning? We can move that up if need be, but if neither Noar nor Brad know anyone's onto them, I'd rather wait and present the king with as much information as possible." He shot her a smile. "That way you can have your Eldovian Christmas weekend." He paused. "If you still want to."

"I still want to." She wanted it desperately, which made her a little wary.

She thought back to the night she'd weaponized her shoe. As she'd told Matteo, the incident had given her an injection of self-confidence. If she could save herself then, she'd reasoned, she could keep doing it. That confidence was what had made her so ambitious, had led to the scholarships, the army, the job, the house. It had been like a low-humming motor always on in the background.

And now she had realized the ultimate achievement—partnership at CZT.

So why did she feel so underwhelmed?

She must have been lost in her thoughts for too long. He shifted as if making to stand—which was entirely reasonable as he had proposed the bath as an indulgent, solo activity. That's what baths were. But she still didn't want him to leave. His hands were on the edge of the tub—he was using it to lever himself up—and before she could overthink it, she rested her hand on his forearm. "Stay with me awhile?"

He looked startled, then pleased. "It would be my pleasure."

Chapter Fourteen

Four days until Christmas

The next morning, walking up the hill to meet Matteo at the appointed time for her sleigh ride—*her sleigh ride!*—Cara was feeling less vulnerable. And smarter about what had happened last night. She'd been literally naked in a tub and she'd told Matteo some stuff she'd never told anyone. Of course she'd been feeling weird. She'd exposed herself in every way. And while that was not typical for her, she was chalking it up to the shock of the news of making partner and to the stress of the whole Brad-Noar-Morneau situation.

She'd spent the morning finalizing her report to the Morneau board, so she was feeling more confident. She was also dressed.

Though she hoped to be undressed later.

Which was a bit confusing.

"Cara!"

There he was, emerging from the ground floor of the stable

building, all pink-cheeked and bundled up, looking like an advertisement for Eldovia. "Good morning," he said when they met at the bottom of the steps. "The horses should be along shortly." He looked over her shoulder as he spoke. "Ah, yes, right on time."

She turned around, and sure enough, there was a woman leading a pair of horses. They were red-tinged dark-brown with even darker brown manes, and honestly, she was a little scared of them. She'd never seen a horse up close, and these seemed bigger than she would have imagined.

"Cara, meet Hilda, one of the palace grooms." She nodded at the young woman. "And may I also present Muskatnuss and Zimt— that's Nutmeg and Cinnamon—a fine pair of Hanoverians."

"Nice to meet you," she said feebly, belatedly realizing that she probably wasn't meant to actually speak to the horses.

Hilda gave over the horses' leads to Matteo and what followed was yet another display of his easy competence. He hooked up the horses to the sleigh and led her to a mounting station of sorts.

The sleigh was really something. It had metal blades that curled up at the ends, just like her mental image of a sleigh. The body of it was red, and the side was painted with what she'd come to recognize as the royal coat of arms. There was a bench up front, which Matteo helped her onto before climbing in next to her. Behind them was an open area, lined with benches around the perimeter. It was from there that Matteo retrieved a heavy wool blanket, which he settled over her lap. "Ready?"

"Ready." She was grinning like an idiot. She could feel it. But she couldn't seem to stop. Matteo made some kind of giddy-up noise and flicked the reins, and the sleigh creaked into motion, the blades making a slicing noise over the snow, which was tightly packed here on the palace grounds. And, oh lord, the horses had jingle bells around their necks.

It should have been too much.

When she was little, her dad used to take her to the Central Park carousel. There had been a period of about a year while her mom was in the process of being diagnosed with rheumatoid arthritis—when her mysterious episodes of pain and stiffness didn't yet have a name—when she spent a lot of time being poked and prodded at Mount Sinai West hospital. Dad and Cara would take the train in with her, drop her off, and walk to the park. Even though those had been somber times, Cara still remembered the liberating feeling of getting on that carousel. Part of it was the splurge. Her parents never spent money on things that weren't necessities. So to have her dad hand over cash for something so frivolous and fleeting as a carousel ride felt like the peak of indulgence. And then there was the actual ride. The novelty of it, the *thrill* of it. The swooping of those horses, the gathering of speed as the ride started.

This felt like that. The snorting of the horses and the whishing of the blades on the squeaky snow. The crisp, pine-scented air, and the coziness of having a heavy blanket on her lap. It was exhilarating. As they picked up speed, she let loose what could only be called a giggle of delight, though Cara didn't like to think of herself as the kind of person who giggled—in delight or for any other reason.

"Well, if I'd known all I needed to do to crack your serious facade was to take you on a sleigh ride, I'd have done it straight away."

She decided to pay him a compliment. "Do you think it's the

sleigh ride that's making me happy, or do you think it's the residue of last night's mind-blowing orgasm?"

He looked down and away, but she caught him grinning. He was embarrassed and pleased in equal measures, she thought.

"No regrets by the harsh light of day?" he asked.

"None whatsoever."

"Well then. Let's not be too long with this little outing."

IT WAS AN ideal day for a sleigh ride. Cold but clear, the sun beat down on them. When they reached the spot Matteo had thought would make a pleasant setting for lunch, he hopped out. "Stay put for a moment, will you?"

Cara nodded, and he had to tear his gaze from her in order to see to the horses. She looked so happy.

And happy looked so good on her.

She'd done her hair in a single, long braid down her back, and it was making him a little crazy. It was the in-between-ness of it. It wasn't her familiar, formal work coiffure, but it also wasn't the messy, free-flowing hair he'd seen last night. It was something else, something casual that felt *more* intimate, somehow, than the postcoital hair had. As if this was how she'd do her hair for a day of leisure with someone she knew well, someone she wasn't trying to impress. Someone she trusted.

Oh, how he yearned to be that person.

And, oh, how alarming that yearning was if he thought about it too much.

So he didn't think about it. He got out the picnic basket and laid out a waterproof mat before coming back to offer Cara a hand—without the block they used to mount the sleigh at the palace, it was a long way down. He ended up sort of swinging her down, and it was all he could do not to *keep* swinging her, to twirl her around as if they were in a movie.

She made appreciative noises as he unpacked the lunch he'd ordered from the palace kitchen. It was merely an array of finger foods—cheeses and cold meats, nuts and dried fruits, tarts for dessert—but she seemed to find it all delightful.

"Before you eat," he said as she filled her plate, "I thought we should toast your promotion." He produced a half bottle of Champagne and raised his eyebrows inquiringly. "I know you're not much of a drinker. I also have sparkling mineral water, if you'd prefer."

"You think of everything, don't you?"

"It's my job."

It was the wrong thing to say, judging by the way her face shuttered, though he wasn't sure why. In the past, she'd complimented him on his thoroughness.

"What an incredible view," she said after a few moments of silence. They were at a lookout about halfway down the hill the palace was situated on. It had been cleared of trees, and there was a view across to the next peak. "What is that?"

"That's a small ski run. Most of the skiing in Eldovia is on the other side of the mountain, but there's a nice little hill over there."

"That doesn't look like a hill to me," she said with what struck him as artificial cheer. "It looks like a near vertical chunk of mountain."

"Ah, yes, you're not a skier. Have you ever tried?"

She didn't answer. She was back to looking shuttered. That was the only word he could think of to describe it. It wasn't the anger or annoyance he'd seen in her earlier in her time here, but something was wrong. "Will you tell me what is troubling you?"

"I went to an elite private high school in New York."

"All right."

"I got a scholarship."

"That's . . . good." It was, yes?

"It paid for my tuition, but my parents killed themselves paying for everything else—uniforms, books. It was the kind of school where the drama teacher didn't think twice about asking everyone to come up with their own costumes, for example. I don't think my parents realized how expensive that school was going to be, even with a full scholarship. They usually made it work when stuff like that came up. They never wanted me to know how tight things were, but I knew."

"Children usually do." He knew that from both his own teen years, when his parents' marriage had been falling apart, and from his current work with families in need.

"Anyway, the senior class went on a trip every year in February. It was usually somewhere drivable, which was the only reason I was entertaining going. We had a bus fee, but that was manageable. But my year voted on a ski trip upstate, at a resort in Lake Placid."

Ah. He saw immediately what the issue with skiing was.

"I'd budgeted for the bus and the accommodations, but they wanted another two hundred bucks to rent skis and for lessons and for the . . . whatever you call it, the slope pass thing. That was not going to happen."

"Of course not."

"The stupid thing was, it never occurred to anyone—the kids, their parents, any teachers—that that might be inaccessible for someone like me. Two hundred dollars was pocket change for these people. Probably they would have 'fundraised' for me if I'd pointed out how inaccessible the trip was. They did that once, when a debate team I was on went to a national competition in California. It was mortifying. No way I was letting that happen again. Alternatively, my parents probably would have come up with the money. They sometimes took cash out against their credit cards to pay for stuff, or went to one of those payday loan places where they advance you money but you have to pay it back with usurious interest rates. That wasn't happening, either."

"Of course not." He would have felt exactly the same in her place. "So you didn't go?"

"I had enough money saved for the bus and the room, so I did go, but . . ." She rolled her eyes. "I pretended to sprain my ankle a few days before. I'd found a pair of crutches at Goodwill. So I went on the trip but I had an excuse not to ski."

"I'd say that's rather ingenious."

"I'd say it's rather pathetic. I should have told them to take their trip and shove it."

"My mother doesn't ski. I can remember trips, in more prosperous times before my father left, when we'd all go to a ski resort. My father and siblings and I would ski, and my mother would visit the spa and drink hot toddies by the fire and read. She used to joke about how much she loved not skiing on ski trips."

"I can see that being a great time with your family, but this trip was a disaster from start to finish. Remember the tattoo?"

She laid her palm over her chest at the spot where the little high-heel tattoo was, and his whole body tensed, as if it some-how knew he wasn't going to like what she said next. "I do," he said carefully. As if he could forget. The image of her sprawled languorously in his bathtub was going to be burned into his brain for all time.

"That story was from this trip. There was a formal dinner the last night. We were supposed to dress up. The boys had suits; the girls wore dresses. Because I was seventeen and stupid, I went to the dinner with my 'cast' on one foot and a high heel on the other."

He could see it. He wanted to ask her if she'd worn her hair up in those days, too, but he didn't want to interrupt what was clearly a story she needed to tell—and a story he very much wanted to hear.

"There was this guy I liked." She rolled her eyes again. "We'd been flirting at school, and on the trip. He invited me to his room after the dinner and . . ." She made a "hurry up" gesture. "You know the rest."

"Is the rest that he attacked you, and you stabbed him with your high heel?" he asked, alarmed.

She blew out a breath he took to mean *yes*. "It was complicated by the fact that I was willingly making out with him. I just didn't want it to go any further than that. I was still very Catholic in those years."

"I don't think your willing participation up to a certain point complicates matters whatsoever."

"Well, now that we live in the Me Too era and we're all en-lightened, we know it doesn't. But *he* didn't know that. And more to the point, *I* didn't know that. I felt terrible when I first started pushing him away. Like it was my fault. I was apologizing, even, if you can believe it. But then things started to get ugly, and instinct kicked in. I grabbed my shoe and stuck it into his thigh."

Matteo thought for a moment that she was about to cry. She was pressing her lips together rather fiercely and her shoulders had risen in such a way that it looked like she was bracing herself.

"Cara." He laid his hand on her shoulder, at a loss for how to comfort her.

She relaxed a bit, leaning into his touch. Perhaps he didn't have to say anything. Perhaps his presence was enough. The thought was buoying. Matteo was used to being needed, but not like this. "It was all pretty terrible, but you should have heard the sound he made," she said, sounding more like herself. She gave a little snort of laughter. "And then he couldn't ski the next day, either, but he couldn't tell anyone what had happened."

"That's a bit of poetic justice."

"Yeah. That part was actually kind of amusing. I know I was supposed to experience it all as a big trauma. It *was* upsetting. But it was also a little bit funny, the next day anyway."

"I think it can be both."

"Both upsetting and funny?"

"Yes."

"You know, you are kind of smart sometimes."

"Sometimes!" he teased, wanting to lighten the mood. He sensed she wanted to be done talking about this.

He was wrong. She turned thoughtful. "It's funny. I never think about skiing. It doesn't come up that much in New York City. And I would have said I was over the whole thing, that even if it was traumatic, it was firmly in my past. But I think that might have been a lie. Because why else did I flip out so thoroughly when any of you mentioned skiing?"

"To be fair, I don't think you flipped out. You communicated that you had no interest in skiing, but I didn't see any flipping out."

"I flipped out internally."

"I think sometimes the burdens that we carry around are invisible even to ourselves."

She looked at him with what seemed an awful lot like tenderness, and said, "Okay, you're smart more than sometimes. You're smart a lot of the time."

"What was this boy's name?" he asked, though he wasn't sure why. It wasn't as if he was going to activate his network and have the man murdered, though part of him wanted to do exactly that.

"His name was Brad!"

"Truly?"

"Truly. Except he wasn't Bradley; he was Bradford. Bradford Worthington III."

"I must say, you do seem to be rather persecuted by Brads."

"Well, this one definitely put me off dating for a long time."

"But you eventually did date?"

"A bit, in college. I was inexplicably popular there."

He was certain her popularity was explicable. "But nothing stuck?"

"No. Guys don't want me." He wanted to object, but she didn't seem upset. It was more that she was stating an unremarkable fact. "They want some version of me that is less ambitious, less brittle, and more . . . malleable. Softer. They want the ballet-pink-nails girl."

He wanted to say that "they" were misguided, that they didn't know what they were missing, but she wouldn't want to hear that. She wouldn't want him to be affronted by her dating history.

"Which is fine," she went on, "because I don't want them, either. Not now. Maybe later in my career, when I . . ."

He was fairly certain she'd been going to say she might have time for dating once she'd made partner and that she'd only belatedly remembered that she *was* a partner.

She looked distressed, so he tried to shift the conversation away from her, wanting to share some of himself in return for her being so forthcoming. "I, too, have found dating a challenge."

"Yes. I gather it's been five years?"

"My last girlfriend was in the army with me. We rubbed along well enough, but it was clear that to her, I was a convenience rather than a long-term prospect, and I'm afraid I rather felt the same."

"Was she the one who gave you the Rilke poems?"

"I beg your pardon?"

"You mentioned that your father had gambled away a first-edition Rilke that had been given to you by someone you admired."

That seemed an odd thing for her to bring up, but he didn't mind answering. He liked that Cara was interested in his life. "That volume was from a teacher of mine. He was the best teacher I ever had. Not to sound too melodramatic, but he changed my way of looking at the world. And he was a constant during a time of upheaval. We kept in touch after I went off to university. He left the Rilke to me in his will, if you can believe it."

She tilted her head and looked at him intensely, in that way she had that made it feel like she was trying to see into his soul. "May I ask you a question?"

"Of course."

"Did you by chance get any condoms? Do you have any condoms at your apartment right now?"

The question jolted him—in a good way. "I did, and I do." He had gone to the village specifically to get some this morning.

When she didn't say anything more, he shot her a wink. "So what exactly are you saying, Ms. Delaney?"

"You're smart, Mr. Benz, you can figure it out."

The bantery reversion to last names felt playful. An interpretation that was ratified when she threw a handful of snow at his head.

"Ah!" He sputtered theatrically. "Now you're in trouble."

She scrambled to her feet and ran. He followed, catching up as she reached the sleigh. She turned, and he slowed his approach but didn't stop until he was right in her space. He lifted the handful of snow he was carrying and held it over her head, a joking threat. But when she reached up, wound her arms around his neck, and pulled his head down to her level, he forgot all about his planned retaliation. Her cheeks were pink, her grin was wide, and her hat was askew. She pressed one mittened hand on each cheek, planted a kiss on his lips that was way too short, and said, "Let's get these sleigh bells jingling."

AFTER THEY HANDED the horses and sleigh over to Hilda, Matteo suggested they retire to Cara's room at the pub rather than to his apartment. He had two reasons for doing so. One, he'd had the recovered panettone delivered this morning, and his apartment was covered with boxes of cake. Two, he had to take delivery of forty-seven geese in the village at four o'clock this afternoon, and it would be easier to extricate himself from Cara's room in order to do so than to eject her from his apartment. He had barely managed to make himself do that last night.

He gave a momentary thought to telling her about his side job. They'd told each other a great deal, and while she would probably tease him, he had no doubt that she would keep his secret. And she didn't live in Eldovia, so he wouldn't have to worry about anyone else finding out from her in coming years. What's more, she didn't meet the criteria for a basket—she wasn't in need of any Christmas magic—so preserving the mystery didn't matter.

In the end, he couldn't quite do it. He and Kai and Torkel had spent years being so secretive that Matteo had trouble dropping the subterfuge.

"But do *you* have condoms?" he asked as he parked near the pub, belatedly realizing the flaw in his plan to move the . . . action to her house. "I can pop over to the pharmacy and get some if need be."

"I have some in my room." She quirked a smile. "I like to be prepared when I travel."

"And here I thought you were all about packing light."

"I'm about packing smart. And I only ever have sex when I travel." His face must have betrayed *something*—he wasn't even sure how he felt about what she'd said—because she added, "Less messy that way." He was tempted to ask her how she was going to square that philosophy with the fact that she supposedly wanted to travel less now that she'd made partner at CZT. But he refrained. If she wanted things not messy, she wasn't going to welcome that line of questioning from him.

"Have you a key for the back door?" he asked as they approached the Owl and Spruce. He gathered that Imogen gave such keys to guests.

"You want to sneak in, do you?"

He wasn't sure how to respond. He didn't want her to think he was trying to hide their . . . relationship. Or whatever it was. But on the other hand, that was exactly what he was trying to do.

Before he could think what to say, she winked, pulled a key from her pocket, and led him around to the back of the building.

They almost encountered Imogen on the way up. They heard her talking as she came from the kitchen, and Cara grabbed his hand and they bolted up the stairs before Imogen emerged. Cara must have been trying to stifle laughter as they ran. Halfway up, a great deal of it burst out of her. It infected him, and by the time they clattered to a halt at her door, they were both breathless with laughter.

It was a strange sensation, both the laughter and this feeling he'd been noting recently of being in league with someone. Of sharing a secret, a jest. It felt in that moment as if he and Cara were allied not just against Noar and the evil Brads of the world . . . but against everything. That they were a unit of two.

He didn't have too much time to expand on that thought, though. She pulled him into the room, slammed the door, pressed him back against it, and kissed him. His last thought, before he lost himself in her, was that losing himself in her was an alarmingly easy thing to do.

They kissed for a long time. Eventually, she grew agitated— with the height difference between them, he thought at first, or perhaps it was the fact that they were still clothed. She was cycling between lifting herself up onto her tiptoes and pasting herself against him and pulling away and making progress in removing their clothing. She would grind herself against him and kiss him for a while, then make a frustrated noise, break away from him, and yank his shirt out from his waistband. Then she'd be back, but just as he was adjusting his body against hers, she would pull away and start working on his shirt buttons.

The back and forth was making him mad with desire—and frustration. "Cara," he muttered, trying to keep her off him. Not that he wanted her off him, not in any elemental way, but he'd be damned if this encounter went as quickly as the last one. "You've got to slow down."

Her eyes narrowed. "I do not."

"You do." He put his hands on her shoulders and, keeping several feet of distance between them, steered her to sit on the bed.

"But—"

"I insist."

She didn't object anymore, probably because he'd gently pushed her down onto her back and reached for the waistband of her pants. They were a soft, athletic variety, and he easily slid them off when she lifted her hips to assist.

With those off, she was splayed out before him, completely naked. He wanted to say that she was beautiful. That every part of her was: her perfect skin and the tattoo on it that covered a complicated scar. Her hair that could be so tightly coiled around her head, like a snake ready to strike, and the brain inside that head that could strike like a snake, too. There was a reason he'd thought of her as a warrior from day one.

He didn't say any of those things. Something caught in his throat. Oddly, he, still dressed, felt more vulnerable than she looked.

She wouldn't want to hear any of his thoughts. They didn't belong in this context. Like him in general, they were too serious.

It was possible he wasn't so good at this time-limited affair business.

"The condoms are in the top drawer of the dresser," she said, her voice a whisper, but one that echoed around the room, and around his chest, like thunder.

Right. He might not be good at this time-limited affair business, but that didn't mean he was going to stop trying.

He took his time fetching the condom, and removing the rest of his clothing. By the time he'd done all that, his penis had calmed down somewhat.

But then when he turned around to find her grinning at him as she undid her braid, it perked right back up. He groaned. At what, exactly, he wasn't sure. Perhaps at how much he was trying to be in control and how badly he was failing.

"What kinds of boxes do you move?"

The word that rose in his mind in response to that perplexing question was the dreaded "Huh?"

"You said yesterday that you move a lot of boxes. That that's how you got your sexy arm muscles."

Dumbly, he looked down at his arms. She thought they were sexy? He could feel his face heating. He also could not answer her question without giving himself away. "Sometimes at events there are last-minute details that get overlooked."

"Last-minute details in boxes?"

"Yes." He tilted his head and regarded her. "Is this really what you want to be talking about right now?"

She dipped her head as if to concede his point. Then she crooked her finger at him, and, powerless against the angel of doom, he went.

It turned out that kissing Cara while horizontal and divested of all clothing was the greatest thing he had ever done.

"Oh my god," he mumbled as he took a breast in one hand while they plundered each other's mouths. It was a revelation, how soft she was. But then as his other hand found her lean thigh and slid upward, how taut she was.

Her hands, which had been clutching at his back, started migrating southward. He wasn't having that, so he let go of her hardness and softness alike and intercepted her. Threading their hands together, he pressed their joined hands down on the mattress above her head. He was momentarily mesmerized by the sight of her hands clutching his own, the black-red lacquer of her nails in stark contrast to the white sheets. She moaned, and he ripped his attention from their joined hands in favor of revisiting the breast he'd unhanded, but with his mouth this time. She moaned again, and louder. He chuckled against the stiff peak, and as her hips chased his, moved his lower body out of her range. When she started to object, he was back at her lips shushing her with his own as he licked into her mouth.

He must have let down his guard for a moment. He wasn't sure how it had happened, but suddenly, there were her legs, wrapped around him. She clasped her ankles behind his back and leveraged herself up so she was rubbing her center against him. She was giving off an incredible heat that he already felt might consume him, and he wasn't even inside her yet.

Inside her.

The very phrase—the shape of the words themselves in his mind—unleashed something inside him. It was as if his control, as she'd called it yesterday, had been hanging on a hook, and those two words somehow had the effect of unlatching that control. Decoupling it from any sense of order or decorum.

He wrenched himself from the grip of her legs, relishing the sound of dismay that resulted. Normally, he sought to soothe expressions of dismay, but not now. Now, he wanted another one. So as he reached for the condom he'd brought with him to the bed with one hand, he used the other to seek out her clit and press down on it with his thumb.

And there it was, another mewl. Not of dismay exactly, but of entreaty. And then another, more frustrated this time, when he needed both hands to unwrap the condom. He sheathed himself, and positioned himself over her. Her pupils were dilated, her hair was spread out on the pillow like a wild crown made of leaves and sticks, and the upside-down heart of her top lip looked as if it were glowing.

She was glorious, and he was lucky, so very lucky.

"Yes?" he whispered, and when she nodded, her pupils almost fully blown, he said a silent prayer of thanks and sank into her.

The relief that slammed into him was stronger and sharper than yesterday, and it came on so fast. He forced himself to move slowly inside her as his fingers found her clit again. From putting his mouth on her yesterday, and paying attention, he'd intuited that a fairly firm pressure was called for. He tried to sync the motion of his fingers and his hips, and he must have been doing something right. She began moaning almost continuously, but she never closed her eyes or looked away. She merely stared at him with that soul-exposing gaze.

Even when she started coming, she kept looking at him. It felt as if it were her gaze rather than her body that pulled his orgasm out of him. When he collapsed, shaking and sweaty and disconcerted, it was all he could do to keep his weight off her. He rolled to his side, keeping his hands on her, but then he thought better of it. She hadn't wanted him touching her last time, afterward.

It was difficult to take his hands off her. To put space between them and to smile at her across that space as if his world had not just been utterly upended.

She smiled back.

"What is this called, this part of your lips?" he suddenly asked, pointing to the top edge of her upper lip but not actually touching it. "This part that looks like an upside-down heart?"

"I think they call that a Cupid's bow."

"Why do I only see it when you're not wearing lipstick?"

"Because I draw my lipstick on in such a way as to obscure it." She demonstrated with her fingernail.

"Why?"

She shrugged. "I feel like it makes me look . . . unserious. Like, it's too cute."

No it isn't, he wanted to say. Well, it *was* cute. But not *too* cute. And *cute* might not even be the right word, given that he wanted to drag his teeth along it pretty much all the time. It made him a little crazy. But it also made him a little sad. The idea of Cara painting over a part of herself made something in him want to gather her in his arms and . . . he wasn't even sure what.

They didn't speak anymore. He watched her, over the next few minutes, fall asleep, her eyes growing heavy, closing for longer and longer periods, until it was just her black lashes against her skin, her chest rising and falling slowly. He pushed back against his own exhaustion. He would have liked nothing more than to drift off to sleep beside her, but there was poultry to receive. There was Christmas to stage. He avoided waking her as he slipped out of bed and dressed. He left the room with an odd sort of hollowness in his chest.

He didn't have experience with affairs of this sort, but he was fairly certain they weren't supposed to come with hollowness in the chest.

MATTEO WAS CHEERED when, at home to change clothes quickly before meeting the goose man—he had *semen* on his pants!—the phone rang with a call from Torkel.

"I need to ask you a favor," Torkel said.

"Of course."

"Sebastien's ring is being made by a jeweler in Witten. It's done, and he assures me he can ship it to me in time for the ball, but . . ."

"You're worried there will be an unforeseen delay and you'll be ringless for the big proposal," Matteo finished.

"Exactly."

"Shall I pick it up and keep it for you?"

"I was hoping you would. I would come get it myself, but I was hoping to squeeze in a visit to my sister before Christmas."

Torkel's sister lived in Vienna. "Of course."

"Is everything all right?"

"Yes, why?"

"You sound . . . off."

"I—"

He almost told Torkel the truth: *I'm falling for the American management consultant, and I don't know what to do about it.* But that was ridiculous. He wasn't falling for her. He simply wasn't accustomed to this type of affair. He was disconcerted by the intensity of their lovemaking. It had been so . . . satiating. He felt wrung out. Happy, even, when he thought about the fact that he was apparently rather good at making Cara come. And even if he *were* falling for her—which he wasn't—nothing could be done about it, least of all by Torkel. "I'm fine. Send me the jeweler's address, and I'll fetch the ring in the next day or so."

"If you have time. I'm sure you and Kai are quite busy with the Christmas baskets."

He would be up all night the next three nights with those blasted baskets—and of course the night after that, Christmas Eve, delivering them. And that was after making an appearance at the ball.

"Everything is under control," he said to Torkel. He was lying. Matteo had never fallen in love before, but he had a sinking feeling this was what it felt like. It didn't feel like being in control whatsoever.

MATTEO WAS GONE when Cara woke up. She fumbled for her phone to see how long she'd been out. It was only five o'clock. There was no text from him, or—she looked around the room—a physical note. Though had she expected one?

Well, yes. She had. Matteo was usually so thorough, and sneaking out didn't seem like him.

Though why was she so pressed? She was getting exactly what she wanted, what she'd been after since she got here: a tidy little travel fling. No mess, no strings.

No notes.

She got dressed and headed downstairs for dinner. The bar was remarkably empty.

"Where is everyone?" she asked Imogen.

"Outside. The ice slide is up."

"Ice slide? What is that?"

"It is a slide. Made of ice." Imogen shook her head in mock incredulity, but her eyes twinkled. "And here I thought you were supposed to be smart."

"An ice slide. This country is too much."

"Isn't it, though?" Imogen asked cheerfully. "You should go try the slide." When Cara didn't reply—she must have looked skeptical—Imogen added, "Come on. Didn't you tell me this was your weekend for all the Christmas things? What else do you have to do right now?"

"I can think of about a hundred things that are higher on my list than an ice slide."

"Really?"

"I went for a sleigh ride today, and—"

Her body shivered from the memory—of both the chilly ride and the warm conversation they'd had about her high school ski trip. The juxtaposition was confusing. *He* was confusing. She'd never imagined telling *anyone* that story.

"You did? With who?"

Cara ignored the question. "That was enough hurtling through space on ice. And I note that it involved an intimate object between my body and said ice. Putting my butt directly on a death-chute made of ice and voluntarily plunging down it? No thank you."

"Well, you're no fun."

"That's right. I'm not fun. I'm sensible. I'm a New Yorker."

Chapter Fifteen

Three days until Christmas

When Matteo got home in the middle of the night after a long evening working at Kai's, he was surprised to find Torkel sitting on the landing outside his door. "What are you doing here? I thought you were going to your sister's. Don't trust me with the ring?" He meant it in jest, but Torkel didn't crack a smile as he stood. Not that that was unusual.

"I thought you could use some help with the Christmas baskets." Torkel paused. "I told my sister I'd see her for New Year's."

Matteo was a bit overcome. He knew that "help with the Christmas baskets" was code for the fact that Torkel was worried about him and was here to check on him. It wasn't often that people did things like that for him. It was usually the other way around. "I could use some help with the Christmas baskets, actually." Though what he meant was that he could use some friendly company. He held up the bag he was carrying. "There's a goose in here. And there are a dozen more in my car. We needed to make room in the industrial fridge in Kai's workshop for other things, so I need to somehow fit these in my refrigerator."

After they'd fetched the geese, and Matteo had set Torkel to work on stuffing gift cards into envelopes, Matteo allowed himself to be interrogated. In fact, he set himself up. "I'm behind on the baskets because I've been spending so much time with the American management consultant."

"I thought she was here to overhaul Morneau."

"She is. But things have become . . . complicated."

"Ah. I see."

"Personally, I mean. Things have become complicated personally." Though lord knew, things had become complicated on the Morneau front, too.

"I got that."

"Yes, well . . ." He had absolutely no idea what to say next, even though he'd started this conversation.

"You've fallen in love with her."

"What? No! We're merely . . ." He couldn't say it. It sounded so tawdry. "We're merely enjoying each other's company."

"Are you enjoying each other's company horizontally?"

Matteo feared his blush answered for him.

Torkel chuckled.

"It's nothing to worry about. It's a very straightforward arrangement. She's only here a few more days."

"If it's nothing to worry about, why do you seem so worried?"

Matteo dropped the length of ribbon he'd been fashioning into a bow and let his head fall into his hands.

"You *have* fallen in love with her, haven't you?"

He opened his fingers and answered through them. "I didn't mean to."

Torkel laughed, a great big belly laugh. "Well, one never does."

"What do I do?"

"I think you should tell her."

"But what good will that do? She lives in New York. She's going home in a matter of days."

"Daniela lived in New York," he said, "and guess what? She and Max just got engaged."

"That's wonderful news." It was, even if it made him . . . well, it made him jealous, truth be told. The idea of finding your person, the one you wanted to spend your entire life with, seemed like something that happened to other people. "It's different for them. Daniela and Max are both portable. Ms. Delaney is excessively— admirably—devoted to her job, and that job is in New York."

"You could go to New York. Nothing to say you can't make *yourself* portable."

"And abandon Eldovia? Never."

That stopped Torkel. He knew the depths of Matteo's devotion to the country.

"That's the problem. We're both married to our jobs." Well, that wasn't really the problem was it? That would only be the problem if they were *trying* to make something work. "None of this matters, anyway. These feelings are entirely one-sided."

"Are you sure?"

"Of course I'm sure," he said, thinking back to the explicit conversation they'd had on the topic, a conversation that had been initiated by her.

"Have you expressed any of these supposed one-sided feelings? Have you asked her how she feels?"

"Oh for god's sake, Torkel. I'm glad you're happy but honestly, Sebastien has turned you into a starry-eyed romantic." He shoved a spool of ribbon toward him, even though experience had taught him that Torkel couldn't make a bow to save his life. "Are you here to help or not?"

"I'm here to help. I'm just saying that you're allowed to want things for yourself."

"What does *that* mean?"

"You arrange things so everyone else is happy. I know that's your job, but it goes beyond your job. All these couples you've gotten together. These Christmas baskets. When do *you* get to be happy?"

"Service to Eldovia makes me happy," he said, and though he had always believed that to be true, it suddenly sounded like a hollow refrain.

"That's fine, but don't you ever want things that have nothing to do with Crown or country?"

"I—" He did. He just didn't know what to *do* with that want. It was an unfamiliar, ill-fitting thing. "What if what I want is beyond my reach?"

Torkel shrugged. "Well, you'll *never* get it if you don't try."

THE NEXT MORNING, Cara woke up to her phone ringing. It was Matteo. They'd texted a lot, but they'd never talked on the phone.

"Matteo? Is everything all right?"

"Let's go skiing."

Her stomach dropped. "What?"

"Skiing. We can go to the run we saw yesterday. It's nearby. It's good for beginners."

"I don't ski." She heard the ice in her tone, but honestly, had he heard anything she said yesterday?

There was a long silence. She was about to put an end to the conversation when he said, "I know, but I think you don't ski because of Bradford Worthington III, and that seems a shame. Bradford Worthington III doesn't seem like the kind of person who deserves that much power. And you wanted to do all the winter things this weekend, did you not? I can teach you. It'll be just us. No one will see you."

She gasped. Oh, Matteo. Good, kind, generous Matteo whom she had completely misjudged. He was setting up an exorcism for her. Even though, after she left, he would never see her again, he was trying to make things better for her. Because that was what he did. Her throat tightened.

"But of course you'll be busy," he added. "It was merely a passing thought, and probably an ill-advised one."

"I don't have the right gear for skiing." She hoped he would take that as the assent it was. He was giving her an opportunity here, a chance to get rid of this heavy, ugly thing inside her. She wanted to take that opportunity, but for some stupid reason, she couldn't make herself outright say yes.

"You mean there's something you don't have in that bottomless Mary Poppins–style bag of yours?" She could hear the smile in his voice, and something in her chest settled. "We can rent everything at the hill."

Ninety minutes later they were doing just that. After they had all the stuff she needed, he led her outside and sat her on a bench near the base of a small hill. He was kneeling at her feet to help her with her boots, but he paused and looked up at her.

She knew he was asking, without actually asking, how she was doing.

"I'm okay," she said. And she was. It was a little odd how okay she was, actually, but she wasn't going to question it.

"Are you sure?"

"Yes. I thought this was going to be a big deal. An exorcism. And maybe it is an exorcism, but apparently it's not going to be a big dramatic one."

"A quiet exorcism," he said thoughtfully. "I like that idea."

They smiled sort of goofily at each other for a moment before he finished getting her into her boots and leading her to a very small hill. She almost laughed. This hardly counted as skiing.

"We'll start here," he said. "And perhaps end here. We needn't tackle any of the bigger hills today."

The way he said "today" made her wish there was going to be another trip sometime in the future. Look at her, *wanting* to ski.

Well, what she really wanted, she feared, were more outings with Matteo. When he wasn't in work mode, he was . . . Well, he was the best.

She eyed the gentle slope. "Everyone on this hill is a literal child."

"Everyone in Eldovia learns to ski at a young age."

"These are all Eldovians? There are no tourists here?"

"There's some winter tourism closer to Riems, where the hills are bigger, but even there it's limited."

"So this hill is going to be me and Eldovian toddlers."

He smiled, and her breath caught. The sun was shining down

on him, making his hair glow golden. "Everyone starts somewhere. There's no shame in being a beginner."

"I'm not good at not being good at things."

She wouldn't have thought it possible, but his smile grew even
wider, and, she thought, maybe even fonder? "I know that, but I
have faith in you."

"You have faith in my ability to not be good at something?"

"I have faith in your ability to not be good at something the first
time you try it, but to do it anyway." He offered her an arm.

"It feels weird," she said, looping her arm through his and taking an experimental step.

He led her to the base of the hill, clipped her into her skis, and
demonstrated how to walk up the hill with the skis at an angle.

"So we just walk up?" she asked, mimicking his turned-out stance.

"We just walk up."

"That's a little disappointing."

"Don't you have an idiom for this? You have to walk before you
can run?" He started up. "Use your poles like this." He showed
her how to dig them in as she went.

"I'm not sure walking is the best metaphor for . . . walking."

At the top of the hill, he gave her a little lesson and took her
poles from her. "You traditionally learn without poles."

"What kind of sense does that make? I thought this was the
beginner hill. Why take tools away from beginners?"

"Learning without poles teaches you balance and encourages
you to develop a more pure technique."

She gave a little snort. "Okay. Here goes nothing." She pushed
off—and skied down the hill. She skied down the hill! Her de-
scent was shaky, but she didn't fall. Not knowing how to stop, she

kept going until she ran out of momentum. She turned, triumphant, and Matteo, still at the top, raised his poles in celebration, took off, and swooshed down the hill, coming to a tidy stop right next to her.

"You did it!"

"I did it! Take that, Bradford Worthington III! You have been quietly exorcised!"

He sniffed, and she caught a glimpse of the old, stuffy, disapproving Mr. Benz. "Indeed."

"Why do you do that sometimes? Flare your nostrils like you're mad?"

"That," he said, "is not an expression of anger, but a relaxation technique. I learned it from a therapist when my parents were splitting up." He demonstrated, but did so in an exaggerated fashion, taking a deep inhale through his nose and then pursing his lips and exhaling through his mouth. "It calms me when I'm . . . riled."

She wanted to laugh at all the times she'd seen that and thought he was asserting his superiority, when really she had just been getting to him. She turned back to the hill. "That was fun. Let's do it again."

They did. And then they did it again. And again. Who knew a quiet exorcism could be so much fun?

"Forget skiing, can we just ride this chairlift thing around and around?" There was something incredibly uplifting—no pun intended—about slowly gaining elevation in the cold sunny blue of a perfect winter day. This really had been an exorcism. Cara wasn't sure when she'd felt so free. Possibly never.

"This ride does afford a lovely view, doesn't it?" Matteo asked, eyes impossibly green under the bright blue sky.

"Yes," she agreed, "though I think everything in Eldovia has a lovely view. But this is more than the view. There's something about moving through the trees and smelling the air—in addition to always looking stunning, Eldovia smells good. How do you guys do that?"

She'd been kidding, but he took her question seriously. "You know, when you first got here, I was determined to show you Eldovia, to make you really *see* it."

"That's why you tried to get me to go to that village, why you took me to the portrait gallery."

"Yes. I should have known that Eldovia's charms cannot be forced." He tilted his head and looked into the distance, as if he were contemplating a mystery. "I should have known that Eldovia didn't need my help in that regard."

At the top of the hill, Cara began to lose her nerve. Not because of the symbolism of skiing but because of the *actual skiing*. This was the smallest of the hills that required the chairlift, so it was still classified as easy, but it looked a lot steeper from this vantage point than it had from the bottom. "Yikes. How do you do this?"

"You just . . . go."

"Is that the technical term?"

He smirked. "It is."

She tamped down the flutter in her stomach. "I'll try."

"Cara," he said with a note of urgency in his tone. When she looked at him he was wearing an extremely serious expression. "There is no try."

She cracked up. "All right, Master Yoda. If go we must, go we shall."

They went. She concentrated on incorporating everything she'd learned. Matteo paced himself and stayed by her side, and why was that so hot? Before she knew it, they were at the bottom.

A spike of pure triumph rose in her chest. "I did it!" she exclaimed, which she realized was the same thing she'd said after her first run on the baby hill. But she had!

"You did indeed!" He seemed as excited as she was.

The next time they went, she was able to focus a bit more on the actual experience, the sensation of zipping along the packed snow, the sharp cold of the air in her nostrils. When they got to the bottom, she said, "I think I like skiing!" A few more runs solidified that stance.

On their fifth trip up the hill, the chairlift shuddered to a halt when they were halfway up.

"This happens when someone has trouble getting on or off," Matteo explained. "Or, actually, when the lift itself malfunctions, which does happen at this hill. This really is the workaday local ski hill."

"Well, no complaints here. Even though I've sort of got the hang of skiing, this chairlift ride is still my . . . favorite part." She'd trailed off because something appeared to be wrong with Matteo. He looked severely distressed, in contrast to the way he'd been the rest of the day—happy and smiling and joking. "Is everything all right?"

"I must speak with you." He shifted as much as possible on the bench so he was partially facing her.

She did the same. "All right." Her heart kicked up. She was

suddenly afraid that something terrible had happened with respect to Morneau. Maybe they *did* need to tell the king about
Brad before tomorrow morning.

"Cara, I have come to admire you a great deal. I greatly . . .
esteem you."

"You greatly esteem me?" She blinked. This was not where she
thought they'd been headed, but okay. She supposed she esteemed
him, too, now that she knew him better. "Wow, and here I thought
you didn't like me." She was kidding, of course. They had long
since dispensed with the idea that they didn't like each other. She
was trying to lighten the mood.

It didn't work. He continued earnestly. "I do like you. In fact,
that's what I'm trying to say. I have endeavored to resist, but I find
myself in the uncomfortable position of liking you very much."
He huffed an annoyed sounding breath. "This is extremely inconvenient."

"What is?" She was confused.

"My feelings for you!" he said, like it should have been obvious.
"My regard."

Okay, now she was getting annoyed. "Your regard for me is *inconvenient*?" And here she would have thought the whole point
of a fling, or, as he called it, a time-limited affair, was that it was
convenient. It was about taking advantage of a situation that was
right in front of you.

"Yes, life was much easier when I could think of you straight-
forwardly as the agent of Eldovia's destruction. But now that there
aren't going to be any layoffs, you're so much easier to like." He
shot her a sheepish smile.

"What?" She was still confused about what he'd said before,

but now he was talking about the company? "Of course there are going to be layoffs."

"But you said . . ."

"I said what?" She had never told him there would be no layoffs.

"When we discovered this business with Noar, I thought . . ."

"You thought that meant everything was magically going to be fine?" She tried to keep herself, and therefore her tone, calm, but her head was spinning. Matteo was usually so precise in his speech, and so attuned to the emotional undercurrents of any situation, but here, now, he had her completely bewildered. "Your incompetent CEO aside, you're still looking at a company that makes one product. One product for which demand is down. Of course there are going to be layoffs. If you're lucky, there will be fewer than there otherwise would have been had we not discovered Noar's misdoings." He looked utterly stunned, as if she'd slapped him. "Look, I know this is upsetting, but—"

"What's upsetting is having a declaration of love ignored in favor of a discussion about corporate downsizing!"

A declaration of what now?

Now she felt like *he'd* slapped *her*.

She suddenly understood what he was saying—or trying to. And this could not happen. This was not in the plan.

Cara thought back to the first day she'd met Matteo. One of the things they'd sparred over had been the difference between castles and palaces. Castles were defensive structures, he'd told her snarkily.

It was time to become a castle. She didn't do this. She didn't do feelings and commitments and encumbrances. She didn't make herself vulnerable to these kinds of attacks.

So how had she been caught with her drawbridge down?

That was a question to be examined later. For now, that draw-bridge had to come up. And so it did. Crocodiles tossed into the moat and archers lined up at the embrasures.

"Let me get this straight. You 'greatly esteem' me"—she could not make herself utter the L-word—"but you are inconvenienced by that fact." She could hear the ice crystals forming in her tone, as cold and hard as any of the snow they'd been skiing on. Good. Her castle could be fortified with ice. Princess Elsa had nothing on her.

"That's not what—"

"This happened in *Pride and Prejudice*."

"I beg your pardon?"

"Mr. Darcy makes this big speech about how he likes Elizabeth in spite of his good judgment. He finds his feelings inconvenient-bordering-on-insulting."

"That's not what I'm doing."

"That's what you *just said*."

"Only because you have apparently been sitting on the news that you're going to lay off hundreds of people!" He threw up his hands.

"You know what Lizzy does when Mr. Darcy makes his speech about how vexing it is to have 'great esteem' for her?" Cara said, letting her ice walls grow thicker, methodically draining herself of all emotion.

"I'm not sure that's an apt—"

"She throws his declaration back in his face."

He was silent for a long moment, and when he spoke, his tone was as cold as hers had been. "For someone who hasn't read the book, you certainly have a good memory of the plot."

That iciness from him was a bit shocking. Their early bickering had been different, had been almost exhilarating. This felt . . . terrible. She forced herself to de-escalate. She was lashing out at him, but this wasn't only his fault. *She'd* let the drawbridge down. *She'd* let the embrasures go unmanned. "I have read the book," she said carefully. "I read it a few weeks ago." She'd read it to get to know him better. To try to solve the puzzle that was Matteo.

"Miss Bennet does throw Mr. Darcy's declaration back in his face," Matteo said, quietly, as if he, too, were trying to disarm this . . . thing between them. "But it all works out in the end."

"Right. Because she has to marry. I, on the other hand, don't have to, and don't *want* to. I'm married to my job—as you are to yours, I would have thought." When he didn't say anything, she added, "And my job is in New York, and yours is here." As if he didn't know that. And as if that were the only barrier. She didn't do relationships. Yeah, maybe it was time to slowly start thinking about dating now that she'd made partner. She had always said that was the plan. But that wasn't the same as signing up for a transatlantic relationship with the guy she happened to be sleeping with when partnership landed in her lap. "It doesn't just 'all work out in the end' in real life," she added gently, because she didn't know what else to say, how to end this excruciating conversation.

The universe must have been looking out for her, because the chairlift lurched into action. She looked away, and they made the rest of the ascent in silence. When Matteo pushed himself off the chairlift at the top of the hill, she did not. She left him standing there, which she realized was a shitty thing to do, but she could not bear to ski with him anymore. She could not bear to *be* with him anymore. She rode the lift down to the bottom, returned her ski gear, and called a taxi to take her back to the village.

WHEN MATTEO GOT to the bottom of the hill, he fished his phone out of his pocket to find a series of texts from Cara.

> **Cara:** I've gone back to Witten.

> **Cara:** I'm sorry if I gave you the wrong impression about things between us. And I'm sorry I left you at the hill. I just thought it was best that I leave. I'm not looking for a relationship right now.

> **Cara:** I think it's best if we return to our previous way of interacting.

Our previous way of interacting. What did that mean? His mind skipped back to all the times they had proclaimed their dislike for each other. Initially, they'd been in earnest, and then it had become a joke.

He could not go back to disliking her, as much as part of him wanted to. It would be so much easier. That's what he'd meant, on the chairlift, when he'd used the word *inconvenient*. But there was no going back. He wasn't sure how it had happened at all, much less so fast, but he *loved* her. Part of him feared he always would.

After he left her bed last time, he'd noted a hollow sort of feeling in his chest. He hadn't been able to make sense of it, because they'd had such an amazing time together. He understood now that that hollowness had been about the mismatch between his actions and his feelings. He loved her, but he hadn't been allowed to express it. He hadn't even admitted it to himself at that point. So he'd *acted* like someone who loved her—he had literally made love to her—but had been suppressing any impulse to *articulate* that love. The result had been an unsettled, ominous feeling he hadn't understood.

The only way he could make sense of what had happened today on that chairlift was to reason that he'd been trying to fix that sense of unease, that mismatch. He'd thought being honest about his feelings would do it. How wrong he had been. Not only had he managed to completely botch his declaration, he had somehow deluded himself into thinking he should make one at all. There could be no way forward for them, even if she *had* returned his affections. His life was in Eldovia. No, it was more than that. Eldovia *was* his life. And Cara never stopped moving. She didn't do long distance. She didn't do *any* distance, because she didn't do relationships at all. He thought back to the conversation in which she'd blithely said she liked to be "on to the next thing." He'd asked her what happened to the first thing when she was on to the next, and she hadn't answered.

He knew now.

What made him feel the worst was that none of this was her fault. She had explicitly asked him to name what they were doing. A time-limited affair. He, by contrast, had gotten swept up in . . . what? Torkel's romantic ideals? Some muddled notion that since she wasn't going to lay people off, it was safe to love her?

It didn't matter. None of it was real. Cara had set out her terms, and he had agreed to them. And then he'd tried to unilaterally change them. No wonder she'd run away.

So what could he do but agree to what she was asking? He took off his gloves to type a reply. His fingers were clumsy, and not from the cold. They were resisting the message his brain was ordering them to send.

> **Matteo:** Of course. My apologies for making things awkward.

He stood there in the cold, staring at his phone, for a long time, but she did not reply.

Chapter Sixteen

Two days until Christmas

Telling the king that Noar Graf had been conspiring with Brad Wiener—fucking Brad—to fleece Morneau was unpleasant.

But it paled in comparison with having to do that with Matteo seated silently at Cara's side across from the king, who was sitting behind his desk in the library. As Cara spoke, she half wished Matteo would say something, even something antagonistic, but he just sat there, mute, expressionless.

The king handled the news well. Or at least he didn't fly off the handle. He didn't do much of anything. Like Matteo, he remained impassive. She supposed the bigger blow had been the initial news about Noar. Brad was merely the cherry on top. Fucking Brad.

"I am aware," she said, after she'd laid out what they knew, "that you hired CZT to help, and that what we have in effect done is the opposite of that." She was treading carefully here. She and Tonya and some of the other partners—the other partners; it was still

hard to wrap her mind around the fact that she was one of them—
had talked through various scenarios, including the possibility that
the Eldovians might bring legal action against CZT. "We're prepared to refund you everything you've already paid, and to help
you manage any of the fallout. I'm personally prepared to let Mr.
Graf go on your behalf, if you'd like me to. And as for the actual
work we were hired to do, I am still ready to hand in my report
anytime. And, of course, to be back after Christmas to discuss it if
you like, or to help in any way I can. Any further work by CZT on
this file will, of course, be carried out at no charge to Morneau."

The king turned an assessing gaze on her. "I had assumed your
work would come to a halt, at least temporarily, given all this business with Noar."

"I'm sorry to say that although Noar certainly had a draining
effect on the company's balance sheet, getting rid of him isn't going to be enough to right things. When you read the report in full,
you'll see that the pivots we're suggesting aren't going to happen
overnight. A leaner workforce is called for in the short to medium
term."

The king looked at Matteo, as Cara had been doing at various
points during their meeting. There had been so many instances
when she'd expected him to chime in with his disagreement. Perhaps the king was feeling the same.

"I have the report with me." She got it out of her bag. "I know
the plan was for me to present it to the board at this afternoon's
meeting—"

"I think the agenda for that meeting has changed. It's nothing
personal, Ms. Delaney, but my feeling is that we need to handle
the Noar situation before we do anything else. And while I ap-

preciate your offer to assist in this matter, we'll be handling it ourselves. We know where to find you if we need help."

All right then. "Shall I leave this with you?" She slid her report, the culmination of so much work, unceremoniously across the desk to him.

He picked it up. "I can't say I look forward to reading it, but I look forward to having this exercise behind us."

Ugh. Cara was accustomed to being unpopular, in some settings. It wasn't like she expected people to jump for joy when she suggested they needed to cut their workforce, but she was usually better at this than she apparently was today. Today she felt *shitty*. "Mind you, my recommendations are not all around the staffing issue. I make some other suggestions as well."

"Good," the king said flatly. "If that's all?"

"Yes, thank you." Well, that wasn't quite all. She had to say one more thing. "I wanted you to know that . . ." The king raised an eyebrow. "I wanted you to know that I couldn't have uncovered all this without Mr. Benz's help." Because Matteo had sat in complete silence during the meeting, she feared it looked like he hadn't had any involvement. Her feelings about Matteo were complicated, to say the least, but allowing that conclusion to stand wasn't fair.

"That's not true. You were well on your way to the truth." Hearing Matteo's voice ring out across the room, when he had been so quiet, was a bit of a shock. She loved his voice. It was deep and sure—and full of shit, in this particular instance.

"You were an enormous help. At Daniel—"

"You would have arrived at the same conclusion, Ms. Delaney," he said curtly.

Ms. Delaney. The formal form of address felt like a blow, like he'd insulted her. But she was the one who had asked that they revert to how things had been before.

She turned to the king. "Your equerry's help was invaluable."

The king nodded, and as she got up to leave, Matteo rose, too. Now they would have to be alone together.

"Mr. Benz, will you stay a moment?" said the king.

Thank goodness for small mercies. As Cara made her way down empty corridors, she thought some more about Matteo's voice. About how shocking it had been to hear, at the end of that meeting, but also how familiar it was. About how many times, these recent weeks, she'd felt as if his voice was sentient. As if it could touch her.

It was entirely likely that she would never hear it again.

She picked up the pace, and she managed to hold back the tears until she made it out the main door.

"Benz, how are you holding up?"

Matteo *wasn't* holding up. His heart was broken, and it was all the more painful knowing he'd brought it on himself. Once again, he had to concede that Ms. Delaney had been scrupulously honest from start to finish. A moment ago, she'd even insisted on crediting him for his help.

But that wasn't what the king meant. He was talking about Noar. Morneau. The layoffs that were coming. "I'm fine, thank you, Your Majesty. It's a blow, of course, but—"

"No, I mean you. How are *you* holding up?"

"I beg your pardon?"

"Something's clearly bothering you, something beyond today's news. You don't seem yourself."

"My apologies, Your Maj—"

"There's no need to apologize. Just tell me what it is."

Could he actually . . . do that?

"Out with it, Benz." The king's tone had taken on an annoyed edge.

"I'm afraid I've fallen in love with someone," he blurted. "It's entirely unexpected and terribly inconvenient."

The king smiled, a warm, wide one at odds with the day's grim news, not to mention the monarch's usually taciturn personality. "It's wonderful."

"It isn't, though. She doesn't feel the same."

"Do you know that for a fact?"

"I do."

"How do you know?"

Good lord. Were they really going to do this? Have a conversation about poor Matteo and his hurt feelings?

The king was looking at him expectantly. "Well?"

Apparently they were. Well, he couldn't make himself more abject if he tried, so why not? "I made a mortifying declaration only to have it thrown back in my face."

The king winced in sympathy.

"Indeed. And to make matters worse, we still have to—"

He'd been going to say they still had to work together but that would come too close to letting it be known that the object of his affection was Cara, and he couldn't let the king know how utterly he had taken leave of his judgment.

Also, *did* they still have to work together? Perhaps if she came back in the new year. But for now? It was sinking in that he wasn't going to see her again on this trip. She was flying out tomorrow, and since she'd been dismissed from today's board meeting, she was not likely to cross his path again.

And if she *didn't* come back in the new year, he would *never* see her again. He'd been thinking, a moment ago, about how Ms. Delaney had been scrupulously honest with him from start to finish.

It appeared this was the finish.

His chest felt like it was going to crack open. The sensation was so strong that he doubled over in place, folding himself over his lap.

"Benz, I'm far from an expert on matters of the heart."

Matteo was making an utter fool of himself. He forced himself to sit up in his chair and pay attention.

The king was looking at him with a kindness in his eyes that Matteo had previously seen directed only at his family. "But," he went on, "it would seem to me that a person would want to be *entirely* sure he had exhausted all avenues, that he had made his feelings *crystal* clear, before he gave up."

He had done all that. Hadn't he?

As he took his leave of the king, he cast his mind back to the chairlift. He had told Cara that he . . . Well, he'd told Cara that he greatly esteemed her. But he was almost certain he'd used the phrase "declaration of love."

But . . . he had referred to having made a declaration of love. Had he actually *said* he loved her? Had he said why?

It was almost amusing, or it would have been if it wasn't so pathetic. Matteo was so good at bringing other people together, but apparently he didn't know how to take his own advice.

It probably didn't matter, wouldn't make a difference, but the king was right. He had to try. At the very least, he couldn't let her leave like this.

HAVING NOTHING TO do was an odd feeling. But as Cara walked down the hill, she realized she was free. The report was done, and she didn't have to attend this afternoon's board meeting. She was leaving tomorrow morning, but between now and then, there was nothing she had to do.

Why didn't it feel better, being free?

As she approached the village, she decided she would buy some Christmas presents for her parents. She drifted around and picked up a few things—some leather gloves for her dad, a teapot for her mom. What she really wanted, though, was one of Kai's snow globes, she thought, as she plopped onto a stool at the pub.

"Coffee?" Imogen asked, strolling over to greet her.

"I think I'll have a pint of that pumpkin stout." Yes, it was eleven in the morning, but she was free, right?

Imogen raised an eyebrow. "All gone, I'm afraid. The seasonal tap at the moment is a cranberry ale. It's brewed with cinnamon and honey—and of course cranberries."

"Great," Cara said, and she was aware that her tone didn't suggest "great" at all.

"Here you are," Imogen said when she was back with the beer. "Ale for what ails you." When Cara could only manage a weak smile, Imogen asked, "What's got your knickers in a twist?"

"Nothing."

"Having some trouble surfing the waves of change, are we?"

Cara gestured at the snow globes behind the bar. "I know Kai doesn't want to sell his snow globes, but how come no one around here sells anything similar? If I want to ride an ice slide or drink some seasonal beer"—she lifted her glass and took a sip—"I can do that. This country seems to be full of Christmas experiences—and consumables. But where's all the *stuff*? I've been poking around in the shops trying to find something Christmasy for my parents, and there isn't much. What I did find was kind of generic."

Imogen shrugged. "I guess people who live here already have all the Christmas stuff they need, so there's not a market for it?"

"And you don't have tourists, it doesn't seem." She thought back to Matteo talking about how all the ski tourism was on the Riems side of the mountains.

"Not many. There's a reason I had a room free for you so close to Christmas. We're not really a tourist destination."

"But you're so stinking cute."

Imogen preened. "Well, thank you very much."

"You know what I mean! Why *don't* you have more tourists?"

"If we had more of a Christmas industry, like one we were known for, we might have more tourists."

A Christmas industry. Hmm.

"Would that be a good thing, though?" Imogen went on. "Would it ruin the actual, I don't know, spirit of Christmas? If every corner had a stall selling 'Christmas in Eldovia' T-shirts?"

"I don't know." Cara would have to think about it.

And she did think about it. She thought about it while she sipped her eleven a.m. beer. She thought about it while she pushed back her stool.

Imogen came over and nodded her thanks for the cash Cara laid on the bar. "Headed upstairs? Will I see you before you leave?"

"I'm headed outside, actually. I'm going to try the ice slide."

"Are you now? I thought you were a sensible New Yorker who didn't go in for hurling your body through space or what have you."

"Yeah, well, sometimes you gotta change things up."

She thought about it—the idea of a Christmas industry in Eldovia—as she climbed the long staircase to the top of the slide. Something not schlocky. Something centered around the experiences that the country was already so good at providing its own citizens. She thought of how beautiful the holiday decorations were at the palace. She thought of Matteo saying that he was always turning down requests to film at the palace.

She thought of Matteo and how much he loved Eldovia, how he cared about its people so much.

She thought of him talking about his expanded mission.

Could she take the same approach with her project here? The charge had been to look at how Morneau could modernize, diversify its operations beyond its historically limited product categories within the context of watches.

But what if the context *wasn't* only watches? What if she thought more broadly, and asked how Eldovia, not just Morneau, could diversify its operations?

No one had asked her to do that, but equally, no one was stopping her.

She reached the top of the slide. She'd been thinking so hard that she hadn't had time to be scared.

She could do this. She could leave Matteo with some hope for his beloved Eldovia.

She sat on the icy slide and whooshed down.

Chapter Seventeen

One day until Christmas

Cara worked late into the night, in her room, researching and running some rough numbers and feeding them into a new report. Amendment. Addendum? She wasn't sure what to call it. When she was done, she felt as though she'd run a marathon. She was wrung out, but in a good way, as if she'd spent all her energy on a good thing.

As she opened her email to send the new report to the king, she noticed the clock had turned over. It was Christmas Eve. Well. She took a deep breath and pressed send. She hoped that whether the king bought into it or not, he would discuss it with Matteo.

Because he was the one she was really doing this for. He had taught her to do this, to think expansively and generously. He had taught her to care. And she wanted to thank him by showing him that she had learned from him, that she was trying to do right by the country he so loved.

She had this odd feeling about him, like she owed him so

much. It was hard to put to words, but when she thought back to all his kindnesses—bringing her tea in the bath, defending her against Noar's sexist remarks, teaching her to ski—her heart filled. But it hurt, too.

She laid on the bed and tried to focus on her happy news. She was a partner at CZT! This was what she'd wanted for so long. This was *everything* she'd wanted. The job itself, the duplex it would allow her to buy, her parents squared away. Less travel.

Right? She'd always said she wanted that, too. She'd told her mom countless times that once she made partner, she'd travel less. She'd stop.

But she was scared to stop.

Scared shitless.

Because if she stopped, she suddenly had time for all the stuff she'd resolutely shuffled into the "later" category. Was she ready for "later" to be here?

She heaved a shaky breath, and closed her eyes.

She fell asleep. She hadn't meant to, but when she jolted awake, it was two in the morning. A close call—she was meant to get up at four to get on the road to the airport, but she hadn't set her alarm.

She hadn't packed, or done anything to get herself ready to go, either. First, she needed a shower. She opened her door, and nearly tripped over something at her feet.

It was a basket made of wicker and adorned with a dark-green velvet ribbon.

She gasped into the empty hallway.

With shaking hands, she brought it inside, her shower forgotten.

She thought of Erika Ulmer, the university-bound girl she'd met at the pub, explaining the baskets. She'd said, "It always seems like the people who need them, get them. Everyone always says that the baskets appear for people who need a little Christmas magic."

People who need a little Christmas magic.

Inside hers, Cara found a bunch of different things. There was a growler of Imogen's pumpkin stout, which Imogen had said was sold out; a book of sudoku puzzles; a bottle of fancy bubble bath; and . . . "Oh my god!" It was a copy of *Pride and Prejudice*. Not a new one, but a well-worn hardcover edition. The cover featured a gold peacock whose tail feathers covered the entire front and spine of the book. She flipped it open to the copyright page, which said 1923. A piece of paper fell out.

Dear Cara,

The problem was that I, like Mr. Darcy, was trying to apply logic to a situation that resists logic. I love you, and if to do so is inconvenient, it is only insofar as I'm painfully aware that an accomplished, confident, independent person such as yourself is unlikely to love me back. And of course I am aware that even if you could be persuaded to, the matter of you living in New York and me living in Eldovia is no small thing.

But then, hope is another state to which logic doesn't apply, don't you find?

While you and Mr. Spock are no doubt correct about almost everything, I did some research into your captain

*Janeway, and I thought perhaps you might consider her
words alongside Mr. Spock's. I know I will.*

> *yours, with all my love,*
> *Matteo*

*P.S. This was my grandmother's copy of Pride and
Prejudice. It was a gift from her mother. Whatever
happens, I would like you to have it.*

At the bottom of the letter he'd stuck a Post-it note, identical in color and size to hers. On it he had written:

*You can use logic to justify almost anything. That's its
power and its flaw.—Captain Janeway*

She burst into tears. Dear, dear Matteo had curated a collection of things he knew she would like, because he had paid attention to her. He had watched her carefully and done what he always did—tried to arrange things so she was pleased and comforted.

And loved.

Cara was certain she had never been loved by anyone other than her parents. She hadn't *let* herself be. But somehow Matteo had stormed her fortified castle.

The bravery of this gesture took her breath away.

She thought about all those books and candles she'd stumbled on in his loft. She'd wondered in passing if he was the mysterious Santa behind Eldovia's Christmas baskets but discarded the notion. When did he have the time?

Maybe he was himself a little magic, like Santa.

She rolled her eyes at herself. The truth was he was a hard worker, and a selfless, compassionate person. To think of him delivering all these baskets in one night—though presumably others' didn't come with declarations of love.

They'd better not. The very thought sent a hot jet of . . . something through her. She was pretty sure, if she was being honest, that it was jealousy.

Because she loved him back. That's what that odd feeling had been earlier, the one she hadn't quite been able to get a handle on except to think that it felt as if she owed him something.

Holy shit. She loved Matteo Benz, the equerry to the throne of Eldovia.

She had always said she would slow down, make time to date, when she made partner. She just hadn't expected to make partner so soon. Or for the man she wanted to slow down *for* to be *right there* when that happened. That's why she'd flipped out on that chairlift, because Matteo had been poking at an uncomfortable truth: she loved him.

An idea took root. He had made this astonishing, brave gesture. Now it was her turn.

But first she needed to call her mom. She laughed out loud, through tears, into the silent room.

Her dad picked up the FaceTime on her mom's phone. "Hello, lassie!"

"Where's Mom? Is everything all right?"

"I'm here!" Her mom edged into the picture. The two of them were in their pajamas—her mom's was a Rudolph nightie—and Cara's heart throbbed. "We can't wait to see you!"

Shit. "About that . . ."

Her mom's face fell. Absolutely crumpled. "You're not coming home for Christmas?"

"I wanted to talk to you about it."

"What kind of job doesn't let you go home for Christmas!"

"It's not the job. I'm done with the job. It's actually . . ." Ugh, why was this so hard? She looked away from her parents and at the note from Matteo. If he could be brave, she could, too. "It's actually a man. I actually . . . fell in love. Which I know sounds bananas— I've only been here a month. But somehow it happened. But then I screwed it up. I'd like to stay another day and try to make it right."

She had stunned her mother into silence, which was a new one on her. Mom sat there with her mouth hanging open while a smile slowly blossomed on Dad's face.

"But if you're not okay with that, I completely understand. I can be on my plane as planned."

That jolted her mother to life. "No! You stay there and work things out!"

"It's just that . . . This thing that I screwed up—I want to fix it today. I want to fix it at Christmas."

"You do that, then. You call us tomorrow! Introduce us to your man."

Her man. She could only hope.

"Thanks, Mom. I love you guys both so much."

"We love you too, lassie," her dad said.

And from her mom: "Merry Christmas, my girl, my greatest thing."

CHRISTMAS EVE DAY. The biggest day—and night—of the year for Matteo. He had the Cocoa Ball to attend, and this year that came with fairy godfather duties as it related to Torkel's proposal. Then he'd meet up with Kai to deliver the baskets.

Which was a good thing, he told himself as he crunched across the snow from the stable to the palace, because this year he needed the distraction. He needed to keep busy, because otherwise he feared he would lose his mind.

He had thought Cara would call, at least, or text. He wanted to tell himself that perhaps she hadn't received the basket. Perhaps she had already been gone when he delivered it. But he'd seen the light under her door, and her winter hat had been hanging on the knob, as if she'd left it there to dry.

Then he told himself that perhaps she was gathering her thoughts and would text him from the airport, even if just to say goodbye.

She had not.

Now a whole day had gone by with no word from her. Which meant he had to accept her verdict, had to accept that he had tried and failed.

And he would, but not yet. He had Christmas to get through. He would accept things later, when he was back at his apartment watching Star Wars. That's when he would break down.

And then he would pick himself up and get on with his life. He had done it before—his whole family had—and he could do it again.

The footmen were setting up the arrival area inside the main entrance. He eyed the decorations that had been added since he'd been here this morning. The ball's theme this year was Silver Bells, and there were indeed silver bells hanging from nearly every surface, most of them trimmed with flowers and ribbons. "It looks wonderful," he said to Frau Lehman as she approached in a simple maroon evening gown. "As do you, if I may say so."

"Thank you, Mr. Benz. You're looking rather smart yourself. I'm here to tell you that His Majesty would like to see you in the library."

"Yes of course," he said, but inwardly, he sighed. He didn't want to talk about Morneau, or Cara's report, or layoffs, or any of it. He wanted one day off from thinking about it all. But there was no use wanting what you couldn't have—he had learned that the hard way these last few days.

He found the king dressed in his full ceremonial regalia. It was always impressive to see, even after all these years.

"Benz," the king said, dispensing with any greeting, not even waiting for Matteo to sit down as he usually did. "I should like to appoint you Eldovia's ambassador to the United Nations."

"I beg your pardon?" He couldn't have heard that correctly.

"You know my daughter's involvement with the UN's High Commission on Refugees has been a central part of her life these past few years." Matteo nodded, unsure why they were talking about this now when there was so much else to do. "She has convinced me we should be a more active presence there, and frankly, Hugo has been nothing more than a warm body."

Hugo Egli had been Eldovia's ambassador to the United Nations for going on twenty years, and it was true that he wasn't known for his intellect or dynamism. All right. Matteo had misheard there. The king was asking for his thoughts on who should replace Egli. Matteo, being as well-connected as he was, was often asked to consult on these sorts of things. "I can draw up a list of names for you. But off the top of my head, I think an excellent, if slightly unconventional, choice would be—"

"I don't want a list of names, Benz. I want *you* to do it."

"*What?*"

"I need someone there who can make things happen. A statesman."

"You . . . think I'm a statesman?" He was dumbstruck.

"Of course you are. You've kept this place running nearly single-handedly for years. And not just the palace. Witten. Hell, the whole damn country in some ways."

"But . . ."

"And if you accept, we'll have the advantage of having you there to advance Morneau's interests, too. I am in receipt of Ms. Delaney's two reports, and—"

"I beg your pardon, *two* reports?" This was all too much confusing information being tossed at him.

The king looked like he was trying not to smile as he picked up a stack of papers stapled neatly in one corner and handed it to Matteo. "Yes. As for Morneau, you know we had a board meeting yesterday—without Hauser, of course, whom we still need to deal with—but we had a quorum. We decided we're going to go ahead and make a blasted smart watch. And trim back the traditional line. There *are* going to be layoffs." He held a hand up as if to forestall a protest he knew was coming, but Matteo was too mixed up to register an objection. The king pressed on. "But last night, Ms. Delaney sent me *that* report, in which she proposes the creation of a Christmas industry. A new company, and a nonprofit tourism board." He nodded at the document. "It's all in there. In broad strokes, mind you. It will require a great deal of work, and a lot of fine-tuning, but she's convinced me that Eldovia has a great deal of unexploited potential in this area. If we can build that up while retooling Morneau . . ." He held out his hands. "Well, it's worth a try, don't you think?"

"I . . . don't know what to say." Matteo flipped through the pages. They were full of numbers his eyes scanned but his mind didn't register. What did register was that perhaps this was why he hadn't heard from Cara. Could she have been busy working on this utterly unexpected report? It probably was not wise to hold out hope on that front, but as he had so recently learned, hope was not subject to logic.

"Say yes."

Right. The UN appointment. The *UN appointment*! So much astonishing information was coming at Matteo so fast it was starting to make his head spin. "You should consider some other candidates, not merely make a rash decision. The person I was thinking of—"

"It isn't rash. It's the least rash such appointment I've ever made. I've been working with you daily for five years. Can I say that about any of the other ambassadorships we've filled?" He smirked. "Of course, parliament will have to approve you, which is rather amusing, isn't it? Generally when I need to make sure something will go smoothly in parliament, I turn to you." The king had a chuckle while Matteo continued to gape at him. "So I'm sure you can see that when I consider the question of who is best suited to advancing Eldovia's interests on the world stage, and when I think about who might be open to an appointment that will mean a great deal of time in New York, well . . ." He spread his arms as if making a proclamation from on high.

"New York," Matteo echoed dumbly. Of course, the UN appointment would mean splitting his time between New York and Eldovia.

He reminded himself once again that hope was not logical.

"Yes. You love so many American things, so it works out perfectly. American jazz, those ridiculous movies . . ." He trailed off with a smirk that suggested he was purposefully leaving something off his list of American things Matteo loved.

A terrible thought occurred to Matteo. "Did Cara Delaney say something to you . . ." Ah, this was mortifying. ". . . about me?"

The king looked like he was trying very hard not to laugh. "She did not."

"But—"

"Do not be so astonished. You have been meddling in my affairs for years. Now it's time for me to do some meddling of my own. And I learned from the best."

Chapter Eighteen

*M*atteo had trouble focusing his attention on the ball. Which didn't bode well for his second shift this evening. He had a literal night of work ahead of him. He pulled out his pocket watch. It was—finally—approaching ten o'clock, which was when Torkel was set to make his quiet proposal to Sebastien. After that, Matteo would slip out and make his way to Kai's workshop, where they would spend a few hours finalizing the baskets. Then they'd head out in the wee hours to deliver them.

And then Star Wars at home.

And then what?

Normally, the relief of sinking onto his sofa and cueing up a Star Wars movie marked the end of the holiday season for him. It was a bookend. After Christmas Star Wars viewing, life returned to normal.

But this year?

Matteo had asked the king for a day to think about the UN appointment, and the king had told him to take a week off and do exactly that. Matteo had protested. He didn't want a week off;

he truly didn't. He didn't need a week to make the decision. He merely needed to call his family and talk through it, to make sure they saw the offer the way he did: as an incredible opportunity he'd been blessed with.

He wanted to do it. He wanted to move to New York and advance Eldovia's interests on a global stage. It was the perfect situation for him. This past year or so, he'd been restless. He could do his current job in his sleep—even though his expanded mission meant that he got very little actual sleep. But he hadn't imagined ever doing anything else, at least as long as the king lived. When Matteo and Cara talked, in the pools at Biel, about what it meant to serve one's country—through military service or otherwise—he'd said that being equerry to the throne of Eldovia was a unique opportunity. He'd thought it so, in the truest sense of the word. It had felt like a once-in-a-lifetime job.

It turned out he'd been wrong. That there was at least one other job in the world that had the same characteristics.

Interestingly, though, he was fairly certain that if the king had suggested he go to New York and get a job as one of those ridiculous dress-up characters in Times Square, he might have considered it. Well, he'd have considered it if Cara wanted him.

He sighed from the corner of the ballroom where he was . . . well, where he was brooding, he supposed. He couldn't leave until after the proposal, but what he really wanted to do was go home and let himself fall. Let himself really *feel* what having a broken heart was like.

It was amazing to him how all these people could be dancing and drinking and laughing while he was standing here . . . ruined.

Or about to be. No ruination until he got home after delivering baskets. He had to hold it together until then.

"Is everything ready?"

Matteo turned, pasting on a smile for his old friend. "It is. Though I have to say, I'm surprised you chose a traditional waltz for your big moment."

"Sebastien loves waltzing."

Was Matteo mistaken or was Torkel blushing? It was difficult to hold on to his own pain when something so wonderful was about to happen. "You have the ring?" Torkel nodded. "All right, it will be the next song. The bandleader is expecting me around this time." He laid a hand on Torkel's shoulder. "Congratulations, my friend."

"Thank you," Torkel said, infusing the two syllables with a kind of fond urgency Matteo felt—and appreciated.

Though it did occur to him that he had spent a lot of time at this ball over the years arranging other people's grand gestures and declarations of love. He didn't begrudge any of it, but he was, suddenly, so tired.

He had felt tired a great deal lately. Cara had called it burnout. He wondered now, though, if it wasn't tiredness he was feeling so much as loneliness. And not the generalized variety. It was focused on one particular, extraordinary person he already missed as if she'd taken part of him home with her. Well, he supposed she had: his heart. He could only hope that she was happily reunited with her parents, cozy at home in New York.

He watched as the familiar strains of Strauss's "Blue Danube Waltz" rang out over the ballroom and Torkel approached Sebastien. He watched Sebastien express surprise at being asked to waltz. The two of them had danced together earlier, but not to one of the more traditional, formal dances that always dotted the ball's program. He watched Torkel convince Sebastien, and Sebastien allow himself to be led out to the middle of the dance floor. He watched the two men put themselves into position and begin to move in the one-two-three step of the dance.

And then, in the distance, at the far end of the ballroom, a mirage. A woman making her way down the stairs that led to the dance floor. She was wearing a classic ball gown: capped sleeves and a fitted bodice atop a big puffy skirt. It would have looked like a Cinderella dress, except it was pure, jet black. A dress fit for an angel of destruction.

All right, enough. He had officially cracked up. His poor, tired mind was hallucinating.

Except . . . he gasped. She started moving, crossing the dance floor, turning her head from side to side as she surveyed the cavernous room. She was looking for someone. Did he dare hope? He started walking, too, pulled by invisible strings.

Perhaps she felt those strings, too. The moment he started moving toward her, her gaze landed on him. She smiled.

Oh, she smiled.

He was overcome.

He started dodging waltzers in earnest. Once they got close enough to talk—though they were still a ways away from each other, separated by some members of the crowd—she stopped and said, "Mr. Benz, there you are. I almost couldn't find you in that tuxedo. It makes you look very handsome, but it *also* makes you look the same as everyone else, which is funny because you're not the same as everyone else, are you?"

He stopped, too, as his chest imploded. *Everything* imploded. He hardly recognized his voice when he said, "Ms. Delaney. I thought you'd gone home." He smiled at their use of last names. They had done that so many times in the past month, first out of formality and then, at times, in anger, or in jest. Now, it felt . . . tender.

"I realized I couldn't leave yet, because I forgot something."

He kept his cool. "Oh? What's that?"

"I forgot to tell you that I love you, too."

It was only then that he realized the reason they could hear each other was that the music had stopped. The waltz was over, and they were standing in the middle of the dance floor, though there was still a good six feet between them. He was having that very public moment that Torkel had wanted to avoid.

This was the opposite of the way things usually went with him. In his role as equerry—and his role as Santa—Matteo worked in the background. Quietly made things happen for other people. He preferred it that way.

Usually.

Now, though, he found he didn't mind at all that the crowd had come to a standstill, that everyone's attention was on him and his angel of destruction.

Another thing he didn't do? Dance. He was always far too busy working to dance at the Cocoa Ball. And yet. "Ms. Delaney, would you care to dance with me?"

She grinned. "I would." She began moving toward him, and the music started up again. It was another waltz—he couldn't have arranged it better himself. To his absolute astonishment, the crowd began *cheering*. It started small, with some clapping, but soon the applause was punctuated with cheers and whistles.

By the time she reached him, she was laughing, and, he thought, crying a little, too. She looked exactly like he felt. As she put her hand in his, she said, "I don't know how to waltz."

"Would you perhaps then consider standing in place, right here, and kissing me?"

"I would."

And so they did.

"Tonya always used to tell me that fairy tale endings were for cartoon women," Cara said breathlessly as Matteo hustled her across the snow to his apartment, "but I don't know, attending a ball at a freaking *palace* then being rushed home for what I assume is going to be some very hot makeup sex? That seems pretty fairy-tale-esque to me."

"Oh, no, we're not going inside," Matteo said with a grin—he had been wearing a downright goofy grin nonstop since they kissed in the ballroom. "We're just here to get my car." He held the passenger side door open for her. "We have work to do."

"We do?" She was confused for a moment, but then she caught on. "Oh, yes, we do! I'm onto you, you know. I even had my suspicions before I found your basket. Should I change, though, before this mysterious work?"

"Probably, but you look too good. I want to keep looking at you in that dress. Until we get home, at which point I plan to remove it posthaste."

As dirty talk went, it was mild, but coming from Matteo, such a threat made her face heat and her stomach go fluttery.

"Where did you get that dress?" He started the car, but he kept staring at her. "It's gorgeous."

It was. It made her look like Cinderella's vampiric sister, and she loved it. "I got it from a shop in the village."

"Lorelei's? I thought she was out of town and had closed up for the holidays."

"Somehow Imogen got in touch with her and arranged for her neighbor to let us in. I tried on a few dresses, found this, and left her payment. I also found these." She kicked a leg out from beneath her voluminous skirts to show Matteo a shoe. She was wearing glittery black flats. "My own shoes would have worked fine. In fact, they would probably have been more appropriate to the occasion. But I decided maybe it was time to retire the high heels."

He glanced over at her. "No longer need a weapon at hand?"

Yes. He understood perfectly. He always did. She nodded, suddenly a little choked up.

He started the car, reached over and grabbed her hand, and drove down the hill holding it. How many times had she perved on his hands in this very car? And now it was hers. *He* was hers. As they approached the bottom of the hill, she said, "I suppose we should talk. In the fairy tales, you never get to hear about how it all works out logistically, after the happily ever after. Like, sure, Cinderella could probably move into the palace right away, but what if she'd had a job she really loved on the other side of the world? Or what if she was just afraid of moving too fast? What if she hadn't ever loved a man before, and she didn't know if—"

"Hush. I have it all worked out—no, I have some of it worked out, and we will work out the rest together. But let's get this other thing done first." He glanced over at her, concern in his eyes. "I promise we will talk soon. Trust me?"

"Yes. Unreservedly." How remarkable.

"I feel the same," he said. "And I can't lie: it's a little bit scary."

"It sure is."

Eventually, they turned off a dark, forested road onto a long drive that opened onto a clearing containing two log cabins. Matteo parked, and they made their way to the larger of the two structures.

Inside was Kai, who appeared to be moving boxes from one end of the space to the other. A table contained several hundred of the same kind of basket she'd found outside her door.

"You really must trust me if you're letting me see your workshop, Santa."

"I'm not Santa. If anyone's Santa, it's Kai. This is his workshop."

"And *this* is what you meant about moving a lot of boxes!" Matteo's physique was due to his job as Santa. It boggled the mind.

"That was a bit of a slipup. But yes. Christmas Eve in Eldovia is rather a lot of work. By tomorrow morning you'll be sore in places you didn't know existed." There was a pause while he absorbed what he'd just said. "I assure you I didn't mean that the way it sounded."

She was about to say that she liked the way that sounded, when Kai realized they'd arrived and made his way over to them. "I wasn't sure you'd come."

"I'm afraid I haven't been the most reliable this year," Matteo said, "and for that I'm sorry."

"That's probably my fault," Cara said.

Kai looked down at their joined hands—Matteo had retaken Cara's hand on the way in and was still holding it—and said, "Ah."

"But you know I'd never miss tonight," Matteo said. "What's left?"

"I was about to add the geese to the baskets that are getting them, then we're ready to go."

Cara was amazed. She had so many questions, but she started with "Why doesn't everyone get a goose?"

"When we started, the baskets were for people in poverty, people who needed material help. That's still a large proportion of the baskets, but some people are on the list because they're lonely, or otherwise in need of help that isn't food-related."

"They're people who need a little Christmas magic," Cara said. People like her.

Matteo winked at her.

"And some people are vegetarians," Kai said, handing Cara a box that she was pretty sure was some kind of Tofurkey-style vegetarian roast even though she couldn't read the German label. "See those baskets over there with the silver ribbons? Those all need one of these."

Gathering that she was being unceremoniously put to work—and happy to help—Cara stuffed baskets with fake meat. And after that, she helped check the baskets against a list the men had.

"This is *exactly* like Santa," she said to Matteo. "You have a list and you're checking it twice." He rolled his eyes affectionately, and they all got to work loading a cargo van that was parked outside the workshop.

They spent the next few hours delivering baskets. It felt like they were doing something important. Matteo told her a bit about some of the families that occupied the houses they were visiting. Kai even got into the spirit of the thing. He wasn't exactly chatty, but he answered her questions about some of his handmade treasures that had gone in the boxes, and he and Matteo occasionally traded dry witticisms.

In her ball gown, spending the night delivering Santa baskets: this was not how Cara had ever imagined her trip to Eldovia ending. She probably looked like she was starring in a montage in one of those stupid Hallmark movies.

She felt like it, too.

When they pulled up to Kai's cabin just before dawn, Matteo said, "Thank you for another good year." Kai nodded and made to get out, but Matteo continued. "We can discuss it later, but I need to tell you that I won't be here next year." Kai raised his eyebrows questioningly, and Cara could feel herself doing the same thing. It was impossible to imagine Matteo bailing on his Santa duties. "The king has appointed me ambassador to the United Nations. I'm moving to New York."

Cara shrieked, and she was not a shrieker.

Kai cracked a small smile, and said, "Well. Congratulations." From him that seemed like the equivalent of a ticker tape parade.

"I think we should enlist Imogen to replace me," Matteo said.

Kai made a vague noise that was hard to interpret and said, "We'll talk later."

"Merry Christmas!" she called after Kai, and when she and Matteo were alone again in the car, she shrieked again. "*UN ambassador?* Why didn't you tell me that earlier?"

He shrugged as he put the car into gear. "I thought we'd agreed to talk about it later."

"Well, it's later, isn't it?"

"Indeed. So let's go home and hash out all the details. We can get out our calendars. Perhaps you can even write a report on the logistics associated with the launch of our relationship and my transatlantic move."

"Well . . ." When he put it that way, perhaps they didn't need to talk about it right away.

"I am teasing. Of course we can talk about whatever you want, whenever you want. I want you to know that I'm delighted to be moving to New York for a job that excites me, but I'm even more excited that I'll be where you are—where you are at least some of the time. I'm happy to go as fast or as slow as you like. This is new for me, too." He grabbed her hand. It was starting to feel normal. "Let's go home and hash out all the details."

"Actually, maybe we can hash out the details tomorrow morning."

"I think it is tomorrow morning," he said.

"Maybe we can hash out the details this afternoon."

"When do you fly back to New York?"

"Tonight. A red-eye out of Zurich. Do you want to come?"

"Yes."

"Look at us. We're turning out to be very efficient at hashing out details." She grinned. "Which might mean we can hash them out here in the car on the way home, and just be done with it."

"Whatever you like."

"I would prefer to do all the hashing now. Because when we get home, we have Star Wars to watch, do we not?"

"Yes, I believe we do. Also perhaps some seldom-used muscles to find."

"Well, let's get a move on then."

Epilogue

One year later

His Majesty King Emil and Her Royal
Highness Princess Marie
request the honor of your presence
at the Eldovian Cocoa Ball
at the Royal Palace
on December 24 at seven o'clock in the evening.
Kindly RSVP.
****

You are cordially invited to
a Boxing Day reception
at the residence of the Eldovian Ambassador
to the United Nations
in New York City.
December 26 at four p.m.
RSVP by December 11.
****

One thing I didn't really think through in getting together with you was how much Christmas hustle was going to be required," Cara said as she did her makeup in the mirror in one of the palace guest rooms. She and Matteo were back in her old guest suite, in fact, having spent the week leading up to the Cocoa Ball vacationing in Eldovia. Vacationing!

Well, *she* was vacationing. Or at least she was trying to—she was still pretty new to the concept. It helped that her parents were in town, installed in the suite next door. Matteo was working, and his schedule had been wall-to-wall meetings. Cara and her parents had been doing all the Christmas stuff in the village, had taken the baths in Biel, and had even gone to Gimmelmatt, aka the cutest village in the world, along with Matteo's mom.

"I know," Matteo said from where he was perched on the edge of the tub watching her get ready. "And here I thought that giving up my Witten Santa duties would make the Christmas season *less* hectic." He leaned forward and studied her reflection. "Don't paint over that Cupid's bow," he said with a kind of growly urgency that made her want to jump him even though she had done just that not an hour ago. She met his eyes in the mirror, and in typical Matteo fashion, he added, "Ignore me. Of course you should do as you like."

She rolled her eyes but proceeded to overline her lips, exaggerating the V at the top of them. She secretly loved how obsessed he was with little bits of her—that Cupid's bow, her nails. Well, her entire self, really. He was always there with an admiring word or a thoughtful gesture. That's what happened when you entered a non-time-limited affair with a former equerry, she supposed. The man had an eye for detail.

Her cheeks heated as she thought about the details he had attended to over the past hour, after he'd come rushing in from a meeting declaring they had only a small window of time before they had to be at the ball and that they'd better make the most of it because it was going to be all royalty and parents and airports and parties for the next few days.

Being back at the palace was surreal. She'd been in such upheaval when she was here a year ago. Now, she was firmly established as a partner at CZT. She had found a balance of traveling less, but not a ton less, it turned out. With Matteo and Mom and Dad in New York—he was, of course, excessively devoted to her parents—she was less stressed about being gone. She *liked* traveling for work.

She also liked coming home from traveling for work.

"Oh, don't you look so handsome," her mother cooed over Matteo as they swung by her parents' suite on the way to the ballroom. Cara rolled her eyes fondly—the excessive devotion went two ways. "What?" her mother said. "Don't you think he looks handsome?"

He did. He was in his tux, and his hair was his usual short style, but somehow, in her eyes, the whole look was overlain with a kind of sexiness that only she could see. Well, she *hoped* only she could see. As if he could hear her thoughts, he caught her eye and smoldered—there was no other word for it. "He looks okay, I guess," she said, answering her mother as she made a silly face at him.

They moved on to collect Matteo's mother and sister, and the pack of them entered the ballroom together, Matteo taking her mom's arm and Cara's father taking Inge's. That left Cara and Martina to bring up the rear, which was fine because Cara had come to adore Matteo's younger sister.

"Why do you always look so amazing?" Martina mock complained. "You have such a consistent sense of style."

"I don't think it's that so much as I just always wear black." This year's ball gown was less Cinderella-y than last year's, being a sleek, one-shoulder number.

Armend had not made the trip home. He was interning in LA and up to his eyeballs in helping with an album by an up-and-coming pop star. They would see him the day after tomorrow, though, because he was flying into New York for Matteo's party—as were they. The whole lot of them: Cara and Matteo, Cara's parents, Martina and Inge. Matteo's older sister and her family were even coming.

Matteo was mobbed as they crossed the floor to their table. He was fielding political and business inquiries—he'd only been at the UN gig a year, but he had been remarkably successful in raising Eldovia's profile on the world stage. But he was also being hailed by friends. Some she recognized—the Duke of Aquilla and his now-wife Daniela, Torkel and his now-husband Sebastien, the princess and her husband Leo—but there were a whole bunch of people she didn't know. Everyone seemed to radiate goodwill toward him. He had earned it.

She allowed the crowd to hijack him and got their families settled at their table. She didn't get a chance to speak to Matteo before the king made his formal predinner remarks. In addition to welcoming everyone, he ceded the stage to the CEO of Eldovia

Noel, the new company that was being launched this very evening. Cara beamed like a proud parent at the CEO that she had personally recruited as part of CZT's ongoing contract with the fledgling company.

Matteo slipped into his chair beside her as the ribbon-cutting ceremony began. The crowd cheered as the king cut a ribbon that had been tied around a gingerbread replica of the new company's headquarters. The building was in Riems, which had made one Mr. Leon Bachmann very happy.

The evening was fun if a bit too much. Too loud, too hot, too much talking. Someone was always wanting a drink refilled, or to dance, or for her to translate—she was doing pretty well with her German if she did say so herself.

She glanced at her watch—Matteo had given her an antique Abendlied when she moved in with him in New York a month ago. It was only ten o'clock. She sighed.

"Ms. Delaney." A voice in her ear, one that made her shiver. "May I borrow you for a moment?"

She turned, and found him right there in her space. All she had to do was lean forward a little, and they'd be hugging. "I'm not waltzing," she said.

"Good lord, no. But I was hoping you'd come with me for a moment."

"Okay," she said, understating the matter entirely. She would go with him for a moment. Or a million moments.

He led her to . . . the ladies' room? "Change into this." He handed her a big bulky bag, and murmured, "Trust."

The bag contained her own clothing—casualwear and her winter outerwear. When she reemerged from the restroom dressed for the elements, she said, "Do I gather we are abandoning this party?"

"We are."

"And do I gather you have made arrangements for our parents?"

"I have."

Of course he had.

He led her along dim palace corridors to a side door—the front of the palace was crowded with security and valet parking for the party. They emerged into the icy night, and Cara inhaled a big breath of that clean, cold Eldovian air. Eldovia Noel needed to figure out a way to bottle this stuff.

"Oh!" she exclaimed, catching sight of Hilda the groom and her charges. "A sleigh ride!" As she climbed on and Matteo took up the reins, a thought occurred to her. "Oh my gosh"—she whispered so Hilda wouldn't hear—"are we doing Santa duty?"

He flicked the reins, and the sleighbells jingled as they set out into the starry night. "We are not. Kai and Imogen have that under control. I thought perhaps you would appreciate a reprieve from the palace. I thought perhaps I would appreciate a reprieve from the palace."

They didn't talk. She sighed and let the slicing sounds of the sleigh's blades and the snorting of the horses soothe her party-jangled nerves. Look at her, being soothed by horses.

"What are you smiling about?"

"How can you tell I'm smiling? Keep your eyes on the road, Mr. Ambassador."

"I am. I don't have to see you to know you're smiling, I can sense it."

"Oh, I forgot, the Jedi have nothing on you." He needed both hands to drive, but he bumped his shoulder against hers, which inspired her to take his arm and snuggle up against him. "I was just laughing at the idea of me, the confirmed city girl, *enjoying* horses. And look at this!" She snuggled harder. "I'm all cuddly. What happened to me?"

"I don't think anything happened to you."

"*You* happened to me."

"I think we happened to each other."

She grinned into the darkness. "Yeah, okay, I will accept that answer."

After a while, they came to a stop at the spot where they'd picnicked a year and a bit ago. A fire was laid but not lit. Matteo had clearly been here ahead of time—or sent minions. He produced a blanket from the sleigh, settled her on it, and got to work on the fire.

"I don't suppose you brought a giant wheel of cheese?" she joked.

"No, but I did bring some snacks," he said, magically producing a picnic basket.

"That's our hill," she said, pointing into the darkness. "Or it would be, if we could see it."

"Our hill." He chuckled. "Yes, so many wonderful memories from that hill."

She swatted him. "I told you I was sorry about that. I was scared."

"I know. I was scared, too, and I botched it."

"We both botched it. But then we un-botched it." And she was so glad they had.

"Then we un-botched it," he agreed. "There's nothing a pair of workaholics can't figure out if they put their minds to it." He got the fire going, and soon its cheery flames were throwing warmth and light onto their little party of two. He unpacked old-fashioned cast-iron sandwich makers. "These are preloaded with cheese sandwiches we can toast in the fire. Not raclette, but perhaps an acceptable substitute." Next he produced a growler. "This is the last of Imogen's fall pumpkin beer. I asked her before we came to make sure she saved some for us."

Of course he had. "You think of every last thing, don't you?"

"I can't help it."

"Once an equerry, always an equerry, I guess. You're an equerry without a kingdom."

"Would it be too cheesy for me to say you are my kingdom?"

"Way too cheesy."

He winked. "Luckily I didn't say it then." He stuck the sandwich irons in the fire and poured their drinks, but instead of giving her one, he set both glasses aside and said to her, with a kind of strange intensity, "I have a very important question to ask you." He reached for her hand.

"Oh no," she blurted, totally ruining the mood. But *crap*. She wasn't ready for this. She had no doubt this was where things were going, that someday she would marry him, but it had only been a year! She had only moved into his UN residence a month ago. She still hadn't found a tenant for her half of the duplex she'd bought with her parents six months ago. She still got spooked sometimes when she thought too hard about how tidily everything had worked out—almost like she *was* in one of those TV Christmas movies.

It was too soon! So much for Mr. Emotional Intelligence, thinking of everything, anticipating her every desire.

He squeezed her mittened hand and regarded her with such

open adoration that she knew she was in trouble. "Are you ready?"

"I . . ." How did you tell someone not to propose to you?

"I love you, Cara Delaney, my corporate goth angel."

"Your what?"

"This is the part where you say you love me, too."

Oh, *shit*. "I do love you. So much. I never thought—"

"You know how it's been such a grind lately, with all the Christmas ado?" He didn't wait for an answer. "Not to mention your new position. And my new position. Moving in together. It's been an intense year. So with that in mind, I'd like to propose something bold."

She braced herself.

"An idea for after the party in New York on the twenty-sixth," he went on.

Oh my god! He wanted to get married *now*? Like the day after tomorrow? "Okay, listen. You know—"

"Just let me finish, will you?"

She could at least do that. She needed to take a breath and gather her thoughts anyway, to make sure this didn't turn out like a year ago on that ski hill. She had to think of a way to say no without saying no.

"Cara Delaney, after the party in New York, once we've gotten rid of our families, will you . . ."

She braced herself.

"Stay up all night watching Star Wars with me?"

"Ahh!" She actually screamed. While he laughed at her. It wasn't a moment, though, before she was joining him. He'd gotten her good there. He grabbed her and started kissing her, and just when she was getting all breathless and befuddled, he pulled away. "You never answered my question. Will you stay up all night watching Star Wars with me?"

"Trek," she countered.

"Wars."

"Trek."

Mr. Benz, her very proper equerry, smiled at her like she'd hung all three moons of Tatooine, and said, "Okay. Trek."

Acknowledgments

My thanks to:

The team at HarperCollins: Elle Keck, who from the very beginning understood the "Hallmark but make it spicy" vibe of this series as well as the way I wanted it to toe the line between bonkers trope-iness and genuine romance. Nicole Fischer for inheriting me with grace and good cheer. Madelyn Blaney for making things go smoothly. Emily Fisher for steadfast, thoughtful advocacy. Yeon Kim for the cover design.

Carina Guevara for another gorgeous cover illustration.

Marion Kuhn for help with the German dialogue.

My friend Sandra Owens and my agent Courtney Miller-Callihan for commentary on early drafts as well as cheerleading when my Christmas spirit flagged.

About the Author

JENNY HOLIDAY is a *USA Today* bestselling author whose books have been featured in the *New York Times*, *Entertainment Weekly*, the *Washington Post*, and on BuzzFeed. She grew up in Minnesota and started writing when her fourth-grade teacher gave her a notebook to fill with stories. When she's not working on her next book, she likes to hike, throw theme parties, and watch other people sing karaoke. Jenny lives in London, Ontario, Canada.

ALSO BY JENNY HOLIDAY

A delightful contemporary Christmas romance, set in the heart of New York City, about a playboy baron and a woman who has said goodbye to love.

"Another confection of a novel that gives readers the fuzzy feelings of a Hallmark movie with a heck of a lot more steam."

—*Entertainment Weekly*

A modern fairy tale about a tough New Yorker from the other side of the tracks who falls for a princess from the other side of the world.

"A perfect combination of sweet and sexy moments makes *A Princess for Christmas* an unputdownable read!"

—Mia Sosa, *USA Today* bestselling author